*THE SECOND LIFE*
*OF JOHN WILKES BOOTH*

## Other Books by Barnaby Conrad

### NOVELS

The Innocent Villa

Matador

Dangerfield

Zorro: A Fox in the City

Endangered *(with Niels Mortensen)*

Fire Below Zero *(with Nico Mastorakis)*

Keepers of the Secret *(with Nico Mastorakis)*

Last Boat to Cadiz

### TRANSLATIONS

The Wounds of Hunger *(Spota)*

The Second Life of Captain Contreras *(Luca de Tena)*

### NON-FICTION

La Fiesta Brava

Encyclopedia of Bullfighting

Gates of Fear

The Death Of Manolete

My Life as a Matador *(Autobiography of Carlos Arruza)*

San Francisco: A Profile in Words and Pictures

Tahiti

Famous Last Words

Fun While It Lasted

How to Fight a Bull

A Revolting Transaction

Time Is All We Have

Hemingway's Spain

Name Dropping

The World of Herb Caen

# THE SECOND LIFE OF JOHN WILKES BOOTH

## BARNABY CONRAD

A KANBAR & CONRAD BOOK

COUNCIL
OAK BOOKS

SAN FRANCISCO & TULSA

First printing, first edition, 2010

Printed in Canada

Cover design by Tom Morgan
Interior design by Carl Brune

LIBRARY OF CONGRESS CATALOGING-IN-PUBLICATION DATA
Conrad, Barnaby, 1922-
The second life of John Wilkes Booth : a novel / by Barnaby Conrad.
-- 1st ed.
    p. cm.
ISBN 978-1-57178-225-0 (hardcover : alk. paper)
1.  Booth, John Wilkes, 1838-1865--Fiction.  2.  Fugitives from justice-
-Fiction.  I. Title.

PS3553.O515S43 2010
813'.54--dc22

                                                2010028651

*For my mentor Sinclair Lewis,*
*who told me this story so long ago*

*Many, I know—the vulgar herd—will blame me for what
I am about to do, but posterity, I am sure, will justify me.
Right or wrong, God judge me, not man.*

JOHN WILKES BOOTH
April 14, 1865

## AUTHOR'S NOTE

The reader is asked to remember that while many of the characters in this book are historical figures, this is a work of fiction. I have simplified some of Booth's escapades during the twelve-day manhunt, but all of the assassin's writings are quoted verbatim. The reporter Langford Upham, Jr. is an entirely fictitious character, as are most of the characters whom Booth encounters after the scene at Garrett's farm, with the exception of Robert E. Lee, his son Custis Lee, and photographer Matthew Brady. Wherever possible the author has endeavored to remain true to the facts of the assassination and to the well-documented personalities of the conspirators and the soldiers who pursued them.

# PROLOGUE

*After being hunted like a dog through swamps, woods, and last night being chased by gun boats till I was forced to return wet cold and starving, with every mans (sic) hand against me, I am here in despair. And why; For doing what Brutus was honored for, what made Tell a Hero. And yet I for striking down a greater tyrant than they ever knew am looked upon as a common cutthroat. My action was purer than either of theirs. . . . I struck for my country and that alone. A country groaned beneath this tyranny and prayed for this end. Yet now behold the cold hand they extend to me. God cannot pardon me if I have done wrong. Yet I cannot see any wrong except in serving a degenerate people . . . I do not repent the blow I struck. I may before God but not to man. . . . I have too great a soul to die like a criminal. Oh may he, may he spare me that and let me die bravely.*

JOHN WILKES BOOTH'S DIARY
Friday, April 21, 1865

# CHAPTER ONE

Though the night was cool, the mood in Washington on this Good Friday evening of April 14, 1865, was light-hearted and festive. A drunken revelry spread from the capital's taverns into its unpaved streets. Mindless of the deep mud left by the day's heavy rain, bar patrons embraced and sang on the sidewalks, while a few inebriated men wrestled in the street slime over perceived deficiencies in patriotism. The Civil War was over, or nearly so. General Robert E. Lee's dignified surrender of the Army of Northern Virginia five days earlier had drained the fight out of all but the South's most passionate idealists and fiery apologists, and only a few scattered Confederate troops fought on.

John Wilkes Booth was one of those passionate believers in the unconquerable South. Immaculate in a custom-tailored black frock coat, he wore his fashionable dark felt hat at a rakish angle. That evening he wove through the careening crowd of revelers with sure-footed grace in spite of the thigh-high cavalry boots and his own heavy intake of whiskey. This determined dreamer, an acclaimed stage actor from a family of noted thespians, marched along Tenth Street as if he were leading a Rebel army. Indeed, in his roiling mind, he was. The twenty-six-year-old actor was about to create his most memorable role in a one-time performance lasting only seconds. He was on his way to Ford's Theater.

Pulling his gold watch from his vest he checked the time—one minute after ten. He quickened his pace up Tenth Street, trying not to be angered by the gaudy patriotic pageant. He looked away from the flaming gas jets erected on buildings spelled the word "VICTORY!" and portrayed the Federal Eagle with wings spread triumphantly.

Three tipsy Union soldiers walked abreast, arms flung across meaty shoulders, leaving no room on the sidewalk for Booth to pass. As he stepped aside, one of his spurred boots sank into the street mud, and he muttered, "Vainglorious vulgar swine." He wanted to thrash the louts, but there could be no deviation from the script. "Focus on the play," he reminded himself. "Act One, Scene One. Hew to the script as written!"

To all appearances, John Wilkes Booth was the epitome of polish, refinement, elocution, manners, and style. The newspapers called him "The Handsomest Man in America." Charm was his currency on stage and off, and his ten years on the boards, from San Francisco to Savannah, had brought him extraordinary fame and fortune, elevating him into a privileged world of elite friendships spanning the Union-Confederate divide. It was a world that was as near to being his oyster as any he might have hoped for, save for one crushing new reality: his beloved South had lost the war.

The sidewalk in front of Ford's Theater was quiet, befitting the establishment's high reputation. Booth had trod its boards many times, playing the gamut of Shakespearean characters, particularly those suited to his dramatic intensity. Tonight's play-goers had endured four bitter years of astonishing bloodshed that left over six hundred thousand men killed. There were many combat veterans in the audience, mostly field officers, with an empty sleeve pinned up against a shoulder or a pant leg similarly shortened. This was not an audience for *Henry IV* or *Macbeth*. Tonight's audience was here to forget for a while, to laugh at the farcical *Our American Cousin*.

Booth stopped short of the entrance and surveyed the street. An elegantly dressed man and woman approached, offering a familiar nod to him. Though they were strangers, Booth tipped his hat and issued a few words from his repertoire of pleasantries. His smile faded just as quickly as the couple passed by.

At the curb, directly in front of the theater's entrance, stood a new, dark green Wood Brothers carriage, a barouche with its folding top up against the drizzle. The four-seater was attended only by a spit-and-polish Union officer and a stocky muscular man in a wrinkled wool suit. On the carriage's maroon door was an elaborate cursive monogram: *A.L.*

Still chuckling at something that had passed between him and the soldier, the civilian glanced sharply at Booth, looking him up and down. A Pinkerton detective, Booth surmised. Another of Lincoln's mercenaries.

He has the face, mused the actor bitterly, of a vulgarian who has never thought to attend a play. *But he'll remember this night's performance forever.*

Booth checked his watch again: five minutes after ten. He wiped its glass with an Irish linen handkerchief, as if he had all the time in the world. The detective's inexplicably sudden glance had spooked him, but he wouldn't show it. He took out his pocketbook, pretending to read a small folded paper he withdrew from it. In fact it was a young woman's name, and the address of her rooming house, that had been offered with an inviting smile a week ago. It happened often. Booth pretended to study it as if it were something more. When the detective and the officer no longer paid him any attention, Booth stepped into the foyer of Ford's Theatre.

The old ticket collector John Buckingham stood at his usual post, serving little purpose at this hour other than to welcome the occasional late arrival. At the sight of Booth, he snapped to attention.

"Good evening, sir!"

"Good evening, Buckingham," said Booth, as a burst of laughter surged from inside the theater.

"We're well into the third act, Mr. Booth."

"Yes, I know."

"If I may be so bold to say so, sir, I would much prefer to have seen you in the lead."

"That's kind of you, Bucky. But I seldom have the privilege of enjoying a play from out front. Always something to learn as a groundling."

"Well, you need no ticket here, sir. Please be our guest."

As he spoke, the older man was suffused with a vicarious excitement over the life this smart young man had before him. *A Booth!* There were many fine actors, as he often said to others, but few with the appeal of this high-strung thoroughbred from the finest acting family in America. A ladies man, a rake, but always the gentleman, even with the small folk. And generous with his purse.

"You're aware, sir, that the President has reserved your usual box?"

"Yes, I heard," said Booth. "I believe some friends of mine are up in dress circle. I thought I might look for them."

"I can check for you, sir." But before Buckingham could retrieve the reservation list, Booth had already ducked through the lobby curtains.

Just at that moment a dapper young man in a bowler hat, a smallish fellow with quick eyes, stepped out of the washroom, wiping his hands on a monogrammed handkerchief. The man's eyes widened and a smile spread across his face. "What luck, Mr. Booth! I am a great admirer— your Macbeth stunned so many and—"

"Thank you for your kindness."

"I'm a reporter with *The New York World*, down here in Washington for a few days, and I would greatly like to interview you. Langford Upham's the name."

"I am meeting people upstairs just now, Mr. Upham."

"Perhaps after the play?"

"Yes, perhaps later," said Booth. "Now I'd best attend to my guests."

Before Upham could say another word the actor turned and disappeared.

Booth stood for a moment at the top of the stairs, letting his eyes adjust to the dim light. On stage, Harry Hawk was playing the title role of Asa Trenchard, the "American cousin" of the play's title. To his right was Helen Muzzey, using her best sing-song warble to convey the snobbishness of British aristocrat Mrs. Mountchessington. A pretty younger actress, Laura Keene, played the woman's scheming daughter, Augusta, who hoped to marry the American for his money.

As Hawk affected the provincial twang of a roughshod Vermonter hopelessly out of step with British society, Booth moved his head contemptuously to the actor's journeyman cadences.

"Wal, I guess shootin' with bows and arrows is just like most things in life. All you've got to do is keep the sun out of your eyes, look straight, pull strong, calculate the distance, and you're sure to hit the mark in most things as well as shootin'."

He has skill, but no gift, thought Booth, irked that Hawk's interpretation nevertheless elicited chuckles from most of the thousand-odd people in the house, a near-capacity crowd.

*They're not here to see you, Hawk.* The main attraction on this Good Friday, typically a slow night, was not even the President but rather his victorious commanding general, Ulysses S. Grant, being hailed as the Hero of Appomattox. After a White House messenger delivered Mary Lincoln's request for theater reservations, the Fords alerted the *Washington Evening Star* that Lincoln, a frequent Ford's patron, would be in his usual box above the stage with General Grant, both accompanied by their wives. The newspaper notice triggered a flurry of ticket sales, most from people eager to glimpse the flinty lieutenant general who had broken the back of the Confederacy. But at the last minute, Grant and his wife had backed out, disappointing many.

By contrast, the president was a far more familiar sight in Washington, often spotted in his carriage or astride his horse, or on his solitary late-night walks from the Executive Mansion to the War Department to check battle reports, and always willing to strike up conversations with ordinary folk.

Booth knew the president's theater-going routine well. Just a year ago he had starred in another play at the Ford that Lincoln attended. During that performance he'd let his hatred of The Tyrant get the better of him. Positioning himself below the State Box, which he also often reserved, he had delivered his threatening lines directly to the Commander in Chief. Many found this transparent innuendo disturbing and offensive. As Booth challenged him, shaking his finger at the President, Lincoln responded diplomatically to a companion's whisper of concern, conceding that the actor's glare was indeed "sharp."

Climbing the dark curving stairs to the dress circle, Booth was startled by a stern voice from the shadows.

"May I help you, sir?"

A tall, powerfully built man peered down at him. Booth's heart beat hard. A burst of laughter from the audience sent another wave of anxiety through his spinning mind; for the progress of the play was integral to the timing of his actions.

Now he was delayed. Yet his vanity demanded satisfaction. A slow balletic turn brought him under a dim gas lamp, where he pointed his toe regally and poised a hand on his hip. He waited with raised eyebrow for the other to recognize him.

The big man squinted, then drew back.

"Ah, Mr. Booth!"

"Indeed."

"I'm sorry, sir—I meant no disrespect." Booth recognized him as a recently hired stagehand, apparently drafted to serve as an usher.

"I'm hoping to find some friends," said the actor. "Up top."

"Of course, sir. Would you like me to bring up a chair?"

"I'll stand. It will soon be over."

When the usher retreated down the stairs to the lobby, Booth resumed his ascent to the first balcony.

Emerging from the passage, he paused to collect himself. At the other end of the curving dress circle were two doors, one opening into the vestibule of the presidential box. He was surprised to find no guard stationed there. Lincoln's valet, Charles Forbes, was seated nearby, his attention fixed upon the stage. Booth had met Forbes before, when the president had attended plays, exchanging the usual perfunctory greetings and handshakes that came with his celebrity.

Between them was a gaggle of theater-goers, who had moved their chairs up onto the aisle for a higher view of the play. Booth inched by with whispered apologies and handshakes for those who recognized him. Forbes looked up with a start. Tipping his hat, Booth formally presented his calling card. "I received an invitation to join them," he whispered. "But I was delayed."

Forbes, a man rendered unquestioning by a lifetime of professional obedience to his superiors, nodded and smiled, accepting the card as a souvenir. The way was clear.

Stepping past Forbes, Booth stood with his back against the wall, striking a pose of nonchalance, as if interested in the play unfolding below. Forbes turned his eyes back to the actors. But Booth noted that more than a few opera glasses were still aimed at him from the gallery on the other side. *There will be no doubt as to who stole the show.*

The comedy was nearing its denouement. The American cousin, up to now believed by his snobbish British kin to have inherited a fortune, had finally confessed to being a pauper. It was this part of the play that American audiences especially enjoyed—when the British cousins' fawning hypocrisy was abruptly replaced by haughty disdain for the homespun Yankee. Listening to the familiar lines, it occurred to Booth, with a sudden, stomach-turning sensation, that he might never have the opportunity to play this or any other role on the stage. *Mine from now on shall be real, the leading character always myself, the world my audience.*

He gazed down at Harry Hawk, as he made his plaintive confession to Mrs. Mountchessington's gold-digging daughter, Augusta.

"You crave affection, you do. Now I've no fortune, but I'm filling over with affections which I'm ready to pour out all over you like apple sass over roast pork."

The audience's sympathetic laughter at the hapless suitor's clumsy metaphor was Booth's cue to open the door to the vestibule leading to the presidential box. In his hand now was a long knife, its blade honed to razor sharpness. If a bodyguard were posted inside, he would plunge it into his heart. In Booth's mind, he was not a mere five feet eight inches and 150 pounds; he embodied the Avenging Fury of the South, a term he had coined and often used in fervid, liquor-fueled conversations with like-minded compatriots.

But there was no bodyguard. In two seconds he slipped into the vestibule and silently closed the door behind him.

Booth bent low in the darkness and felt for the sturdy pine post he had taken from a music stand and hidden under the carpet that afternoon. Finding it still there, he seated one end in a notch he had scraped into the wall's thick plaster. The other end he silently wedged firm against the passageway's outer door. His motions were practiced, assured, and swift. There was no turning back.

Waiting in the pitch-black chamber he heard Helen Muzzey chastise Hawk's hapless Vermonter: "You will please recollect you are addressing my daughter, and in my presence!"

Moving close to the State Box door, he found the peephole the theatre had installed. It enabled officials' aides and bodyguards to keep watch on their charges without interrupting their privacy.

Booth's reconnaissance was brief. On the other side of the door, against the right front wall of the box, a Union Army officer sat alone on a love seat. To his immediate right sat a young woman, her chair set next to the flag-draped balustrade. Seated to their left in separate chairs were Abraham and Mary Lincoln. The president's broad back and large head cut a looming silhouette against the dim glow of stage lights below. The sight of his big roughhewn hand affectionately clasping the pale little paw of his diminutive wife came as a shock to Booth. He felt a sudden chill in his gut. It dismayed him that his loathing of Lincoln could be so easily rattled by cheap sentiment.

He drew a long, deep breath, then winced as a droplet of sweat ran into an eye. Wiping it on a monogrammed cuff, he steeled himself. *This is how history turns, as a great bank vault door swivels on a tiny jewel bearing. I am no longer merely a man. I am destiny.*

He took out his ornately engraved Deringer and carefully cocked it, placing a thumb between the hammer and the firing cap until he heard the faint click of the trigger lock engaging.

He twisted the doorknob slowly, to minimize any sound from the latch mechanism. Then he waited for his cue.

"I'm offering her my heart and hand," said the American cousin, "just as she wants them, with nothing in 'em!" There were gasps, groans, and even an indignant "boo" that earned its own laughter as Mrs. Mountchessington ordered her disappointed daughter off-stage. The girl flung a biting insult at her now-rejected suitor, and left.

Booth listened intently to Helen Muzzey's voice:

"I am aware, Mr. Trenchard, you are not used to the manners of good society, and that, alone, will excuse the impertinence of which you have been guilty."

In his mind, Booth saw the actress bustling offstage in a crinoline huff, leaving Hawks alone before the footlights. He silently opened the State Box door and slipped inside. None of the four in front of him heard or noticed.

Booth took a step toward Lincoln, freezing at the faint creak of a floorboard under his boot. He aimed the short muzzle of the single-shot .44 caliber Deringer at the back of the president's head, marveling at the great size of The Tyrant's cranium.

Hawk's voice seemed to thunder in his ears:

"Don't know the manners of good society, eh? Well, I guess I know enough to turn you inside out, old gal—you sockdologizing old man-trap!"

Then the husky bark of the black powder pistol.

The shot filled the box with smoke. Lincoln slumped forward. The

Union officer, Major Henry Rathbone, jumped up and rushed Booth. He saw the knife raised high and blocked Booth's thrust but the blade cut his arm long and deep. Rathbone's fiancée, Clara Harris, sat frozen. Mary Lincoln was speechless, paralyzed with shock.

Booth clambered onto the balustrade. Rathbone, blood dripping from his slashed tunic sleeve, grabbed at the wild-eyed man's coat from behind. Booth jumped from the balcony. His right spur snagged a fold of the Stars and Stripes, which had been draped below the rail. The bunting tore free as Booth plunged twelve feet to the stage. Landing hard on his left leg, he felt a snap above his ankle and a surge of pain.

Raising his dagger above his head, the actor pierced the stunned silence. "*Sic semper tyrannis!*" he shouted. "The South is avenged!"

*Thus ever to tyrants!* It was the state motto of Virginia, and the words Brutus had said when he killed Caesar. Many in the audience wondered if this was some bizarre addition to the night's presentation, or, at worst, a shocking prank by a Confederate sympathizer. A shriek of horror from the State Box—the cry of Mary Lincoln—broke the spell. The audience erupted in pandemonium. Onstage Booth ran past the cowering Hawk, swinging his knife as if at ghosts, and disappeared backstage.

Rising from his chair in front of the orchestra pit, a towering Union Army major, Joseph Stewart, climbed over the backs of the musicians' chairs to reach the stage, and gave chase.

Booth burst from the stage door onto the alley behind Ford's. There, as planned, stood the young stagehand John Burroughs, always called John Peanut, struggling to restrain a nervous bay mare. The rented mount jerked violently, nearly yanking the reins from Peanut's hands.

"Peanut, give me the reins! The reins!" Booth vaulted onto the mare, landing hard in the saddle.

Out the same stage door came the Union major. At six-feet-five, Joseph Stewart was one of the tallest men in the capital. Booth steered the hoof-flashing mare directly at him. Stewart lunged to seize the reins, but the actor yanked the mare around, hindquarters and hooves swiveling, turning her bridle away and out of the soldier's reach. Stewart darted to the mare's other side for another try, but Booth spurred her hard, and away she galloped down the alley, swerved into another street, and disappeared from sight. Lincoln's assassin had escaped.

# CHAPTER TWO

Seconds after Stewart strode across the chair backs to follow Booth, another man—a foot shorter than the soldier—scrambled after the assassin. A trim young man in a fashionable suit and tie, it was the reporter, Langford Upham. He vaulted over the low rail fronting the orchestra pit and began his climb up over the footlights, putting a boot through a musician's drumhead in the process.

Now, Upham stood helpless on stage, below the twin arches of the State Box, hearing the pitiful cries of Mary Lincoln, pleading with her unconscious husband. Then he heard a young Army surgeon ordering whomever was in the box to make room to lay the president on the floor.

More men from the audience climbed onto the stage, all craning their necks to peer into the box above. *All exhibiting the general desire to be closer to and helpful to the wounded president*, observed Upham, making a mental note for the story he would soon write for *The New York World*.

Peering up at the flag-draped balustrade, straining to hear over the general uproar, Upham stepped back in hope of a better view and felt something under his heel. He looked down and saw a piece of metal protruding from the bunting. As the jostling crush surrounded him, he crouched, stood up and held it to the light. It was Booth's spur. Caught in the rowel was a bit of blue cloth.

Booth kept his mare on an easterly course through the capital, turning southeast toward Capitol Hill. The celebrations were behind him now, shrouded by dense fog. It didn't matter that he had lost a spur in his jump to the stage, but the pain in his leg was breathtaking. Nothing to be done.

The mare was lathered and breathing hard. He let her set her own pace as he turned her south. The Navy Yard Bridge would take him across the Potomac to Maryland. It was less than half an hour since he pulled the trigger at Ford's. He was gambling that the War Department's telegraph office had not yet alerted local garrisons to be on the lookout for him. Beyond the river lay friendly country, a region of Confederate sympathies and hatred for The Tyrant. He imagined the welcome he would receive, once his deed became known. *There will be parades. By God, I did it!*

Was ever a night so momentous, so still as this? He rode along the Potomac in the light of a near-full moon. To his side were modest riverfront homes, all but a few already darkened for sleep. He had passed not a single person on the road. Far ahead a point of pale yellow light materialized in the fog. The entrance to the bridge. Booth slowed his pace, reaching into his other bag to withdraw a hat similar to the one he'd lost in his struggle at the theater. He positioned it atop his head just so.

Four men stood in the light of a lantern placed atop the bridge's broad rail. A voice shot out of the gloom.

"Who goes there?"

"A friend, sir!" Booth shouted back. "Good evening!"

He reined the nervous mare to a halt in front of Sergeant Silas Cobb, who looked tired and in need of a shave. His three sentries, all privates, hunched stiffly in the chill.

"Where are you from?" asked Cobb.

"From the city," said Booth, careful to keep his tone cordial and his manner that of a man of no importance.

"Bound to where?"

"Going down home."

"And that would be where?"

"Down in Charles County."

Cobb looked Booth over, noting his fine long boots, which the sergeant knew cost more than four times what he earned every month. He noted the actor's pale, delicate hands. *This one's a stranger to work.*

"The curfew's still in effect, sir. The bridge closed at nine."

"I didn't know."

"It's been so for some time."

"Well, I assumed, with the war almost over—"

"Not all's ready to accept it, sir. So the law stands: no crossings after nine."

Booth heaved a sigh and stared off, composing a story.

"Why travel so late?" the Sergeant asked. "Your horse looks as if you've ridden hard."

"To be frank with you, sir, I dallied far too long in town, you know, celebrating our victory. It's a dark road home. I thought if I waited a spell I'd have the moon. Just didn't think of the curfew."

The soldier stared at him blankly. Booth had the sinking feeling the man was not going to budge.

"Sergeant, I respect your charge. For my part, I have an impatient wife whose wrath I fear more than the Devil himself, and I'm long overdue."

"And where does this Devil woman await?"

"Down near Beantown, in the country."

"Your name?"

"Booth." The actor felt almost faint from the idiocy of his error. For all his planning, incredibly, he had neglected to construct a false identity. Worse, he was a virtual mosaic of monograms, most notably the large B tooled prominently onto the flaps of his two saddlebags, one now staring his inquisitor in the face. He held his breath, smiling at the sergeant, his heart all but seized up.

Cobb coughed deeply and struggled to clear his throat. Then he leaned over the rail to spit into the river. "Well, sir, I'll pass you, but I don't know as I ought to."

"You may well have saved my life, Sergeant."

Booth expected a knowing smile but got only the stare of a weary soldier. His implicit reference to an unforgiving wife rang false to Cobb—from the looks of him, the dandy was riding home to a luxurious life, so how bad could it be?

"Hell," said Booth, now playing his Everyman character, "I guess there'll be no trouble about that. I reckon I'm the least of the Union's concerns these days."

The mare jerked her head against the reins.

"Walk your mount across, please."

"I'll do my best to restrain her, sir. Fighting me all the way north, and now in a shameless rush to her home barn."

The Sergeant could only nod. He was cold, footsore and chilled to the bone.

Tightly reining in the mare, Booth tipped his hat to the soldiers. The Sergeant gave a perfunctory salute with his index finger.

"Congratulations on your victory, men," Booth said. *Ashes in your mouths.* He eased off on the reins and the mare danced sideways onto the planks of the bridge, her hoof beats echoing across the water.

*There will be parades!*

# CHAPTER THREE

From a wooded knoll, peering down at the road from the bridge through his telescope, Booth could not tell if the shakes that overtook him every minute or so were from the cold, or the magnificence of what lay ahead.

*I have done it. By God, I have done it!*

He imagined his eventual meeting with Lee, the great leader of the Army of Northern Virginia welcoming him as a comrade-in-arms, embracing the Avenging Fury of the South with tears of gratitude.

His leg throbbed as if it might burst. There would be time for a painkiller at Mudd's. And some whiskey. He checked his watch, turning its porcelain face to the luminous moon. A minute past eleven. Despite the good moonlight he could not find Soper's Hill, the place where he and Davey Herold had agreed to rendezvous. Good old Davey. The actor feared a man without his own gifts of persuasion would fare badly with Sergeant Cobb, and Davey Herold did not possess them. What Herold excelled at was everything Booth did not: the rustic skills they would need to navigate cross-country and, if need be, live off the land. The man had once killed a deer using only his knife.

The sounds of the woods, a rustling of leaves, startled him, but it was only a small animal in the brush. It had been a long day, the longest day of his life, and he suddenly felt tired. He thought of the beds he had known, beds perfumed, beds cushioned by plump goose down, and a vague sensation of loss washed over him. Rough days lay ahead. And then there was his fiancée, the ambassador's daughter in Spain—how would she take the news?

Booth strained to make out Soper's Hill. By day it was a distinctive shape above the Maryland plain, but now it was hidden in the misty distance. He hoped Herold had brought the compass. He was becoming impatient. He turned his horse to proceed alone, then froze at the sound of hooves approaching from the high ground. *Does it end here?* He closed his eyes to listen carefully. It was a single horse. Its hoof beats slowed from a canter to a walk, then to nothing. An astonishingly tall spectral figure appeared in the gloom before him. Then came the shaking of a bit and bridle.

"John?" said a quiet voice.

"Davey?"

The other man walked his horse forward. Booth recognized Herold's plain, guileless face.

"It's done," said Booth.

"Thank the L-Lord." Herold was a silhouette in the cold blue light of the moon. The butt of his Spencer rifle jutted from its scabbard.

"What did you hear," Booth asked, "about Lincoln?"

"Nothing," Herold answered.

"Did Powell get to Seward?"

"I reckon. Few minutes after he g-got inside the Secretary's house, a nigger woman ran into the street hollering 'Murder! Murder!'"

"Did he come out?"

"Don't know. When she c-come out, I left."

"What about Johnson? Did Atzerodt kill him at the hotel?"

"I don't know, J-John!" said Herold. "Can't be in two places at once, now, c-can I?"

Booth felt a surge of anger. "For God's sake, man! You act as if it wasn't in the reckoning! We had a plan!"

"They didn't meet up with me! I waited more than long enough, but I had to make the b-bridge. I reckon as we'll know everything with the morrow's paper. It's every man for h-his self now, isn't it?"

*The Cause.* Booth fought a sinking sensation of failure. While trying to kill Secretary of State Seward, perhaps Powell had been killed by bodyguards, or captured, or found his escape route blocked. And did Atzerodt get in to assassinate Vice-President Johnson? He'd come to doubt Atzerodt's resolve. The Prussian carriage painter was prone to heavy drinking, but it had been too late to recruit a replacement. Now Powell, there was a born killer, his fury as natural to him as drawing a breath.

"I'll wager Powell got to Seward," Booth said, watching the road ahead, its wheel ruts faint in the moon glow. "But Atzerodt is a throw of the dice."

Herold's only reply was, "Best move on, John."

As their horses walked through the night, it occurred to Booth that in his haste to sabotage the Union victory he had assembled a motley crew of lowlifes. He alone would go to meet Robert E. Lee. He would take the general's great hand, and let it pull him up into the world of consequence, up among the true shapers of history.

Thirteen miles from the Navy Yard Bridge, they came to a crossroad. In one of its quadrants stood a squat two-story building. Its small glass windows were dark.

"That's Surratt's," Herold said quietly, dismounting.

Booth stayed on his horse. His left leg pulsed with a hot pain, the ankle so thick from swelling it pressed hard against the leather of his boot. The mare dropped her head to graze.

The keeper of the inn was John Lloyd, who tended the business for Surratt's widow and her son John, another conspirator, who had exploited his Catholic connections in Montreal for money and support for the Confederacy. Right now Lloyd was snoring loudly in his bed. It took Herold a long time to rouse him, but his steady pounding on the planked side door to the saloon eventually penetrated Lloyd's alcoholic slumber. Lloyd padded barefoot down the low stairs to the door.

"Who is it?"

"Herold!"

Lloyd unbarred the door and pulled it open without a greeting. Herold stepped onto the creaking floor of the saloon. "You still have it all?"

Lloyd grunted in the affirmative and struck a match, lighting a pair of candles on the bar. He slid a full bottle of whiskey and a brace of glasses into the candlelight, then shuffled off into the darkness. Herold poured himself a half glass and drank it down.

Lloyd came back from the darkness with a Spencer Rifle, a small sack of cartridges, and a pair of Lemaire field glasses. Herold collected them, picked up the whiskey from the counter, carried it outside and handed the bottle up to Booth, who appeared to be dozing in the saddle. He was careful not to touch the actor's leg, rousing him instead with a gentle pat on the forearm. Booth's head rose.

"Bottle of Pepper, John," said Herold, holding it up. "Courtesy of the house."

Booth grasped the whiskey and took two eager burning swallows from the bottle. "God," he said, heaving a great sigh. "Oh, God."

He wondered if Oscar Pepper's Kentucky distillery had survived the war.

Herold began to insert the second Spencer into the saddle scabbard on Booth's left, but the actor blocked him. "I can't have it against my leg," he said.

"How bad is it?"

"Bad enough," said Booth. "We need to get to Mudd's."

Lloyd had pulled on boots and scuffed out to the road where the two men sat astride their horses. Booth handed him back the whiskey, then pulled a fold of paper money from his vest.

"No need for that," said Lloyd. But he accepted the three dollars Booth held out to him. "So you've finished your—your business in Washington?"

"Finished it we did, sir."

"Then you'd best ride on, and forget you were ever here."

"Someday, sir," said Booth, "you shall be a footnote to a glorious history, and proud to claim that you did your part."

"Is that so?"

"The Tyrant is dead, and the South is rising again as surely as we stand here."

Lloyd glanced at Herold for reaction, but Booth's companion appeared to be gazing off into the night.

"Time to go, John."


The windows of the War Department Building in Washington glowed with lanterns. A line of well-armed Union soldiers ran the length of the edifice and around both sides: the building was under heavy guard. Langford Upham approached a tall young lieutenant who was reading a message from a runner. The young officer looked down at the reporter with an air of effrontery. "The building is off limits to the public, sir."

Upham handed the lieutenant his calling card. The messenger

obligingly held up his small lantern to illuminate it. The officer glanced at the card and handed it back to Upham.

"Off limits, sir."

"Would you escort me to Secretary Stanton, Lieutenant? I know him personally."

"My orders are to admit no one but the President's cabinet, and officers known to me."

Upham nodded. "Is the Secretary unharmed?"

"What makes you ask that?"

"The Capital's rife with talk of assassination. Secretary Seward, Secretary Stanton, others. I came to assay Mr. Stanton's condition."

"He is unharmed."

"Thank God."

The Lieutenant signed the messenger's receipt book and gave the private a salute. The courier trotted off to his horse.

"Why so many soldiers, Lieutenant?"

"Orders of Secretary Stanton. No reason given. You'll find the same at the Executive Mansion and the cabinet residences—and I assume elsewhere. I'm not privy to more."

The Lieutenant watched as the persistent reporter scribbled notes in a small pocketbook. Upham was by nature a terrier—the affectionate nickname bestowed upon him by friends amused by his irrepressible curiosity.

"Any news of the President?" the Lieutenant asked.

"Nothing new," said Upham. "Gravely wounded by an assassin's bullet, possibly stabbed as well. They have him in a rooming house across from Ford's."

The Lieutenant's face darkened. "He should be at the Mansion!"

"It's my understanding the doctors feared the journey might worsen his condition. He's said to be surrounded by physicians, including Army surgeons. One's named Charles Leale. Do you know him?"

"No." The Lieutenant shook his head. "It's an abomination," he said at length.

"I agree."

Booth's pocket watch read a minute after four. An hour until dawn. The moon rested on the roof of a white two-story residence at the end of the dirt lane ahead of them.

They rode up to the house and stopped. Even the crickets were asleep now. The house was dark. Herold slid off his horse and listened. Silence. His boots crunched over the gravel in the drive. He lifted the brass clapper on the front door and let it fall. They waited. Then Herold began to softly tap a knuckle against the door. Another minute passed. He doubled up a fist and pounded hard.

In a back bedroom, Sarah Frances Mudd was pushing gently against her husband's shoulder, trying to rouse him. The pounding frightened her, for she and Samuel Mudd were used to a prosperous and peaceful routine on their 218-acre farm and tending their four young children.

The doctor awakened with a start.

"What?"

"Someone's pounding at the door."

Mudd pulled a Colt revolver from under the mattress beneath him and tip-toed downstairs through the dark house in his nightshirt. He peered out through a front window to the front yard and saw a man on a horse, and a riderless mount beside him. Moving to another window he saw a man step back and crane his neck to look at the second-story windows.

"What do you want?" asked Mudd through the door.

"We're travelers, sir—one of us is injured. His horse fell on him. We think his leg is broken."

Mudd unbolted his door and stepped outside, keeping the revolver hidden in a fold of his shirt. With the moon nearly down now, they might all have been blind men. Mudd walked to where Booth slumped atop his mare. Mudd saw a man with a thick beard, swaddled in a scarf, hat pulled down.

"Your leg is broken, you say?"

"Injured badly, doctor."

"How do you come to know I'm a physician, sir?"

"We've met, some time ago," said the man, touching his beard.

"And you are?"

"Tyson."

"Forgive me, I don't recall the name."

"I'll forgive if you can put me back together."

"Come in then."

The doctor and Herold eased Booth down from the saddle. Throwing an arm over Mudd's shoulder, the actor hobbled into the house. Mudd could still not see the bearded man's face clearly. Herold was left holding the horses.

The two men shuffled awkwardly, Booth keeping his injured leg bent, putting most of his weight on the doctor's shoulder, and swinging his right forward. Mudd led him into the front parlor and deposited him on a settee. Booth pushed himself up on the cushions. Minutes before arriving at Mudd's he had donned a false beard, but the glue had come unstuck.

Mudd lit an oil lamp and placed it on a side table. Booth watched him closely. The doctor positioned a small chair in front of the settee and sat down to examine Booth's leg. He looked up at the actor's lamplit face and saw the beard come away from his cheek.

"My God! Is it you?"

"Fate has brought us together again, doctor," said Booth.

"Fate?"

"Fate and free will."

"What of the things we discussed?"

"None came to pass."

"It's just as well. This madness is over. The war is over. How were you injured?"

"This was a mere accident. Horse slipped. So with my apologies, if your sleep tonight is interrupted."

Mudd gazed at Booth for a long moment, then turned to the task at hand. Several seasons past, he had been introduced to the actor by a mutual acquaintance who, like Mudd, was a Confederate sympathizer and, until Lincoln's Emancipation Proclamation, a slave-holder. He had agreed to provide Booth a safe house in connection with a scheme to kidnap the president and trade him for thousands of Confederate prisoners. *Kidnap. Not kill.*

He tried to pull off Booth's boot, but the lower leg had ballooned. When the doctor eased off, Booth stopped holding his breath.

Mudd left again for a moment, returning with his doctor's bag. He removed a flat black leather case from it and opened it to reveal a set of surgical knives lying in red velvet.

"Good God!"

"It's for the boot, Mr. Booth."

"Ah. Yes."

With a scalpel, Mudd cut open the front of Booth's boot where the swelling was greatest. His incision was sure; he managed to spare even the stocking underneath. Now the boot slid off easily. Laying it aside, he peeled off the stocking, revealing a darkly bruised and inflated lower limb.

Booth closed his eyes and let the doctor examine him, feeling Mudd's fingers press, probe, slide up and down over the ankle and lower leg.

"I would say that you're in luck, relatively speaking of course."

"How so? It hurts like the devil."

"It could be far worse, if that's any comfort. There's nothing to suggest a compound fracture. Only one bone, your fibula, is broken, a small break. I'm going to try to set it. The process could be painful. Are you ready?"

Booth nodded. Mudd continued to feel for the fracture, working his fingers over the break. Booth was pleasantly surprised by the lessening of his agony as the doctor pulled gently on his limb.

"So what's in store for me, then?"

"I'd say eight weeks on crutches with your leg in a splint. Maybe less."

"In other words, I am a cripple."

"Temporarily. You'll recover fully, with time."

"I had proposed to take a holiday from the stage in any case."

Mudd was putting his knives back in his bag. "You have no choice now. But, then, you could do readings, no?"

"I suppose."

Mudd slapped his thighs. "The leg is set. I'll fashion a splint, but as soon as you return to Washington, consult a physician to make you a proper one, to ensure the bones knit correctly."

Booth's glance at Herold found his accomplice looking hard at him. "We ought to be m-movin' on, John."

"That's out of the question!" said the doctor. "You need to rest. I want to watch this leg for at least a day."

Another glance between Booth and Herold. This time Mudd noticed. "Is there an urgency to your travel?"

Booth gazed off. "No."

Mudd had no splint materials on hand, so he improvised, using wood pieces taken from a crate and split with a knife, wrapping them around the broken leg with gauze, then adding plaster. As the physician worked, Booth's mind filled with drumming hooves.

When the splint was finished, Mudd helped him climb the stairs to a room with two narrow beds pressed to opposite walls. Davey Herold sat on one tentatively, looking out of place. The room was clean and well furnished, the wallpaper bright and stylish. It smelled of floor wax and lemon soap. Booth was vastly comforted. He wondered how long it might be before he enjoyed the luxuries of his former life, and shuddered at the thought that they might be forever behind him. *So be it, Lee is used to tents as well.*

He slept through the morning, but when he awakened he was sick with doubt. Maybe he'd failed to kill Lincoln. Just as he had pulled the trigger, the president had begun to lean forward, turning his head toward the audience below. What if the ball had glanced off him? And what was the fate of the Vice President, and the Secretary of State? With Lincoln alive, he had accomplishing nothing, save the ruination of his own life.

A soft tap at the door roused him. "Yes? Come in."

Frances Mudd opened the door but stood to the side, out of sight. "May I enter?"

"Yes, of course."

Booth pushed himself upright as Mrs. Mudd approached the foot of the bed holding a slice of cake, a sectioned orange, and a glass of wine.

"May I bring you anything else?"

Booth looked at her latest offering without emotion, and shook his head. "Perhaps some whiskey," he said. "Oh, and a razor. I'd like to shave. Thank you."

Even as they rode side by side toward Bryantown, their tired horses at a walk, Samuel Mudd and Davey Herold were in two different worlds. Herold was counting his cash, worried that he might not have brought enough to purchase a carriage to take Lincoln's injured killer deeper into Confederate territory. The doctor, on the other hand, was feeling good about life. The warmth of the spring sun and the scent of new grass and wildflowers filled him with a sense of well-being. The war was done, last year's intrigue with Booth and company put to rest. And even Lincoln, the reviled bogeyman of the North, had lately spoken of forgiveness and reconciliation.

As they turned a corner past a grove of willows, the village came into view, and Herold abruptly jerked his horse to a halt. Bryantown's main street was filled with Union Cavalrymen. Puzzled, Mudd turned in the saddle to look back at him.

"There's nothing to fear. The war in these parts is finished."

Still Herold refused to move. "As I think more about it, we don't need a c-carriage. John can ride a horse and his leg would be fine, right?"

"Best would be to keep the leg elevated, and immobile."

Before Mudd could say more, Herold turned his horse and galloped away in the direction from which they'd come.

The Thirteenth New York Cavalry had occupied Bryantown, setting up a command post in the tavern. The county was known for a sizeable contingent of Confederate sympathizers, and the mustachioed officer in charge stood on the tavern's covered porch, legs planted wide and arms folded across his chest. He surveyed the street as if he expected trouble.

Mudd tied up his horse and tipped his hat to the officer. "Good afternoon, sir," he said affably. "To what do we owe the honor of your visit to our little town?"

The officer waited for the doctor to walk up the steps to the porch. "You're unaware of the terrible news?"

"For the moment, blissfully so."

"The president has been shot, along with the Secretary of State."

"My God."

Mudd's reaction—he appeared to stagger—was satisfactory to the officer, whose judgment of character had been shaped as a hunter of Rebel spies and saboteurs. Appraising the look of horror on this bookish fellow, he saw a crestfallen man without guile.

Mudd's heart raced. Booth! Since when does an actor travel with two rifles and a brace of revolvers in the middle of the night? Mudd felt so light-headed he had to grasp a porch pole to steady himself.

"What of the president's condition?"

"He did not survive the attack. He died this morning."

Mudd could only hang his head and exhale. It was neither grief nor shock, as the Colonel assumed, but a terrible fear for himself and his family. Mudd had conspired with Booth the prior year, as part of what was to be a bloodless coup. The president was to be kidnapped while on one of his solitary rides, held to win the release of thousands of Confederate prisoners. Since then, a stash of whiskey and supplies had lain under canvas in the Mudds' root cellar. Now Booth had betrayed him, ensnared him in assassination. He sat down on the steps and covered his face with his hands.

"It is indeed a terrible shock," the officer allowed, sympathetically. "After all the bloodshed, now this unspeakable thing."

"I am astonished," said the doctor, barely audibly.

"Where do you live, sir?"

The question frightened Mudd.

"A short distance—a half hour's ride. I have a small farm, but I am mainly a physician. I have a wife and four children. The oldest is six. A boy. A lovely little fellow. My daughters—I'm blessed with beautiful children, you see." He was speaking not for the officer's benefit, but compulsively listing all that he cherished—all now hostage to his treasonous folly.

"You have a rifle, or an iron?"

"A revolver and a box of cartridges."

"Well, sir, keep them handy."

Mudd, his eyes still covered, heard the rustle of paper by his ear.

In the officer's hand was the front sheet of the *Washington Evening Star*. Under the headline, "ASSASSIN!" was a photograph of Booth the actor, seated sideways in a chair. "Should this man appear at your door, shoot him."

Mudd did not answer.

It was late afternoon when Booth and Herold, waiting on the Mudds' porch with mounting anxiety, saw a lone rider coming up the road to the house. Frances had taken the children down to the meadow.

Booth rubbed his clean-shaven upper lip, his trademark moustache gone. It alarmed him that the doctor approached so slowly, as if he were reluctant to return. He shot a look to Herold, who shrugged.

Mudd walked his horse to the hitching post in the yard. Two gunny sacks of store-bought goods were slung over his saddle. He dismounted, leaving them there, and walked slowly toward the porch, head down, eyes hidden by the brim of his hat. He stopped at the foot of the stairs and looked up at Booth.

"You have betrayed me."

"I did no such thing," Booth objected. "You've long known what was afoot."

"You proposed to kidnap Lincoln last year. You didn't. I kept my silence, concealed your supplies. But I did not agree to assassination! I would never agree to such a thing—never! You've gone too far!"

"When the news spreads, hope will return to the Confederate cause like the sun after a storm."

"Federal Cavalry are in town. I told them nothing, but they appear to have your scent. They will certainly come here shortly. Pack up now and leave my farm."

"Oh, my good Doctor Mudd," sighed the actor.

"You are a frightful idiot, Booth. You have no idea what you've done." Mudd stamped up onto the porch and passed between the fugitives. He slammed the front door behind him.

Herold rose, stretching. "We b-best be movin' on, John."

Mudd returned to the porch, his revolver under his belt.

"I won't claim to grieve for Lincoln. He was ruinous to us all. But it was over! *Over!*"

"It is *not* over!" said Booth.

"I can't help you anymore. Go now, and I'll say nothing. I want you both away from here in ten minutes." Mudd fixed both men with a long hard look, then stepped back into his house.

Nine minutes later, Booth was mounted, splinted leg extended, his foot in a brogan left unlaced around his swollen ankle. A pair of crude wooden crutches protruded from his rifle scabbard. He sat silently, watching Herold secure his bedroll.

28

Mudd stepped onto the porch. "I will tell them that two travelers came by. Dry goods traders, one with a broken leg. I will tell them that I set the leg and that you rode off in the direction of Washington."

"You don't have to tell them anything," Booth said sharply.

"Neither I nor my family are as schooled in lying as you. If you're caught and betray me, I will hang."

Booth's response was to raise an eyebrow and regard the doctor with an exaggerated expression of ridicule. "Tell your darky he's not to talk on pain of a whipping."

"That time is past, Mr. Booth. He's a free man now, whether we like it or not. I can ask for his confidence, but not command it."

"That time is definitely *not* past," said Booth, turning his horse and spurring him down the drive.

# CHAPTER FOUR

Samuel Mudd watched Booth and Herold ride out of his yard. Touching an index finger to the brim of his hat, Booth shot him a dismissive salute. It was an odd gesture, thought Mudd, but in keeping with the actor's vanity. *We're all stage hands to him.*

Despite his show of bravado, Booth was beset with foreboding, sinking into a morass of self-reproach. After last year's aborted kidnap plot, he should have changed plans to suit the darker agenda of assassination.

With the coming of darkness, federal search parties could no longer spot them at a distance. There were stars overhead. The air was chilly and damp, and the actor's light coat offered little protection. This was unknown territory—the detour to Mudd's farm had taken them far off their intended route of escape, into a region of bogs and swamps.

Though angry, Mudd had offered up the name of a Confederate sympathizer with the connections to get them safely across the Potomac River. The farther Booth went away from his family, the better. He had drawn them a roadmap to the home of Samuel Cox, a prosperous farmer with a fine house on a knoll appropriately named Rich Hill. Cox was also overseer of a network of Rebel operatives. Among Cox's lieutenants in these well-disciplined intrigues was his foster brother, a man named Thomas Jones, whose scows and rowboats had ferried many a Confederate spy undetected across the Potomac.

The lamps were still burning in Cox's imposing home when Davey Herold knocked on the door. Made wary by four years of a dangerous cat-and-mouse game with Union counter-espionage agents, Cox addressed him from the darkness outside his house.

"Identify yourself."

Cox emerged from the shadows, easing the hammer of his Navy Colt back down. Within minutes the fugitives were seated at the spymaster's long kitchen table, wolfing down sausage and bread as Cox's black house man watched silently from a corner. His steady, impassive gaze caught Booth's eye. The assassin stopped eating and straightened up in his chair, glaring back at the man.

"Don't mind him," said Cox. "He knows who he works for."

Booth asked to throw down their blankets in the farmer's hayloft, but Cox insisted they encamp in a thick stand of pines about a mile away, while he arranged for his courier to take them to the Potomac for the crossing to Virginia. "I'm always under the eye of the federals," he explained. "You're not safe here. As for my river man, he's had a rough patch due to his loyalties, and might not be of a mind to help you now that The Cause is lost."

Cox's words stung Booth, but, desperate for his help, the actor thought better of rebuking him for defeatism.

"I'll speak to him," said Cox, "to see of what mind he's in." His gaze turned to Davey Herold. "And what's your story, young fellow?" Herold looked to Booth as if for prompting.

"Davey's a supporter of The Cause," Booth interjected.

"And how have you supported it?"

"I was a ... ph-pharmacist. An assistant." He stopped there.

Cox's gaze at Davey was inscrutable, but Booth surmised the hard-bitten Confederate subversive was unimpressed with his accomplice.

"Davey has served me well as a guide and loyal protector."

After a long moment Cox nodded and cut a slice of sausage with his Bowie knife, speared it on the point of the blade, and consumed it in a single bite —his eyes on Davey the whole time.

In the faint glow of stars, Cox's son led them across a wide tobacco field gone to weed. The stand of pines materialized out of the ground fog as a dark shape with a serrated skyline.

"They ain't nobody goes in there," said the boy, in a thick rural accent. "They ain't nothin' there 'cept' scrub pine an' brush. You want to watch for rattlers. Cain't see but a few feet. Y'all should be right safe, long as you don' light a fire."

He and Davey tramped into the pines, leading the horses through dense undergrowth as Booth hunched in his saddle, leaning away from bent saplings that whipped back at them. A mosquito began to attack his ears. At length they reached a hidden clearing. While Booth stood wearily on his crutches, Herold and the Cox boy unsaddled the horses and spread blankets on the wet grass. The youth left them a canteen of water and a knapsack with some cheese and a loaf of dry bread. His twig-snapping retreat through the underbrush quickly faded to silence.

Booth awoke with a band of sunlight hot on his face and heard the harsh cawing of crows roosting high above. He lifted his head and looked around. He was marooned in an isle of pines. Davey was nowhere to be seen. He felt as if he had barely slept at all, and fell back onto his blanket, thankful at least for the warming air.

Davey Herold lay prone in deep brush at the edge of the little forest, peering through the field glasses at a search party of mounted federal soldiers proceeding slowly along a road about a quarter-mile away. He could hear the faint barking of dogs sniffing for a scent. Heat waves rose from the stubble of the old tobacco field, distorting his binocular image, but one of the soldiers appeared to be aiming his field glasses directly at Davey's hiding place. Another soldier rode up and turned to stare at the pines. Herold's heart was racing. There were at least two dozen cavalrymen. If the dogs came, it was all over. He watched the two soldiers through the quivering air. Finally the first lowered his field glasses and spurred his horse away. The second, after a last consideration of the trees, followed.

Davey rested his head on one forearm. For the first time, his predicament was clear to him. It astonished him that what had begun as youthful hero worship had brought him to this pass. He too had sensed Cox's disapproval of him at the kitchen table, and it shamed him. He knew he was not cut out for what Booth had wrought.

Thomas Jones, Cox's foster brother, was the man to ferry them to Virginia. When Jones arrived at last light to take their measure, Davey did not protest when he was told to shoot their horses, lest they be discovered at the river's edge and identified.

Booth's killing of Lincoln was a momentous crime. But what undid Davey Herold was killing the horses. He had led them to a quicksand bog with a heavy heart, slapped them gently forward into the pond, fully saddled, where their hooves were quickly mired in the mud. Wrapping his revolver in his blanket to muffle the reports, he shot each in the head, their great bodies falling into the dark water. As they slowly sank, the twenty-three-year-old sat on the bank and sobbed like a child.

The third day in the pine stand passed without a threat of discovery. While Davey moved stealthily from one edge of the woodland to another, keeping watch on as many points of the compass as he could, Booth sat propped up against a tree, writing in his diary, occasionally dozing off, always waking with a start, then dozing again. His leg continued to pain him. He was sore from sitting and hungrier than he had ever been. The water Herold brought from a nearby spring in the canteen was their only luxury. Come sunset, they lay unspeaking, each deep in his thoughts.

Someone whistled. They jerked upright. It was the musical password they had rehearsed in Cox's kitchen.

Cox's boy brought a camp tin of cold bean soup, some hard tack, another slice of dry cheese, and a slab of jerked beef. But what Booth grabbed first were the two newspapers the boy carried. As Davey gnawed, Booth read by the light of a candle held in his hand, and learned what had become of his plot. After several minutes, the newspaper shaking in his hand, he fell back against the tree with a groan, letting the candle go out.

"Atzerodt betrayed me."

"He what?"

"That idiot Johnson is unscathed, and Seward lives."

From the darkness where Davey lay came only silence.

"Powell appears to have gone berserk and attacked the entire Seward family with a knife." Booth let the newspaper fall onto the pine needles.

"They have captured him and Mrs. Surratt. That poor woman."

Still only silence from Herold. Booth could sense his discouragement. He pushed the newspaper away. "A fiasco," he breathed. "A total fiasco."

A fourth sweltering day of hiding in the pines was followed by a fifth. The idle numbing hours were twice punctuated by brief terror when Union search parties passed by, the second barely two hundred yards from the thicket. But they rode by upwind of the trees, so their dogs missed the fugitives' scent of sweaty fear.

As each day had passed, Booth said less and less. He lay on his back, his splinted leg elevated on a mound of pine needles Davey had gathered. When Cox's boy brought more newspapers, Booth read each intently, now and then swearing under his breath.

"They have transformed The Tyrant into Jesus on Earth!" he growled. "Pure hagiography! Oh, such saintly virtues he possessed! Such wisdom! Father Abraham freed the slaves and was escorted through the Pearly Gates by a chorus of heavenly angels! And how evil the dastardly Booth! How cowardly his act!" He threw the paper aside. "Cowardly? I did what the frightened masses were too cowardly to do!"

"Well, they're U-Union papers, John. I 'spect you'll read different views once we're in V-Virginia."

Booth made no reply. Then, pushing himself more upright, he rummaged inside his coat, found his diary, fished a pencil stub from his vest and began to write.

*Until to day nothing was ever thought of sacrificing to our country's wrongs. For six months we had worked to capture. But our cause being almost lost, something decisive & great must be done. But its failure is owing to others, who did not strike for their country with a heart. I struck boldly and not as the papers say . . .*

It was after dark when Thomas Jones whistled the three-note musical password. As Herold helped Booth to his feet, it was clear to Jones that the man who killed Lincoln was a poor candidate for a Potomac crossing. The limping man on crutches had haggard eyes and a five-day beard.

"The Union boys got it in their heads you're down in Mary's County," said Jones. "They rode out this afternoon. That's a break. We have a dark night and little wind. It's time to make the run."

It was a slow trek over three miles with Herold on foot, leading Booth astride Jones's nondescript mare. The Confederate led them along cow paths and farming lanes and a dangerous mile of public road. Acting as point man, Jones signaled them forward with a brief whistle.

The Potomac was now only a mile distant, beyond a patchwork of fallow fields cleared from dense woods. They came to a heavy wooden fence that spanned a clearing and disappeared on both ends into the trees. It was too tall for the horse to jump or climb and too stout to break down. Jones and Herold helped Booth dismount and pushed him up and over the barrier. The actor faced three hundred yards of walking on his crutches to the river's edge. His first steps made clear the crutches were useless here. Their tips sank into the soft soil.

"You know the soldier's carry?" Jones asked Herold.

With Booth on his back, Davey followed Jones across the field, staggering under his burden. Several times, he had to stop to catch his breath. Booth's 150 pounds seemed twice that. He plodded on, praying that his burning legs would not humiliate him.

Booth caught his first scent of the river, a cool, stony freshwater smell. The sweet perfume of freedom. He heard the faint rustling of cattails and reeds. The smell of the river and its promise lifted his mood. He began to think lyrically, once again fancying his miserable flight as the stuff of historical, even mythical fables. *Someday, perhaps, I shall write a memoir of this journey—this heroic quest!* He fancied that the ordeal had toughened him as a man, even as Davey Herold struggled on beneath him.

## CHAPTER FIVE

A fog shrouded the broad river. Thomas Jones handed Booth a pocket compass, a box of matches, and a candle. Head west, he told them—just keep the scow pointed west—and row hard. Never mind the current. Hold to the compass heading. Booth handed him eighteen dollars and said, "God bless you, dear friend, for all you have done for me." Then Jones faded into the gloom.

Davey Herold pulled steadily on the oars, pushing the flat-bottom boat across the water as Booth bent over the compass, a blanket draped over him to hide the candle's flame from the wind, and from patrolling Union gunboats. The needle danced delicately on its pivot as the tiny craft lurched forward in the darkness, the river's waves slapping its hull. After a silent half-hour of labor, Herold stopped and turned to look into the darkness ahead of them. "Are we on the right heading?" he asked.

Booth struck a match and checked the compass. The needle swung back and forth maddeningly. "The damned thing has palsy!"

"Best k-keep our voices down, John. They carry on the river. Just keep me p-pointed west."

"We're headed more north, I think. Damn it!"

Davey ceased rowing. He was silent as he peered over the bow. "Damned if I can figure out where we are." He pulled again on the oars. "Just tell me to pull right or left."

Booth's candle had burned far down. It was seated in a clam shell he'd found lying between the thwarts. He tried to hold it steady. "We're going west now, I think."

Davey labored on for another hour, occasionally turning to look in vain for a light on the far shore that might orient them. His oars began to hit the water in an uneven rhythm, now and then splashing Booth.

"About done for," Davey gasped finally. "Need to get to shore."

He resumed his pulling, leaning far back toward the bow. "Used to hunt these parts ... " he panted. "Know it w-well ... friends here ... to help us."

Far off the bow to the right, Booth made out a faint point of light.

"What's that?"

"Probably... Indiantown," said Davey, breathing hard now. "My friends' f-farm."

"Virginia?"

"Maryland."

"This cannot be!"

"Sorry, John, but with the c-current going one way and the river t-turnin' like a snake—"

"Damn it!"

"S-sorry! Just c-can't find my way out here."

Booth strained to keep his temper. "All right! All right! Let's just keep our wits about us."

Davey Herold rowed a ragged course toward the dark shore. In a few minutes the scow thudded against a soft bank, the current quickly turning it parallel to a low bluff. Herold stepped onto the crumbling shore, the mooring line wrapped around his arm. Booth felt the boat lurch sideways. Davey lifted the bow up onto a narrow beach and fell back, exhausted.

"Indiantown, all right," Davey gasped.

"Can we still make Virginia tonight?"

"Haven't got it in me. S-sorry."

"Tomorrow night, then." *I am going to go mad.*

"We're among f-friends, John. We're safe."

The friends, two middle-aged men who farmed the land in a bachelors' partnership, had little to offer save food and drink and the name of a Southern loyalist on the Virginia shore. Over supper, the two men lamented the misfortune of the fallen South, and it occurred to Booth that their spirits were not at all lifted by the presence of Lincoln's killer at their table. He was tormented. *I must get to General Lee.*

They did not cross the river the next night. Davey's back was knotted up. He spent both evenings upstairs in the farmers' copper bathtub, soaking in Epsom salts while Booth slouched in an uncomfortable parlor chair, watching the two farmers silently play checkers. *Get to Lee.*

Their second crossing landed them in territory Davey also knew from his hunting expeditions. The agonizing delays were wearing Booth down. In a kind of detached fog, he stood with Davey at the imposing front door of a Virginia mansion that opened to bathe them in light and welcoming voices and the warm scent of cologne. Surrounded by smiling faces, he shook hands and recited his usual pleasantries, answering questions as admiring hands patted him on the shoulder. A hero of the South is among us! He drank whiskey, glass after glass. He recognized the rosy scent of an aristocratic matron's perfume and heard her cultured Southern drawl—disembodied, lilting words he acknowledged in actorly fashion, saying what was proper and expected, then swallowing more whiskey, noting how the crystal glass glinted in the soft light. Somewhere in the delirium he slept for a few hours on a bed, somewhere. Then came daylight and two new horses, and they were riding again. Jones's compass still did its maddening dance, but they were finally, blessedly, heading south, due south.

On they rode in the full light of day, letting their horses set the pace, using the field glasses to reconnoiter the territory ahead. The absence of Union patrols made this bucolic expanse of the Old Dominion seem as though the war had never been. Birds sang, roadside wildflowers bowed to them as they passed. A short, wizened old man in a weathered buckboard pulled by two shaggy nags tipped his straw hat.

Coming down off a rise they approached a small field where five black men worked with hoes, preparing the ground for planting. They stopped their toil as the white men neared, and watched. Put off by their silent stares, Booth glared at them. "Enjoying your freedom, gentlemen?"

"No need for that, John," warned Herold.

"Life's *so* much better now, isn't it, gentlemen? Full of possibilities! Oh, the world is your oyster now, isn't it?"

"J-John. Don't trouble them."

Booth felt torn between rage and grief. *What worth did the great Saint Abraham see in these baboons? He was Kentucky born! What led him to his poisonous follies?* He entertained a fantasy of talking with Lincoln over glasses of whiskey. *I could have made him see the folly of his ways!* Then he thought—with a pang—for a moment, of Bradley, his childhood playmate, the son of neighboring slaves, his best friend until age ten, until they realized—or were told—that they were different, separated by different destinies. Where was Bradley now? He was free—he was suddenly an equal.

Herold ventured a conciliatory nod at the field hands, who remained still as statues, eyes fixed on them. Then he saw the face of one man change, overtaken by a terrible recognition.

"Lord Almighty, that looks like—"

They stood stricken, watching Lincoln's murderer ride past.

"Thass him," said one of the field hands. "I think thass *him*."

To Booth, the Confederacy seemed alive and well in Virginia. Nearing Port Conway on the Rappahannock River, they passed a contingent of gray-uniformed soldiers, some mounted, others riding in wagons.

"All is not lost, Davey," he crowed as they shook hands with a trio of young Confederate soldiers in Port Royal. They were members of the 43rd Battalion of the 1st Virginia Cavalry, General John Mosby's fabled Rangers. In his exuberance, Booth impulsively removed his glove to reveal the tattoo on his left hand, *J.W.B.*

"Mr. Booth, an honor, sir."

Stunned, the elite guerrilla fighters volunteered to escort them on the ferry crossing the Rappahannock to Port Royal, and to act as a bodyguard until Booth found refuge for the night. The soldiers made inquiries at farms and estates, beseeching their owners to take in a wounded veteran named "Mister James William Boyd," an alias Booth had recently concocted. Theirs was not an unusual request. After Appomattox, many soldiers were forced to wander the roads. Most Virginians considered it not merely a civic duty but an honor to host these heroes on their journey home.

Toward evening, about five miles down the road from Port Royal, the Rangers released their charge to the hospitality of a genteel Caroline County farmer named Richard Garrett. Davey Herold would continue south to scout their route and arrange the next night's sanctuary. Booth embraced him briefly, then eased himself to the ground, unsheathed his crutches, and hobbled off alongside Richard Garrett as Davey and the Rangers departed.

Garrett's 500-acre estate was home to his extended family, including a dutiful son named John, a second son William, and his namesake Richard, Jr. who was not yet twelve. At dinner Booth entertained the family with vivid tales of sabotage missions and evading Union patrols. Booth let the children play with the compass, showing how a knife blade could redirect the needle. He took a shine to one of the daughters, calling her My Little Blue Eyes. To the elder Garrett and his two younger sons hunched over the oval dining room, James Boyd was a Mosby-certified hero, and a refined example of Southern gallantry. Little Dickie hung on his every word. And the women in the family admired his wit and manners. Only the elder son, Jack, a poker-faced man, failed to delight in the actor's stories of derring-do.

Always sensitive to the reactions of his audience, Booth was quick to note Jack Garrett's reserve. To win him over, Booth courted him with questions about his farming, his future marriage, his horse sense, his everything. But this time Booth's instincts had failed him. Jack was not intimidated by their talkative guest's adventures, but suspicious. He did not believe the garrulous Mr. Boyd was genuine.

By the third day he grumbled about sharing his bedroom with the traveler, and resented Boyd's apparent need to dominate every conversation. His father had left the farm for an overnight trip north to buy seed, leaving the farm and family under his stewardship. Meantime, Boyd seemed to have no intention of leaving anytime soon, and no compelling agenda despite frequent mention of a yearning to see his "beloved mother" in Baltimore after so many years of military service.

Seated beside the actor on the family's front porch, reading the new *Farmer's Almanac*, Garrett was perplexed by his guest's sudden alarm at the passage of a Union patrol on the road skirting the farm. His puzzlement turned to fear when Booth sent his younger brother William upstairs to fetch his revolver and a belt of cartridges. As Booth strapped on the belt, Garrett looked at him.

"That's hardly necessary," Garrett told him. "The war is over, and I can assure you the Garretts have nothing to answer for to either side."

"Perhaps," Booth replied, keeping his eye on the blue-clad cavalrymen as they receded into the distance.

Garrett's doubts only increased when, late that afternoon, Davey Herold galloped up to the house, and Booth, using only a single crutch, hobbled across the yard to speak with him, out of earshot. He had not seen Boyd move that fast before.

Davey Herold looked frightened. "The roads are crawling with f-federals, John. Newspaper in B-Bowling Green said they caught Atzerodt. That's him and Powell and Mrs. Surratt in irons now."

The name of his failed co-conspirators made Booth wince. "John Surratt—what of him? And Arnold?"

"Still on the loose—but that was yesterday," said Herold.

"And, by God, they haven't caught us yet. Where are the Rangers?"

"Long gone. John. We p-parted ways down in Bowling Green. They gave me this." He opened his coat to display the handle of a Griswold & Gunnison revolver, the best sidearm of the Confederacy. Booth surprised him by grabbing his lapel and closing the coat to conceal the weapon from Garrett's eyes. Then he looked back at the farmer, and shouted across the yard. "This is my cousin Davey Boyd. He's been with Mosby's Rangers."

Booth was not satisfied with Garrett's sober nod, and turned back to Davey. "We'll stay here tonight and leave tomorrow."

Davey shifted uncomfortably. "I think that's a b-bad plan, John. Riding back here it looks like they're going f-farm to farm."

Booth glanced at Garrett. The farmer's stony gaze was still fixed on them.

"We ought to leave here soon as it's d-dark."

Booth limped back to the porch steps. "Jack, I'd like to stay one more night, and I'd appreciate it if you'd extend your hospitality to my cousin. He has fought bravely for The Cause."

Jack Garrett's expression was cold. "My father is away today. In his absence, I cannot open his home to anyone—yourself included." He saw Booth's mouth open, then close. "I'd prefer you both leave. Port Royal has accommodations and many good people who I expect will welcome you."

"But why not you, then?" Booth said. "Are you not 'good people' as well? What's changed?" Garrett's unblinking stare was beginning to unnerve him.

"Just pack up," said Garrett. "It's time to leave. I believe we all know why."

"Will you put us up in your father's barn, then? Would that be beyond your authority?"

"One night. You and your kinsman can bed down in the tobacco barn. But I'll ask you to be gone by daylight. Is that understood, Mister—*Boyd*?"

Davey Herold had ventured over to the foot of the porch. "We sh-should go now, John."

"I have to think this through," said Booth. He turned back to Garrett. "As you wish. Have you got a map of Virginia—so we may plan our route?"

"The way to Baltimore is simple enough, sir."

"I have business first with Robert E. Lee."

"Oh, do you now," said Garrett.

"Yes, sir, in point of fact, I do."

Twelve miles to the northeast, on the far side of the Rappahannock, as the sun touched the plain ahead, the black field hand who thought he had recognized Booth loped along the road, sweat-soaked and determined to overtake the Union patrol just a half-mile beyond. The two dozen members of the 16th New York Cavalry were under the command of twenty-five-year-old Lieutenant Edward P. Doherty. He had been deployed on orders issued by the War Department, from Colonel Lafayette Baker, head of the National Detective police. The new instructions indicated that Booth was not in Maryland as most had supposed, but in northern Virginia. This was encouraging until Doherty and his soldiers realized the region was vast and its sympathies decidedly Confederate. No one ventured out to greet them. They were the victors, but here they were pariahs.

Now only a quarter-mile behind them, the field hand felt as if his heart were near bursting. He had learned painfully to avoid soldiers, but these wore blue, not gray. He was also a free man now. Once he had answered to the single slave name Cotton, given to him by his master, in whose cotton fields he had labored. But with the Emancipation Proclamation, he was free to take a new name. Cotton was gone. He chose his new first name from the Bible readings he attended at a Negro church. His second from his savior. The newly minted Joseph Lincoln could not read, but on an errand to Port Conway for his former owner, he had seen a newspaper tacked to a wall, its front page bearing a photo-engraving of Booth under the headline: "ASSASSIN!" Hat in hand, he asked a white man what it meant, and the man told him. The next day, he was convinced that the very same man in the newspaper had passed his field.

Now Joseph Lincoln began shouting at the cavalrymen to stop. He loped along the stone-filled road, panting hard and waving his arms. He saw one of the soldiers turn in his saddle.

"Hold up! I got news!"

Then all the soldiers turned to look at him, and Doherty brought the column to a halt.

# CHAPTER SIX

That night Booth lay on his blanket atop a bed of hay in Garrett's tobacco barn. He was breathing heavily, lathered in sweat, tossing fitfully in a frightful dream of riding, *Hoof beats, hoof beats, hoof beats* throbbing in his ears. He woke hard, his heart racing, and looked around in bewilderment at the blue shafts of moonlight falling between the wide-set boards of the barn. Then he remembered where he was, and fell back onto the blanket. It was three in the morning.

Twelve days now since the night at Ford's. Still he heard the clatter of his horse's hooves echoing in the alleyway behind the theater. Sleep did not allay the nightmares, any more than it smothered the pistol shot. He fumbled for his pocket watch and held it in the dim light: past midnight. He twisted, heard himself groan.

Davey's news from Bowling Green had upset him. Atzerodt the incompetent Prussian carriage-painter had failed to kill Johnson. Powell, the muscle-bound thug proved incapable of knifing an unprotected, bed-ridden old man named Seward, then proceeded to bash and slash other members of the Secretary of State's family before fleeing. He knew Atzerodt and Powell would talk. But Mary Surratt, she would be strong. Booth knew she wouldn't crack. She would cling to her rosary beads. Damn it, why hadn't he taken her son John's advice and gone to that Catholic hideout in Maryland? Then to Canada. And Spain. No, it had seemed better to go deeper into the South.

He felt like a wounded fox before the hounds, crossing swamps and rivers, begging help from those dwindling few still loyal to The Cause. Running, hiding, resting. Running. *Hoof beats.*

And now this barn deep in Virginia, the moldy hay was making him nauseous. All this running and cowering, this demeaning flight would end soon—when he reached General Lee. Yes, tomorrow he could be in Richmond.

Middle of the night and yet so humid and hot. He was hungry, but more, he needed a drink. He maneuvered his splinted leg into a more comfortable position, took a swallow from the whiskey bottle, but the ache wouldn't stop. He took another swallow, then corked the bottle and lay down again. He tried to sleep, but he kept hearing hoof beats. His poor mare. He'd hated to kill that good horse in the swamp, but Jones had been right. Toward the end, mostly at night, the mare was raising a fuss, agitating the other as well. Mares fought with each other. She could have betrayed them. What a merciless, unforgiving world he was in now.

He tried to sleep, to erase all the terrible images in his mind which he chose to think of as *The Event*. Concentrate on the good things to come. But he kept hearing hoof beats. He sat up. Now they weren't in his mind. They were real.

He groped for his revolver, then pulled himself up on a crutch. He gasped at the first painful stab in his lower leg as he limped over to the broken slat at the back of the barn. A good exit hole, he thought.

He heard a horse at a trot, slowing to a walk.

Soldiers? No, it sounded like a single animal. Pursuers never came alone. In the cold moonlight: a horse and rider. He couldn't tell if the man was in uniform. Perhaps the stranger would ride by. But no—now he was veering off the road and heading towards the barn. The man dismounted and tied his horse a hundred yards from the barn.

Booth cocked his pistol, stepping back into the shadows behind the bales of hay. He watched the door creak open. A shaft of moonlight pierced a hole in the roof to illuminate the intruder like a theater lamp.

From the shadows Booth could see that the man was a tattered and dusty soldier. Round-shouldered, thin, no taller than he. He wore the gray uniform of a Confederate private.

"Hold it right there, friend," said Booth. "I have an iron leveled at your chest."

The man jerked back. "Who's there? I can't see you."

"What are you doing here?"

"I came from the 62nd," said the soldier. "All the way from Belle Plain today."

"The sixty-second *what?*"

"Virginia Infantry, Company C."

"Is someone after you?" he demanded. "What's your name?"

"Put the gun away, mister," the man mumbled.

"Name!"

"Beech," said the man.

"First name?"

"Wilson."

"Why did you come here?" Booth poked the muzzle of his revolver against Beech's chest. "Why this barn? Have you been trailing me?"

"I'm tired, mister. Told you, I come down from Belle Plain. Why the hell would I trail you? Please put that damn iron away. I ain't hurtin' nobody."

He sagged down onto the hay on buckling legs and wiped his face with the bandanna at his throat. Holding the revolver on him, Booth struck a match, lit a lantern. The man took off his big hat. Now Booth could see his face—sweaty, gaunt, high cheekbones, dark complexioned and about his own age—twenty-six, twenty-seven. No moustache, but dark eyes, blood-shot, strangely familiar to Booth. Like brother Edwin, thought Booth. *Or me on a bad day.* The soldier's tunic was torn open at the neck, the buttons missing. Booth noticed a blotchy scar on his neck.

"Very strange," Booth said. "In all Virginia you just happen to rest at this particular barn. Where were you going? And tell me true, my friend, or I'll shoot you with no qualms."

"I got into—into a little trouble. I'm really heading out West."

"West?"

"Montana Territory." The man finished wiping his face. "They've struck gold big at Bannack. Gold nuggets tumbling out of the creek beds. And a place called Alder Gulch. My cousin Wilma—she wrote me—she's there—she says everybody's getting rich. Now that the war's over, there's where I'm going."

"You expect me to believe these tales of Eldorado?"

"Eldorado? No, it's in Montana territory. Up the Missouri. That's why I got to get to St. Louis—the river boat to Fort Benton, then—"

"You're heading in the wrong direction, friend." Booth uncocked his revolver and pushed it under his belt. *The man is a wastrel, but he has a horse tied up outside.*

About five hundred yards from the barn, Davey Herold sat on the ground, his back against a tree, snoring softly. His .52-caliber Spencer rifle lay across his lap, his Bowie knife in his hand. Oblivious to the faint barking of distant dogs, he dreamed of coon-hunting along the Potomac in simpler times, a life forever lost to him now. *Hoof beats.* Then he heard the horses and awakened.

Davey crept silently to the edge of the woods. The dogs and soldiers were far away. He lifted the field glasses and scanned the road below Garrett's farm from north to south, a blue-tinted tableaux of moonlight. On a distant rise, perhaps a mile distant, he could make out what looked to be the silhouettes of mounted cavalry. There were many. At this late hour, he knew, they were not likely to be Confederates.

*Footsteps.* Booth held up his hand to silence Beech's aimless prattle about Montana's gold. He drew his revolver, limped to a crevice in the wall, peered out at the moonlit road, and saw someone walking toward the barn: Davey. He eased the revolver's hammer back down.

Beech had retreated into the shadows. "Don't tell 'em about me, sir."

"Calm yourself," said Booth. "It's just my friend."

Davey pulled open the door, lurched in. He leaned his back against the door, panting hard, his eyes wild. "Soldiers, John! They're circling the ridge." Even in the lantern light, Booth could see that his face was ashen.

"How many?"

"A lot of 'em! Maybe twenty. Or more."

"Where are they?"

"Across the valley, on the ridge. No more'n twenty minutes, I'd say. Oh, Lord, I got a feeling this is the end."

"The hell it is," said Booth calmly. "We're getting out of here."

The soldier remained motionless in the shadows. Following Booth's eyes, Davey gave a start as for the first time he noticed Beech. "Who the d-devil is he?"

"Just a fellow Southerner in trouble," said Booth. "Mr. Beech, this is my cousin, Davey Boyd."

Beech merely nodded, staying in the shadows. Herold was too

frightened to pay the newcomer any attention.

"Not running any more, John," he said. He had to swallow now to muster courage. "S-stayin' here, give myself up."

"They'll hang you."

"Can't run no more," muttered Herold. "Garrett must have sold us out." He rummaged in his saddle bag and pulled out a pint of whiskey, took a long pull and passed it to Booth. "I'm going out, John."

"Don't be a fool, Davey. They'll hang you sure as we stand here."

"Give yourself up, J-John! You can't run forever." He put the pistol in his belt and lifted the bottle to his lips.

"Don't forget The Cause, boy."

"They'll catch up with you and they'll shoot you down." Herold's voice was hoarse with despair.

"Not if I get to Lee first. We can still turn the tide and rally the South. I know it. Lee will save us."

Booth glanced over at Beech, whose head had been on a swivel, watching their back-and-forth. Booth held out the bottle to him. "Drink, friend?"

"Don't mind if I do," said the Confederate, stepping from the shadows.

Instead of taking the bottle, he raised a large revolver and pointed it at Booth's face.

"Mr. John Wilkes Booth, I do believe," said Beech. "Raise your hands."

Then he yanked Booth's pistol from his belt and pushed it under his tarnished CSA buckle.

"You're making a mistake," said Booth quietly.

"Guess I won't be heading to Montana after all," said Beech.

"A very big mistake," said Booth.

"Mr. Booth," said Beech. "There's a large reward for you. Fifty thousand dollars. You are my own gold strike." He laughed as though he'd said something very clever.

"What exactly do you plan to do?" asked Booth. He spoke calmly, waiting for the man to make a mistake. He had not come this far, overcoming obstacle after obstacle, and risked so much, only to be stopped by this malodorous dolt.

"I plan to take my walkin' gold mine—that would be you—to Washington," said Beech. "Or the nearest Yankee camp. Collect the fifty thousand reward. That's my plan, Mr. Booth. Then I intend to go back to my farm in Front Royal and never work again."

"I dislike spoiling your plans," said Booth. "But I am not going with you."

Beech raised the revolver. "The poster, 'case you don't know," said Beech between clenched teeth, "reads 'Dead or Alive'. And I ain't the least bit fussy which it's going to be."

Herold took a step forward. "You foul bastard!"

Beech turned the muzzle of his revolver away from Booth, leveling it at Herold's chest. "One step more, boy, and I'll blow you to Hell."

Booth shattered the whiskey bottle against the man's head. Even as Beech fell back against the bales of hay, Booth was on top of him, one hand grasping the barrel of the pistol, the other jabbing with the jagged bottle neck at his face. Beech was strong, but Booth was able to force the man's hand back and back until the barrel was against his throat and pointed up under his jaw.

"No!" Beech screamed.

There was an explosion. Beech's head jerked. His body slid over the bales to the ground. He clawed at his bloody neck, a rush of air burbling from his throat. He twitched feebly, convulsed and lay unmoving.

Booth, breathing hard, watched the man's face.

"Dirty skunk," whispered Herold, staring down at him. "He had it coming."

"Poor devil," said Booth. "I didn't mean that to happen. But his bad luck—our good luck." He looked around him and saw a pitchfork, a sledgehammer and a shovel leaning against a workbench.

"Fetch me that sledge," Booth commanded. "Our friend here will be my passport to Lee."

Herold brought the tool. Booth reached down and shoved the dead man's left pant leg up to the knee. He raised the sledge over his head and swung it down hard, striking the leg with a crunch just above the ankle.

He dropped the sledgehammer and quickly began undressing. The ghastly corpse glared up at him.

"And now, Davey, you must give me your help. Your last bit of help. Then if you're not coming with me, I'll be out of your life forever."

"I d-don't understand," said Herold.

"Like Macbeth: 'They have tied me to a stake; I cannot fly, but bear-like, I must fight the course.' There's our motto, Davey. Fight the course!"

"You know I will, Johnny," said the boy. "And G-God help us."

"God can only help those who help themselves, Davey," said Booth, stripping off his clothes. "Put my clothes on that man's body. And here take this. Attach it to his shirt." It was a gold stickpin, given to Booth years ago by a fellow actor.

When Beech's body was dressed, Booth pulled out a bottle of ink and a pen. Then he took Beech's limp left hand in his, setting it on his thigh. He began to punch the pen methodically into the skin like a tattoo artist.

"Why're you doing that, Johnny?"

"Because of this," said Booth holding up his left hand. Tattooed between thumb and forefinger were the faint blue initials *J.W.B.* He had done this to himself as a boy in Maryland. And now he was doing it to the man who would save his life.

# CHAPTER SEVEN

Half an hour later twenty-five uniformed horsemen cantered up to the Garrets' farmhouse, followed by three men in mufti. Lieutenant Doherty and two sergeants swung off their mounts and strode to the front porch. They banged once on the door, then swiftly forced it open. The farmer, Richard Garrett, stumbled down the stairs, nightshirt tucked into pantaloons, an oil lamp in his hand.

"Gentlemen, what is the meaning of this?"

"Where are they?" demanded a voice.

"Who?"

"You know who, Garrett. The two men."

"They've—they left. They went to the woods."

Lieutenant Luther Byron Baker stepped in front of Garrett, pushed him up against the door jamb, and shoved a revolver against his neck. "Where are they?"

"They were here but they left to go to the woods and then they came back for their supper and then they left again—"

"No long stories, farmer! Come hang this rebel," Luther Baker called over his shoulder. "A little stretching will improve his memory."

Four soldiers grabbed Garrett and hustled him down the porch steps and across the yard to a chopping block. His wife and daughter ran downstairs and screamed from the porch as the farmer was boosted onto the block. A soldier knotted a rope and slipped it over Garrett's head. Another man flipped the rope over a limb and pulled it taut.

"Stop!"

Dickie Garrett, the farmer's eleven-year-old son, wearing only a pair of dungarees, bounded down the porch steps. The soldiers kept the tension on the rope, and the farmer was now lifted on tiptoe, his face puffed with blood, eyes bulging.

"Let my daddy go!" cried Dickie. "They're down there! In the tobacco barn!"

Lieutenant Baker holstered his revolver, the soldiers released the rope, and Garrett fell limply to the ground.

Minutes later, twenty-five dark shapes stole down the slope in the moonlight. In black shadows, they surrounded the barn.

They were the Sixteenth New York Cavalry led by Lieutenant Edward P. Doherty. Riding with them were two detectives from the National Detective Agency, Colonel Everton Conger and Lieutenant Luther Byron Baker, first cousin of Lafayette Baker, the powerful federal detective in charge of apprehending Booth and the conspirators. "Lafe" Baker had made it clear that Booth was to be captured at all costs, not only for justice, but for the reward, which would be split among all involved with Booth's capture. Luther Baker would ensure that a large portion of that $50,000 stayed in the family.

Lieutenant Baker was eager for this to end. In his twelve days of running and hiding, Booth had left a hardscrabble trail. Until the clues added up—the doctor who splinted his leg, the boat obtained to cross the Rappahannock, the occasional help from traceable sympathizers, the Negro field hand. Now the manhunt would end. The question that every citizen in America was asking—"Where's Wilkes Booth?"—would soon be answered: the murderer was cornered like a treed raccoon in Garrett's barn near Bowling Green, Virginia.

Lieutenant Doherty directed his men swiftly by hand signals and whispered commands. They crept around the barn, most of them at the back, blocking the woods where a fleeing assassin would try to escape. When every man was in place, Luther Baker crept forward. A few yards behind him crouched a short man in civilian clothes.

It was Langford Upham, Jr., the roving reporter for *The New York World*. Wearing a fashionable New York suit and derby hat, he seemed very out of place. But Lafe Baker, never averse to publicity, had invited Upham to accompany his cousin Luther to record the assassin's capture for posterity. The young reporter had achieved some fame with his eye-witness account of the president's murder—and he would ensure proper credit for the reward when the capture was made. He would record history. Baker had raised the reward stakes higher for every day Booth was free—and made sure his cousin Luther Baker would be part of the take.

When the soldiers were in place, Lieutenant Baker called out, "All right, Wilkes Booth! Come out!"

There was silence. Baker heard the soldiers breathing the night air.

"You are surrounded!"

No answer. One soldier was shifting his feet and coughing nervously.

"Come out, Wilkes Booth," Baker boomed again. "We won't hurt you!"

No answer from the barn.

A small florid-faced sergeant, Boston Corbett, left the side of the barn and slunk back to where Baker crouched. A devout Christian, Corbett had served with bravery in battle. Yet all acknowledged there was something odd about him.

"Lieutenant, I can see one of 'em in there," he whispered. "I can shoot him through a crack in the boards!"

"I want to take him alive," hissed Baker.

"One's leaning on a bale of hay. The other's close to the door." The soldier was panting and his eyes had a demented glaze. "I can get the sitting one easy. He looks half asleep! Lieutenant, let me get him!"

"Back to your post!"

As Baker turned to direct the men, he saw Corbett slide back to the side of the barn.

"Disobedient bastard," Baker muttered to Upham. "Don't care about orders. Just glory." It was well known that the reward would make a man rich, but the orders said "alive." They would need Booth's testimony against the other captured conspirators.

Baker motioned to the soldiers at the corners of the barn. They began gathering brush and logs and piling them up against the planks of the structure.

Upham said, "Let me go in there before you fire it!"

"You insane?" the colonel retorted.

"I'll bet I can talk him out," said Upham. "Appeal to him. His life story in the paper, Booth's view of the assassination. His cause. Brutus, Caesar, The Republic."

"And if you got killed? Your father would have my head."

"Remember, I was at Ford's Theater," said Upham. "I witnessed Booth's grand night, his greatest performance. I can appeal to this man's ego."

Baker shook his head. "City lad, don't play Cicero. Stay out of this. Your Daddy'd have me shot."

Baker shouted behind him at the Garrett family. "William Garrett, come here."

The adolescent approached the detective. "Yes, sir?"

"Mr. Booth won't hurt you. Your family fed him. Gave him a nice hiding place. Now you go in there—to the barn—and ask him for his gun. Tell him to come out peaceable."

Richard Garrett, still rubbing his rope-burned neck, said, "Lieutenant, he's just a boy!"

"I'm warning you, Garrett. You're this close to being considered an accomplice." Then Baker turned and put his arm around the trembling boy. "William, just ask Mr. Booth for his guns. That's all."

The pale boy swallowed. "His guns, sir?"

Baker gave him a slow but firm push toward the barn. The boy took a cautious step.

Then Baker shouted: "All right, Wilkes Booth, William Garrett's coming in there, coming to talk to you. He's just a boy, don't go shooting him."

William walked hesitantly up to the barn. A soldier yanked open the door and stepped back quickly. William stopped in front of the doorway while the soldiers trained their rifles on the void.

"Mister—kin I come in?" The boy's voice quavered. "Don't kill me, please."

"Speak your piece from there, boy," said a voice from the darkness. "Be quick about it."

The boy's legs shook. "The Lieutenant says throw out your weapons and come out clean. They swear you won't get hurt."

A dry laugh came from the barn. "You'd best go back, Billy."

The boy turned and raced back to the farmhouse.

"I want you to surrender, Wilkes Booth," said Baker. "If you don't, I will burn this barn down."

"Give me time to think about it," said the voice.

Luther Baker caught Everton Conger's eye. "How much time?"

"Fifteen minutes," said the detective. "Then we fire the barn."

"We want him alive, don't we?"

"That depends."

"All right, Wilkes Booth! Can you hear me?"

Again there was that voice, "Who are you and what do you want?"

"It doesn't make any difference who we are. We want to take you prisoners."

Then, suddenly a voice from the barn. "Oh, captain, there's a man here who wants to come out!"

Upham strained to hear what was happening. How many men were actually in the barn? How well-armed were they?

"All right, throw your weapons out! Then hold your empty hands out the door. Where we can see 'em."

"He is unarmed," said the voice. "The arms are mine. There is a man here who wants to come out. He is innocent."

"Yes," said another voice. "Let me out. I do not know this desperate character, and he is going to shoot me."

Doherty turned to Baker. "We'd better let him out."

Doherty positioned himself to one side of the barn door, then shouted, "You inside! Show your hands!"

Empty hands were thrust through the aperture. Doherty grabbed them and pulled the man out like an errant schoolboy. Soldiers wrestled him across the yard, his head dangling, his feet dragging. As Upham and Baker approached, the prisoner raised his head.

"That's not Booth!" Upham shouted.

"Who are you?" demanded Doherty.

"Herold," gasped the man. "Davey Herold—and I didn't hurt or kill n-nobody, honest!"

"Tie that man to a tree," Baker ordered. "Booth must still be in there."

"Let's wait until dawn. Let's talk him out," Doherty suggested.

"Don't be a fool," said Baker. "He's heavily armed and could pick us off."

Everton Conger caught his eye. "Let's fire it."

"All right," said Baker.

"Wilkes Booth," shouted Conger. "We are going to fire the barn!"

No reply.

After ten minutes Baker looked at his pocket watch and shouted. "Only five minutes to go, Wilkes Booth. Then we fire the barn."

When there was no response, Conger gave the signal, and four soldiers set fire to the brush piled against the barn. The flames turned the men's faces to orange masks. The other soldiers had their rifles at the ready for whatever should run from the inferno.

"Had enough, Booth?" yelled Baker.

There was a long silence. The flames crawled up the sides of the barn and invaded its innards. The hay was crackling.

Crack of a pistol shot. It came from the side of the barn where Boston Corbett had stationed himself.

Before the Lieutenant could stop him, Upham was running towards the burning building. The flames hadn't reached the doorway, and he backed in, holding a handkerchief to his nose. Through the smoke, he made out a body lying on a pile of hay, a pistol gripped in the right hand. Upham saw a crumpled figure with a grotesque blood-spattered face. The man was dead or dying. Three soldiers grabbed him under the arms, dragged him across the crackling black hay and carried him out of the inferno.

Thirty yards from the burning barn they laid him on the grass.

"Got him, boys!" shouted a soldier. "We've got Booth!"

Lieutenant Baker strode over to the body and looked down at the bloody, cinder-flecked face. "God damn it, men. He's been shot. Who fired?"

Upham also was studying the corpse's head. He'd been in the front row when Booth shot Lincoln twelve days ago in Ford's Theater, he'd seen the assassin close up. He'd actually talked to him. Could this corpse have ever been that man?

"Sir, Booth had a moustache," said Upham, bending over the bloody face.

"He would have shaved it off first thing," said Lieutenant Baker. "Use your goddamned head."

"I saw him in *The Rivals* just last year," said a soldier. "Looked different."

"Death does that sometimes," said Baker.

"It's more than that," said Upham.

"The clothes fit the exact description they gave us," said Baker defensively. "Expensive suit, tailored by the best. That's Booth, all right."

"He was a more muscular man," said Upham. "An athlete. This man is thin."

"He's been on the run for days. Lost weight." Luther Baker ignored him. "Check his pockets for identification."

Upham started to kneel down.

"Get back, sir," said Baker. "Detective Conger, please inspect the man's pockets."

Conger knelt and went through the dead man's torn and bloodstained suit. There was nothing in the pants pocket but a few coins. In the side pockets of the tailored jacket were some tobacco, a compass, and a small knife, but from the breast pocket came a little notebook. Conger flipped it open and saw many pages written in pencil. Upham looked over his shoulder. "May I see that please?" said Upham.

Conger looked to Baker for approval.

"Go ahead, let the reporter do his job."

By the flames' flickering, Upham found the last page and saw it was dated that morning. He straightened up and, squinting, read aloud:

*"Friday, 21st. After being hunted like a dog through swamps and woods, and last night being chased by gunboats till I was forced to return, wet, cold, and starving with every man's hand against me, I am here in despair. And why? For doing what Brutus was honored for—what made William Tell a Hero, and yet I, for striking down an even greater tyrant than they ever knew am treated like a common cutthroat—"*

"All right, that's enough, Upham." Lieutenant Baker yanked the notebook. As he did so, five photographs fell out of a side pocket. Upham bent quickly to gather them up. They were of young women. One he recognized as Lucy Hale, daughter of former New Hampshire Senator John Hale, now ambassador to Spain. Purported to be Booth's fiancée.

"Mr. Upham, I'll take those, thank you," said Conger firmly. He slipped them with the notebook into his pocket. "It's Booth, all right."

Conger nodded to Herold, now bound tightly to a tree. "Let's see what he has to say."

Baker walked over to him. "Prisoner, identify yourself."

"David Herold."

"And do you know this man?" he said, pointing to the corpse.

"I don't know him. I never met him before."

"Could you take a guess? Who do you think it is?"

Herold spat out. "It's the goddamned k-king of England himself."

A soldier struck him across the face. "Answer the Lieutenant proper! Who is it, and tell it true or I'll put a bayonet through your gut!"

Herold bit his lip. "It's who you think it is, sirs." Tears ran down his face. "The best friend a m-man could have, it's—John Wilkes Booth."

"Friend?" said Lieutenant Baker. "*Friend*? He sure got you in a fine mess, boy."

The bewhiskered little sergeant, Boston Corbett, ran up to the Lieutenant, panting, then assumed a more distinguished pose. "I was the one who got him, sir," he said. "I told you I could hit him and I did!"

"You fired," said the Lieutenant quietly, "against my orders."

"I saw him there through the crack, sir. He weren't makin' no move to come out even with the fire comin' around him. He was leaning against a hay bale with a pistol in his hand. Providence directed me."

"He wouldn't make a move," said Upham, "if he was already dead."

Lieutenant Baker stared at Upham and then down at the pistol still in the corpse's rigid hand. He frowned, glancing at Conger. "You think—suicide?"

Conger shook his head. "I don't like that—oh, I don't like that at all, Mr. Upham. The government wanted to interview this man before having the pleasure of hanging him. They won't like it that I let the assassin get away with a nice death like that."

No," said Lieutenant Baker. "The facts speak for themselves. I think Sergeant Corbett here did the job."

"Yes," said Conger. "I'm sure he did."

"Thank you, sir," said Corbett. "Hit him in the neck I did, right in the neck."

"It just doesn't look like him," said Upham.

"Who else would it be?" said Baker. "Who else would have written that diary?"

"Maybe it's one of the other conspirators," said Upham. "Two others are still at large."

Baker knelt down and shoved up the pants on the dead man's left leg. Baker, Conger and Upham stared at the bluish bulge just above the ankle.

"There's your answer," said Lieutenant Baker smugly.

Upham scowled. "Guess you're right." But, he was wondering why a leg broken almost two weeks ago would not be more on the mend.

"And look at this, Upham," said Baker pointing to the corpse's left hand. "Tattooed initials." Upham looked and saw the faint marks. *J.W.B.* But it occurred to him that tattoos were generally bluish under the skin, not gray-black.

"And here we have a stickpin in the shirt. Inscribed 'Dan Bryant to J.W.B.' That should do it." said Luther Baker. "Now, Upham, my good man. Swear to me that you won't put anything in your write-up suggesting suicide."

"Or that this isn't Booth," added Conger, leaning in. "Report what you must report, but don't exaggerate. Don't expand the truth to...something else."

Upham shrugged. "Sir, I've got to write it as I see it."

"This is John Wilkes Booth. We all know that much. Herold has identified him. And the notebook. It's definitely Booth."

But was he? Was *this* body really Booth's mortal remains?

"I spoke with Booth at Ford's, saw him on the stage as he escaped," said Upham. "I got a good look at his face—at his eyes. This man doesn't quite resemble him."

"This man's eyes are closed! And his face is swollen with blood."

"I'm not convinced."

As Upham started to walk away, Lieutenant Baker grabbed him by the shoulder and spun him around. "Now listen, you," he said. "My cousin Lafe Baker gave you the chance of a life to come along. What you saw tonight was the capture and killing of John Wilkes Booth. Do we have an understanding?"

Upham stared back and said calmly. "With all due respect, I'm still not certain this corpse is that man, Lieutenant."

Luther Baker held his face close to Upham's and said coldly, "Write this down, Mister: 'Boston Corbett, a brave veteran sergeant of the Sixteenth New York Cavalry, under the command of Edward Doherty and with the guidance of detectives Luther Byron Baker and Colonel Everton Conger at great risk to all their lives, tonight managed to outwit and kill the wily, heavily-armed John Wilkes Booth, assassin of the sixteenth President of the United States.' Got it?"

Upham gave a little smile. "Got it," he said. The reporter firmly removed Baker's hand from his shoulder. "Goodnight, gentlemen. I've some traveling to do."

Upham turned and started walking back to the farmhouse where his horse was hitched. He knew he had a great story, in any case an exclusive one—even better than his account of the assassination twelve days ago. It would surely bring him a bonus and maybe a promotion. Wait until his father—a man who told people, "My bon vivant son thinks he's a reporter!"—wait till the old buzzard picked up his own newspaper. He could see the headline:

*I SAW THE ASSASSIN RUN DOWN AND SHOT!*
*An exclusive story by Langford Upham, Jr.*

He went over the facts in his head. Two men in a barn. Only two? Only two observed, one alive, one dead. The man was in Booth's clothes. The man was roughly Booth's height and age. Herold identified the corpse as Booth. The dead man's pockets held what was probably Booth's diary along with the *cartes de visite* of five lady-loves.

But what else was wrong besides the broken leg that didn't look right? What else? Granted, he'd been shot in the neck and the face was swollen, but the corpse simply didn't resemble the man he'd seen close-up at Ford's Theater. Booth was a thoroughbred; this man looks like a hardscrabble mule.

Still, what would a newspaperman's opinion count against Baker, Conger, Corbett, and the official report that would be published? What did the public want? An assassin on whom to vent their anger for the killing of a beloved president. Baker needed a corpse, Baker got a corpse. And he'd share in the reward.

As Upham was tightening the cinch on his saddle it came to him. The revolver! Clenched in the corpse's *right* hand!

Upham mounted his horse, then looked back at the gathered men, the corpse, and the prisoner bound to the tree, all framed by the burning barn beyond. The soldiers were still trying to put out the fire while the Garrett family stood to the side.

The corpse on the ground. The pistol had been found in his right hand. Hadn't he read that Booth was left-handed? And hadn't he held the dagger in his left hand when he slashed his way across the stage of Ford's Theater?

Was it possible—just possible —that Booth had been in that barn with two accomplices instead of one and escaped before the soldiers arrived? Beyond the burning barn lay dark protective woods that stretched for many miles. To the south, the welcoming heart of the Confederacy. It was possible. Not probable, but possible.

"Wilkes Booth, are you alive?" he muttered. "If so, God damn you!" He dug his spurs into the horse and was gone.

A minute later, a soldier crouching beside the man who had been dragged from the barn shouted, "Lieutenant Baker, sir!"

"What is it?"

"Please come quick, sir—this man is not dead. I just felt a pulse. And he said something."

# CHAPTER EIGHT

Three miles away, Booth cantered down the moonlit road. Minutes before Boston Corbett fired at Beech's body, propped up on a hay bale, Booth had crawled through a hedge behind the barn and slithered into the woods to find Beech's horse.

He turned in the saddle to glance at the flames of Garrett's barn still clawing the pre-dawn sky.

"God," he said aloud, "I hope they didn't kill Davey."

He reminded himself that he was responsible. Herold knew little of war or politics or life. He'd followed Booth into the conspiracy out of blind hero worship. Perhaps it was better for him to die quickly in the barn, before they could make him talk. Better for The Cause they both believed in so fervently. And certainly better for John Wilkes Booth, alias Wilson Beech.

The splint on Booth's throbbing ankle and lower leg banged painfully against the stirrup leather with every lunge of the horse. Mudd had done a good job; the leg was knitting, but it was swollen, purple, and far from healed.

A mile on he pulled his mount up and patted the animal's lathered neck. His family had always kept good horses on the farm in Maryland, and he appreciated fine bloodstock. As a boy he'd spent hours drawing pictures of horses in his school books, often with a knight or soldier astride them. This high-stepping gelding was too good to have belonged to a private in the Confederate Army; obviously, Beech had stolen well.

He let the horse walk down the road, a road that led to Richmond. He massaged his leg above the splint, inhaled the cool pine air and listened to the night's silence. Not even an owl's hoot. No one was following him. But how long would Beech's body be accepted as his?

My God, you—little Johnny Booth—have killed two men in the last two weeks.

Lincoln, a political tyrant, was one thing. A killer of hundreds of thousands, not to mention slaying Constitutional rights. But Beech had also been willing to kill—for money. How vulgar. Still the man's bloody face haunted him. He had to force the image out of his mind, along with other terrible images from *The Event*. Yes—he who had never killed any living thing had now slain two men. Justified by higher motive—they were for The Cause.

And what a piece of luck Beech had turned out to be, providing not only a reliable horse, but a uniform, albeit tattered and stinking. A couple of miles down the road would be a good time to use that vial of bleach to lighten his hair. He almost felt far enough away from the soldiers to relax. A few hours hence he would be safe in Richmond in the protection of—indeed, basking in the admiration of—Robert E. Lee.

Lee! Though he'd never met the general he could already hear the great man's voice intoning: "So you are the brave soldier—a Knight of the South!—who risked his life to kill The Tyrant! You have given new hope to all of us! You shall be decorated and join me in rallying the troops left to Jefferson Davis!" *There will be parades.*

He was jolted from fantasy: behind came the sound. Faintly, then louder, a galloping horse. *Hoof beats.*

Mother of God, how did they get on to him so fast?

Booth spurred his horse off the road into the trees, his pistol drawn. The horseman kept approaching. Booth made out a lone figure, small, like a monkey bareback on a pinto pony. The horse looked like Peacock, Booth's beloved childhood pony. In a moment he recognized the farmer's youngest boy, Dickie Garrett.

"Halt!" Booth commanded as he urged his horse out of the shadows, onto the road. The boy pulled up, his pony sliding on its back legs.

"What are you doing, boy?"

"Mister John," panted the young man. "I saw you sneak out the back."

"Anyone follow you?"

"They's too busy firin' the barn and fussin' with Mister Davey."

"Davey's alive?"

"They drug him out—he's alive, yessir."

Thank God, he thought. And then wondered if that was for the best. Davey might talk.

"And the other man," said Dickie, "they think it's you."

"Do they?"

"Yes sir, but it ain't final. One of them don't think so."

"Who?"

"The one that's not in uniform. The newspaperman."

Booth wasn't quite sure whom he meant. At any rate, Davey would hang. *Better to have been shot.* This boy—had he been sent by the pursuers? Booth's fingers shifted on his pistol.

"Why are you following me?"

"Had to tell you, Mister John." The boy's face was spectral in the moonlight. Tears glinted on his cheeks. "Just had to explain—" He faltered.

"What, boy, what?"

"We never would've turned you in! Never in a million years! But it was Pa—they was goin' to hang him if I didn't tell! They had a noose 'round his neck!"

Booth lowered his pistol, but kept it by his side.

"Mister John, you are my hero, you got to know that. You did the bravest thing—you killed the mighty Tyrant. The man that ruined my Pa. What good's the farm now, our slaves is gone?"

"Go back, Dickie. They'll shoot you if they see you with me."

"They said bad things about you, them soldiers, and I said, 'S'posin' one of you'd killed Jeff Davis, why you'd be a big hero!' I said, 'Mister Booth done a great thing himself and that made him a hero to us.'" He swallowed. "When I said that one of the soldiers hit me hard."

The boy was going to talk till doomsday, or at least till the army caught up.

"You're a fine lad, Dickie," Booth said. "But I've got to move on."

"What about the dead man?"

This boy, he suddenly felt, might have to die. For The Cause. "Let it be our secret. Just the two of us. Swear to God?"

"I swear."

"Go on home, Dickie. Before they come to kill us both."

67

"Mister John," Dickie said tearfully, "The South will rise again, won't it?"

Clumsily he handed Booth something wrapped in brown paper. "Chicken's all I had time to grab."

He stared at Booth with bright eyes, as if memorizing him, then reined his horse around. As he galloped away, Booth had a clear shot in the moonlight. They might make him talk. For an instant he saw not Dickie Garrett, but himself as a boy on Peacock, and he holstered his pistol.

Booth spurred his horse into action once more.

It was Harry Hawk's ghostly voice intoning over and over, "Well, I guess I know enough to turn you inside out, you sockdologizing old mantrap...."

Booth was virtually asleep in the saddle, rocking back and forth as his wet horse plodded steadily on mile after mile in the gray morning's drizzle.

"Sockdologizing old mantrap —"

Then an image came to him from the box at Ford's: "What will the young people think of my holding your hand?" Booth remembered Mary Lincoln's affectionate joke, the last words her husband would ever hear from her.

"They won't think anything about it," Lincoln replied. Just before the shot.

Bang! Sudden crack of a whip and Booth was jerked wide awake as his horse shied. He pulled his pistol from his belt. In the morning light he saw a wagon drawn by two mules. An elderly black man was driving a load of broken-down furniture and three women with a child and a dog.

"No cause to shoot nobody," said the old man, scowling as he pulled up. "Jus' headin' north."

Booth put up his pistol. "Which way is Richmond?"

The man jerked a thumb over his shoulder and muttered, "Thataway. What's left of it." He slapped the reins on the mules' backs, and the wagon rattled by.

As the morning wore on, a weary Booth passed more wagons loaded with black and white families and their belongings. Some were riding mules, other men and women pulled carts on foot. Children, old people, cripples, goats, oxen, and more dogs trotting behind wagons. Finally Booth came up over a hill and saw below him the small town of Manchester. Beyond, across the James River, lay Richmond.

He'd made it. Many times in the past thirty-six hours he'd thought he wouldn't. By a zigzag route and back roads he'd avoided the pockets of Union soldiers. He'd only stopped twice for two hours of wary sleep. His leg throbbed. He was famished and exhausted.

He slid off his lathered horse and limped down to the river. He knelt and plunged his head into the water. Oh God, how wonderful it felt. He looked down at his mirrored face. Where was John Wilkes Booth? The person who stared back was not the man who had made history at Ford's Theater. His moustache was gone, his thick eyebrows shaved thin, his long dark hair cut short. He wore Beech's big black hat and tattered uniform instead of a tailored suit. He'd easily lost ten pounds from the stress. Under the hat, his once-vibrant face was pale and gaunt with fatigue and pain, the black eyes sunk in dark hollows. The face of a god-like poet (as one favorable critic had described him) bore now the haggard look of a vagrant. Dipping his head into the water, he poured bleach into his hair, rubbing it in, eyes stinging from the acrid fumes. He repeated the process twice, then once more, until the bleach was gone and his curls were transformed into the dull blond tones of a derelict who slept in the sun.

He sat on the riverbank and gazed across the water at his goal. In the gray mid-morning, he could see that both bridges had been destroyed by Lee's army as it evacuated Richmond. Muddy wagons and dozens of ragged soldiers jammed the makeshift pontoon bridge that the Union forces had thrown across the river two weeks ago. Ahead of him was a city he could not recognize. He'd been in Richmond only years before when his theatrical group had played there. Booth had received good notices as Mark Antony, but as usual the critics had compared him to his elder brother Edwin and found him "very handsome, very athletic, but wanting the genius that the role cried out for." He remembered the review; he remembered all his reviews, word for word. A trick of memory that was annoying more than useful, making it hard for him to forget anything he had ever said, read—or done.

Now as he rode into the gaping ruins of downtown Richmond, he saw an alien city. Broken brick chimneys and jagged blackened walls reared above the charred wreckage of buildings, homes, and tobacco warehouses. Streets once broad and grand were now muddy trails meandering through rubble. It might have been Pompeii.

Above the ruins, completely intact, rose the handsome Capitol Building of the Commonwealth of Virginia. Blindingly white, with tall Ionic columns under the portico, it had been the legislative seat of the Confederate States of America for four years of war. Miraculously, it still stood.

The drizzle stopped and the sun, in one awe-inspiring minute, emerged in glory. Booth's spirits soared as light fell like a benediction on the building. Surely this was an omen! By God, the war was not over, not by a long shot! Yes, General Lee had surrendered at Appomattox three weeks ago, but that did not mean the end of the Confederacy. President Davis was still fighting. Lee's army might rise again. The South could still triumph!

Three days ago Booth had read in a newspaper that Lee had "rejoined his family in a rented house in Richmond." But it gave no address and what was left of Richmond was still a big city.

As he rode up muddy Main Street, the devastation became less horrific. Some buildings stood apparently untouched by the fire. One was the Hotel Richmond Palace, where he and Edwin had often stayed. Booth recalled a fetching—and obliging—chambermaid who might conceivably still be there, who might recognize him in spite of his new appearance. For that matter, so might local theater-goers.

In front of the hitching area stood what had once been an ambulance carriage, hitched to two cavalry horses. A crude sign on the side said *Taxi*. A young man in Confederate uniform with a lieutenant's insignia dozed on the driver's seat.

Booth pulled his horse alongside. "Excuse me, sir." Belatedly, he remembered he was now a soldier and saluted. "Sorry to bother you, sir, but I'm looking for the house of General Robert E. Lee."

"You too?" growled the man.

"I'll pay you to lead me there," said Booth. "It's vital that I see him."

The shabby lieutenant shook his head. "Can't lead anyone anywhere.

I'm retained all week. Matter of fact, Mr. Brady and I are photographing General Lee today."

"You mean—Mathew Brady?"

Just a few years before, Booth himself had been photographed by Brady. And who hadn't been moved by Brady's images of war? Photography—a strange, compelling art, thought Booth; the camera had recorded him and his brothers many times, but no one had done it like Brady. A fellow artist, Brady was, no doubt about that.

"Got all his damn equipment here. Plates, chemicals, tripod. Right here in my taxi. Never get the stink out."

"Sir, if you won't take me there, at least tell me the address," said Booth.

"You'll never get in to see him," said the man. "The General's seen enough shabby soldiers to last a lifetime."

"The address, sir, please."

The man gave a sigh. "Keep straight on this here street. All the way up to Franklin. Then go left four, five blocks. You'll see Number 707 soon enough."

"Thank you, my friend." Booth spurred his horse into a trot.

He passed a tavern whose sign proclaimed "The Black Rooster." He yearned to stop and have a drink. Several drinks. To share with other Southern sympathizers the joy of having got rid of The Tyrant. A thousand tankards. But there'd be plenty of time for celebration after he'd joined himself with General Lee.

Passing a fence he suddenly found himself face to face with himself—a huge reward poster promised: *$50,000 for the assassin John Wilkes Booth and $50,000 more for his fellow conspirators!* Below this some wag had crudely scrawled, *And 50 cents a pound for General Grant.*

He had expected reward posters in the North. It was a shock to see them in the South. Of course, Richmond was a captured city. Lincoln himself had visited the ruins less than a month ago. Thank God he'd been spared that sight, The Tyrant strolling about, rubbing his hands together, gloating over the corpse of Virginia's once beautiful capital.

In fifteen minutes Booth was in front of a three-story brick house. It remained untouched by the flames even though the house next door was a black skeleton. A sergeant in a clean uniform stood guard in front of the iron gate.

About fifty people loitered outside—old women dressed in black, tattered soldiers in gray, some missing limbs, with sleeves and pant legs pinned up neatly. An old black man, a few school children sat patiently nearby in the shade.

Booth tied his horse's reins to the hitching post and limped up to the sergeant. He saluted sharply.

"I must see the General," he demanded. The soldier looked at him with bored, heavy-lidded eyes and a bemused smile.

"And who might you be, soldier?"

"Beech," said Booth with no hesitation. "Wilson Beech."

"And your business with the General?"

"Personal."

The sergeant gestured at the waiting crowd. "All of 'em have personal reasons for seeing him."

"But mine are urgent."

"Theirs are also urgent."

"Please, sir."

"Give me your pistol and wait your turn," snarled the sergeant. "Hell, the man's lost his war. He's tired, depressed. Can't see everyone who wants him."

Booth handed over his pistol. "I can relieve his depression, I swear."

"Get in line, soldier," said the sergeant, tossing the pistol into a box with other sidearms.

"Listen, sir," Booth said in desperation, "Look at this injured leg—I was wounded at Petersburg!"

The sentry had turned away.

Booth's hands tightened into fists. If they only knew who I am, he thought. As he started to join the group of waiting people he saw the taxi-ambulance clattering down Franklin Street. The team pulled up in front of the house. An imposing, well-bellied man in a black suit jumped out of the back of the vehicle. His long face ended with a little skunk-like beard, a dark stripe between two white ones.

"You are late, Mr. Brady," admonished the sentry. "I have you listed for an hour ago."

"I know, I know," said Brady with exasperation. "My damned

assistant turned up drunk. Three cups of coffee later he is still in the hotel, drunk."

He reached back into the wagon and struggled to lift out a heavy leather case.

"Mr. Brady," said Booth. "May I help you with that?"

"What?" said the photographer eyeing him closely. "Who are you?" For a moment Booth wondered if Brady might recognize him.

"Wilson Beech, sir," said Booth, saluting. "An honor to meet you, sir, after admiring your scenes of the war for such a long time. I could help you with the plates and the tripod. I've assisted in the studio before, sir."

"Did you now?" said Brady. "Then heft this big case, will you?"

Booth nodded, keeping his eyes lowered. "Why, yes, sir." He stepped forward and grasped the case with both hands.

"Easy with that, son!" barked Brady.

Booth set the case gently on the ground. *He hasn't recognized me.*

"Thank you, sir," said the photographer. "Damn that boy anyway. Drunkard. What's your name again, young man?" said Brady, squinting into the sun.

"Beech, sir."

"Well, Mr. Beech, I'll reward you later for helping me. Come along." His eyes took in Booth's limp. "Where'd you get it?"

"Petersburg, sir."

"Stout lad. Come along now."

If Brady, with his discerning eye, hadn't recognized him without moustache, perhaps no one would.

The photographer elbowed his way through the crowd with Booth carrying the case behind him. The sentry pushed open the ironwork gate for them, and they went up the steps to the portico. Before they reached the stained glass door it was opened by a black servant in livery. In the foyer stood a huge man in the uniform of a major general.

"Custis Lee at your service, Mr. Brady," he said. "My father was expecting you earlier."

"General, I'm most sorry for the delay. My assistant neglected his duty. I have enlisted this kind gentleman's help."

"Follow me, sir," said the big man.

He turned and walked through the house, followed closely by Brady. To Booth the case's weight caused excruciating pain, but he bit his lip and hobbled after the photographer. They went through the parlor, full of red plush furniture, and past a sitting room where a girl brushed the long gray hair of an aristocratic woman in a wheelchair. It was Mary Custis Lee, the general's wife.

At the end of the house was a guest room set up as an office. A white-bearded man in a gray uniform sat writing like an accountant at a cluttered desk that did not fit the room's ornate decoration.

Booth found it hard to believe this was Robert E. Lee himself. For years a large photograph of his hero in a silver frame had traveled with him in his theater dressing rooms and in his hotel rooms, never far from his sight. "Do it, my boy!" the black and silver image had whispered. "Pull down the evil colossus, and you'll go on to the greatest glory!"

Face to face with his hero at last, he felt a little faint.

"Father," said Custis Lee, "Mathew Brady is here."

Without looking up, continuing to write, the bearded man said, "You are late, Mr. Brady."

"My apologies, sir. An unreliable assistant, General," said Brady. "But I have a replacement."

The old soldier put down his pen, took off his glasses, and glanced briefly at Booth. Then he frowned.

"Mr. Brady, how can I possibly sit for a photograph at a time like this? I assure you I'm doing this only because my friend Judge Ould requested it."

"It is greatly appreciated, General Lee, greatly. I won't be long about it, I promise. And be assured, General, I shall not speak of the war."

Lee nodded and said softly, "You are considerate, sir. And I ask your forgiveness for my melancholy. I'm not myself."

"None of us are ourselves these days, sir. We all share dreadfully sorrowful feelings at this time."

Lee's beard and hair were almost white yet the dark eyes set in his grief-lined face still flickered with determination.

Here was a noble man! Booth's heart went out to him. Oh, to have had a father like him instead of the strange, suicidal tyrant of his childhood! He took off his hat in respect. He longed to speak, but Brady opened the large case, motioned briskly to Booth, and handed him the tripod.

"Be a good fellow, ah, Beech," said Brady. "Set this up."

Booth put his hat down on a chair. He pulled out the legs of the tripod and set the screws so the tripod stood level on the carpet. Brady busied himself with his big square camera and glass plates. Booth stood alert, ready to carry out cues from his master. As his father had once told him years before, "minor actors may activate the stage in a way unbeknownst to the audience, simply by being *alive*."

Then as the photographer mounted the camera on the tripod, Lee said, "My condolences for your President's death. I know you were close to him."

"A great tragedy," said Brady, adjusting the black cloth of the camera over his head. "There is a rumor that soldiers captured the assassin yesterday." His head popped out of the cloth. "Would you mind standing, sir?"

Lee rose and frowned uncomfortably into the lens. He was six feet tall and still ramrod straight. Watching him, Booth stood up straighter.

"Now turn ever so slightly to the left, General."

"My left or your left?"

"Your left, sir," said Brady.

Lee shifted his weight.

"Would you mind wearing your sword, sir?"

"No sword," said Lee.

"As you say, General," said Brady with a dip of his head.

It pleased Booth that this famous photographer had recognized the majesty of Lee.

"Please remain still, sir, until I tell you. Your eyes may blink, but keep them always on me. Do not avert them. Always on me."

Lee did that.

Brady had to look away from the dark eyes twice.

Finally Brady said. "Good. One more, sir."

The general indulged him and the camera clicked again, the plate was withdrawn and another inserted. Click.

Then Lee raised his hand. "Enough."

"One more, sir—this time with your son by your side."

Lee abruptly sat back down at his desk, put on his glasses, and picked up his pen. The interview was clearly over.

Booth helped the photographer pack his equipment, but he deliberately left his hat sitting on the chair.

"Thank you, General Lee," said Brady. "I wish you well, sir, in your new life of peace. I will provide you a print of the best photograph we took today."

Lee glanced up with a hint of a smile. "Thank you—I shall send it to my little Markie."

Lee went back to writing, and Brady, escorted by the General's son, backed out of the room followed by Booth carrying the case. At the front door, Booth put down the case.

"Mr. Brady, I forgot my hat," he said. "One quick moment, sir."

He turned and limped quickly back to the office. Lee barely glanced at him as he retrieved the hat. Then Booth strode over to the desk, abruptly conscious that he looked like any refugee from the war, another ragged soldier.

Bowing he said, "General, I must speak with you."

Lee's eyes narrowed.

"Soldier, I don't have time."

"My General—Appomattox was not the end of the war! Lincoln The Tyrant is dead—but Jefferson Davis lives! Andrew Johnson is a poor thing. The people will sweep him away if we just rally the troops. If we fight on for a great last push!"

"Fight on, my young advisor?" Lee gave a resigned sigh. "Fight on with what, may I ask? With fists and teeth and broomsticks? It takes a great deal of money to run a war. The South has none. Our factories are gone, our people are hungry, our currency is worthless, our ports blockaded. Our government is in flight. Fight on with—what?"

General Lee was listening to him! Breathless, Booth could not contain himself. His theatrical voice reached full volume. "With the new rallying cry, sir—the Scourge, The Tyrant is dead! Without Lincoln the South can rise again and prevail!"

A sad smile came to Lee's face. "You are misguided or misinformed, sir. Had he lived, Lincoln would have been the best friend the South could have at this time."

Had he heard correctly? Friend? Friend of the South? The Tyrant!

"General Lee, with all respect, how can you say that? Lincoln's saint-hood is a hoax." The words poured out. "His egomania cost six hundred thousand American lives! He's responsible for the rape of the South!"

Lee stood up and said quietly, "Who are you, soldier?"

"I am no soldier, sir. Look at me. Do you not know my face?"

Lee studied the man in front of him silently.

"Have you not seen my face on the posters—"Wanted dead or alive?' The man who killed the Monster?"

"Monster?"

"Abraham Lincoln."

"Booth killed Lincoln," said Lee gravely. "According to a dispatch this morning Booth is—"

"Booth is not dead, sir—look closely at me!"

"I am looking."

"I am John Wilkes Booth!"

Lee stared at him and managed a slight smile. "You really believe you are Booth?"

"Together, my general, you and I can rally the South and march to victory. It's too soon to give up, sir. As Macbeth says: 'We must fight the course!'"

Lee looked hard at him, then yanked open a drawer in his desk and took out his long-barreled Colt. "My poor friend, Abraham Lincoln and I had vastly different political ideas, but he was one of the finest men America has ever seen." He cocked the pistol. "If indeed you are convinced that you are the maniac who killed him, you should be hanged as an example from the nearest tree. Booth deserved far worse than a merciful bullet." He pointed the pistol at Booth's chest. "Now get out of here before I kill you myself, you poor mad creature."

Booth staggered back. "I am not mad, sir."

"Out!"

"General Lee, sir," he gasped. "You don't understand—"

"Get out!" roared the General.

Booth turned away, blinded by sudden tears. He stumbled out of the office to the front door, mindless of the pain in his leg, down the steps and into the street.

Brady and the ambulance-taxi were gone.

Across the street a stylish little man wearing a black bowler leaned against a lamp post, reading a newspaper. Through his tears, Booth saw the newspaper's headline.

*LINCOLN'S ASSASSIN KILLED IN BOWLING GREEN!*

The man holding it casually looked up. Their eyes met for a fleeting moment. He looked vaguely familiar to Booth. The man went back to reading as Booth, choking back a sob, limped to his tethered horse, and put his foot in the stirrup.

# CHAPTER NINE

Dazed, Booth rode past the houses along Franklin Street, his horse's hooves making sucking sounds in the mud. He was suddenly exhausted. The endless days of flight came down upon his body. He felt close to fainting. He needed rest, food, and time to assess his terrible situation. Perhaps it was true—the war was over. If Lee said so, the Southern Cause was lost.

What a clod he must have seemed to Lee!

But how could Lee have done this to him? He had risked his life as much as any one of Lee's soldiers at Gettysburg. Yet Lee treated him like a dog, a madman. The general was not the man he had envisioned at all. He was a politician. Where was the fire, the dedication to the Cause, the raw courage, the unquenchable will to win no matter what? He was old and sick and beaten. Pathetic. Who could Booth turn to now? Only one man. Jefferson Davis. But he, too, was at the end of his rope, in full flight with a handful of troops in the deep South. No one knew for sure his whereabouts.

Had it all been in vain? Had he thrown his life away for nothing? Surely people would soon realize he had purged the world of a monster. The South especially was well rid of Lincoln, even if the war was ended. He suddenly remembered that his pistol had been left with the sentry at Lee's headquarters. Just as well. It would be too easy to turn it on himself.

He came to The Black Rooster tavern. Through the swinging doors he could see men drinking at the bar. Dear God, he wanted whiskey. It was almost a prayer. Once a particularly virulent theater critic had quipped,

"All the Booths seem to have been born two drinks below normal."
It was certainly true now. First he needed to bathe, lie down, get his
throbbing leg up for a while. Yet he must keep moving, somewhere;
Beech's faithful horse kept a steady walk forward, to nowhere.

The Richmond Palace hotel loomed up uselessly before him. He
couldn't stay anywhere fancy. It would not be wise.

He guided his tired horse down a side street and in two blocks came
to a gray clapboard house with a sign: *Rooms. One Dollar*. He tethered
his horse to the hitching post, loosened its cinch, and gave the lathered
neck a pat.

"I don't know your name, good beast, but thank you."

He opened the door and limped into a dark and musty foyer. The air
stank of cigar smoke and boiled cabbage. The walls were covered with
red flocked paper. An old man dozed on a divan. Behind the counter sat
a fat pink woman, her bulk covered with a tent-like gingham, a white
bonnet on her head. Spread in front of her was a newspaper.

"I'd like a room," said Booth. "And I'd like my horse taken care of,
please."

The woman kept reading intently.

"Madam, do you have a room for me?"

"Excuse me, sir," she brightened. "Your name, please?"

"Beech," he said. "Wilson Beech."

He noticed on the wall behind her a photograph of several soldiers
and "Battle of Petersburg" scrawled underneath.

"Card, please," she said.

"Card?"

"Identity card," she said. "There's still a war on, y'know."

He fumbled in his pockets and found the dead man's wallet. There he
saw a folded card with Beech's name on it. He handed it to her.

The woman barely glanced at it, wrote down the number and handed
it back.

"Where'd you get it?" she asked.

"Get it?"

She pointed at his leg.

"Oh, that," he said. "Petersburg."

"Land sakes!" exclaimed the woman. She brightened, and the mouth between the great cheeks widened. "My husband was at Petersburg! He'd want to talk about the battle with you."

"Well," said Booth, "it's still very painful to—to talk about."

"I understand," she said, studying the stranger's face. "Don't worry. You won't have to talk about the battle with my husband. He didn't come back from it."

"I'm very sorry to hear that. A terrible loss, I'm sure."

"Well, thank you kindly. But it was a time ago, wasn't it? Least it seems so." She smiled. She had a nice smile. There was a rather pretty face hidden somewhere under the fat. "I've got a nice room for you, Mr. Beech, my best one. Number three. Down that hall. Soup?"

"I beg your pardon?"

"Wonderful mutton broth a-simmerin' in the kitchen," she said pleasantly. "I'll bring you a cup. Mutton's mighty hard to come by these days."

"Madam, you are very kind," he said.

"Name's Florie."

He gave a little bow. "At your service, Florie." And though he yearned to read her newspaper, he added, very casually, "Oh, and when you're through with that periodical I wouldn't mind a glimpse at it."

She tilted her head, smiled, and handed him a key.

An hour later life seemed almost worth living again. Booth had bathed in the tub down the hall and gulped down two cups of mutton soup in the sitting room at the back. When Florie began to tell him her life story, he yawned, apologized, and finally managed to extricate himself, trudging upstairs to his small, bare room. He lay down on the cot with a groan of pleasure and was just dozing off when there came a knock on the door. Florie sashayed into the room with a blue suit on a hanger.

"I've been waiting for this very moment, Mr. Beech," she said. "You're just the right size."

Uh-oh, thought Booth.

"No earthly use of this suit going to waste. Only wore it once before he went off to war."

The suit looked almost new, and with it was a white shirt and black string tie.

"You are being most kind to a stranger," said Booth. "I would gladly pay you for it."

"Oh, we'll work something out. You must be dying to get out of that old and—if you don't mind my saying so—smelly uniform." She hung the suit on a peg. "And I bring you big news: they finally got him, thank God."

"Who?"

"The killer, of course."

She handed him the newspaper that she'd held clamped under her thick arm. As she went out the door she said, "You get some rest, Mr. Beech, and if you feel like it, later we might just have us some dinner."

"Enchanted, Florie, enchanted."

He bolted the door and quickly spread the *Richmond Dispatch* on the bed. Screaming from its front page:

*The Actor Booth Killed, Accomplice Herold Taken!*

There were three engravings of Booth, one done after a studio portrait, ironically taken by Brady himself. The others depicted him in the roles of Hamlet and Romeo. Obviously, Florie had not recognized him. There were likenesses of Davey Herold and a detective, Lieutenant Luther Byron Baker. A sergeant with the absurd name of Boston Corbett rated a separate column under the claim: *"I am the man who shot the murderer!"*

*Well, at least my ruse worked.*

A small engraving of a reporter in a black bowler hat accompanied his account, which covered much of the front page. The journalist's face looked vaguely familiar. Could that be the man he'd seen when he left General Lee's home?

*"I Saw the Great Capture!" An Eyewitness Report By Langford Upham, Jr.*

*" . . . It was then that Lieutenant Baker produced from the assassin's breast pocket a small notebook with these words . . . "*

It had been wise to leave his diary with the dead man. He read his own words avidly: *"I struck for my country and for her alone . . . "*

Someday, Booth knew, he would be vindicated and hailed as a hero. He was certain there were tens of thousands in the North as well as the South who privately celebrated the death of Lincoln, and regarded the man who slew The Tyrant as a patriot. But nowhere in this corrupt newspaper was there a hint of that. Instead there were more florid odes to Our Fallen Leader, nauseatingly obsequious paeans to Father Abraham's singular greatness, and sickening details of the Emancipator's mortal remains lying in state in the Capitol, and "soon to be transported by railcar to his beloved town of Springfield, Illinois in an elaborate and heart-rending hegira." Booth fumed at the cheap sentiment of the masses, fed by the purple prose of third-rate scribes. Only one voice stood apart from the chorus of certainty. It was Upham's:

*"Though the pistol was found in the corpse's right hand, and Booth was known to be left-handed, Lieutenant Baker was quoted as saying that the actor was thought to be ambidextrous. The famed detective ventured no comment on the fact that the corpse had a prominent scar on the right side of its neck . . ."*

From his breast pocket, Booth took the worn leather wallet of the man he had killed. Who exactly was his late alter ego, Wilson Beech? There was his identity card. Folded inside the wallet was a soiled envelope marked "Charlotte." He gasped at the contents: three one hundred dollar bills, not in useless Confederate money but solid Union currency, redeemable in gold.

Where did a private in the army get that kind of money—a week's stage pay for Booth, perhaps—but more than a Union sergeant's annual income by half. Had he stolen it? Was that why he was on the run that night in Garrett's barn? Of course. And a fine stolen horse.

There were two letters in his wallet. One, signed "Ever yr. affectionate cousin, Wilma Harrison," urged Beech to come to Bannack, Montana Territory, where "everyone is getting rich in the mines."

The other, enclosing a lock of auburn hair, was written in a scrawl: *"My dear husband: I hope you are well and coming home soon to me and our Johnny now that the war is almost over. We need you bad. Yr. Loving wife, Charlotte. Post Script: Do not secum to temptations, dear Wilson."* A lump formed his throat as he read the letter. Here was a simple, loving wife, whose man he had killed. Beech's boy would grow up without a father. Worse, neither she nor his son would ever know what happened to him. He would soon be buried in a grave marked "John Wilkes Booth." Doubtless Beech had intended to send them this money.

Booth gazed at the bills. He would need the money certainly in the days to come. The Cause. But Beech's wife and child needed it too. Certainly they were part of The Cause. He pocketed one bill and inserted the other two back into the envelope.

Sleep was impossible now. Terrible visions danced before his eyes. Beech's face kept appearing before him, along with the shattered head of The Tyrant. Booth felt a terrible craving for whiskey. He thought of his lovely sister, Asia, and his mother, envisioning how they would read the graphic accounts of his body being found in Garrett's barn. He didn't really care about his pompous older brother, Edwin, the great Edwin, the successor to the Booth theatrical throne. But Asia—what a lovely sister. His friend through thick and thin always. And his mother—his lonely, grieving mother. How could he let them know that he loved them dearly and regretted the anguish he'd caused them? Not till his supposed death was officially and universally accepted. But couldn't he tell them at least that he was alive? With a private signal? He could do that much.

He tore off a piece of the blank margin of the newspaper. He found a stub of pencil in the drawer of the table and sat down on the chair. Any note might be intercepted. Only Asia should know it was from him.

Then he thought of Peacock. Their little dappled pony on the farm in Maryland when they were children. When Peacock died suddenly, they gave it an elaborate funeral. Mrs. Booth had tried to soften their grief by repeatedly assuring them that one day in the future they would "once again ride Peacock over the clouds in Heaven."

He put the pencil to his lips, wet the lead and wrote:

*"To Mrs. John Sleeper Clarke: Dear Asia – heavenly Peacock is not being ridden nor is the future cloudy. (Signed) A True Friend."*

Not exactly a Shakespearean sonnet, but it would do the job.

He folded the paper. He would get an envelope and mail it, but perhaps it would be better to wait a few days.

He put on the clean shirt and the suit supplied by his new benefactress. Though tight in the shoulders, it fit reasonably well. At the mirror he knotted the tie. He was amazed how different he looked clean-shaven, with bleached, shortened hair and abbreviated eyebrows shaved into weak crescents. *My own mother would not know me,* he thought. Thinking of her again, he felt a pang over her own suffering.

He went out into the foyer. Seated at the counter, Florie looked up at him with a smile.

"My, don't we look refreshed," she said.

"Thanks to you, Florie." He picked up the pen lying on the open register, took the envelope from his pocket and wrote:

*Mrs. Charlotte Beech.*

*Butt's Farm, Lot 2, Front Royal, Virginia*

He handed it over along with a coin. "Would you be good enough to mail this for me? It's important."

Florie looked at the address and frowned. "Your wife?"

"My sister," he said. "My dear sister. Charlotte."

She smiled.

"I'm going out for a bit of air," he said.

"Don't forget our dinner engagement."

He turned at the door. "How could I forget, madam?"

It was dusk now and the air was warm and smoky from all the ruins. The Black Rooster was only a few blocks away, but his leg was throbbing badly by the time he made the tavern. He limped through the swinging doors and sagged onto a stool at the crowded bar.

The bartender had more hair on his eyebrows and lip than on his head. He smiled at Booth, wiping the varnished counter between them with a rag. "Stranger, you look as much in need of a drink as anyone I've seen today, and I've seen a lot."

"Whiskey," Booth said, pronouncing the word with reverence.

The barman slid a glass in front of him and placed a full bottle beside it. "You look like an honest man who'll keep track."

Just closing his fingers around the glass made him feel better.

"I'll buy the bottle," Booth said. "Simplify matters." The barman nodded assent.

Booth looked down the long bar at the clientele. Of all ages and attire, they were quiet, even somber. *And why not? Most of their city has been destroyed.*

Apart from his newly acquired one hundred dollar bill, Booth had $160 of his own, and paid for the whiskey out of this. He threw the burning liquor down in two gulps and poured another. He was a habitué of restaurants and saloons, a connoisseur of pleasure, but on closer examination this one appeared too rough even for his tastes. The customers were uncouth working men and soldiers—and there were no women.

He liked women. He got along with them better than men. He could use a woman now, not for sexual release but for comfort, care, the gentle caress, the intelligent listener, the feline sensuality. It had been a long time. Bessie Hale: he'd wanted to marry her and she'd loved him, given herself to him, oh so privately, for six lovely months. But she wouldn't marry him—said he led a strange life in the theater, that he drank too much. She had gone off to Madrid with her diplomat father last year, telling Booth to "grow wise." Hah! Grow wise! What would she say now, that he had killed the head of their nation?

If she only knew what he'd done! How proud she'd be of his courageous act. David and Goliath. Perhaps not. Her father was a Unionist. Across the Atlantic, she would soon learn of his fate and perhaps weep for him. Curious how seldom he thought of Bessie; his obsession with the war and Lincoln had driven any other passion from his mind. Damn Robert E. Lee! How could he have treated him this way—like a common murderer instead of a patriot? He poured himself another shot. Better take it easy, laddie. Sip it.

Customers at the far end of the bar were talking about "that man"— he could hear the words "Booth," "Lincoln," and "Herold." He heard someone say, "The trial of the conspirators starts in three weeks." Another laughed bitterly. "Why bother? They're all going to swing!"

As Booth drank, the whiskey dulled the pain of his leg, but not the terrible hurt of Lee's rejection. He had anticipated everything but that— planned for all failures, all unexpected disasters. How shabbily he had been treated! Lee had no idea of the great motivation, the patriotism that had gone into the planning. No clue as to Booth's integrity and worth. Suddenly Hamlet's words to Guildenstern came to him, and he muttered them aloud angrily.

"'Why, look you now, how unworthy a thing you make of me! You would play upon me, you would seem to know my stops, you would

pluck out the heart of my mystery, you would sound me from my lowest
note to—'"

"You all right, mister?" The bartender was looking at him curiously.

Booth collected himself and nodded. "Fine, sir, just fine." But he
knew he was not fine. What would he do now? There was always Mexico
or Cuba or Spain. Maybe Bessie would think about marrying him now.
He could give up liquor anytime he wanted. Maybe tomorrow.

He poured another shot.

Supposing he went to Front Royal, presented himself to Mrs. Wilson
Beech as—let's see—Mark Anthony Smith, a great friend of her
husband. *With him when he died. Brave fellow, noble fellow! Last words:
"Mark, take care of Charlotte!"* He could hear her saying, "Wonderful,
come right in, Mr. Smith. You can use the back bedroom long as you
like."

Not a bad idea. Women always had the right idea. For awhile. He
could hide out until all this hysteria blew over, then, in a few weeks he'd
go to Spain and Bessie. A horse, a train, a fake passport, a ship, and he
would be in Madrid within a month's time.

A callow youth next to him at the bar was sipping beer with a straw. It
reminded him of the time when he was young, about fourteen, the year
before his father died, and the old man had been locked in his dressing
room in the theater by the impresario so that he couldn't go out and get
drunk before the performance. The old man had slid money under the
door to young John and ordered him to get a bottle of whiskey and a
straw. When he brought it back, Booth senior angled the straw through
the keyhole to drain the bottle. To everyone's puzzlement and dismay
the actor appeared on stage gloriously drunk. *Yet the audience cheered.*

It made him angry just to think of his father. When he was a boy his
father had tried to hang himself. Somehow they'd stopped him, and the
old man went on to think nothing of it. But everyone else remembered.

Booth had another drink, put the bottle in the pocket of his new suit,
and headed back to Florie's. He felt better than he had in weeks; a good
dinner awaited him and who knew what else.

Florie was not exactly Jenny Lind—the great stage beauty had once
briefly been the object of his youthful fantasies—but she had a pretty
face, and her body looked as full and ripe as a persimmon. It had been a

long time since he'd had a woman, of any size. After a good night's rest he'd be off early to Front Royal.

As he neared the rooming house he saw another horse tied next to his. Quietly he went up the steps and listened at the door. He heard voices. He opened the door a crack. He saw Florie in the foyer talking to a trimly attired man whose derby sat beside him on the settee. The same little man he'd seen outside of General Lee's house this morning. The same man whose picture headed the by-line of Langford Upham, Jr. And hadn't he briefly encountered someone very much like him in the lobby of Ford's Theater the night of *The Event*? Florie was talking a mile a minute, flirting with the enemy: the hunting wordsmith.

Booth eased the door shut and went quickly down the steps to the street. Better to leave the horse as a placeholder, a sign that he was coming back. He limped away as quickly as he could. He remembered the direction to the train station from his previous visits.

Stay calm. No panic, but radical change in plans. No Front Royal now. Where to? They would expect him to go south, very far south to Mexico. Or even Spain. He would fool Mr. Langford Upham, Jr. And anyone else.

He would go where no one in the world would imagine him going.

# CHAPTER TEN

"Such a nice gentleman, your friend Mr. Beech," Florie was saying at the reception desk. "Were you at Petersburg with him when he was wounded?"

"No," said Langford Upham. "Haven't seen him for years. When I spotted him on the street today—I would have sworn he was my old friend from school. But I lost him in the crowd. Luckily I tried here."

"What a lovely voice Mr. Beech has," said Florie dreamily.

But what first name is he using now, thought Upham.

"Yes, old Beech was good at acting at school, very good." He made a show of looking at his pocket watch. "Afraid I won't be able to wait for him," he said. "Let me get his address."

She turned the open register around.

"Wilson Beech, Front Royal, Virginia," she read aloud.

"Ah yes, still in Front Royal, I see," said Upham. "That's where old Wilson and I went to school together."

"And his sister," she said, holding up the envelope Booth had left to mail. "Is she as fine-looking as her brother?"

Upham glanced at the envelope. "Dear Charlotte. She's, ah—every inch a lady. Just as you are, madam. Well, I have to go."

"Wilson should be here any minute," she said.

*So it's Wilson already.*

"Madam, what makes you sure he's coming back?"

She looked coy. "We have a dinner engagement."

"I have an engagement myself," he said, turning to go. "Thank you for your help."

"Who shall I say was looking for him? If you don't find him?"

"Tell him an old friend," said Upham at the door. "Better still, don't tell him anything. I'll surprise him tomorrow at breakfast. That's better, don't you agree?"

Upham walked out into the warm night. He looked up and down the street: no one about. He hurried across to a cannon-shattered office building and settled himself in the shadows, sitting on a granite lintel blasted from its entrance. He could see the rooming house from here, and he was prepared to wait as long as it took. Booth would surely return; his horse was still tied to the hitching post.

And just what would he do when Booth showed up?

"Excuse me, sir, but I'm from *The World*. And I think you're John Wilkes Booth. Remember me, old boy? I watched you kill the President at Ford's Theater. Then I saw Davey Herold come out of the burning barn. And I'd like an exclusive interview with you before you shoot me dead."

And suppose, thought Upham, just suppose he's not John Wilkes Booth, but really one Wilson Beech?

The letter the woman had shown him had shaken his conviction considerably. Unless it was a clever subterfuge—Booth was not stupid, after all.

Neither was he. He was smart enough to have deduced that Booth would head either for Jefferson Davis, President of the Confederacy, or for General Robert E. Lee, spiritual leader of the South. Davis was in hiding, whereabouts unknown, so naturally Booth would seek Lee for asylum first. Which, clearly, he hadn't received.

Could the blond-haired, crestfallen figure he'd seen limp out of Lee's house today really be Booth? If Lee had spurned him, it made sense. Upham had tried to worm information from Lee's sentry, but he'd made the mistake of saying he was a newspaperman.

"General Lee's staff has issued orders," the sentry snarled. "No journalists allowed in to see him. Not now, nor in the immediate future. Goodbye, sir."

All Upham learned was that the blond man had assisted the photographer, Brady. This evinced more doubts—Booth suddenly an assistant to the great documenter of the Union's struggle? On the other hand, Brady's wagon had left without the blond man in the soldier's uniform; easy enough for Upham to find out what Brady knew of him.

One of Upham's first reportorial assignments—which he'd requested—had been an interview with Brady. It was well-received and gave *The World* a good excuse to run half a dozen poignant battlefield photos, reproduced by the newspaper's new photo-gravure printing process.

The interview had been more than a day's work to Upham. He felt passionately about the war, about Lincoln, about the Union. With the rebel shelling of Fort Sumter four years ago, Upham, just turned twenty-one, had left Yale and hurried to a recruiting station to enlist.

A short sprint up and down a dirt hill carrying a forty-pound sack of sand had left him wheezing, nearly unconscious. He was rejected for asthma. With volunteers comprising ninety-two percent of the Grand Army of the Republic, and their paid substitutes another six percent, the surgeons who poked and assayed the recruits could afford to be choosy. He was determined, however, to take part in the war, or failing that to be close to it. He decided to take a job with *The New York World*.

His job at the newspaper was not benefited by the fact that its publisher was his father, Langford Upham, who shared his editors' general assessment of Junior: clever, educated, and eager, but fortunate to have been born wealthy.

This prejudice blinded most to the fact that Junior had been the first to report that General James Ledie spent the Battle of the Crater well behind the lines, drunk, while 5,100 of his soldiers were massacred for lack of leadership. Junior's discovery that the Navy's new vaunted ironclads were barely seaworthy embarrassed War Department officials. "These fearsome inventions," he wrote, borrowing from Shakespeare, "show mastership in floating only when seas are calm."

His resentful colleagues at *The World* and his rivals at the Washington bureaus of *The New York Herald* and the *Times* pretended not to notice that, unlike most, Upham frequently traveled at his own expense and considerable peril to the front lines. It was a heady time for Upham, who for the first time since his admission to Yale sensed a small—very small—note of approval from his remote father.

So here he was embarked on his—or any reporter's—career moment. He felt ridiculous waiting for a phantom. He waited for an hour. No one showed up at the rooming house. Where would Booth have gone at this time of the evening? Not far, because his horse—or Beech's horse—was still there. A restaurant? There were so few still operating in Richmond. Besides, wasn't Mr. Beech scheduled to dine with the opulent Florie?

Booth was known to be a drinker. What about a saloon? It would have to be close because of his bad leg—he hadn't taken his horse. Upham had seen a tavern a couple of blocks away.

He pondered his approach: "Excuse me, sir, aren't you the brother of my friend Charlotte Beech?"

He remembered that voice he'd heard only two weeks ago, shouting powerfully from the stage at Ford's.

And if it were the same voice, he would ask him point blank, "Sir, have I not seen you on the stage?"

If Booth were to show alarm, bid him farewell, and stroll away calmly, would he summon soldiers or a policeman to arrest him?

He stood up and headed for the Black Rooster.

# CHAPTER ELEVEN

By the time Booth reached the Richmond station, it was midnight. He bought a ticket on the first available train going west.

His coach was less than half full. A few Confederate soldiers, two old ladies, a woman with a baby, and an old Negro. Booth was not so drunk as to be indiscreet or incautious, and studied the car's occupants before choosing a seat. There appeared to be no threat here—no Union soldiers, no nosy reporters like that bastard Langford Upham.

He took a seat in the back, finished off his whiskey bottle, then curled up on the wicker seat. He quickly fell asleep, oblivious to the train's jerky departure from Richmond. He dreamed he was leading a mounted parade. Suddenly, hands were reaching for him, pulling him off his horse. He dreamed that he had been caught by a mob led by Robert E. Lee. They were going to hang him. In the crowd he could see his father laughing, his mother crying, his brother shaking his head. He awakened briefly, shook off the nightmare, and soon fell into a deep sleep.

The next morning the sun burned through the window, but it did not wake him. Rocked by the train, he slept on, making up for two harrowing weeks of sleepless nights. He awoke with a moan when a rotund conductor shook him at noon.

"Wake up there, sir," said the man. "Need to see a ticket."

"Where are we?" Booth mumbled. He was trembling.

The conductor glanced out the window as though looking for a sign on the landscape flashing by.

"Kentucky, near Owensboro, reckon."

He looked down at Booth. "Say, don't I know you?"

Booth pulled himself together and looked up at the conductor innocently. "Don't believe so, sir."

"Know your face." The man kept staring at him. "From somewhere."

"Maybe my cousin," said Booth. "Happens all the time. We look alike."

"Maybe," said the conductor, not entirely convinced. "Maybe that's it."

The train was slowing. Booth craned his head out of the window. To his astonishment he saw people standing along the tracks in the noonday sun, hordes of people, all standing quietly in line, holding their hats.

"What are they doing?" he asked. He could see many strewing flowers along the tracks, some weeping. "Why are they there?'"

"The cortege is right behind us," said the conductor. "From Washington."

"Cortege?"

"Funeral train for the president," said the conductor. "To Illinois. They're going to bury Lincoln in Springfield. Twelve days to cover seven states—more'n sixteen hundred miles. Plays hell with our schedules, no disrespect."

Booth gazed in wonderment at the crowds. It was incredible. More than half the faces were black, of all ages, but many were white. The men stood with hats held over their hearts, the women with handkerchiefs to their faces, or clasping children. Booth was astonished.

He felt the train lurch to one side as it turned onto a siding and jerked to a stop. Leaning out his window, he could hear another train approaching from behind. Soon the gleaming locomotive and nine ornate coaches were clattering slowly by, causing Booth's window to rattle. The funeral train was draped in black bunting. It passed so slowly he could see into the windows. In the first cars were men dressed in black, looking solemn and important. And—*oh, God*—in the middle car he glimpsed a great silver catafalque in the center of wood-paneled splendor. An honor guard stood at attention behind it. To Booth's horror, the lid of the coffin was open—he quickly averted his head, but not before catching a fleeting glimpse of that terrible waxen brow, the sunken cheeks and bearded jaw, restored by the embalmer's art.

For one horrible moment, he saw his derringer pointed at the back of that great head and felt the explosion. He saw Lincoln lurch forward in the smoke, felt that soldier grabbing his coat, and heard Mrs. Lincoln scream in terror. The final leap to the stage, and the twelve days of running and hiding.

He did not look back at the funeral train. In a few seconds the last car was receding out of sight. His breath was coming very fast. He fought an insane urge to leap to his feet and shout to his fellow passengers, "See that, you people? I did that! Caesar is dead!"

He noticed a thin woman across the aisle. She pressed a handkerchief to her face as she wept quietly. A sudden rage suffused him. "May I inquire, madam," said Booth coldly. "Are you a Southerner?"

Startled by the stranger's question, she hesitated before answering, looking Booth over. "In a manner of speaking."

"And you weep for the enemy?"

She didn't answer, but appeared to be studying his face.

"I ask you again, madam," said Booth, "Why do you weep for The Tyrant?"

"I wanted Mr. Lincoln to lose his war," she replied, "not his life."

"For a tyrant," Booth said, straining to moderate his tone, "war and life are one."

"I need not justify my feelings to a stranger, sir, nor do I wish to discuss them further."

Booth turned angrily away, staring out the window. He could see the passing crowds beginning to disperse, many weeping, shaking their heads, some with their arms around each other.

"Poor, ignorant people," he said between clenched teeth. "Why do you cry?" But he couldn't stop staring at them.

Mile after interminable mile went by. Because his train trailed the funeral cortege, the tableaux of sorrowing people on both sides of the car seemed endless—mourners chanting, throwing flowers, waving pitifully. In rural regions they stood beside the tracks in groups of a dozen; as his train neared towns, they closed ranks, becoming an unbroken crowd of hundreds, then thousands. More and more of them, Booth saw, were white. Long before the funeral train was switched off to the right to head north to Illinois, Booth had yanked down the shade.

He wanted a drink. He was vaguely alarmed to find the woman across the aisle looking at him. Does she recognize me? Perhaps she suspects. Maybe I should change my seat. *I should change my face again—perhaps grow a beard*. After a long, uncomfortable moment, the woman's hawk eyes turned away.

Then, as though in front of a blackboard, he forcibly erased *The Event* from his mind before it could engulf him in its horrible passion. As the train rolled on, its noisy swaying motion lulled Booth to sleep.

# CHAPTER TWELVE

Upham had no difficulty getting a train out of Richmond for Front Royal, and it was only a matter of hours before he was rolling through the outskirts and into the small Virginia town. He stepped down onto the depot's brick platform and hailed the sole carriage-cab.

"Where to, suh?" asked the old black coachman, tipping a forefinger to his high silk hat and bowing slightly. But when Upham showed him the envelope with the address of Charlotte Beech, the driver frowned.

"Suh, that's a far piece from town."

"I have the time, sir," said Upham, "and the money."

"Well, suh, then I have the means," chuckled the driver. He slapped the reins down on his horse's back, and they were off.

Upham put the envelope back in his pocket and patted it. It had taken some doing to acquire it. After going to the Black Rooster to learn from the bartender that a blond, well-dressed man with a limp had indeed been there and left, Upham hurried back to Florie's boarding house. Mr. Beech had not returned, Florie said. Upham booked a room himself and spent the night there, rising before dawn to watch for the elusive Mr. Beech.

"I can't imagine what happened to him," Florie said with a mixture of resentment and hurt. "And after I gave him a suit of clothes, too."

"I regret your disappointment, ma'am."

"You just cain't tell about people anymore. He didn't even pay his bill!" She looked near tears.

"Perhaps something of importance came up," said Upham. "I will pay his bill and collect from him when I see him."

Florie brightened. "So kind of you, sir. I'm glad to see there's still gentlemen around."

As Upham was leaving, he said very casually, "You know, Florie, I happen to be on my way right now to Front Royal on business. Why don't I take that letter to his sister and hand-deliver it for you?"

She hesitated. "Mr. Beech was very concerned that I mail it."

"Of course! But think how much sooner it will get there with me—and how much safer, given these uncertain times. I won't let you down, Florie."

On the train Upham held the envelope up to the light. It appeared to hold currency, but whether it also contained a letter he couldn't tell.

As the cab rolled over a rough country road, Upham pondered the likely outcome of his expedition. Would Charlotte Beech prove indeed to be the sister of the blond man with the bad leg who called himself Wilson Beech? If so, Beech was not Booth, and the trail would not only be cold, but dead-ended. He certainly wouldn't mention this to his ever-skeptical father.

Upham smiled wistfully at his memories of their contentious relationship. Reading Junior's acceptance letter from Yale, his father had grunted a grudging approval. Yet that first autumn in New Haven, the old man had fumed when his son announced his intent to study Greek. "For God's sake, why not pursue something useful?"

He wished his mother had lived to see him become a man. She had died when he was fifteen, after a year of sickly decline. Her death left him feeling bereft, but his father, whose own sorrow, if any, was kept hidden behind his gruff public face, had waited only a month before marrying a show girl. Blanche disliked children and referred to her resentful step-son as "the troll."

"So what's the little troll going to be when he grows up?" she'd giggle. "A chimney sweep?"

The senior Upham had not helped matters, charging his son with being a sybarite, a dandy, and a fop. The accusations were not entirely unfounded; his armoire owed much to the tailors at Brooks Brothers. But with the outbreak of civil war, Upham began to change.

"I will try to do in prose what Brady's stark photographs of the war do," he'd told Chadwick Tompkins, *The World*'s managing editor, but so far, in Upham's view, even his best work failed to meet that standard.

This story, however—tracking down and exposing Lincoln's assassin—would make his byline famous.

The cabbie's horse clopped along steadily through the green countryside. Three ragged soldiers trudging along the winding dirt road were a jarring reminder of the war. Upham also noticed the absence of livestock, surmising that the region's sheep, cattle, and pigs had been slaughtered to feed the troops of both armies.

The buggy rounded a bend, passed through a stand of trees, and emerged into a shallow farming valley. On a hill overlooking them stood a large white clapboard house.

"This be Butt's Farm," said the driver. "Number Two Lot be down further."

They continued for another half-mile past unplanted fields to a squat log house set back from the road. A yellow dog slept on the front steps.

"Yo' destination, suh," said the cabbie.

"Wait for me, please," said Upham, stepping down from the carriage. The cabbie tipped his hat in assent.

The reporter knocked twice on the door. The dog woke up, barked once, whined, and dropped its head onto its paws. No one answered. Upham walked around in back of the house where a very thin woman was taking clothes off a line. Her face was gaunt but held a faded prettiness.

"Charlotte Beech?" he asked. "My name is Langford Upham."

At the sight of the dapper man in the black derby she dropped the shirt she was folding.

"Oh God," she said. "What's happened?"

"Don't be alarmed," said Upham. "A friend of Mr. Beech asked me to deliver this." He handed her the envelope, and she took it gingerly, as though it might explode.

"Go ahead, open it."

"Is Wilson all right? I mean, nothing's happened to him?"

And with her mention of Beech's name he knew this was all a wild goose chase. But he had to play out the game.

"Far as I know, ma'am, he's fine. Open it."

"Where did you see him?"

"I bumped into him in—in Richmond."

"He's not wounded or anything?"

"Fine—except for some trouble with his leg."

"Wilson's tough. He'll get over that. I was just afraid you were going to tell me some awful news, you know ...."

"Nothing like that, I'm glad to say."

"And he's not in some trouble? Wilson can get himself in trouble when he drinks."

"Do open the envelope."

Although she looked to Upham to be about twenty-five, her freckled hands were like those of an old woman. She tore open the envelope and slid out the money slowly.

"Good Lord," she whispered, looking at both sides of the bills, as if fearing they might not be genuine. "Good Lord."

"A thoughtful gesture," said Upham.

"But wherever did he get this proper Union money?"

"I've no idea, ma'am."

"So much money! I do hope Wilson come by it honest."

"Is there a note with it?"

She shook her head. "Never much for writin'. Haven't heard from him for months—didn't know for sure he was alive."

"Well, I believe—I would say he is very much alive."

"Was he headed here, do you know?"

Upham shrugged helplessly. The depth of his deception was getting to him. He had the stomach-turning thought that he might be doing this poor woman a terrible disservice.

"I'm grateful to you for takin' the trouble to come all the way out here, Mr. Upham."

"It's nothing."

"Let me take you in the house and get you some water or maybe somethin' stronger for your trouble. Got a little corn whiskey put away for special occasions."

"I would be pleased—madam."

"Call me Charlotte."

The question jumped from his mouth before he had given its absurdity any thought: "By any chance, Charlotte, were you or Mr. Beech acquainted with—" he cleared his throat and gave a little apologetic laugh, "John Wilkes Booth?"

She looked at him in bewilderment. "You mean—the murderer? The actor?"

"I do."

She turned and strode into the house, murmuring, "What a question, Mr. Upham. How on earth would we get to know someone like him?"

"A silly question." He dejectedly followed her through her tiny kitchen and into a drab parlor. A doorway revealed a prim little bedroom, barely large enough for its bed and the trunk at its foot.

"You make yourself comfortable and I'll get us somethin' cool," she said. She took the envelope from a pocket and pondered it.

"Two hundred Union dollars. That'll buy us a year's worth of foodstuffs, even in these times." She sighed, shook her head in wonder, and padded back to the kitchen.

Upham took off his hat and morosely surveyed the room. A little pedal organ in the corner was the only extravagance, a book of hymns on its music stand. Two high-backed upholstered chairs flanked the fireplace. A print of praying hands hung above the sooty mantel. On the mantel sat a glittering rock. He picked it up and sat down in one of the chairs, turning the heavy jagged stone in his hands. It appeared to be laced with intricate veins of gold. Charlotte returned with two glasses of brown liquid.

"Isn't that something?" she said, handing him a glass. "That little bitty piece of rock has about eight dollars worth of gold in it. Wilson's cousin Wilma sent it to us from the Montana Territory."

Upham heard a small noise from the bedroom. He had the feeling someone was eavesdropping. A wave of terror swept through him: *Could Wilson Beech be here? Is this a trap?*

"They say the streets of Bannack are cobbled with chunks like that one," Charlotte explained, entirely at ease, not seeming to notice Upham's apprehensive glances at the bedroom doorway. "Our cousin keeps tellin' me and Wilson to come out there and make our fortune. Maybe we will, if Wilson ever gets out of the army and comes home. I'd like it fine to go to Montana Territory." She slumped in her chair, her face a portrait of yearning. "Been a powerful long time since we've seen him," she said sadly. "Johnny misses him very much."

"Madam—Charlotte," asked Upham. "Are we alone in the house?"

The woman put a hand to the side of her mouth. "Hey, you Johnny, you come out, I know you're there a-listenin'!"

A ferret-faced boy of four stuck his tousled head out from the bedroom, flashed a toothless grin, and just as quickly withdrew, with a giggle of delight.

"I can get that boy the food he needs now," she said, raising her glass as if to toast her good fortune.

"Johnny's his name?" said Upham, clinking his glass against hers.

"Our boy," said Charlotte, smiling for the first time. "I wanted to name him after his daddy, but Wilson says a boy should have his own name, so he's John James Beech."

Upham choked on his drink, the whiskey burning in his nose. "Wilson Beech is *not* your brother?"

"What ever gave you that idea?"

"Well—the letter." *The son of a bitch wanted to bed Florie, so he claimed the letter was to his sister, not his wife.*

"I don't have a brother, Mr. Upham—just a pair of sisters and a husband I want to welcome home from the war."

Upham put down his glass, his heart racing.

"Mrs. Beech," he said, collecting himself. "It seems I have been misinformed."

"I should say so."

Retrieving his hat, he stood up abruptly.

"I must apologize."

"Not at all—but do you have to leave so sudden-like?"

"I have a cab waiting and a long journey ahead of me." Upham's thoughts were spinning. "Before I go, however, may I ask a favor?"

"Of course."

"If you have a portrait of your husband, I would very much like to see it—for reasons I shall explain." A grim thought came to mind: Exhumation.

He saw Charlotte's expression change. "Wilson's in trouble, isn't he?"

# CHAPTER THIRTEEN

The riverboat *Yellowstone* glistened in her berth on the St. Louis waterfront, filling the air with the scent of varnish and fresh paint. Gleaming white with blue and red trim, she was designed to navigate the shallow waters of the upper Yellowstone River. Two hundred feet from bow to stern with a thirty-foot beam, she drew only three feet of water. Ten soldiers were posted aboard, to protect the vessel from Indian attack along the way to Montana Territory. Two days before, stevedores had unloaded a thousand buffalo hides fresh out of Fort Benton, the line's northernmost port in the territory. Now she was scrubbed down, re-stocked with food for her passengers and fuel for her two boilers—ready for the month-and-a-half long voyage upriver. Loaded to the gunwales with freight, she had a near-capacity passenger list, a hundred and fifty people filling the cabins and forty-nine who would sleep on deck for half price.

Booth had no sooner stepped off his train when he heard a shrill blast of the *Yellowstone's* whistle. He offered a cab driver a double fare to get him to the river at a trot.

A band played "Hail, Missouri" as Booth wove his way through the crowd that had gathered to see the paddle-wheeler off. The gangway was still on the dock, and he was relieved to learn that the boat didn't sail for two more hours. Booth sat down on a barrel of pitch to catch his breath. He gazed over the waters of the Mississippi to a low green line of trees marking the Big Muddy's confluence with the Missouri.

The purser at the gangplank, resplendent in a brass-buttoned tunic, striped pants and a conductor's cap, rubbed his tiny moustache as he took stock of the slight, weary man standing before him. "You're in luck, sir," he said pridefully, indicating the handsome vessel behind him.

"We have but one more deck space available, at one hundred dollars."

"That's a fortune!"

"For a journey so great, and replete with such exotic wonders, sir, it is a pittance."

"Perhaps to a plutocrat."

"Would you prefer the alternative?" sniffed the purser. "There's a very uncomfortable and extremely slow wagon train leaving next week. Indian attacks are *gratis*, I might add. Aboard the *Yellowstone* you dine and sleep like a gentleman, as the American panorama presents itself for your pleasure and awe."

"I'll take a place on deck," Booth said, reaching into his breast pocket for Beech's wallet. He patted all the pockets of his jacket. The dead man's wallet and one hundred dollar bill was gone. His heart began to pound in his ears. *I truly will go mad.*

The purser looked away, as if embarrassed by this patently phony act.

Booth turned his coat inside out, then gave up. *A pickpocket, probably while I slept on that infernal train. The woman, perhaps. That hawk-like gaze might have been the predatory stare of a grifter.*

He fumbled in his pants pocket and pulled out a sheath of crumpled bills, his own money. He counted them hastily—only sixty dollars left —and offered them to the purser. "I have but this left, sir. It appears I was pick-pocketed on my train."

"The deck fare, sir, is one hundred dollars."

"I could work off the rest on the trip. I'm able-bodied."

"We have a full and able crew," the man said. "One hundred dollars for the ticket, sir, and you'd be lucky to get it."


Booth walked along the dock, his mind spinning. *Where to find forty dollars in two hours?*

Robbery? He had no weapon, and he was not a thief. A political assassin, a murderer, yes, but never a thief. Gambling? Could he hold his own in one of the many poker games in the waterfront saloons? No. He had never been good at cards.

His aimless walking brought him to the gaudy tents of a carnival. He stood dejectedly in front of the freak tent. A barker urged passersby to step right up and see the pin-headed boy, the bearded lady, Mister Skeleton, and the two-headed calf.

"—and all of these astounding sights for the unique price of only one thin dime, the tenth part of a dollar!"

Booth started to move on when farther down the street his eyes caught the sign over another tent:

*Win Big Money!*
*20 Whole Dollars For Every Round You*
*Can Last With Spider O'Sullivan!*
*Gentlemen, Test Your Manhood!*

Booth stood before the sign, assessing its written challenge. He was athletic and he knew how to box—he had been a champion in his preparatory school. For two and a half years his father had made him take daily boxing lessons from the retired former middleweight champion, Irish Danny Cohelan. The elder Booth was determined to make a man of his slight, overly sensitive boy. As Junius Booth had cruelly told him, "It'll be good for you! You're starting to act like a nancy boy!"

Thank you, dear father, he thought bitterly.

Booth stood outside the red and white striped tent. He could hear shouts coming from inside, bursts of blood lust and the dull thud of fists on flesh.

"Kill 'em, Spider!"

"Brave lad—good blow!"

"Hit him harder!"

Booth confronted the old barker. "How much to enter?"

"Spectator, one dime," rasped the old man, "participant, five dollars. Which is it?"

Boxing with a hired tutor or against schoolboys was one thing. But fighting a professional pugilist—with his leg still healing?

"Make up your mind, my good man. Fish, or cut bait!"

Booth reached in his pocket and held out a five-dollar bill. The old man looked down with mild surprise, took the money and said dryly, "Big enough, are you?"

Just then there was a great shout. Two men lurched out of the tent, the older holding up his friend, who was naked to the waist, gleaming with sweat, and careening on rubber legs. Islands of red blotched his muscular torso. His eyes were nearly swollen shut.

"Ya did fine, Ned," said the helper. "Just fine while you lasted. Now we'll get a little whiskey for you, clean you up."

"Did ma best," mumbled the other between swollen lips as they staggered off.

The old barker grinned at Booth, baring gruesome teeth. "Sure you want to go through with this, sonny?"

Booth nodded.

"Then you're up next."

Inside the sweltering tent he recoiled from the stench of sweat and liniment, sawdust and cigar smoke. As his eyes grew accustomed to the gloom, he guessed about one hundred men sat on benches surrounding the ring. Smoke swirled in lazy blue patterns around lanterns strung overhead. The ring was empty save for two stools in opposite corners. Blood spotted the pale canvas. There was no sign of Spider O'Sullivan.

A round, bald man with a fringe of white hair stepped from behind a canvas curtain, waddled to the ring, and climbed through the ropes. He held up his fat hands like two pink starfish, opening and closing them to call for attention. The crowd quieted.

"Gentlemen! We are ready for bout number four this afternoon! Remember, the munificent prize of twenty dollars"—he pulled a fold of green bills from his shirt pocket and held them up— "for anyone who can go one round with Spider O'Sullivan, forty for two rounds, and so forth. And a bonus! For any man gifted enough, brave enough, and strong enough to knock the Spider out, one thousand whole dollars!"

The crowd buzzed in anticipation.

"Our next brave lad is—" The fat man turned to Booth. "What's your name, son?"

"Wilson Beech."

"Give a hand to brave Wilson Beech! All right, lad, take your coat and shirt off and climb in the ring."

Booth handed his hat, coat, and shirt to a man in the front row and climbed through the ropes.

"Mr. Beech, however briefly—"

The audience laughed.

"—will engage in fisticuffs with the one, the only, the peerless and the unbeaten ..." He flung out his arms theatrically ... "Spi-der O-Sull-i-van!"

The crowd broke into applause and cheers. From the back of the tent a strange-looking creature strode briskly toward the ring. He was bare-chested, with skin the color of mahogany and a massive frame. To Booth he looked neither like a spider nor an O'Sullivan. His black eyes were slanted and his glistening shaved head rested on a neck wider than his skull. The fighter's arms were the size of fire logs, and his pectoral muscles protruded like a woman's breasts. Though no taller than Booth he clearly outweighed him by thirty pounds. To Booth he resembled a Nubian genie out of a very large bottle. He was terrifying.

Spider lifted the top rope to climb into the ring. The sight of his biceps and triceps might have evaporated Booth's resolve, but for the reason he was in this spectacle: *If I can last, I will be free.*

Reaching his corner, Spider didn't even glance at his opponent. His back to Booth, he took hold of the top rope and did knee bends. He rolled his tree-trunk neck one way and then the other, shadow-boxed, and did more knee bends. Then, slowly, he turned and stared across the ring at Booth. There was no expression on his face as he ground his huge right fist into his other palm. Booth was trying to remember some of the advice he'd had from his boxing instructor so long ago.

"A maximum five-round contest," boomed the fat man, a brass gong in his hand. "One minute per round, one minute rest in between. And may the better man win."

He rang the gong, and both men left their corners.

Spider shuffled out into the ring on thick legs, his fists held disdainfully at the level of his blue tights. Booth held his hands high, as he'd been taught, his left extended toward his opponent, his right on his chest ready to block a punch to the chin. The words of his coach, Danny Cohelan, came to him: Always try to get in the first punch, your calling card to your opponent, and aim not for the chin but the nose.

107

Circling to Spider's right, Booth stabbed his left out in a straight jab that landed on the bridge of Spider's nose.

And almost simultaneously something hard exploded on the left side of Booth's jaw, slamming him to the canvas. He lay there, sprawled on his back, motionless.

The world swirled around him. He dimly heard the roar of the crowd and over it, the faint drone of the referee's counting the seconds.

"Three, four ..."

*Get up, got to get up!*

At the count of six he rolled over and pushed himself up on all fours.

"Seven," tolled the referee. "Eight—"

Fighting for breath, Booth struggled to his feet. He shook his head to clear the fog, saw the referee leaning close.

"Want to continue, Beech?" His voice sounded far away.

Booth nodded and assumed his fighting stance. As Spider advanced toward him, Booth suddenly realized what he had done wrong—he heard Danny Cohelan's brogue: "Laddie, when yer circlin' yer opponent, waitin' to throw a punch, always circle to his left—otherwise you'll be extendin' a warm invitation from your jaw to his right fist."

Which was what he'd just done.

Now he moved around the ring to Spider's left, away from that terrible right hand, cocked to deliver another punch. He never stopped moving to his own right.

Frustrated by this maneuver, Spider jabbed out with his left several times, but Booth snapped back a token punch, or ducked down. Spider's haymakers swung harmlessly by his head. Booth guessed that the huge overhand right, not his muscle-bound left, was the key to Spider's fearsome career. *As long as I can circle away from it, I might survive.*

But the constant movement around the sluggish behemoth was taking its toll on Booth. His leg was hurting terribly, even though he avoided putting his full weight on it.

When he didn't think he could endure another moment of agony, the gong rang.

He hobbled to his corner and collapsed onto his stool. The referee squeezed a sponge over his head. The cool water felt good.

*One round, twenty dollars! Two more to go!*

Another gong. Booth got up and started out with the same tactic, circling to his own right. Spider clumsily tried to trap Booth in a corner, blocking him so that he could unleash his mighty right from close range. But Booth escaped the trap, ducking under his opponent's arm and moving swiftly to the center of the ring.

Back in safer territory, he felt confident enough to attempt a combination of his own—a left jab to the jaw and a right to the belly. To his dismay, the veteran fighter shrugged off his blows as if they were bites from a horsefly.

It was clear to Booth that he could not punch hard enough to hurt Spider, let alone ward him off. The voice of Danny Cohelan again: "To cut his face, twist your fist."

When Spider missed with a wild left hook, Booth jabbed out with a straight left high on Spider's forehead. Just before he felt his knuckles hit the bone beside the man's eye, Booth twisted his wrist sharply, and felt his knuckles open the skin.

Blood spurted and ran down Spider's brow, filling his eyes. Something unexpected: Spider simply stopped fighting. As if in stunned disbelief, he put his hand to his face and stared at his bloody fingers.

Then, with a bellow, he charged Booth, bulling him into the ropes and pinning him there, pumping savage blows to his face and body. Booth tried to block the barrage, even as it brought on a mind-numbing darkness.

Knowing he'd won, Spider stepped back. Booth's legs buckled, and he pitched forward. He lay crumpled and unmoving at the referee's feet.

He did not move until the count of seven. Then, using the ropes, he pulled himself up to his knees. He struggled to his feet at the count of nine and fought for balance.

Spider was on him again. Another vicious right put Booth down again just as the gong rang to end the round.

The referee dragged him to his corner and helped him on to the stool. One of Booth's eyes was totally closed, the other cut and bleeding.

"All right, fella," said the referee. "That's it for you."

Booth shook his head.

"Look," said the referee, sponging Booth's battered face. "You got yourself forty dollars—nobody gets that fightin' the Spider."

"Not enough," mumbled Booth through swollen lips.

The referee shook his head. "It's your funeral, son." He rang the gong for round three.

Booth struggled to his feet. Looking across the ring he saw two Spider O'Sullivans. He stumbled forward, his desperation banishing all fear. With all his remaining strength he swung a roundhouse punch at Spider's head. The boxer ducked it easily, and Booth toppled to the canvas. He heard laughter from a long way off.

Spider and the referee dragged Booth back to his corner. Spider himself dumped the bucket of water on him.

"Got to get—out there—and fight," Booth mumbled as he struggled to rise from the stool.

"It's all over, Beech." The referee took out his roll of bills, and peeled off two twenties. He held up the money and yelled at the crowd, "See how easy it is?"

He handed the money to Booth and turned back to the crowd. "Who's next?"

Booth realized that Spider was down on one knee in front of him, smiling. "Hey, mon, you sure want da money bad, hey?" His accent was sing-song Jamaican, a high voice that surprised Booth with its gentleness. "You want buy somethin' bad, yes? What for?"

Booth put the bills in his pants pocket. He struggled to his feet. "Boat," he said thickly. "Ticket for a boat."

"Well, now you got it."

Booth shook his head. "Short. Five dollars short."

He struggled through the ropes, his knees buckling. There was scattered applause—he'd cut the face of the great Spider O'Sullivan and lasted two horrendous rounds. Floating in a kind of dream state, he put on his shirt, coat and hat, not caring how he must look. A few spectators smiled at him, some gave him a nod, but most had already forgotten him. Another nervous challenger was already climbing into the ring.

Booth held onto a tent rope, waiting for his double vision to come together. He heard a voice behind him.

"Hey, mon!" It was Spider.

"The ref don' count you out, hey?" said the boxer. "Spider is honest mon, right?"

Booth nodded, at a loss for his meaning. The Jamaican discreetly pressed two folded bills into his hand. "Good fight, mon. Good luck, hey?"

He was gone before Booth could thank him. He opened his hand to find two ten-dollar bills—Union banknotes. *A darky from the Indies had saved him. A mulatto!*

Emerging unsteadily from the tent into the sun's blinding glare, he put a hand to his swollen jaw. It was numb. He wanted a drink, and saw a saloon's swinging doors a few steps away. Then came a whistle blast from the *Yellowstone*. Hurrying as best he could to the dock, Booth shuffled up to the purser with one hundred dollars held tightly in a bruised and swollen hand, the other twenty was deep in his pants pocket, beyond the reach of pickpockets.

The purser reacted in alarm to Booth's battered face.

"What in hell happened to you, sir?"

"I tripped on a rope."

He handed the money to the purser, who regarded him with a look of disbelief.

"And what name do I write in the manifest?"

Booth was about to say, "Beech" when he recalled the close encounter with Upham in Richmond.

"I need your name, sir," said the purser.

For a moment Booth drew a blank. Then, from his time on stage came "Marlowe."

"First name?"

"John." Then, thinking better of it, he said, "Richard."

"Well," said the purser, his patience with this strange fellow wearing thin. "Which is it?"

"John—Richard—Marlowe," said Booth.

The purser wrote it carefully in the register. "Very good, Mr. Marlowe. You will have space 32 on the aft deck. After nine o'clock you will find a blanket and pillow placed there."

Booth drew himself up to respond as a gentleman might, but he could not manage it. He was a fugitive beaten nearly to a pulp, and down to his last few dollars. He walked slowly up the gangway, the pain in his leg breath-taking. Finding space 32, he gingerly eased himself down onto the deck; this would be his home for the next six weeks and twenty-three hundred miles. *Welcome to the Wild West, John Richard Marlowe.*

# CHAPTER FOURTEEN

Minutes later, the steam engines began to rumble and chuff. The crew hauled up the gangway, mooring lines were cast off, the whistle blasted twice, and the *Yellowstone*'s huge paddle wheel churned the muddy water. As deckhands coiled the dripping lines, the great ferry slid away from the dock, out into the brown stream of the Mississippi River.

Through swollen eyelids, Booth watched the shore recede, half-expecting Upham and a dozen Union soldiers to charge down the dock yelling for the boat to return. They wouldn't recognize his battered face. *Thank you, Spider.*

Sitting on a crate of cargo, ignoring the stares of other passengers, he massaged his throbbing leg and took stock of his situation. Despite Upham's suspicions, only one person—besides young Dickie Garrett—knew for certain that he had not died in the Bowling Green barn. He'd learned from yesterday's newspaper that Davey Herold would stand trial with Mrs. Surratt, Powell, and Atzerodt in four days, on the tenth of May. *My twenty-seventh birthday.* Davey wouldn't talk, but he lacked guile. On the stand he might be badgered into contradiction, revealing the truth.

The outskirts of St. Louis faded away when the *Yellowstone* veered ponderously to the left and entered the mouth of the Missouri. Booth put Upham from his mind. It had been three weeks since *The Event*. Here, on the broad wild river, it seemed certain that no one could get at him. The river would liberate him. He was headed for a new country as a new man—John Richard Marlowe. He smiled slightly, thinking of the motto on the Booth family's coat of arms: *Quod ero, Spero. I look forward to what I shall become.*

The gold of the Montana Territory, such as it might be, awaited him. His stage career had always filled his pockets as quickly as he emptied

them. He'd spend his fortune on women and The Cause. Now he was virtually penniless. He marveled now at his spendthrift ways. But that was
the old Booth, a man who was dead. He was John Marlowe now: entre-
preneur, explorer, adventurer, bound for a distant, wild territory where
gold would pay for the most precious things, isolation and freedom.

At first Booth contentedly watched the farms go by and waved to the
villagers on the banks. The land-bound citizens watched in awe as the
great white ship huffed up their river, bound for the fabled West, the new
Promised Land.

After the first week shipboard, he grew restless. Pushing against the
Missouri's strong current, the *Yellowstone* made about fifty river miles
a day, with occasional stops to exchange mail sacks and buy fuel from
wood hawks working out of forlorn outposts on the muddy bank. Despite
the packet's steady progress, the landscape seemed unchanging. There
was nothing for Booth to do aboard the boat. His bedroll space on deck
lodged him between two large, loud-snoring, and flatulent miners. The
blanket provided by the steamboat company was thin, offering little
cushion against the bare deck, and when sleep did finally come, Booth's
mind was beset by nightmares—ghastly images of Ford's Theater, of
his heartbroken mother, of Garrett's barn, and of poor Wilson Beech's
bloody face. Then those thousands of mourners standing alongside the
railroad tracks, grieving over what he, Booth, had done.

He was able to banish troubling images from his mind while awake,
but in the night they returned to torment him. Sometimes waking in a
sweat, his heart racing, he would be utterly astonished to find himself
on the deck of a river boat.

As the great ship labored northwest, Booth's boredom grew acute, and
so did his yearning for drink. He was determined, however, to husband
his dollars, the hardest-earned wages of his entire life. He didn't want
to arrive in Fort Benton penniless. He steeled himself against the
temptation, watching with detachment the other men in their endless
gambling sessions and horseshoe pitching contests on the stern deck,
repelled by their predictably coarse talk of female conquests, and how
they would spend their fortunes in gold.

One day, a miner lounging next to Booth leaned over and pointed to the tattoo on Booth's left hand. "Whose initials are those? Thought your name was Marlowe."

Booth resisted the instinct to withdraw his hand. "Oh, this? Just a . . . memory of a long-lost love. Beautiful girl—Jenny. Jenny Wilma Brown."

The miner laughed. "Well, pardner, I'll tell ya, no future gal of yours gonna be too happy to see J.W.B. tattooed there."

"So right. Thanks for the advice."

But it made him think. The initials drew attention to his past life. And he couldn't wear gloves all the time. That evening he made his way down to the boiler room of the ship. There a bare-chested stoker was feeding chunks of wood into a burning maw of flame. Booth stood idly by the door, smoking a cheroot, until the man stopped work, wiped his brow, and went topside for a breather.

With only the briefest hesitation, Booth grabbed a pair of tongs, scooped up a hot red ember and pressed it to his left hand. There was a sizzling hiss, a steam of vapor, then a hideous, searing pain. He gritted his teeth and kept pressing the tongs to his quivering hand. The smoke of burning flesh stung his nostrils. He felt faint. Then it was done. He dropped the tongs. Between his thumb and forefinger appeared a dollar-sized mark resembling burnt steak.

He wobbled up top and found a wooden bucket of water to soak his hand. That night, even with a bottle of whiskey purchased from a miner, he could barely sleep. The hand throbbed all night and the next day. He finished off the whiskey to make it through the night. After the large oyster-like blister had wept its juices, a crusty scab formed. A week later when it peeled, the tattoo was invisible in the raw pink flesh. *I now have the hands, or hand, of a working man*, he thought, *without having worked.*

The third week brought some excitement. Three Indians on painted ponies rode alongside the steamboat, whooping and shooting arrows that, save for two, fell harmlessly into the water. The soldiers on board fired shots in the air, and the braves veered away with triumphant, melodious yells. On deck there was a scramble to retrieve the arrows as coveted souvenirs of the true West, such as it was.

To Booth the passengers appeared to be a mix of the rough and the refined. Among the uneducated types were a few made of sterner stuff. They were all hopeful misfits, united only by their faith in the promise of the Montana gold fields. There were a few women aboard, including a half-dozen decent-looking mail-order brides on their way to unknown husbands, as well as several painted ladies, obviously prostitutes.

If only he'd been able to bring some books. Few passengers, he noticed, were readers. One exception was an older woman, always dressed in gray or black, who was traveling with a young boy, Tommy. She had an inscrutable face, inexpressive and as pale as a marble statue. She sat on the upper deck, reading for hours at a time. Occasionally, he noticed, she would become so engrossed in a book that she would suck the end of her pinkie finger. She rarely glanced at the passing scenery or her fellow passengers. She read Dickens and Wilkie Collins. He longed to get his hands on her copy of *The Woman in White*. He had once tried to start a conversation with her, about the pleasant weather, but that elicited a glacial response, something he was not accustomed to from women. He couldn't fault her, though. He was an unkempt stranger in sweat-stained clothes; his face, still distorted from Spider's blows, now sprouted an untrimmed beard while his bleached hair showed dark roots.

One day, however, in their fourth week on the river, he happened to find himself on the aft deck sitting two chairs away from her red-haired boy, Tommy, who had a drawing pad on his lap and a large box of watercolors. He was trying to draw something, but kept slapping his pencil down on the paper in frustration.

"I want to draw a proper horse," he complained, "but I can't!"

Booth craned his neck to look at the pad. The horse looked more like a pig. "If you don't mind my saying so, son," he offered, "you've got his head too big and his legs too short and his body too fat." He smiled and held out his hand. "May I?"

The boy regarded him suspiciously, but handed over the pad and pencil. Booth flipped the paper over to a new page.

"Let's start with a couple of circles, shall we? One for the rump area, like this, and another for the chest area, then we just connect them with a line for the back and another for the stomach and we have the body. Extend two lines for the neck, and a kind of triangle here gives us his head. Now, shall he be running or standing?"

Booth had grown up with horses on their farm with Maryland and knew their lines and conformation.

Tommy, eyes wide, was mesmerized as the realistic horse suddenly materialized on the page. "How about trotting, sir?"

"Right!" said Booth. "Now watch how the fetlock is bent, just so. And watch the hocks." He was enjoying this. At one point in his life there was nothing he'd wanted so much as to be an artist. He had done caricatures of all the boys at St. Timothy's, and took a month-long class at the Baltimore School of Art where he learned to draw at thirteen. But he was a Booth, and Booths, as his father never let him forget, were "of the theater, my boy!" He was fourteen when his father died and he gave up his "doodles." He was forced to learn the theater and to practice always in the critical shadow of his two famous brothers.

Now he quickly sketched in the horse's legs. "And finally the tail!"

"Excellent, sir," said the boy, "First rate! Now what color shall it be?"

"What color would you like?"

"Brown, with a white face. Like my little bay mare at home."

Under the boy's direction, Booth opened the fine watercolors and brushed in a background, green fields with a red barn on a hill. As he painted, he felt a kind of lost youth coming back to him. And he realized that Tommy, the only child on board, was probably lonely and bored. While Booth painted, Tommy chattered on, saying that he and his mother, Emma Ledyard, were going to Fort Benton, where his father, Tobias Ledyard, had just been appointed Collector of Customs for Montana and Idaho territories.

"What exactly does a Collector of Customs do?" Booth asked.

"I'm not sure," said the boy. "But he's *wery* important. *Wery.* He's finding a house for us up there now—and a pony for me, I hope."

At this juncture, Tommy's mother, Mrs. Ledyard, appeared. She frowned at the unkempt stranger. The heat of the day had led Booth to take off his shirt, so that he was clothed in just an undershirt, his well-muscled shoulders tanned by the sun.

117

"Good day, madam," said Booth. He stood up, bowing slightly. "Your fine son has been entertaining me with his art supplies."

"Look at what he's drawn for me, Mama," exclaimed the boy. "It's wery, wery good!"

Mrs. Ledyard examined the drawing.

"Yes," she said. "Quite."

She studied Booth now, coldly. "And you are Mister—?"

"Marlowe," he said. "John Marlowe."

"Mr. Marlowe," she repeated, taking inventory of Booth's face. Her eyes roamed his muscular chest and shoulders. "Like the dramatist."

"Precisely," he said.

"And do you do portraits of humans, Mr. Marlowe?"

His most successful efforts in his small experience at art school had always been head studies. He found himself saying "Well, yes, actually I do. That is, I could."

"I would like to commission you to make a little drawing of Tommy," she said with a suddenly happy look on her face. "For which I shall compensate you."

She turned and strode away.

He started the portrait immediately. This, he thought, might bring enough money for a bottle of whiskey and some cabin-class dining. Booth was finding it increasingly difficult to swallow the tasteless greasy slop ladled out to deck travelers on tin plates.

It had been at least four years since he had drawn anything, save for an occasional working sketch to illustrate an idea for a stage set. But the boy proved a good subject, sitting as still as a ten-year-old could. As Booth worked, the basic craft he had acquired at the Baltimore School of Art came back to his hand. He could hear his old professor walking from student to student, commenting in his thick Bavarian accent, "Der eyes comink in da middle of da head, ja? Make da eyes one width of eye apart, ja? Top of ears comink in line mit eyebrows, *und so weiter*."

Booth had to erase and redo many lines—it had been many years since those lessons—but eventually he had an accurate likeness sketched in. Then, with the brush he daubed in color—the boy's blue eyes, the bright red hair, the freckles, the green of his jumper. A group of passengers gradually assembled behind him and watched each stroke with rapt

118

interest. One of the prostitutes nudged a girlfriend and whispered, "Ain't he cunning?"

It was after five when Mrs. Ledyard returned. She looked at the completed sketch.

"Do you approve, madam?" he asked, finally. *I am painting for my supper.*

"It is quite good, I must say," she said with genuine delight. "What do I owe you, Mr. Marlowe?"

He wanted to say three or four dollars, which would buy him a fine dinner tonight and a bottle of whiskey at the next port. "I would like these pencils, the watercolors and the pad," he said instead. "If it seems a fair exchange to you. I will give Tommy lessons with them, *gratis*, of course."

She seemed bemused by this. "Is that all right with you, Tommy?"

"Oh, yes," he said. "If Mr. Marlowe will give me another lesson tomorrow."

"Very well," she said, taking the boy's hand. She turned to Booth, regarding him with her heavy-lidded eyes, and said with a smile, "Glad to have met you, Mr. Marlowe. There's so little for a boy to do aboard ship. You've brightened Tommy's trip."

The next day Booth gave Tommy another drawing lesson. Afterward, a miner with a beard like a gray hedgehog sidled up. "Do one of me for the missus back in Texas," he said, "and I'll give you four dollars. Five if you make me look handsome."

Five dollars!

"Handsome you will be, sir."

The man positioned himself on a rope-bound bale, the backs of his hands together between his knees, and Booth began to sketch.

"Where are you headed?" asked Booth, as he outlined the mass of hair and beard with the burnt umber pencil.

"Bannack, out in the Montana Territory."

"Is there really as much gold there as people say?"

"Son, I tell you true, out there, the nuggets line the road like horse turds!" Then he added, "Course I ain't been there yet."

Booth laughed, a strange sound he hadn't heard in a long time. There was a newspaper sitting next to the miner and the word *Lincoln* in a headline caught his eye. During a break, he turned the pages of the three-week old paper:

*From now until God's judgment day, the minds of men will not cease to thrill at the killing of Abraham Lincoln, by the hand of Booth, the actor . . . Some will regard it with all the horror of the most wicked assassination, others will feel it to be that righteous retribution which descends direct from the hand of God upon the destroyer of human liberty, and the oppressor of a free people . . .*

*Not a soldier, nor a woman, nor an old man nor a lisping child with a true heart for this Southern land but feels the thrill, electric and divine, at this sudden fall of our oppressor. Monomaniac, assassin, and villain Booth may have been . . .*

*Villain?* Where in God's name was the word "patriot"? Yet this article approved of his act—or did it? How could they approve of Lincoln's death but not approve of the man who caused it? It beggared the imagination.

Booth looked up from the newspaper to find the miner studying him. *I still must be watchful even way out here in no man's land.*

He went back to drawing with a trembling hand and a strange feeling of exultation in his heart, an ebullience mingled with guilt and fear. Fear of what? Fear of—the Providences of God? And just what does that ponderous phrase mean?

There was a rightness to The Tyrant's death. Yet try as he might, his mind could not erase from memory those thousands of mourners weeping as they watched Lincoln's funeral train pass.

# CHAPTER FIFTEEN

Langford Upham walked down the broad oak stairs to the basement of the War Department Building and prepared to do battle with a man known for his ruthlessness.

It was the tenth of May, John Wilkes Booth's twenty-seventh birthday, as several newspapers noted. A week after he'd left Richmond, Upham was finally granted a meeting with Colonel Lafayette Baker. As chief of the National Detective Police, Baker had personally directed the efforts to capture Booth and the conspirators, and reported directly to Secretary of War Edwin Stanton. He had stalled Upham and canceled two appointments, but the reporter had persevered.

An adjutant opened the door, looking the journalist up and down. Upham was nattily dressed in a yellow suit, his black bowler cocked on his head, and strode confidently into the office.

Baker was seated in his dark uniform behind a massive desk. His foot-long auburn beard was thick and curly. Ice blue eyes glared at Upham through a haze of cigar smoke.

"Colonel Baker," Upham began, deliberately. "Thank you for this opportunity."

"You son of a bitch," growled the officer, taking the cigar from his mouth.

Upham's narrow face flushed. "To what do I owe that cordial salutation?"

"You know damn well what I mean. Look at you sitting there in that— that canary yellow outfit of yours."

"I know not of what you speak, sir," said Upham innocently.

"I allowed you to tag along with my detectives, Colonel Conger and my cousin Luther. You were to report the Booth mission accurately. I told you pointedly, clearly, not to mention certain things in your goddamned newspaper, and you went ahead and did it anyway." The big man swiveled in his chair, tugged on his full beard, and said to his young adjutant, "Tom, how about you go get yourself some lunch."

"Yessir," said the adjutant, and stepped quickly out of the office.

Upham seated himself in an uncomfortable chair facing Baker's desk. "I merely reported a few rumors, Colonel."

"You damn near cost me my job, you sawed-off little popinjay."

"For reporting a few *theories*?"

"That jackass Johnson had me in the White House the next day." Baker's voice went falsetto to imitate the new president. "'Is that corpse you've got over there *really* Booth?'" He shook his head and rasped, "He's something from hell, that Johnson. To think he sits in Lincoln's chair now! Even his worst enemies admit what a great man Lincoln really was."

Upham was amused. The scuttlebutt was that Baker had actually made money on the side, in the early part of the war, giving information to the Confederates. Useless information, of course. And Baker and his henchman had arrested hundreds of people in the capital after the assassination, including the entire cast and stage crew of *Our American Cousin*, who, fortunately, were released quickly. Yet the rumors continued as evidence was uncovered, then buried. A sense of paranoia ran through the capital as the Radical Republicans, no doubt encouraged by Edwin Stanton, jockeyed with Johnson's executive branch.

"And, of course, that corpse really is Booth, isn't it?" said Upham.

"You know it is! You were there."

"I know Booth was left-handed. He didn't have that scar on his neck. In addition, he had a moustache."

"Oh, a moustache? You don't say? And I know," said Baker, pointing a finger at Upham, "that Booth was ambidextrous, that he *did* have a scar on his neck—tumor operation with a certain Dr. May—and a moustache is the *first* thing he would get rid of. He shaved it off at Mudd's. Use your goddamned head, man! And what about the fact that Booth had a tattoo on his left hand—'J.W.B.'—his initials? My cousin Luther said even *you* saw and acknowledged that at Garrett's farm."

"Yes, well," said Upham. "But what about that broken leg?"

"What about it?"

"The bone was sticking out. It looked fresh, with no sign of healing."

"So now you're a medical expert as well?"

"Where was the splint Doctor Mudd admits he put on the leg?"

"It probably fell off during the man's flight. He rode a considerable distance. It makes perfect sense. He probably re-broke it along the way."

If only Upham could get him to admit that there was a *possibility* that the body wasn't Booth's. "One other thing, Colonel. Please simply hear me out. I am not here as your enemy."

Baker shifted with an air of impatience. "All right."

"I can't help but note that the corpse, one could say very conveniently, had Booth's diary on it and sure, pictures of the ladies in his life were tucked in it. But no cash? Not one dollar! Wouldn't Booth have had escape money on him? After all that elaborate planning? He was a man of considerable means, and he had backers in this scheme."

Baker countered, "We've confirmed that was Booth's suit of clothes. We found his tailor in New York."

"But you saw that it was loose-fitting. It didn't fit the corpse very well," said Upham. "This is what tailors are for, sir—your own uniform fits you handsomely—and Booth was known to be a dandy."

"It fit as well as most people's," Baker said defensively. "The man had lost weight."

"Sir, did anyone *positively* identify the body? I mean a close friend, a family member, or someone who knew him well—say, the tailor, perhaps?"

"His mother asked to see him, and one of his brothers," Baker said, his manner softening. "By the time they got to Washington it was too late. We had him in the ground."

"Why so much hurry?"

"It was Secretary Stanton's order to get the job done."

"Stanton's? Not President Johnson's?"

"We had no appetite for keeping the bastard above ground indefinitely. It was time to bury him. He was getting ripe."

"How soon was that done?"

Baker chewed his cigar. "Fairly soon."

"The next day?"

"You'd better ask the Secretary yourself."

"Within twelve hours?"

"I don't have to answer your questions, Upham."

"But sir! Consider: No wonder no one could identify him! He was in the ground before his family or close friends could get there."

"What does it matter? You know, after you left, he came to. Regained his senses."

"Who came to?" asked Upham, incredulous.

"The man you saw dragged from the tobacco barn," said Baker. "John Wilkes Booth."

"I don't believe it."

"He did! Luther told me all. He made notes, too."

"That man was at death's door, sir. Actually he *was* dead."

"Wrong you are. It was after you and detective Conger rode off," said Baker. "Luther and the soldiers carried him up to the farmhouse and laid him on the porch. Luther heard him say, 'Useless.' He raised his hands."

"'Useless?'"

"Just that word—he said it twice. Then he said 'Mother' once. That's all. He only lived a short time. Well, a couple of hours. Actually, three hours. They gave him water, but there was nothing to be done. He died. The story ends there."

For the first time Upham felt Baker was telling the truth. "Forgive me my simple-minded questions, Colonel, but I must be clear. Did anyone actually ask him if he was John Wilkes Booth?"

"One of the men asked him to identify himself."

"And?"

"He said one more word. Luther and Conger couldn't rightly make it out."

"What do you think he might have said?"

Baker hesitated. "It sounded like 'harlot.' Others were in agreement."

"Harlot! Sir, that's a very strange thing for a dying man to say."

"That's what we believe he said. His very last word. Harlot."

"Could he have said 'Charlotte?'" Upham asked as calmly as he could.

"Christ, man! I don't know! Harlot, or Charlotte, or maybe 'hurts a lot'—they couldn't tell. Then Luther said he coughed and died. Hell, even Herold said he was Booth. You heard him yourself! At least you got that part right in your cursed article."

"Herold has every reason to cover Booth's tracks. It's called loyalty. What did they do with the body?"

"Sewed it up in a blanket. Commandeered a darky's market wagon. Drove it to Belle Plain. Put the corpse on a steamer to Washington. Then transferred it to an ironclad, the *Montauk*. I was on board by then."

"And then you got him into the ground as soon as possible. Before his family or anyone else could identify him."

"The man's face was a sorry mess. Puffed up with blood. Hell, the neck half blown away. You saw it. We wanted to spare his family that horror." The soldier shrugged. "Civilians aren't used to such things."

"How considerate of you." Upham leaned forward in his chair. "Suppose I told you something, Colonel Baker—something that would set the nation aflame."

"I'm all ears, Upham," his tone implying the opposite.

"I don't know how it all came to pass, but I swear to you, sir, that Booth is alive, and that he went to see General Lee in Richmond."

"And Lee made him a general, and the two of them are dancing a jig as they rally the Army of Northern Virginia to take up arms again."

"I am serious, damn it, sir!" said Upham. "The man I saw leaving Lee's house, I'm sure, was Booth, in disguise."

"Ah. Disguised, is he now?"

"He stayed at a boarding house under the name of Beech. There was a real Wilson Beech. I suspect he was the man in the barn—the man you buried. I learned that Booth sent money to Beech's wife. Two hundred dollars."

"Who goes around sending money to another man's wife? Escaped assassins? Or perhaps you think of Booth as something of an idealist."

"I went to Front Royal to see the woman—"

"You've become quite the roving detective, haven't you?"

"She showed me a picture of her husband, taken four years ago. It did not remotely resemble the man I saw in Richmond—the man I am certain is Booth, but claims to be Beech."

"And?"

Upham took a deep breath. "Major, Beech's wife is named Charlotte."

"So?"

"That dying man didn't say 'harlot.' With his last breath, he said his wife's name: 'Charlotte.'"

For a moment, Upham believed that Baker was on the brink of being persuaded.

Then the soldier slapped his knees briskly and stood up. "You've lost me, Upham. Too complicated. I have work to do. Good day, sir."

"Colonel, the man posing as Beech also had a bad leg!"

"Do you realize how many men have wounded legs these days?" Baker said. "Even you might have earned one if your father hadn't paid to keep you out of uniform."

"No one paid a nickel on my behalf, sir. I volunteered and was rejected on account of my asthma. But I will let your insult pass."

Baker colored, but said nothing.

"Colonel, I demand that you order an exhumation of the body you buried as Wilkes Booth."

"You 'demand?'" Baker said, drawing himself up. "You *demand?*"

"All right then; I beseech you as a concerned citizen."

"There will be no exhumation by my order. Booth is buried, the President is satisfied, Stanton is satisfied, and the case is closed. All we need to do is hang the conspirators."

"Do you know what they're saying about the Secretary of War?"

"Who," Baker said between puffs of smoke as he re-lit his cigar, "are *they?*"

"People. Prominent people."

"Do tell me what *people* are saying about Mr. Stanton."

"That he was in on the conspiracy."

"Hogwash!"

"They say that's why Lincoln's guard at the theater—Parker—conveniently disappeared to a bar across the street. They say that's why every road out of Washington was blocked after the assassination—all except Booth's route to Virginia. They say Stanton tore eighteen pages out of Booth's diary. I myself read some of those pages when I handled the diary at Garrett's farm—it mentioned Senator Conness of California, Benjamin Wade of Ohio, and Zachariah Chandler of Michigan—all Radical Republicans—and it mentioned Stanton himself—"

"I forbid you to talk that way about the Secretary! This is the worst form of treasonous slander!"

"Have I hit a nerve, Colonel?"

"God damn it, you impertinent bastard!"

"There were photographs taken of Booth's body taken aboard the *Montauk*," said Upham. "People on shore have told me of seeing the photographer, Mr. Alexander Gardner."

"Upham, I was there, remember?"

"I'm told the Gardner plates were developed immediately and handed over to the Secretary of War—placed on Mr. Stanton's desk—and have not been heard of since."

"The public can hardly expect to be privy to such ghastly things, man. I really must ask you to leave."

Upham stood up. "I could petition the President for that body to be exhumed. My father will talk to Johnson and ask him about the photographs." He hated invoking his father, but he knew it would intimidate Baker. "Booth's mother will certainly conclude that the corpse is not her son. When Mrs. *Charlotte* Beech views the body, she will confirm that it is, or was, her husband."

A hard look came over Baker's face, a narrowing of eyes and a slow elevation of his chin. "Nobody can dig up that body."

"And why not?"

"It's buried in a secret place—deep—in a burlap bag. We poured a thick slab of cement over it."

"Cement?"

"Security. So it can't become a shrine to the Confederacy."

Upham took out his watch. "The trial begins in an hour. The conspirators. Aren't you attending, Major?"

"Why bother? We're going to hang 'em all anyway."

"Even Mrs. Surratt?"

"Especially Mrs. Surratt. Damned Catholics! You have no idea what kind of ring we shattered when we got Booth and the others. There's a Montreal angle to all this."

Upham, who had studied the conspiracy's every known detail, hadn't made up his mind about Mrs. Surratt. Certainly the conspirators—how many were there, ten, twelve, including her twenty-year-old son John?—met in her boarding house. Booth himself had stopped by the very day of the assassination. And they nabbed Powell there. How much had she herself known? She was possibly in favor of kidnap and overthrow. But murder? Her son had fled to Montreal.

"What happened to the presumption of innocence?"

"That's inside the courtroom. Out here they're guilty as sin. Or hadn't you reporters heard by now?"

"May I quote you, Colonel?"

"Listen here." Baker yanked the cigar from his mouth and stabbed it at Upham. "If any more of your tripe mentions me, I'll personally break both your arms."

"Well, sir, on that note I shall leave." Upham opened the door, but turned for a parting shot. "When I find Booth and bring him back, you're going to have to dig up that block of cement."

# CHAPTER SIXTEEN

Standing on the deck of the *Yellowstone,* Booth was astonished to see an immense herd of buffalo crossing the river. They came plunging off the grassy banks by the hundreds and swam across the steamer's bow— cows, calves, and huge shaggy bulls moving in a steady bellowing wave that blocked the steamboat's passage. A soldier shot a bull near the boat. Deck hands lassoed his neck and horns and hauled the half-ton animal aboard. While it was being butchered, Booth made a pencil sketch of its great head and curving black horns, and then water-colored it.

Every day, after giving Tommy Ledyard an art lesson, Booth had made quick sketches of the deer and buffalo that he'd seen feeding along the banks. The graceful pronghorn antelopes excited him the most, and he made several action studies. It saddened him when two soldiers shot three of the animals for sport, leaving their carcasses to rot on the prairie.

Booth's colored sketch of an eagle perched on a dead tree with a fish under one claw sold for an astounding eight dollars to a passenger headed for Bannack with mining equipment. This was important to Booth. This was a real picture, a finished painting, and an exhilarating transaction: eight whole dollars!

For only four hours of doing something he enjoyed so much. Maybe he would be an artist. Maybe he would dedicate his life to art.

"Welcome to the world's innermost port!" shouted the purser through a tin megaphone as the *Yellowstone* huffed its way around the last bend of the Missouri before arriving at Fort Benton. The steam whistle blew three blasts. The six-week journey was over.

Booth joined the other weary passengers as they gathered along the starboard rail to cheer the frontier settlement. Across the water stood the crumbling adobe fort which had given the town its name. Surrounded by tall cottonwood trees and flanked by high clay bluffs, it appeared as an oasis, resplendent in the late afternoon sun. Apart from his time to draw, to learn a new, strangely silent craft, this had been a tedious journey. Benton loomed as a relief, the start of a new life for John Richard Marlowe.

He studied the crowd and the wooden storefronts and saloons behind them. Stevedores milled among the horses, wagons, barrels, sacks, and piled buffalo hides. There were buckskinned mountain men with their wolf dogs and long rifles, trappers with racks of fur on their shoulders, and four prostitutes—"soiled doves"—in their best finery. Indians stood nearby, watching impassively. All were curious to review the latest load of human cargo—their future neighbors, customers, marks, concubines, or mail-order brides.

"I can't believe this is the same place!" said the age-worn miner whose portrait Booth had sketched. "Old Pierre Chouteau and the Frenchies got the fur-tradin' fort going, then Culbertson showed up in Forty-Six and rebuilt it. That's when I come out as a lad—for the furs. Pelts and plews made me some money. And now the gold bug's got everyone dancing. Includin' me!"

"It seems an exciting place," Booth ventured. *And strange.*

"Will you look at Benton now! New buildings everywhere. Gold's a mighty strange thing, mister. They say Bannack and Alder Gulch are pure bedlam these days. The inmates rule the asylum."

Booth scanned the crowd warily. He spotted no soldiers, no lawmen, and no one resembling that cursed reporter. He chided himself: how could anyone ever trace him to this obscure refuge? He didn't look even remotely like he had two months ago, with his moustache replaced by a full well-trimmed beard, and a nose that had been reshaped by Spider O'Sullivan. *That mulatto boxer gave me twenty dollars on a point of honor. Thank you, Spider.*

Feeling in no immediate danger, Booth was determined to relax and enjoy the panorama, a Wild West every bit as colorful as magazines described it, and the vast landscape was splendid.

The steamboat's big rear wheel stopped, reversed, and swung the vessel parallel to the dock. The crew tossed mooring lines to men ashore, who deftly wrapped them around stout posts driven into the river mud. The paddle wheel ceased to turn. The crowd cheered as the gangplank dropped to the heavy plank dock with a thud.

Tommy and Mrs. Ledyard stood at the rail waving to a rotund, gray-haired, well-dressed man on the dock. His face was flushed, and he was waving his arms over his head.

"All ashore!" boomed the purser's voice. "And don't forget your belongings or you'll never see them again!"

Passengers disembarked carrying their luggage, while stevedores unloaded the freight. Booth's belongings were slim and all fit into a bag he'd bought from an Indian woman at Cow Island, thirty miles downstream. Inside was a buckskin shirt from the same woman, the drawing pad and watercolors, as well as a hairbrush, a towel, and a bar of soap acquired through trade on the boat. The steamboat line had given him the filthy blanket he'd slept in for almost two months. Bathing in the river as often as he could, he'd somehow avoided the bedbugs that inflicted many on board. Tommy and Mrs. Ledyard waved briefly at Booth before walking down the gangplank.

He suddenly realized how far away he was from his former life, a world away. *Quod ero, Spero. I look forward to what I will become.* He was now John Richard Marlowe, man without portfolio. How would he survive here? Mrs. Ledyard had suggested that, once they arrived in Fort Benton, the instruction in art and poetic recitation for Tommy might continue if Mr. Ledyard agreed. Booth had replied that his plans were, alas, to press on by stage to Bannack for its promise of gold. But he was worried about his cash. He might not even have enough for the two-hundred-mile journey by stage.

Booth stepped down the gangplank onto the dock with barely a limp; his leg had mended well in two months. He made his way through the throng still milling on the dock. The braying of mules, the rattle of wagons, the barking of dogs, the crack of a bullwhacker's whip over a bellowing team of oxen—a discordant symphony, full of life and madness. Booth felt invigorated as he picked his way through the muck toward the nearest saloon. Its large sign proclaimed it *The Star, Benton's Finest.* He'd run out of whiskey several days ago, but he hadn't really missed it, so involved was he in his drawings. Now, seeing the saloon, he decided he could use a drink.

As he crossed the street, an open buggy drawn by two handsome sorrel horses cut in front of him and stopped.

"Mr. Marlowe!" said a hearty voice. It was Tobias Ledyard, Tommy's father at the reins. Tommy and the prim Mrs. Ledyard sat beside him.

Booth doffed his hat, gazing up at the older man's round, florid face.

"My wife tells me you've been a good tutor to Tommy, and I wish to thank you."

"My pleasure. He's an apt student."

"Have you a place to stay the night? We have a large enough house back against the hill, should you need a room."

*I need a drink.* Booth shook his head. "Kind of you, sir, kind indeed. But I'm going to catch the stage to Bannack early tomorrow."

"Very well, Marlowe," said the man genially. "But do feel free to call upon us at any time. And I love the portraits you did of Tommy. Change your mind about Bannack, come see me."

"Most generous of you, sir. Thank you." Booth tipped his hat, stepping back as Ledyard slapped the reins. As the carriage drove off, Tommy stood up and waved. Booth stopped and waved back, waiting until the carriage had turned the corner so that the boy wouldn't see him enter a saloon. *Whiskey!*

Even at five o'clock, The Star was already full and active. Through a haze of fragrant cigar smoke Booth saw that many tables were occupied by card players. Two scantily upholstered women, one old and busty, one young and scrawny, waited on the patrons. A black piano player at the end of the long bar was mechanically banging out a tremolo version of "Beautiful Dreamer." Mounted above the ornate mahogany back bar were crudely stuffed heads of elk, moose, and antelope. Good models for paintings, he thought.

Booth stood at the middle of the crowded bar and ordered a whiskey. As the bartender returned with a bottle and glass, Booth noticed that the man had no ears. Frostbite, perhaps. Or an unpleasant encounter with the Red Man. Were all those stories about heartless savages really true? He had been in hundreds of saloons in the South and the East, but never had he chanced upon one populated like this. He looked around in wonder at the tableau of human destinies.

Next to Booth stood a large man with a mane of pigeon-gray hair and a raptor's nose. Like many here, he wore a heavy revolver seated in a holster on his hip. He swiveled his bulk to face Booth, announcing with stale breath, "Suh, Where y'all from?"

Before Booth could answer, the man jabbed out his hand. "Suggs here—Moody Suggs from Jackson, Mississippi, and God bless the Confederacy."

Booth took the big hand and cringed as the man clamped it like a vise. When he let go, Booth said, "Marlowe, Front Royal, Virginia."

"I knew it—a fellow Southerner! There's a few of us up here. Makes the Yankees uncomfortable." His hand swept through the cigar smoke to take in the whole room.

Booth could tell by the bloodshot eyes that focused tightly, intently, then lost their bearing, that Suggs was quite drunk. His father's eyes had behaved that way just before he would pass out.

Booth started to rise from the stool. "Excuse me, friend, but I'd better find out about the stage to Bannack."

Suggs clamped a heavy hand on his shoulder and shoved him back. "Stage don't leave till tomorrow, Mr. Marlowe." He gestured to the bartender. "We'll drink to Jefferson Davis—God bless him in his time of trouble! You heard the news?"

"Probably not." Booth had heard no news for weeks.

"Captured in Alabama. Davis and what was left of his army. Terrible thing."

*President Davis captured! Of course, it was inevitable. Now the war was truly over.*

Booth slumped on the stool. It had all been in vain. Lincoln's murder, Beech's death, everything. *Useless.* He picked up the drink the bartender set in front of him and took a gulp. Then he pulled a coin from his pocket and put it on the bar.

"Next one is on me, Mr. Suggs."

"Call me Moody," said the man, raising his glass. "To old Jeff Davis."

"Will they hang him?"

"Most likely. Same as the others."

A chill grabbed at Booth's stomach. "Which others?"

"The ones who killed that baboon Lincoln. The federals are goin' through the motions of a proper trial, but I'll wager a double eagle they'll hang 'em all."

"Which—how many are they?"

Cox rubbed his face. "There's Powell, Herold, and Mrs. Surratt," said Moody. "And the Dutchman, what's his name."

"Atzerodt," said Booth automatically. He didn't care about Powell, the madman, or the feckless dull-witted German, but Davey Herold's guileless face appeared before him. Good old loyal Davey.

"There's others in the dock."

"I expect they cast a wide net."

"That doctor who fixed his leg—they'll probably string him up, too."

"Mudd didn't know who he was treating," Booth blurted, remembering Mudd's dismay, and his wife's solicitous attentions. Moody studied Booth with a renewed curiosity.

"I mean," said Booth quickly, "I read that the assassin wore a false beard."

"The way I see it, Mudd only done what a doc is supposed to do."

"Poor Mrs. Surratt," Booth said dully. He saw the face of the kind boardinghouse keeper. She had treated him like a son. A good churchgoer. And beautiful in her way. A loyal sympathizer of the Confederate cause, she had harbored spies in her H Street establishment, including three of the Lincoln conspirators. But Booth, not wanting her implicated, had seen to it that she knew little if anything about the plot. And now they were talking of hanging her.

"They're all innocent, if you ask me," muttered Moody, pouring himself a shot from Booth's bottle. "And as for the late Johnny W. Booth, I say give the man a medal and put a statue of him in every town south of the Mason-Dixon."

"So Booth is really dead?"

"No doubt about it. Them sons of bitches trapped him like a rat in Virginia and a bluecoat named Boston Corbett shot him."

Moody pulled his long-barreled revolver from its holster and laid it gently on the bar reverently, as though it were a piece of the True Cross.

"See that? That fine weapon killed Yanks—five of 'em—at Chancellorsville. Damn right!" Moody pounded on the bar. "I was ten feet from Stonewall Jackson when he was done in, and I got me a bullet in the gut the same morning, but by God I took five of 'em bluecoats with me that day."

Maudlin tears welled in the man's bloodshot eyes as he stared morosely at the weapon. Booth started to move away, but suddenly Moody grabbed his glass and raised it. He leaned past Booth and shouted down the bar, "Hey boys, tell the nigra to play Dixie! Here's to Jeff Davis and Robert E. Lee!"

The men stared back at him. None moved to raise a glass. The pianist stopped playing.

Moody's eyes narrowed. "Perhaps you fellows didn't hear me. I said here's to Jeff Davis and Robert E. Lee."

Then one of the muleskinners at the bar, said, "Moody, did I hear you say here's to General Grant and Abe Lincoln?"

"Why, you son of a bitch!"

Moody snatched up his gun and leveled it, wobbling, at the man. Without thinking, Booth slapped his hand down on the barrel of the pistol, and the deafening blast sent a bullet through the floorboards. The bartender vaulted the bar, wrenched the revolver from Suggs's grasp as a cowboy pinioned his arms.

"Moody, you crazy bastard," he said. "I warned you!"

The cowboy and the bartender frog-walked Moody to the swinging doors and heaved him out into the street. Moody stumbled off the wooden porch and fell on his hands and knees in the mud. After a string of profanities, he stood up, careening wildly, and shouted, "Long live the Confederacy!" He fell backwards in a growling stupor.

When the bartender came back behind the bar he extended his hand to Booth. "Name's Luke, and this round's on me."

The big man in a buckskin shirt, who would have been Moody Suggs's victim, came down the bar to Booth and thanked him.

"Moody's a crazy son of a bitch when he's drinking." He laughed. "Matter of fact, he's a crazy shitter when he's not drinking. I'm Tim

Winters, and I'm buying this drink."

"I'm Marlowe," said Booth. "John Marlowe."

"And what brings you to Benton, Marlowe?"

He was going to answer "gold" but he found himself telling Winters he was an artist.

"No bull?"

"Truly."

"What kind of artist? Never met an artist before."

Booth opened his bag and showed some of his drawings. A few men gathered around and seemed impressed.

"That antelope," said one. "Shot a dozen just like him."

"And the buff. I shot one like that yesterday."

"Could you do a picture of me—for my mother?" asked Tim Winters.

"When I'm sober," said Booth. "Right now I couldn't do you a picture of a dead woodchuck."

"Tomorrow then," said Winters, and they drank to that.


It had been a long time since Booth had felt such camaraderie or, at least, any personal associations outside of conspiracy. As the drinks kept coming, thoughts of Jeff Davis, Davey Herold's trial, poor Mrs. Surratt, and *The Event* itself were pushed to the back of his mind. Soon he was very drunk, but kept putting them down. He had no place to go. So might as well stay here.

"Mister, it's time," said the bartender.

"For what?" said Booth, his eyes now half-shut.

"Closing time."

He looked around. All his new friends had left. Clutching his bag of belongings, he walked uncertainly out of The Star, bumping through the swinging door and into the night. The afternoon had been hot, but now the air was cool.

Tim had told him of an inexpensive hotel, the Metropolitan, and he ventured along the empty street in search of it. He saw no hotel, only darkened shop fronts. Then he stood at what looked like the edge of Benton. Maybe the man had meant the other end of town. Booth wheeled and followed the river bank, the edge of the Missouri, until he came to a stand of cottonwoods. By now, he was exhausted. From his knapsack he pulled the thin blanket he'd been given aboard the steamboat. He wrapped the blanket around him, tucked the knapsack under his head, and fell sound asleep.

# CHAPTER SEVENTEEN

By noon on Friday July 7, the keeper of the official thermometer at the Smithsonian Institute had recorded the hottest day of the year in Washington. Seated under a protective canopy in the broad prison courtyard of the Federal Arsenal, Langford Upham sweltered in the midday sun. Fifty armed guards were stationed atop the high red brick walls enclosing the yard. The heat had led most to drop the butts of their rifles to the ground and grasp the railing, lest they faint.

Only two hundred passes had been issued to witness the execution. All the observers were men dressed in dark suits, some fanning themselves with their hats.

"This heat!" one man observed, mopping his brow. "The fires of Hell are bein' stoked up for the wicked."

Before the witnesses loomed the gallows, newly carpentered for the momentous occasion. Upham was close enough to smell its fresh-cut pine timbers sweating in the sun. Four nooses made of stout, bright manila hung down twelve feet and coiled beside four chairs. Standing below the platform, a quartet of soldiers stood in the shade, ready to knock away the long posts supporting the hinged trap doors. Behind the gallows one could see four waiting coffins and four graves with shovels planted in the freshly-dug piles of earth.

Upham had never witnessed a hanging. His first encounter with violent death came after the Battle of Bull Run. Hunting for battle stories, he had come upon a platoon of surgeons working under an open-air tent over a half-dozen tables. One was amputating a screaming soldier's shattered leg above the knee with a long curved saw. Finished, the surgeon tossed the limb onto a pile of severed arms and legs that lay on the blood-soaked grass. Its meaty landing made a ghastly smacking sound. Upham stepped backward, turned and retched into the bushes.

That incident, and the churning in his stomach now, mocked his once-grand notions of what kind of soldier he would have made. As much as he claimed regret at being declared unfit to serve, deep down Upham suspected himself to be a physical coward.

Now he was going to witness not only a hanging, but the execution of someone he briefly knew, and for whom he felt considerable pity. Davey Herold. After his unpleasant meeting with Baker, Upham used the letterhead of his newspaper and his father's influence with The White House to win grudging permission for a five-minute prison session with Herold.

Seated in a drab anteroom next to the cells in the bowels of the Arsenal, Upham heard the clanking irons of a heavily shackled prisoner approaching. Herold appeared, flanked by two guards who roughly shoved him down onto the chair across the table from him. The reporter was shocked to see how pale and thin he was. He seemed little more than a hapless, none-too-bright farm boy swept up in Booth's colossal debacle for the most pathetic of motives: hero-worship. Haggard from weeks of sleepless nights, Herold was sweating, and his face twitched constantly.

"David," said Upham, "I'm here as a journalist, but not without sympathy for your plight."

Herold lifted his gaze from his shackled hands to meet Upham's earnest face. "I thank you, sir."

"I credit the possibility—no guarantee—that, if you tell me some truths, it may go better at your sentencing."

A sad smile formed on the prisoner's pale face. "You know they're g-goin' to hang me no matter what I say. Or what you say, sir. I'm as good as d-dead right now."

Upham had never met a man who appeared so forlorn. "Have you always had a stutter, Davey?"

Herold nodded, looking down again. "Can't h-help it."

"Are you a man of faith?"

Herold glanced uneasily at the soldiers flanking the table. "I reckon. But I d-didn't go to church r-regular, that is."

"Tell me then, before you meet your Maker, sooner or later as we all must, and have to atone for our sins, who was that man they shot in the barn?"

Herold seemed surprised by the question. "Why, John Wilkes Booth."
*No stutter.*

"John Wilkes Booth. No one else, Davey?"

"J-John it were, for sure."

"Will you swear to the God you will one day face that he was Booth?"

Herold's eyes flickered. "It was M-Mister Booth, I swear. I ain't dumb like that d-damn lawyer keeps tellin' everybody. I was a pharmacist's assistant! I know what I did! I g-gave my word of honor to John Booth, and I kept it!"

Upham felt a fathomless pity. He could not help but admire the poor boy's hapless loyalty to the man who'd got him into this fix. It also occurred to him that Herold, at twenty-three, was hardly a boy, yet that seemed to be most everyone's impression of him.

"David, I have to tell you that I believe your hero Booth is still alive." He watched Herold closely, but his face was inscrutable.

"Oh?"

"I am quite sure he went to see Robert E. Lee immediately after escaping Garrett's barn."

"Uh-huh."

Was that a hint of a smile at the corners of Herold's mouth?

"Tell me, Davey. Supposing, just supposing now, that Booth had somehow escaped—where do you think he'd go?"

Herold shrugged. "I don't know. Mexico, maybe, or Spain, S-South 'merica." Then he added wistfully, "That's where I'd go if they weren't going to h-hang me."

"Maybe they won't," said Upham. "It hasn't been decided."

"Oh, it has been decided." Herold smiled sadly. "But to answer your question: Booth's d-dead, mister."

"Time's up," said one of the guards, snapping shut his pocket watch.

The trial went on for two more weeks, until the last of two hundred and sixty-five witnesses had testified for or against the eight defendants. Many thought Mudd, the doctor, was not telling the truth. And there were doubts about Mrs. Surratt's role, even if she had kept a photograph of

Booth hidden in her house. Upham begrudged the time he was ordered to spend reporting every detail of the plot for *The World*, when he yearned to be out on his own, tracking down leads to Booth's whereabouts—leads growing colder by the week. In the end, as predicted by the defense lawyers and prosecutors he questioned, four of the conspirators were sentenced to hard labor, and four were sentenced to die.

Now, a day after the judgments, Upham sat in the baking prison yard, dutifully making abbreviated notes. He dreaded what was coming, but as a reporter he was shamelessly thrilled to witness this gruesome historical rite.

As one o'clock neared, the spectators grew silent. Then came the hinge-groan of the heavy iron gate swinging open at the far end of the yard. Out of a dark passage lurched a woman dressed in black, supported by two priests. To Upham, Mary Surratt looked younger, thinner than her photographs, almost elegant with her dark hair parted in the middle, but her chalky face was taut with terror. Behind her, four soldiers with bayoneted rifles walked in step.

Trailing them was the feckless carriage maker, George Atzerodt, glancing nervously from side to side. The German wore a knotted handkerchief on his head, from which his filthy hair stuck out wildly. Upham made an entry in the notebook on his knee. *He slinks like a frightened rat. Beady eyes.*

Four more soldiers followed Atzerodt, and behind them shuffled David Herold. Upham watched him closely. *Weak in legs—face white as suet —eyes bulge w/ fright—sees the great gallows awaiting—his gateway to Judgment Day. Hesitates—almost faints.*

Then came Lewis Powell. *Brings up rear—strides cockily—LP professional soldier. As he passes officer he snatches off sailor's straw hat & puts on own head, bravura gesture, Grand Guignol style. Amazing.*

Mrs. Surratt fell to her knees at the bottom of the stairway to the gallows. She hugged the leg of a priest. She had to be held erect, lifted up the steps to the platform. She walked slowly up the thirteen steps and was lowered into a chair. Someone held a black umbrella over her, to shield her from the searing sun. *What a lovely, considerate gesture.*

Powell, still smirking, was strong-armed onto the chair beside her. He shot his handlers a defiant look and wrenched free of their grasp. Then a quivering Herold was seated next to him, his hands shaking as if palsied. Neither man appeared to acknowledge the other. Last to climb the steps was Atzerodt, looking around with an expression of puzzlement, as if unable to comprehend what was happening. *His eyes seemed to ask: why exactly are we gathered here today?*

General John C. Hartranft read the Order of Execution in a monotone barely audible to the crowd. No one asked him to speak up. What did it matter? Three clergymen then spoke in turn, piously beseeching divine forgiveness. *Predictable platitudes from clerics as whimpering M. Surratt covers a crucifix w/ frantic kisses.* Upham's determined note-taking held at bay his own dread.

Captain Christian Rather ordered the prisoners to stand. Powell rose immediately, showing no sign of fear. The other men rose more hesitantly. Mrs. Surratt had to be helped up from her chair. All were swiftly bound with rope.

"It hurts my wrists," said Mrs. Surratt.

"It won't last long," said the guard.

They fitted loose hoods of heavy white cloth over their heads. Mesmerized by the awful ritual, Upham stopped writing.

The nooses were slipped over the condemned heads. The executioners adjusted the ropes around four necks, giving each knot a final tug. Mrs. Surratt, teetered, as if about to collapse.

Captain Rath surveyed his men. They nodded and backed away from the four prisoners. There was a long moment during which time stopped. No one moved or spoke. Then Captain Rath clapped his hands once. Twice. Thrice.

Under the platform four soldiers hammered the supporting posts sideways. The hinged platforms dropped. Four bodies plunged, hit the end of their ropes, and were yanked upward. They hung twisting and jerking.

Lewis Powell's thick neck was unbroken by the fall. He fought the strangling rope, jackknifing his body over and over. *Like a trout hooked on a trotline.* Upham looked at his watch. Four minutes had passed, and yet Powell was still squirming on the rope.

Upham began to take deep breaths, determined not to humiliate himself by vomiting. The reporter next to him did so, noisily.

Swallowing bile, Upham collected himself. *By all rights there should be only one man hanging here.* Booth surely deserved to die, if anyone on Earth did—not only for killing the greatest American leader since Washington, but for the curse he had brought upon so many. *Rest in peace, poor Davey Herold.* Upham was no longer certain about inflicting such a death on any human being, no matter what the crime. He snapped his notebook shut, stood up, and strode from the yard without a backward glance at the swaying bodies.

Now there was only one person left who could help prove his theory about Booth. And, by God, even if he had to swallow his pride and ask his father for help, he would get to him.

# CHAPTER EIGHTEEN

*Hoof beats*. Booth awakened with a start. *Where am I?*

He saw first the cottonwoods, the ripples on the Missouri and the bluffs beyond. He turned his eyes toward the commotion behind him. A horseman in buckskins and a coonskin hat trotted beside a team of eight bellowing oxen, shouting obscenities. Behind came six more teams pulling heavily-loaded wagons. A muleskinner's whip cracked in the morning air.

Booth stood up, brushed himself off, and felt his head knocking from all the whiskey. Not a good feeling, but one he knew well. He remembered the evening at The Star, the bartender with no ears—Luke—and that crazy Moody Suggs firing his pistol. Then more drinks, laughing faces of strangers, and the rest was erased by whiskey. Somehow he'd ended up here on the river bank. Like a vagrant. He looked out over the yellow hills across the river and felt bile in his throat. A hawk, no, a buzzard looking for carrion, wheeled in the huge sky. *How did I get here?*

His mother's sweet voice, with its repeated warnings, rang in his ears: *Darling boy, remember always to be careful of your predisposition for drink. You don't want to be like your brother and your father. It may drive you to the wrong kind of woman.*

Booth felt self-reproach asserting itself, once again. If he hadn't gone to The Star—if he hadn't got himself drunk, again—he'd have caught the early stage to Bannack. He might be on his way to gold and glory. Instead he was standing by a wide river, wiping the dew off his face, and swatting the last of the morning's mosquitoes.

He walked down Front Street, watching the shopkeepers opening their doors. He found the Metropolitan Hotel easily enough, a one-story log structure with a false front to make it look more impressive. All the buildings in this town were this way. It seemed to be the way of the West.

145

He took a room. There was a tin pan and a chipped pitcher of river water sitting on a small table. He stripped and washed himself thoroughly then dressed again.

He remembered telling his fellow drinkers at the saloon that he was an artist. But what would that mean out here? This wasn't exactly London or Paris. Fort Benton was a transportation hub, a place of movement, action. Horse, mules, and oxen were what made this town function.

In the hotel's front room—which gave on to a butcher shop—Booth paid one whole dollar for a breakfast of biscuits covered with gravy and bits of antelope meat, washing it down with harsh-flavored coffee. He asked the proprietor for directions to Tobias Ledyard's office.

Ten minutes later he found a one-story log cabin marked *Customs* down by the levee. He knocked on the door, holding his hat in his hand.

Tobias Ledyard himself opened the door. "Well, if it isn't Mr. Marlowe, Fort Benton's first artist!"

"Sorry to disturb you, Mr. Ledyard."

"No trouble at all. Come in, come in. So you haven't gone to Bannack?"

"Not yet," said Marlowe, following Ledyard into the simple office. "I've been thinking to first work in Benton. Earn some money, build up a reserve."

"Yes, yes, amass a *grubstake*, as they say out here. Gold mining's a chancy enterprise. So, for that matter, is the stage to Bannack. Quite dangerous these days. The Blackfeet have killed five passengers in the last month."

"For the gold?"

"No, for revenge. One of the fur-trading men killed eight of the braves in a dispute over stolen whiskey. Shot them and threw their bodies in the river. A ghastly event that has riled them, understandably. The Blackfeet are a fearsome people. Not all, but most."

Booth shifted on his feet. "I'm hesitant to ask such a favor, sir, but would you have a suggestion about work?"

"No doubt this town seems ripe for artistic record—and it is!— but the bread and butter of Benton is freighting and shipping. Rough work. Do you know anything about livestock, horses?"

"I do," said Booth, brightening. "I'm descended from centaurs."

"You're what?" said Ledyard. "Oh, yes, I see, yes, amusing!"

"I grew up with good bloodstock on our farm," said Booth. "Without boasting, I can ride any spirited horse. And I could certainly learn to hitch an ox team."

"Rough work, but steady," said Ledyard, seeing that Booth was in earnest. "There must be five hundred oxen and as many horses moving through this town every week, heading west out the Mullan Road or down to Bannack or Helena. Many of the horses are unbroken or misfits. Often they've been stolen by the Blackfeet, then recovered. Here's what I'll do." Ledyard picked up a pen, dipped it in the well, and quickly drafted a note, signing it with a flourish.

"There," he said handing the page to Booth. "Your *bona fides*. Go see Mr. Carroll of Carroll & Steele. They're the big liverymen in this town. Tell them I sent you."

"Thank you so much, sir," said Booth rising from his chair. "And please give my best to Mrs. Ledyard and Tommy. I'll stop by soon, if I might."

"I know Tommy'd like to see you again. You've got him drawing horses of all kinds. And good luck, Mr. Marlowe."


By the end of his first week at Carroll & Steele's, Booth felt as if every muscle and joint had been bruised, wrenched and pushed to the limit. His hands were rope-burned in spite of his gloves. Many of the horses had barely been ridden and few were trained to be hitched. Mr. Carroll didn't bother to name the horses; they were either known as Mare Twenty-three, Gelding Fourteen, or "that son-of-bitch with the four white socks." One crow-hopping mare ran around the log corral twenty times before rubbing Booth off on the fence, and when he caught her again, she bit him on the shoulder. But he got back on, beat her with a quirt, and after ten minutes she gave up, huffing and wheezing with exhaustion. "Mr. Marlowe," said Carroll. "For that ride, I will buy you a bottle of bad whiskey at The Star."

It was tough work, and Booth's ankle ached so much every night he needed a couple of shots of whiskey to ease the pain. But every day he felt his leg getting stronger. He spent his first paycheck buying a new pair of boots and spurs of a kind he'd never seen before, silver with large rowels like an eight-leafed clover. He also bought two clean white shirts which he kept neatly folded on his table in the room at the Metropolitan. During his off day, he sat on the front porch of the hotel and sketched the passing scene of loop-horned oxen, big-bearded fur trappers, and the Blackfeet men and women who came through town. Then he slept deeply.

The weeks went by. It was now August and the days were hot. "I'm gonna need your help with this one," said Carroll. "My partner won this stallion in a poker game. Ain't been ridden in six months after coming up lame, and we've got to get him shod. We plan to breed him to a couple of mares then sell him. And next spring the foals come."

"You're going to shoe him before gentling him?"

"I just want him shod, bred, and sold."

The gray stallion wasn't tall but he was big-shouldered and powerful. He was standing statue-still when Booth and Carroll slipped into the corral. By sheer luck, Booth eased a rope over his neck. Just as he bolted Carroll cast a big wobbly loop that the stallion couldn't avoid. The men pulled tight on either side.

"Got him!"

"Watch him, Marlowe. This one sees ghosts everywhere."

The bug-eyed horse suddenly went passive, as if resigned to the captivity.

"I know he's been shod before, but look how long his hooves are," said Carroll.

"Good, boy," said Booth in a soothing manner. "You're all right, aren't you, fella?" He clutched the rope with one hand and held out some oats in the other. The horse sniffed, lifted his head in suspicion, snorted, then began to nibble the oats. "All right, Pegasus, just keep walking this way."

They had almost coaxed him into the blacksmith's shop when a squawking chicken exploded into the alley, chased by a dog. The stallion spooked nearly wrenching the rope from Booth's hands. Carroll yanked back, but the horse reared high, hooves flailing, swiveling toward Booth. He tightened his grip, but the great horse reared again, and when he came down a hoof struck Booth's skull with a sharp thud, and the world went dark.

Sometime later, he felt himself being lifted up with great difficulty. He managed to open his eyes against the harsh light—was it morning already? He could not keep them open. A red vapor, like a sunset of blood, swept through his brain.

Booth vomited, fell back on the bed, and felt the world spinning around him. In that short moment he had the distinct impression of a human face very close to his, saying, "Mr. Marlowe, can you hear me?" The face was vaguely female, with long hair, the ugliest scarred face he had ever seen.

Then he passed out again.

"My, my, he's waking up."

These were the first sounds Booth could hang onto—faint, indistinct words after what seemed a long time adrift in a dream world. He struggled to raise his head from the pillow, coughing and looking around with bleary eyes. He lay on a rough deerskin mattress, a kind of daybed, covered with a blanket. Sunlight streamed through a window. He took in his surroundings: white plaster chinked between walls of stripped yellow logs.

Tobias Ledyard was peering over him. "Can you hear me, Mr. Marlowe? Tobias Ledyard here. Do you hear me?"

"Where am I?"

"You are in my house," said Ledyard. "You have been unconscious for four days. Dr. Canby says it's a coma. He's not here right now. Do you remember the accident?"

"What accident?"

"With the stallion. With Mr. Carroll. You were wounded in the head."

Booth tried to sit up but his head banged with pain. The sunlight was too bright. He covered his eyes with his hand.

"Don't try to move, Mr. Marlowe. Lie back. Rest up."

There was another indistinct figure standing next to Ledyard, a young woman, with long brown hair hanging down one side of her face, pinned back tightly on the other side. She stood at the foot of the couch. He blinked and squinted. She was beautiful. He wanted to cry. He felt weak. Drunk-brained. A head full of blood. *I am the wrong person, and everything is wrong and hurts.* He became nauseous and retched bile into a bucket, which miraculously appeared under his mouth.

"Has he done this before?" said Tobias Ledyard.

"Yes," said a woman's voice. "It's the concussion."

The woman wiped his mouth with a wet cloth.

"Who are you?" Booth croaked at last. "What is this?"

"You've been sick," she said. "Out of your head."

"How long?"

"Four days."

"Where is this place?"

"Mr. Ledyard's house." The woman frowned and glanced at Ledyard as if to say, he is not right in his head. "You will need plenty of rest."

"Who are you?" he asked again, He felt a piercing pain behind his eyes.

"Fern Jamison," said the woman. "Fern to most. Tommy's new tutor. But I also assist Dr. Canby as a nurse. He's come every day since you went out."

"And is this a hospital?"

"It is a house, Mr. Ledyard's house," she said, sitting down on a chair in front of him. "Do you remember Mr. Ledyard?"

"He gave me a letter. To George Carroll." Fern looked up at Tobias Ledyard, who nodded.

"What's *your* name?" asked Fern.

It took him a moment to remember. "Marlowe."

"And your first name?"

"John...." Booth swallowed. "John ... Richard ... Marlowe."

"What are you doing in Fort Benton, Mr. Marlowe?"

"I'm an artist." It felt good to say that.

"And what do you most like to paint?"

"Animals," he said. "Mostly animals."

"Ah, said Fern. "And I've seen the portrait of Tommy."

"Yes," said Tobias Ledyard, leaning in from the other side of the bed. "I've told Miss Fern a great deal about you. How you taught Tommy aboard the packet. Art and poetic recitation."

"You saw my drawings?"

"The tips of an antelope's horns point backward, Mr. Marlowe," she said, "not forward. My only criticism."

"They move…," he said, "very fast."

"Well, you'll have plenty of time to observe the antelope once you're better. Drink a glass of water. Then lie back and rest."

Who was this woman? She had a low voice, musical. And where was the one whose ugly face he vividly remembered now—the one who had spoken harshly as he lay in the mud? Those terrible, disfiguring red and purple scars on her cheek and jaw. Or was it a drunken hallucination? A demon. How had he gotten here?

He slept again for what seemed like a few hours.

"Good morning, Mr. Marlowe," said the woman. "That was quite a long nap you took. A full day has passed. Do you know what day of the week it is?"

"No."

"It is Wednesday. Would you like to get up so I can change the bedding?"

Booth pushed himself up on his elbow and swung his legs off the couch. He felt faint, but it had to be done. He sat up. The room swirled around him, and he had to lie down again. A series of hefty coughs wracked his lungs.

Fern returned with a tray, placing it on the table next to the couch. He stared at a bowl of what looked to be stew, made with a dark red-brown meat. He felt nauseous. "What is that?"

"Buffalo," she said.

"I'd like a drink," he said.

"You have water there," she said, pointing.

"I meant a *drink*."

"There's no liquor in this house," she said sternly. "And certainly not for a man who has sustained a concussion."

He picked up his bowl with shaky hands and sipped from it. The broth was rich and meaty, scented with barley.

"Thank you, madam." He had to set the bowl down, and coughed again, and again. "Please excuse me." He lay back on the daybed. "Still a bit shaky."

"Are you interested in the theater, Mr. Marlowe?"

"Why do you ask?"

"When you were out of your head, you talked a lot about Abraham Lincoln."

"And what did I say?" He affected a casual tone, but feared the worst. *I am doomed to betray myself.*

"Just ramblings, mostly about the President and Ford's Theater. You kept saying 'sockdologizing old mantrap.'"

Booth nodded, looking away from her.

"That was the line in the play when the President was murdered, wasn't it?"

"Maybe," said Booth. "Yes, I believe it was."

"I find it curious that a Southerner would take Lincoln's death so hard."

"Well, he was the President, wasn't he?" said Booth.

"The greatest who ever lived," she said. Her voice suddenly went tremulous: "Booth didn't really kill Lincoln, you know."

"I believe. . . . the fact is that he did, madam."

"You don't understand," she said, drawing herself up. "He made Lincoln immortal. For the ages. He robbed him of life but gave him immortality!" She was flushed, triumphant. She appeared about to say more, then turned away and began to make preparations to leave.

Booth watched her, fascinated. A beautiful, challenging woman, and, like so many, under the spell of The Tyrant. "When will you come back?" he asked.

"Three hours, thereabouts."

"And the other woman, who was she?"

"What other woman?"

"The one I saw. The one who helped me after the accident at the blacksmith's shop. The one who pressed a wet rag to my head. Perhaps before you came?"

"There was no other person."

"Are you sure?"

She looked intently at him. "Only Mr. Ledyard and I came to you, Marlowe. There was no one about. Mr. Carroll called us. The men carried you here. Then Dr. Canby came and examined your pupils. An insult to the brain, he said."

"Well, then, perhaps I only dreamed it. But I remember this strange woman's face."

"Yes?"

"I remember it quite well."

"And what was it like?"

"It was a ... scarred face," he said. "Cruelly disfigured."

She turned her head away and gathered the fall of hair on the left side of her face. "Did it look," she said, turning back to him, her voice cold, "like this?"

# CHAPTER NINETEEN

Langford Upham was once again perspiring in the sun, this time outside Lee's house in Richmond, Virginia. Through his father's friend, President Andrew Johnson, he had managed to arrange an interview with the General. But he was kept waiting for over an hour before being ushered into the house.

Lee, immaculate in his gray uniform, sat behind a stack of ledgers on his desk.

"Mr. Upham, I will give you a few moments in a very busy morning, whose urgencies are not of my making. What is it you wish to discuss that is so important that President Johnson himself requests it?"

Upham remained standing. "Well, sir—"

"Sit," Lee commanded, and Upham sat. "Anything we talk about is not for publication. I must tell you, I do not care anymore for newspapers or reporters, although I should like to hope you may prove an exception to my experience."

"Sir, Thomas Jefferson said he'd rather have the press and no government than government with no press."

"That was Jefferson, Mr. Upham. Another age. Not a word of what we say here will appear in a newspaper—understood?"

"Agreed, sir." Upham had the all-too-familiar sense of losing control over yet another crucial interview. "I merely wished to ask you one thing. It may seem a frivolous question, and I mean no disrespect to you. But —sir—have you any knowledge, or heard any talk, or seen any report—even speculation—that John Wilkes Booth might still be alive?"

Lee snorted. "What brings you to ask a thing like that?"

"Well, sir, some weeks ago, I saw a man leave this very house who I have reason to believe who—I know, hard to believe—who might have been John Wilkes Booth."

Lee leaned back in his chair, a small smile on his face. "This house?"

"Yes, sir."

"I see a great many people here every day."

"Do you remember a person resembling Booth?"

"I do not."

"A strange man on the same day that Matthew Brady took your photograph? I believe your son Custis was present, too?"

The General's brow furrowed. "Well, there was an odd creature. I remember a man who rambled, who claimed to be Booth, but he didn't look at all like the actor, if that's what you mean."

"What did this fellow want, may I ask?"

"He professed some insane fantasy about killing the late President and reviving the Confederacy, about our continuing the war. Clearly out of his mind. I ordered him to leave immediately."

"So you do not believe it was Booth."

"Mr. Upham, war makes people do strange things. Four years of war such as we have suffered can break the mind. I see many strange people and hear many strange and pathetic stories, every day, and I cannot trouble myself with the whys and the hows of them."

"I see."

"Now then," said Lee. "Dismembering an army is not an easy task. One simply does not tell an army to go home, thank you very much. Thus, I must ask you to leave and let me get on with my sad hard duties to this nation."

Upham stood up promptly.

"Thank you, sir, for generously giving me so much of your time."

*I've learned absolutely nothing.*

Upham left Lee's house sick with discouragement. The heat of the sun burned through the dark cloth of his suit. He found a shade tree and sagged into a chair that a sentry had likely left there. Now there was nowhere else to turn for confirmation.

# CHAPTER TWENTY

"You didn't come to Benton to draw pictures," said Fern, the next day as she wiped Booth's brow.

"No I came for the cathedrals. I'm an itinerant monk and a sinner."

"Please, Mr. Marlowe. Have you ever seen a cathedral? I haven't. Just in pictures. They are so beautiful."

"Sorry. Only in pictures." *Can't tell her I've been to St. Paul's and Nôtre Dame.*

"So why are you here then?"

"On my way to Bannack."

She snorted with disgust. "So you're one of them. Every n'er-do-well in all America is coming out to the Territory to get rich."

"And you? Why did you come here?"

"Personal reasons." As she spoke she repeatedly ran her hand down the long strands of hair that covered the left side of her face—beautiful hair, thought Booth, the color of the darkest clover honey. But the other side of that face—what did the scars mean? What caused the disfigurement?

"And when do you plan to go?" she asked. "To Bannack."

"When I am … better. I'm still a bit weak," he said, putting aside the wet cloth she had placed on his head. "Perhaps next Tuesday."

"There's no stage Tuesday. And you are in no shape to travel two hundred miles in three days over bumpy roads with little or no sleep."

"Ah, my luck… then I'll go to the hotel for a few nights," he said.

"Mr. Marlowe, I suspect you have little money."

"True," said Booth. "But Mr. Carroll owes me wages. I will figure something out. I am not yet at the glue factory."

"I have an idea. I own a small cabin west of here, on the edge of town. I was given it by—by somebody. But as a woman in this part of the world I could not live there alone. Quite frankly, it would be dangerous. There are only twelve white women in Benton and several hundred men. That's why I live with the Ledyards … now."

"Yes," said Booth. "I understand."

"I would like someone to occupy it. I could rent it to you. You would do me a favor to be there, like a watchman."

"I don't have much money," said Booth. "And I can't work at the livery, for awhile. So I would be happy to accept."

"We'll work something out. Far cheaper than the hotel."


Ten days after the accident with the stallion, Booth's head was still bruised and painful, but after examining his pupils and his reflexes, Dr. Phineas Canby declared him "fit as a slightly battered fiddle." He could go outside for a short walk or ride in a buggy. "But no strenuous exertion—and no stallions, Mr. Marlowe."

Fern Jamison drove Marlowe in the buggy out to her cabin on the north side of town. The roof was willow and wattle with an overlay of sod. There were two rooms and a lean-to kitchen off the back. The logs were chinked with mud and the inside walls had been plastered and white-washed. It was surprisingly clean and sun streamed in from the single glass-paned window in the front room. There was an iron stove, a table and two chairs, and a wooden bed. A shelf held thirty or forty books.

"Ah," said Fern, "I see the mice are back. All the more reason to have a man—someone—here in charge. What do you think, Mr. Marlowe? Could you kill a mouse or a packrat?"

"It's a fine place. I will keep the mice at bay and send the rats packing."

"Then it is yours."

"At what price?"

She picked up his drawing pad and flipped though the pages. "You can pay me by helping me. Behind I.G. Baker's store, I have a miserable little log cabin schoolroom in which I am tutoring three white children, including Tommy, and one clever half-breed. I want to make it a real school. I want to give the children inspiration. On either side of the flag I want pictures of two presidents—General Washington and Mr. Lincoln."

Booth was repelled by the thought. Washington? Yes, the greatest of American presidents. But he could never render The Tyrant. "I have no presidential portraits to work from."

She walked to her bookcase, selected a red buckram volume and handed it to him. It was a slim school primer entitled *Our Presidents.* Inside were engraved portraits of the nation's leaders, ending with Lincoln, an engraving based on his first inaugural photograph. He leafed through the book, studying the images morosely, avoiding the last portrait in the book as long as he could.

"I can copy Gilbert Stuart's engraving of Washington easily enough. There is enough detail," he said finally. "But the one of Lincoln is not good." He tried to say it off-handedly. "Should we not use this fine portrait of Thomas Jefferson instead? Look at that handsome brow, those eyes! And a Virginian. What a wonderful president he was."

"Lincoln," she said. "The incomparable George Washington and the great Abraham Lincoln." She handed him the pad.

Booth hid his inner turmoil. He was trapped, and in any case he knew he owed anything that this fine woman might ask of him. "When do I start?"

"Tomorrow. We'll go back into town now to get some supplies and food. Then I'll drive you out here in the morning, and you'll be on your own. I'll stop by every now and then to see that you're all right. And to see if the deer have eaten up my vegetable garden."


After moving in the next day, Booth started with Washington's portrait, and by late afternoon, after several discarded sketches—the mouth was difficult—he had finished a drawing that worked. Fern came in from weeding her vegetables and studied his idealized portrait of the Founding Father, noting how his slightly hooded eyes peered at eternity with a commanding glint.

"You really are very good, Mr. Marlowe."

Booth shrugged. "I'm no Gilbert Stuart. But I can copy."


The next day he faced the second part of his task. *The Tyrant.* Booth's mood darkened as he fanned the pages toward the chapter entitled "Our

159

16th President." *What is going on with me, for God's sake? I'm shaking like a dog in a snowstorm.*

Lincoln's image leapt out at him. A three-quarter engraving based on a photograph by Matthew Brady. Finely attuned to the expressions of the human face by his years on stage, Booth was unsettled to perceive in Lincoln's frank, war-weary gaze into Brady's lens a sad forgiveness. A humility. A tragic comprehension. The man's deep-vaulted eyes gripped the actor. With a sense of awful clarity, he realized that if Lincoln had been facing him that night in Ford's Theater, looking directly at him as he did here from a small page in a book, he could never have pulled the trigger.

On the facing page was a quotation:

*Whenever I hear anyone arguing for slavery, I feel a strong impulse to see it tried on him personally. — A. Lincoln*

The old anger rose in him. *How noble—you hypocrite! Once, you wanted to send them all back to Africa! Then suddenly, in '62, when it was politically expedient to free them, you did!*

Fiercely, Booth began to block in the shape of his victim's head, scratching hard for form, almost carving the pencil into the paper.

He was suddenly reminded of the time that he appeared in Charles Selby's "The Marble Heart," playing a Greek sculptor who made marble statues come to life. It was at the debut of Ford's Theater, November 9, 1863, with 1,500 people in the audience. Lincoln himself watched the play from his box—the same box in which he would be shot.

*And now here I am, bringing a dead tyrant to life through art.* Booth put aside his emotions, surgically focusing on the task: a man's face. But his fingers defied him; when his pencil point came to the ear, neck, and back of Lincoln's head, the pencil lead veered off course and the skull bulged.

*I must get my mind off Lincoln's head—and out of my own skull.*

"Tomorrow," he said, putting the pad down with a trembling hand.

*Am I going insane?* He wondered. *Have I been insane? My father was insane. But if I thought I might be insane, that would mean I am not. Lunatics always fancy they are perfectly rational. But I have done what the papers call an insane thing, one mad act.*

Fern had left him a pot of venison stew on the stove. That night Booth restlessly browsed her bookshelves, finding mostly school texts, histories, and biographies. One volume brought back memories: the painter George Catlin's *Life amongst the Indians*. The vivid illustrations first captivated him as a boy, a discovery in his father's library. Time and again he would look at those images and imagine living in the world of Indians—the noble savage!—freed from rules, restrictions, and dominating fathers. A world of careening horses and feathered crowns. Edwin now has that book, he remembered. *But I have the real landscape! I am here!*

He was astonished to find another fine book, *The Animals of the American West*. It was a comprehensive survey of the anatomy and habits of dozens of creatures—the iconic bison, grizzly, cougar, and wolf, as well as the plodding porcupine and elusive wolverine, and the impossibly fleet and graceful pronghorn antelope, whose antlers, as Fern declared, did indeed point backward. And here was the chipmunk, its knobby-knuckled little hands depicted in a prayerful pose. These wonderful creatures! He immediately made a sketch of the chipmunk. It brought him satisfaction.


The next afternoon Fern appeared at the cabin with another delicacy: a brace of prairie hens and boiled carrots.

As he took his place at her humble table, he was struck anew by her beauty—the unmarred part of her face she allowed the world to see was exquisite. From where, he wondered, came such serenity and maturity? She seemed to him much like his beloved sister Asia, but riper, more seasoned, perhaps by pain.

"What brought you to Benton?" he asked.

"Not a very interesting story," she said. "Eat, please, before it gets cold."

Booth had noticed that, unlike Fern, many of the people he'd encountered along his odyssey from St. Louis had been eager—too eager, in his view—to announce their motives for abandoning the East. They'd all been men.

"Are you happy here?" he asked her.

"Lincoln once said that people are as happy as they make up their minds to be."

*Lincoln! Spare me.*

"So then, Fern, have you made up your mind to be happy here?"

She nodded and smiled, showing white, even teeth. Booth was struck by the irony of such beauty paired with such awful disfigurement.

They ate in silence, but it was not an uncomfortable silence. Booth felt at ease with the woman opposite him. Now and then she would meet his eye. Save for Booth's compliment on her tasty meal, for which she shyly thanked him, neither said a word until she had cleared the dishes and was washing them in the wooden sink.

"You asked what brought me to the Territory," she said, her back to him. She had paused in her work and appeared to be looking out the window at the evening light.

"Two years ago, when I was nineteen, I answered an advertisement in *The Boston Globe*. A forty-year-old man wanted a 'healthy young bride.' Healthy and young I was, and also very naïve—stupid, really. When I wrote to him, I didn't tell him about my face. I don't know what I was thinking. When I came off the boat he was shocked. I hoped he'd get used to my face—but Jack didn't want me. He wasn't a bad man at all, but he just couldn't look at me. Poor fellow. I can't blame him. He went over to the gold strike at Helena—not Bannack—and was lucky in Confederate Gulch. Like you, he was a gentleman."

*Poor fellow? A gentleman? A despicable oaf!*

"So he left you?"

He saw her head nod.

"Did you ever see him again?"

She shook her head. "But after he'd made his fortune, he was happy enough to leave me this cabin. Mr. Ledyard was kind enough to lend his legal advice. And I've been grateful ever since. I forgot to mention that Jack is Tobias's half-brother."

"And Ledyard advised his brother to do that? To give you the cabin?"

"Yes. And I am grateful. Even if I can only come out a few hours during the week to plant the garden. One day I'll be able to live here."

Booth touched his temple, feeling the scar from the accident. "How did you—how did it happen?"

"My face?"

"If I may ask."

She spoke without self-pity. "My stepfather. A monster." Her voice took on a tremble. "He drank. Oh God, how he drank. On my sixteenth birthday, he fell into a rage over something I'd said—I don't even know what it was that set him off. He pushed my head down on the griddle when I was cooking."

"You needn't say more," said Booth, to be polite, but he wanted to hear everything. "I'm so sorry."

"He held my face there forever. I can still smell the flesh burning."

Booth remembered the stench of his own flesh as he burned the tattoo off his left hand just two months ago.

She took a deep breath. "But he did worse to me." She dropped her head for a long moment. "Much worse. Glad to get out and come West."

He saw her wipe her eyes.

"To me," said Booth hesitatingly. He'd never had trouble complimenting a woman, but now found himself searching for words to match an unaccustomed sincerity. "To me—I think you are—"

"You needn't say anything, Mr. Marlowe."

He stood up from his chair, awkwardly. "I think you are lovely. I think you are the loveliest, finest woman in the Territory of Montana!"

She turned to look at him, then gave a mirthless laugh. "As long as I keep moving counter-clockwise."

"No." He didn't know what else to say. He placed his hands on the back of the chair. "Your whole being."

She came back to the table and sat down with one foot under her. It was a girlish posture that suited her. He adored it.

"Before Jack left, he gave me a horse and a rifle besides this fine cabin. I've got no complaints. And, I've come to love this country. I really do love it."

Booth nodded, still at a loss for easy words, fearing any comment he might make could sound trivial alongside her tale. He kept his hands on the rough wood of the chair's back.

"So, there, Mr. Marlowe. Now you know my story. And you?"

He shrugged. "A commoner's tale, really. Nothing grand."

"You must have a history. Everyone who comes to Benton has a history."

"Just a craftsman. Not a miner yet, just a minor artist," he said with a laugh. He flipped his hand into an indeterminate space. "Sign painting, decorative work. Just sketching my way through an uneventful life of little consequence and unforeseen beauty."

"Married?"

"Oh, several times in the mind. But no, not really. I'm only twenty-seven."

"You just arrived. How'd you get into such a fix so quickly?"

"I didn't mean to get my head crashed in."

"And what about your limp? You were in the war?"

"Another equine collision," he said carefully. "Before the recent unpleasantness."

"You're educated, aren't you," she said, with a tone of wistful envy.

"A little art school," he said. "Trade school. Little else. Anyone can read a few books, can't they?"

"I would suspect a great deal of reading—along with the 'little else.'"

"I find it enjoyable, calming, to read great works."

"I revere education," she said. "When you were not yourself, you quoted Shakespeare."

"What did I say?"

"You kept saying 'Is this a dagger which I see before me, the handle toward my hand?' That is from *Macbeth*, yes?"

"I did some set painting for small theater troupes. Good pay. But strange people, actors. Better simply to read Shakespeare on one's own."

"My students haven't reached that level," she said. "I do my best. We don't really have a school. The last teacher left in May for the gold strike at Helena. With a man, of course. I just try to stay a chapter ahead of my students. I use the *McGuffey Eclectic Reader*, do you know it?"

Booth shook his head.

"Well, it's quite good. First published in 1836. Teaching, helping the children learn, watching their world enlarge—it's become my life. And

I've got some clever ones. That's a great responsibility, you know. I'm all they have out here on the prairie."

"I'd wager they're all in your thrall," he said.

She straightened up and looked at him differently. "Speaking of which, I have a school session tomorrow. So I must depart, while it's still light, and read the lesson. We're agreed then, that you're my lodger here?"

"Yes."

"You have enough money?"

"A little," he said.

"Very little, probably. Today I told Mr. I.G. Baker about your drawings. He suggested putting them in his store window. He thinks they might be bought by people going down-river, as souvenirs—people with too much gold dust in their pockets. As people come in, they also leave. This is a harsh world, Marlowe. But it has its moments of beauty."

"That was kind of you. Too much gold dust in my pockets would be a welcome worry."

She smiled at him. "You know, Mr. Marlowe, if I were you, I would entertain the thought that you might find more gold here in Benton, with your pencils and brushes. And now I must leave you to your solitude." She stood up from table. "Good night."

Booth stood and walked her out to the horse and buggy. He reached for her warm hand and helped her climb up into the seat. But he didn't let go of her hand.

"Thank you, Miss Fern. For your faith in me."

"You are welcome, Mr. Marlowe."

"Drive safely."

"I will," she said. "Remember, the rifle is always behind the door. And it's loaded."

As the sound of the horse and buggy faded in the twilight, Booth went back inside the cabin. In the flickering glow of the oil lamp, he looked at the Lincoln portrait with an eye more clinical than artistic, and compared it to Lincoln's image in the book. He tried another version, but tore it up in disgust. *I will conquer this—I will finish this goddamned picture and never again think of the man.* Then he closed the book and turned down the oil lamp.

He felt his way to the bed. He lay there for a while thinking of Fern. Disfigured was too harsh a word. *Marked by life, as all of us are, eventually*. And my own scars? *They are not just on the surface*.

He resolved not to think of Lincoln, to banish the man from his mind forever. Drifting off, he imagined himself at a blackboard, erasing the haunting images of his past as they appeared, ghost-like, on the dark slate. All to be forgotten. Finally he fell into a dreamless sleep.

# CHAPTER TWENTY ONE

Summer in Manhattan was ending and the morning air was crisp. Opening a closet in his Manhattan apartment, Langford Upham picked out a conservative suit and tie for an important interview. Even in the best of circumstances, Upham was warned, Edwin Booth was testy and short-tempered. The assassin's brother was America's foremost Shakespearean actor, but since the tragedy at Ford's Theater he had scarcely uttered a public word.

Upham's Manhattan apartment, his primary residence since leaving New Haven, was small but "well-appointed in an odd way," as his infernal stepmother insisted on describing it. A pastoral watercolor by his late mother, in the Romantic style of Samuel Palmer, hung over the fireplace. There was an antique writing desk, a divan, and a small piano covered with sheet music, most of it by Chopin.

Books lined three walls, unread volumes—Goethe, Trollope, Dickens, and others—titles hinting at the better writer he aspired to be. There were well-thumbed volumes concerning the French Revolution, a collection of Greek classics, and another shelf devoted to books and news clippings about Abraham Lincoln and the Civil War.

On the walls hung engraved likenesses of Upham's favorite performers, including the Australian diva Fiona Rutherford, the Italian tenor Boldini, the actress Laura Keene, who had been in the cast at Ford's the night the President was murdered. Among them was a vacant dark rectangle of unfaded wallpaper, marking the place where a photograph of John Wilkes Booth as Hamlet had once hung; though not destroyed, it had been sent to Purgatory in a drawer.

A lady would have appreciated the neatness of the apartment, but save for his maid and his stepmother, no woman had yet visited here. Despite his social connections, his name, and his byline, most of Upham's interactions with ladies ranged only from the chaste to the courtly. He did not yet feel he'd earned the right to pursue them seriously.

Then, too, there was the business about his height. A painful issue in boyhood, it was less so now that his professional confidence and reputation had grown. Men seemed not to notice. Women, however, he sensed, only pretended not to notice. His dampened ardor in the company of women was finally broadcast to an old Yale classmate over a drink at the Brevoort. "I am less than a man to these ladies."

"With all respect, my dear Uppy," said his friend, "that is horseshit. You are not meant for a spinster's life."

Save for occasional liaisons with prostitutes, true romance eluded him. Still, he dared to believe a great love might eventually cross his path.

For now, his favorite female resided in a brass cage in the corner of his living room. Calpurnia, a large white sulfur-crested cockatoo of indeterminate age, was an inheritance from his mother. The bird had gone with him to preparatory school—Deerfield—and Yale. Her cage door was left open, and Calpurnia came and went as she pleased. Every morning that he spent in New York, she decorously ate her breakfast toast and apple off a China plate alongside his own. Other days, his housekeeper, Mrs. O'Neill, attended to "the lady of the house," as she called the bird. Upham noticed that Mrs. O'Neill would siphon whiskey out of his decanter, and water it afterward. No matter; Calpurnia was well cared for.

As he shrugged on his overcoat this morning, the parrot screeched in protest, for she knew he would be leaving the apartment. As usual, she croaked, "Once more into the breach, dear friends." She only had three or four phrases, but she enunciated these intelligibly and with feeling.

"Unto the breach," said Upham sternly but affectionately. "*Unto!* How many hundred times must I tell you? Arriving unto the breach is not the same as entering it!"

He gently ruffled the cockatoo's chartreuse head feathers. "Such a beautiful girl you are, Calpy, and yet only a bird brain behind those lovely eyes."

Now, dressed in a gray flannel suit and his trademark black bowler, Upham locked up his apartment, walked lightly down the two flights of stairs, and strode out into sun-swept Fifth Street. There was a waiting cab, but he decided to walk the nine blocks to Edwin Booth's townhouse, intending to work off his tension and apprehensions. He could also use the exercise. He prided himself on maintaining his wiry physique and collegiate fitness. At Yale, despite his asthma, he'd been a successful coxswain, goading eight burly oarsmen in a thin wooden shell to repeated triumphs over Harvard's much-vaunted crews.

He marched uptown past the imposing Brevoort Hotel on Fifth Avenue, skirting the house where Edgar Allan Poe had lived, past the home of the novelist Herman Melville. Someday, mused Upham—perhaps when his account of Booth's escape was published to acclaim—he might also enjoy a lasting reputation as a writer, not just temporary newspaper fame.

Melville's curtains were drawn. A few weeks before, the author of *Moby-Dick* had published an ode to Lincoln that was garnering great praise and being quoted in the papers, clubs, schools, and saloons of America. Entitled "The Martyr," Upham had already memorized the haunting start of it:

> *Good Friday was the day.*
> *Of the prodigy and crime,*
> *When they killed him in his pity,*
> *When they killed him in his prime ...*
> *they killed him in his kindness,*
> *In their madness in their blindness,*
> *And they killed him from behind.*

Upham mused over whether, somewhere, John Wilkes Booth might be reading that same poem. He hoped the verses would stab into the assassin's soul and rob him of sleep forever. A romantic, Upham loved Melville's books on the paradise islands of the Pacific, *Typee* and *Omoo*. Booth would have read those books, too—could he be headed for the "fairy isles of the South Seas?" Would the murderer soon be lazing on a tropical beach in the amorous company of Melville's beautiful native women who "wore the garb of Eden?"

He arrived at Edwin Booth's imposing three-story brownstone exactly at eleven o'clock. Nervous, he rang the doorbell twice. He did not, of course, expect John Wilkes Booth to be hiding inside. But Upham hoped to glean a hint of where the man's infamous sibling *might* have gone into hiding. All he knew for sure was that the man—"Beech"—who had abandoned his horse at Florie's boarding house, had probably left Richmond. But for where? South of the Border, as Davey Herold opined? Or indeed for the South Pacific?

A liveried butler opened the door, took Upham's hat, and led him into a sumptuous drawing room.

"Mr. Booth will be with you shortly, sir."

The big room reeked of stylish acquisition, of rare English antiques and leather upholstery, of furniture polish, cigars, and cognac. Upham admired a wall covered with inscribed photographs from Edwin Booth's illustrious friends, including Queen Victoria and Lincoln himself. On a bookshelf were scripts of the many plays in which he had starred, leather-bound and gold-stamped. There was a human skull mounted on a board with a bronze inscription: *Junius Brutus Booth (1796-1852)*.

Upham was wondering about the skull's provenance when Edwin Booth strode into the room, attired in a red velvet smoking jacket with black lapels. The actor was thirty-two but already graying, and to Upham looked as if he might be in his late forties. Edwin Booth was not tall, but he projected a formidable presence that filled the room. He sipped from a large coffee cup, from which Upham caught the scent of brandy.

Booth nodded at the skull. "My father's," he said in his theatrically English accent.

*My God.* John Wilkes Booth would have been fourteen when his father died. *And left this skull to Edwin.*

Then Booth held out his hand to shake Upham's. "Hah! Not his *own* skull, of course." He tried, but could not quite manage to smile. "The one he used for poor Yorick's. His London *Hamlet*. Do sit, Mr. Upham."

Upham settled into the high-backed embroidered chair opposite Booth. The actor sat for a moment, then rose and paced.

"Sir, it was good of you to—" Upham started to say. Booth interrupted with a wave of his hand.

"I'm doing this only for my old friend, your father," he said into his

170

coffee cup, in the resonant baritone of a trained actor. "His newspaper has been remarkably considerate to me over the many years of my career. Especially now, in this ghastly time."

There followed a silence. To break it Upham said, "I must tell you how I enjoyed your performance in *Othello* in Richmond two years ago."

Booth brightened. "Ah, did you? I was pleased with it myself. Of course, I took the lesser part of Iago to help Johnny, to give him a leg up, y'know. For a young fellow I thought he did surprisingly well as Othello, didn't you?"

*Enough of this polite talk.* "Sir, I hear you have quit the present play you were appearing in."

The actor put his fingers to his forehead, a gesture Upham found artful, if artificial. "I shall not act again in this life," said Booth, with the tone of a man delivering a eulogy. "You must know how shattered our old mother is, how we all are. Upstairs, she recoils from the world, devastated. And our sister Asia! You see, we admired Lincoln. A great man, I voted for him. We all did. The fact that our brother—"

He was not able to finish. He sagged on the red sofa, rubbing his temple with his fingers. He looked to Upham as if he were posing for a photograph.

The reporter waited a long moment. *This interview's not going to last. Got to be careful or he'll shuffle off to get himself another drink and never return.*

"Mr. Booth, how do you explain your brother's actions?"

"Explain?" Booth stood up quickly and paced the room. "How does one explain such a mad act? Murder! The one crime for which the perpetrator can never make restitution to his victim—the extinction of a living flame, which can never be relit, as our friend Othello so well knew." He held up one arm dramatically, looked heavenward, and recited: "'If I quench thee, thou flaming minister, I can again thy former light restore.'" Then, quietly, for the smallness of the audience, "'Should I repent me; but once put out thy light, Thou cunning'st pattern of excellent nature, I know not where is that Promethean heat That can thy light relume.'" Booth paused, the arm still uplifted.

*Am I supposed to applaud now?*

Upham cleared his throat. "Bravo, sir. Bravo." Booth took several

171

seconds to deflate, then took his seat.

"Mr. Booth, do you consider him—your brother—a madman?"

Booth's eyes flashed. "Insane? No, no! Impulsive, yes, very impulsive, yes!"

"But you called the murder a 'mad act.'"

"Johnny was far-reaching, filled with quixotic notions. When he was a child on the farm in Maryland, he would gallop through the woods on his beloved pony —Peacock was her name—shouting heroic speeches with a wooden lance in hand. One day he was Lancelot, the next El Cid. We thought him a good-hearted, harmless boy." He snorted. "Harmless! My God."

Then he held up his hand again and declaimed to the second balcony: "'Murder most foul, as in the best it is. But this most foul, strange, and unnatural!'"

He slumped down in a corner armchair and drank deep from his cup. Upham studied him. *Actors.*

"Look at the harm he has done the world," Booth muttered. "He wanted great fame, that is true. Once when he was young, he startled me by saying, 'I wish there were still a Colossus of Rhodes and that I could topple it down—then all the world would know my name!' That troubled me, but I let it pass. He was just a boy, a gentle boy, after all."

Booth stared off for a long moment, his face pensive. "Well, he has certainly toppled his colossus, hasn't he?" He brooded on this, drank again, and said morosely, "I've written Asia, our beloved sister."

*He punctuates each word as though chiseling it upon some marble mausoleum.*

"I told the dear heart, 'Think no more of him as our brother, for he is dead to us now, as soon he must be to all the world, but imagine the boy you loved to be in the better part of his spirit in a better world.'"

He dropped his chin upon his chest and flung an arm across the back of the divan, his fingers arrayed just so. Upham suppressed an impulse to smile at Booth's theatricality, but it was clear that the man was genuinely devastated by his sibling's crime.

"Sir, do you think your brother might have gone to—"

"I overheard a man say something unkind at my club the other day," said Booth. "The fellow didn't see me, I was seated on the other side of a column—he turns to another member, saying, 'Can you believe what this fellow Wilkes Booth has done?' The other man replies 'Of course I can, old boy, all those damn Booths are loony.'"

The actor snorted. "Probably true. Father was loony, the greatest actor of all time, but a loony like grandpa. Some legacy for me and Johnny, eh? Something in the blood. But I swear, Johnny is not at bottom insane. What he is, I believe, is obsessively ambitious, idealistic to the point of blindness, and frustrated—about what, I can't say. Everything, probably, in some way. He was never really, you know, *satisfied*. Very fanciful man, certainly. He had, I believe, an incapacity for happiness. It was always the past, or the future, or ever-lasting glory. The present was never enough."

Booth drank deeply from his coffee and cognac.

"Once, as a young man I saw him dressed in a toga with angel wings strapped to his shoulders, cavorting about in a field around some cows. When I asked him what in hell he was doing, he said, 'Can't you see I'm dancing with God?' I never forgot that phrase. Well, I suppose he's dancing with God now—or more likely, Lucifer."

"Could it be, sir, that he envied the great fame that you and your late father enjoyed?"

"He had his own fame! Not inconsiderable, I assure you. It was not as if he were a failure. He once said theater stood between him and life; yet it gave him life! He also had a talent for drawing, sketching, you know."

"I didn't know that."

"Oh, yes, quite a talent when he was young. Often said he wished he'd become an artist instead of going on 'the cursed stage', as he called it. Seemed to prefer painting the sets to acting in front of them. Father cut off his obsession with the details of backdrop ... the words, the acting of course, were the important thing. But John's fervid obsessions for this or that always got in the way of ... of ..."

"Would you say that—"

Booth shook his head. "To think we used to laugh at his patriotic froth whenever Secession was discussed. He was indeed unbalanced on that one point, I'll grant you that, and no one knew why. Because our own family never had slaves. When I told him I had voted for Lincoln's re-election he became furious and spouted some nonsense about Lincoln intending to declare himself the king of America. I sent him a transcript of Lincoln's beautiful Second Inaugural Address, cut from your newspaper, actually. He sent it back in an envelope, torn to bits."

"And after that?"

"He avoided us. If he consented to act in a play with us, after the performance he would disappear to consort with those subversive, plotting friends of his. God, what rabble! He fancied he was doing his part for the South. He called us traitors more than once. No secret that he hated our late father. I expect that somehow—I don't understand the mental workings of it—he may have transferred that very hatred of—of a patriarch—to poor Lincoln. Don't really know what in hell fastened itself on his mind. I am torn between great anger and great pity—and—and—great anguish."

He stared out the window.

"Did he ever tell you—"

"Yet what a good and jolly companion he could be at times! I remember once in the Adirondacks, when we were out in a canoe. A flock of geese appeared overhead and ..." A chuckle suddenly came into his voice at the memory. "Johnny pretended to us that he would—that he would fly like a—"

Booth closed his mouth tightly and began to breathe hard through his nose. Tears filled his eyes. The actor took a few moments to inhale deeply and compose himself.

"Upham, my friend, the world should know that Johnny was truly of a gentle, loving disposition. His mother's darling boy. And perhaps someday, God only knows, we might understand this one awful mad act of his. I cannot speak the word 'forgiveness' in connection with him. I wish I could but I simply cannot. For the nation's sake. It's too much, what he did."

"You talk of madness, his and your father's. Would it be too rude, sir, to ask if your father really was—insane?"

Booth's cheeks tightened, and he gave a mirthless laugh. "Ask anyone. Everyone has a 'mad Junius Brutus Booth' story." He pointed at the skull that Upham had noticed. "That was the head of one of his best friends, killed in an accident. Father varnished it himself! I ask you, is that a rational act, to acquire and keep such a skull? At our farm he would hold elaborate funerals, with music and all, for dead squirrels and birds, and he'd weep copiously at the ceremonies. He named my brother after the infamous John Wilkes, the London agitator, and hoped that the boy would grow up in that rebellious mode. Thank you, dear father. Think of what my poor mother has had to bear. That husband and, now, *this* from her favorite child!"

"And what was your brother's reaction to the bizarre things your father did?"

"Generally? Appalled, of course, except that Johnny *liked* father's animal funerals. That was the only activity he enjoyed doing with him. You see, John loved animals. He was always kind to them."

Loved animals, thought Upham. *Hated presidents. Killed presidents. Loved animals.*

"Johnny loved all funerals, now that I think of it—like father. You can't believe the things our father did, drunk or sober. Once when we were crossing the Atlantic to appear in a play in London, Father suddenly exclaimed, 'I must give a message to Conway!' Conway was a friend of his who'd jumped off a ship and drowned years before. Whereupon, Father put his hands on the rail and leapt overboard. This is true. It took a long time to launch a lifeboat and save him. It was not certain he would be found, but he was. Mad! So the answer to your question is a qualified 'yes.' But not Johnny, oh, not Johnny. Johnny is not mad. He is something else."

"Why, sir, do you say, 'he *is*?'"

"Excuse me?"

"You said, 'Johnny *is* not mad.' *Is*."

Booth sagged. "Was."

"He did a very violent thing, shot the President, stabbed the soldier in the box. Would you classify him as a violent person, if not mad?"

The actor seemed taken aback. "No, but as I said: Impulsive? Yes. Driven? Yes. He would get carried away, sometimes even on stage. Once, in Richmond, we were in a play which called for us to have a duel. These sword battles are always tightly choreographed. You know, leg, leg, neck, neck, turn, cross swords—and so forth. Yet Johnny, perhaps a bit taken in wine, I don't know, fought me fiercely, as if he meant to really kill me! Perhaps he did want to kill me a little. People said he harbored some jealousy and animosity toward me. I am, of course, the older brother. But that's another story. In any event, I suddenly had to fight for my life. He's a very good fencer, a wonderful athlete, but I was always better and so to quiet him down I pricked him hard on the right shoulder. More than a prick, a real cut. At the sight of blood staining his shirt, he seemed to come to his senses. He stopped slashing and returned to acting. Of course the audience thought it stage blood and just part of the performance, and they cheered as he lurched off the stage. That was a disturbing incident to me."

"Then he must have had a scar on his shoulder."

"Oh, yes, a considerable scar, I'm sorry to say."

"The right shoulder?"

Booth nodded and stood up. He seemed to falter and clamped a steadying hand on the back of a chair. *Theatrics or genuine?*

He cleared his throat and said firmly, "Now, sir—Mr. Upham—you will please forgive me, but I must ask you kindly to leave me."

Upham had not obtained the answers he'd hoped for, nor asked all the questions he'd prepared. He wondered if Booth's up-and-down, walking-around-the-room histrionics were an elaborate performance designed to obscure the truth about his brother.

As Booth showed him to the front door, Upham chanced a final, incendiary question. "Mr. Booth, I have heard a rumor that your brother was not the one they apprehended in Virginia—that he might still be alive and on the run."

Booth stopped and turned, a look of pained astonishment on his face. "Who says this?"

"Rumors. People."

"Preposterous," snapped Booth.

He shook his head and groaned softly. "Oh, the horror of all this." He looked at Upham as if searching for sympathy. "Do you know, they did not even allow us, his kinfolk—no one!—to identify the body. Then they buried him with unseemly haste. Why? We wished to take him home, to be buried in the family plot in Baltimore."

Upham wondered how much of the grief this man evidenced was sorrow for a lost brother, or engendered by the shame brought down upon the House of Booth. Standing just outside Booth's broad doorway, he ventured a final question.

"Let us suppose, sir, that your brother did not die as they claim. If a fugitive, where would you expect him to go?"

Booth's face grew dark as he gripped the open door.

"I will not entertain that ludicrous thought, sir."

"Would he contact you?" Upham managed from the top step.

"Goodbye, Mr. Upham!"

The door slammed. As Upham descended the townhouse steps, he muttered, "If you ask me, all the Booths are dancing with God."

At least he'd learned something here. *A considerable scar on his right shoulder!* That might be an important fact. Or not.

# CHAPTER TWENTY TWO

Two days later Fern arrived in the mid-afternoon to check on her lodger, but without her buggy. Standing in the doorway, Booth watched her ride up on her little blue roan, Sagebrush. He'd never seen a woman straddle a horse before. What would they think back in Maryland? She looked so at home on the horse, so much in harmony with her surroundings, that she could just as well be a native Indian. She wore a long black skirt, a buckskin jacket over her high-necked blouse, and a gray broad-brimmed hat with a thong that dangled under her chin. Her thick hair draped over the left side of her face, the other side was pulled back and held with a silver clip. There was nothing conventionally fashionable about her, and yet she pleased Booth.

She didn't stay long. On her way out the door she stopped and turned to him. "Will you keep our bargain about the portrait?"

"I will finish the portrait." He could not bring himself to speak Lincoln's name.

"Do take your other drawings to the store," said Fern. "Mr. Baker is a solid sort. He won't cheat you."

"I'll do that. Next time I walk into town."

"Finish the portrait," she said, reining in the eager horse. "And no liquor. Are we agreed on that?"

The irony of his situation made him smile. As a famous actor, sometimes proclaimed "America's handsomest man," he had generally dictated to women, even when he pretended to be complaisant. Now he was doing whatever this woman asked. But why give in to her and complete this loathsome drawing task? All he had to do was get up and go down to town, have a drink, and hop the stage to Bannack. *Gold.*

He watched as she trotted away to the smoking chimneys of Fort Benton. It was a beautiful clear day, and the sun striking this stretch of the Missouri below the cabin turned the water a blinding white. Twenty

179

yards away a woodchuck, a brown furry lump, lay stretched out on a boulder near the little circular corral. Booth thought of making a sketch of the animal, then remembered his assignment. He sighed and went back inside the cabin.

By noon the following day he had finished the portrait of Lincoln, mentally closing the invisible but remembered gash in the back of the skull. He even added the unsightly wart on the man's right cheek. It chagrined him to admit that this portrait was better than the one he'd made of Washington. He studied the photogravure of the Illinois lawyer's face, a visage so relentlessly ridiculed by his enemies. Looking at it now, with his artist's eye, Booth had to concede that it radiated strength and character. As an actor, he knew that a face could not lie as easily as a voice, no matter what people supposed.

What a tragedy for the Nation that this gifted man had been so misguided.

In the afternoon, he gathered together the best sketches made during his weeks steaming up the Missouri. With the packet under his arm he began the trek to Fort Benton. Walking past The Star saloon, he fought the compulsion to go in, but remembered Moody Suggs and kept walking. He felt, oddly, as if he were under the protective shadow of Fern's admonition. He did not want to be banished from her cabin.

She was much in his mind. He wanted her approval, like a child wanting to please his teacher. But maybe it was more than that.

He easily found the wooden façade of the I.G. Baker Company warehouse, a block off the waterfront. The lofty, spice-scented space inside was crowded with miners, trappers, settlers, merchants, and Indians trading furs for "many-shots" rifles. As Fern had assured him, Isaac Baker, a tall middle-aged man with the confident air of a boomtown merchant, was enthusiastic about adding art to his inventory.

"Anything to please the beautiful schoolmarm," he said, chuckling as Booth put the pile of papers on the back counter. "We carry whiskey, rifles, traps, ox bows, wagons, chewing tobacco, buffalo robes, and dried beans, flour—and a hundred more things. So why not pictures, eh, Marlowe?"

As he examined Booth's drawings, his jocular manner faded. "These are quite good, sir," he said earnestly. "You have an eye for animals, I must say. These are refined." It struck Booth that his pictures probably seemed extraordinary here, at the edge of civilization, because no other kind of art existed.

Baker paused to scrutinize a drawing of a chipmunk. He carefully set the sheet of paper aside. "I'll take this one home—for my wife. She loves art."

"And is your wife here in Benton?"

"Oh, no she's back in St. Louis," said Baker. "This is no town for a lady."

The merchant sorted the rest of the sketches into two piles, then surprised Booth by offering him $135 for all. Astonished, Booth accepted immediately.

"Bring me more, Marlowe," he said, a mercantile glitter in his eyes. "Indians and animals especially. I will sell some here, but also downriver in St. Louis." They shook hands.


Booth left, ecstatic over the sale until, passing the row of saloons, he saw a hulking figure thumping down the plank sidewalk. He pulled his hat over his face and crossed the street, but Moody Suggs spotted him and loped across the mud to overtake him.

"What do you know!" he rasped. "It's the Virginian!" He gestured toward The Star with a newspaper folded in his hand. "Have a drink on me, my friend." He thrust his face close to Booth's. "I have news!"

"Sorry, Suggs," Booth said. "I have an appointment."

"You've heard the terrible news?"

Booth shook his head.

Moody slapped the newspaper into his hand. "Just in on the packet boat."

Booth unfolded the paper with that familiar sense of foreboding. On the front page was a large drawing of four hooded bodies hanging from a gallows. His heart pounded as he scanned the caption below them.

*Justice is Done! Surratt, Powell, Atzerodt, and Herold Pay with Their Lives!*

"Didn't I tell you the bastards would hang those fine patriots? They didn't have the chance of a snowball in Hades."

Booth's head was spinning. A wave of nausea rose into his throat, and his knees felt as though they might buckle. *I caused the death of those people. Forgive me, God. Forgive me.*

Moody's ragged voice penetrated the fog of his dismay. "You all right?"

Booth nodded.

"I feel the same as you, old man." Moody slapped a heavy arm across Booth's shoulders. "We need a drink."

Booth allowed himself to be led into The Star. As they stood at the bar, Moody pounded his fist on the counter and bellowed, "Luke, you're about as useful as teats on a bull! Get over here and pour drinks for two old Rebels."

The earless bartender came down the bar and stood in front of them, his arms folded. "No whiskey unless you promise to behave yourself, Moody."

Suggs put his hand to his chest. "Upon my honor as a Southern gentleman."

"Not joking, Moody. Do I have your word? For the twelfth time?"

"You got my god-damned word, good sir! Now pour the god-damned drinks!"

As Booth threw down a shot of whiskey, the image of the gallows filled his thoughts. He ordered another and knocked it back. Suggs was already pouring his third and beginning to talk to himself in that strange croaking mumble.

Booth started to read the article under the ghastly drawing. He saw that it was written by Langford Upham, Jr.—*"An Actual Eyewitness to the Hangings!"*

*"Spectators felt cheated,"* wrote Upham, *"that the assassin and ring-leader John Wilkes Booth did not occupy a place of honor on the gallows and dance his own gavotte at the end of a rope for all to see.*

*"To the public's vexation,"* the reporter continued, *"details of Booth's*

*purported capture and death remain obscured by a peculiar official secrecy. Meantime, the unreliable and mercurial Sergeant Boston Corbett continues to claim it was his bullet, fired at Garrett's barn, that brought down the man alleged to be Booth."*

Booth shoved the newspaper back to Suggs. *Purported death?*

"I don't blame you for being disgusted like any good Southerner," said Suggs. "I'd shoot that Yankee scribbler if I saw him. That son of a bitch took pleasure in that hangin'." He raised his glass, a catch in his voice. "Join me in a drink to those brave four who have gone over to Glory."

Booth drank and fought the tears starting in his eyes.

"And here's to John Wilkes Booth!" said Suggs, pouring his fifth drink.

Booth put down his glass. "I'll be going now."

Suggs fixed his bloodshot eyes on Booth, trying to focus.

"You'll drink this with me, by God, or you're not a true son of the South." His voice had become an animal growl.

Booth obliged him by hoisting his glass and quickly downing his drink. Then he stood up. "Got to go."

Suggs grabbed his arm. "You'll have another, suh! We got to show respec' for the—the fallen."

"Certainly respect, Mr. Suggs," said Booth, twisting his arm from Suggs's powerful grip. "I mean no offense, but I am obliged to be somewhere on time."

Moody waved him off in disgust.

Booth strode out of the bar into the warm afternoon. By the time he reached Fern's cabin it was almost dusk. The brisk walk across the plains had cleared the whiskey from his head. He chewed a sprig of spicy sagebrush to blunt the scent of whiskey and took a moment to savor the silence. The news of execution had shaken him, but the landscape of this strange world of the Great West renewed him. The Missouri's great flow had come from Eternity and would continue into it.

He saw Fern's horse tied up at the fence. Smoke from the chimney was curling up into the blue-gray sky. It was good to see the lighted lamp in the kitchen window and to glimpse the young woman moving around inside.

He entered after a knock and greeted her awkwardly. She came out of the kitchen, wiping her hands on a towel.

"I finished the drawing for you," said Booth.

"Saw it. Mighty fine. You have captured his great soul. Thank you."

Her praise seemed genuine, so he told her about his success with I.G. Baker and his ideas for more pictures. "I want to go up into those mountains to draw the wild sheep and the mountain goats. I hear they are white with black horns. And the bison out on the plains. And the great shovel-like horns of the moose. What creatures!"

"You are in a poetic mode, I see. And Bannack?" she said. "What about the gold?"

"I like it here," he said, sitting down in a chair.

As she moved behind him to set plates on the table, she made a face. "I smell whiskey. You said you wouldn't, Marlowe."

"No," he retorted. "*You* said I wouldn't."

She stared at him sternly. "You promised me. And I took it as a promise."

"I was invited to have a drink in town," he said. "I agreed only out of courtesy."

Her gaze at him was full of disappointment. "Perhaps I was mistaken."

Suddenly, the words came out of him with no previous thought: "I will never drink again, Fern. Never. On my honor."

She looked hard and long at him, then accepted his declaration with a shrug. "If that's the case, you may stay on here. It's certainly less than what you would pay at the hotel."

"What will people say if you keep bringing me such lovely home-made meals?"

"My reputation may suffer," she said. "In a small way."

As she moved to go by him, he rose from his chair. Impulsively, he put his arms around her waist. She looked startled as he pulled her to him.

"Thank you," he said. "For everything."

She drew away. But not far.

"I say thank you from the bottom of my heart." He kissed her lightly on the cheek, then again, finally on her mouth.

This time she did not pull away. He kissed her again, a little harder fervently. She kissed back, but her eyes were closed, as if she were afraid to look at him. Or to see him looking at her.

Then he gently lifted the hair from the covered part of her face and looked carefully at it without flinching, lightly touching the scarred flesh with his fingers. He kissed her there until he began to taste her tears. Surprisingly he felt his own eyes blur.

# CHAPTER TWENTY THREE

On this last day in September the very last steamboat from Fort Benton was due to depart. In a week the Missouri would be too low for passage. As Booth rode Sagebrush into town, he felt safe. No boats would be able to make their way upriver until next April's snowmelt and rains.

These summer months at Fort Benton had been the happiest time of his life. The ghastly nightmares of *The Event* and Beech's face came only sporadically now. He had kept his bargain with Fern and had not taken a drink since that last encounter with Moody Suggs at The Star. Nor did he even want a drink.

He also had come to the conclusion that he was not insane and had not been insane. It had, however, become abundantly clear to him how liquor had dominated his life and, indeed, dictated its course. Yes, he had seen Lincoln as The Tyrant. It was a political decision to kill him. But he never could have pulled the trigger that Good Friday night at Ford's if he had not been drinking heavily for days, weeks, and months before. He had hid his drunkenness well, most of all from himself. He had appeared in plays drunk without missing a cue or forgetting a line, but he now saw that made him no less a drunk. Now, Booth believed, he saw the world clearly, a world bearing scant resemblance to the one through which he had strutted in a self-centered manner for most of his adult years.

At the mail order counter at the back of Baker's store, Booth addressed an envelope to Mrs. Wilson Beech in Front Royal, Virginia. He folded a sheet of blank stationery around a hundred dollar bill and inserted it into an envelope. Affixing double the required postage for good measure, he handed it to Baker's clerk. "Just make sure it gets on board."

He had repaid a small, but significant debt. Relieved, Booth strode along the town's muddy main street, a great weight lifting from his heart.

He had returned the money he'd taken from Wilson Beech's wallet to send to his widow. It eased the gnawing at his soul.

Life was looking better. He was now a bona fide artist. He would hurry back to the cabin and begin another series of drawings before sunset. Perhaps the woodchuck would return to his rock the next day and pose for him.

As he rode up to the cabin, he saw Fern waving, smiling at him in the doorway of her little house. She only came out for an hour or two in daylight. But every time she left him, he missed her. He didn't want to be alone in the cabin. He wanted her with him.

He dismounted, tied the rein to the fence, and walked towards her. Taking her hands, he felt the words appear in his mouth of their own accord.

"Dearest Fern," he said, "You have given my life the greatest fullness. I've wanted to ask you to marry me for some time. Will you have me? Will you marry me?"

"Perhaps you would give me a few weeks to consider the idea."

"But darling I need—"

Then she was crying, clutching him tightly. "Of course, I shall marry you."

The next morning Booth drove into town and bought a ring at I.G. Baker's. Then he went to the Ledyards' house where Fern was waiting for him, clutching a bouquet of flowers from the prairie. Tobias, Emma, and Tommy Ledyard were also there. All of them walked over to the little office behind the jail to meet Judge Mack, justice of the peace. Tommy was the ring-bearer. It took only minutes. When the thin young judge said, "I now pronounce you man and wife," the newlyweds kissed, and Booth felt such overwhelming love for her that tears came to his eyes.

They spent their honeymoon patching the roof. The following week Booth bought a gentle saddle horse from Mr. Carroll and daily rode to the distant hills in search of animals to draw. This worried Fern.

"Marlowe, you shouldn't be going alone. There are grizzlies out there, not to mention the Blackfeet."

"I thought they had a trading agreement with Fort Benton."

"That's only inside Benton. Outside the town, they do as they wish. There are bad Blackfeet. How do you think the bartender at The Star lost his ears?"

It pleased him that she was concerned for his safety. It had been a long time since a woman had cared whether he lived or died. For all his public acclaim, he could not recall one of his paramours taking him seriously as a man. Even his former fiancée Lucy Hale considered acting a low trade. But now he was an artist, like Catlin or Bodmer. And a husband to a woman who loved him.

He'd seen no Indians on his forays and only one old limping grizzly at a distance. This particular Saturday was a brisk, sunny fall morning. As he mounted his horse, he waved goodbye to Fern. Following the trail along the Missouri, he felt glad to be alive.

And what a crystalline clear October day it was. He had come to love this land more than any he'd known—the distant mountain peaks always flecked with snow, the mighty river flanked by limestone ramparts, and the huge sky above; the spicy scent of sagebrush, the heavy whirring of wings as the grouse exploded from brush. Northern geese honked high overhead, in lacy V formations. And the teeming populations of badger, antelope, and bear, all to be marveled at, and sketched.

He especially liked the sudden dark storms that would advance across the vast plain on dancing legs of lightning, heralded by the loudest thunderclaps he had ever heard.

And, of course, it was Fern who opened his eyes and his heart to this astonishing world of inexhaustible treasure. He'd never known real love and trust before. Acclaim, fame, and yes, romance, but never simple love. He'd been too deep in his mad political obsessions, too intoxicated by his own false notions of himself to love anyone else.

He knew that she felt a powerful attachment to him, something she did not try to put in words. Her reticence was not a deficiency of emotion. Instead she showed her love in actions. She no longer hid the left side of her face from him, now pulling her hair back in a bun when she was working around the cabin. For his part he barely noticed her scars, no more than he might have noticed a freckle on her cheek.

He could not believe his good fortune. He wanted to spend the rest of his life this way. Sometimes, in a meditative mood while sitting before his easel out on the Montana wild, listening to the sigh of wind through the grass, or the clatter of water over a pebbly shallows, he felt a desire to confess his dark secret to her.

What would confession accomplish? He had been a murderer. He was a murderer still. He had killed a man and, he had since learned from the newspapers, he had also murdered history. According to some, he had assassinated the best hope for the South in its abysmal defeat. Johnson was proving to be little more than a placeholder, a shadow of the man he replaced, and a hostage to the vindictive forces intent on punishing the rebellious Confederate states. Lincoln had promised reconciliation and a new partnership. Johnson promised nothing—and delivered it.

# CHAPTER TWENTY FOUR

Months after the hangings, Upham still couldn't banish his suspicions about Booth's escape. Every day he thought about Ford's Theater, the twelve-day flight into Virginia, and the smoke-stained, swollen face of the man dragged from Garrett's barn. He declared to himself that plain good sense required that Lincoln's killer was dead.

Then, after a day of routine reporting at *The World*, as Manhattan's warmest November suddenly turned cold again, Upham climbed the stairs to his apartment to find a letter slipped under the door. Postmarked Front Royal, Virginia, it appeared to have been fashioned from used wrapping paper. Cutting it open he found a letter crudely written in pencil on a fragment of double-lined paper, the kind issued to schoolchildren learning penmanship. It was signed "Mrs. W. Beech."

Upham had written to Charlotte Beech some weeks before, in hope of tying up a few last loose ends in his abandoned quest, but expecting no response.

*Dear Sir—You axed me to contack you if I heared from my husband. I have. No more can be said in a letter if you take my meaning.*

Upham was astonished. *Wilson Beech is alive?*

"Once more unto the breach," croaked Calpurnia when the bird saw Upham pull his suitcase from the closet.

"Exactly right, Calpurnia," said Upham absently. "*Unto*, indeed!"

On the overnight train to Front Royal he mulled over the new scenario, searching for flaws. According to Charlotte Beech, her husband was alive. This shot to hell his theory that Wilson Beech was the man who died in the burning barn, and whose persona Booth assumed while at Florie's boarding house. Nevertheless, the man calling himself Beech,

191

whom Upham had followed to Richmond, looked nothing like the picture of the hapless Confederate soldier his wife had shown him.

To compound his confusion, Upham had received a curt note from the photographer Matthew Brady the week before:

*Sir: In answer to your query, it was a total stranger who so briefly helped me take my equipment into Gen. Lee's house that day. I do not recall knowing any Wilson Beech. yrs, M. Brady.*

As his sleeper car clattered south from Alexandria to Front Royal on the Manassas Gap Railroad, Upham lay on his berth, smoking a cheroot, and pondering the slim possibility that two men named Wilson Beech had somehow crossed paths. But that would still not explain why one had claimed to be Charlotte Beech's brother, or sent her two hundred dollars. Upham recalled his speculation that he might have wished to conceal that he was married in order to seduce the rotund hotel clerk Florie—God forbid. The aesthetics were abominable. He drifted off to sleep, once again troubled by dreams of a conspiracy of *doppelgängers*.

At precisely nine the next morning, Upham stepped down onto the red brick platform of the Front Royal station. By chance, the same elderly black cabbie was waiting for a fare, dozing over his whip, and once again guided him out to the Beech farmstead.

Charlotte Beech's little boy was playing in the weeds of the front yard with the yellow dog. The boy looked up and greeted the reporter with a shy smile, but did not respond to his greeting.

His mother was in the back yard, feeding chickens. She was startled by the appearance of Upham around the corner of her house, hat in hand.

"Hello, Mrs. Beech."

"You got my letter!" she exclaimed, wiping the sweat from her forehead with her apron. She had a pretty smile. He had not noticed that during his first visit.

She led him into her run-down cottage by the back door and invited him to sit at her kitchen table, pouring glasses of cellar-cooled water from a clay jug.

"After I wrote you that letter, I axed myself, 'how come all this interest in my husband?' You a lawyer?"

"I'm a newspaperman."

She frowned. "Not a lawyer?"

"I'm a reporter for *The New York World*."

"What in heaven's name would some big-city newspaper care about us?"

"I'm doing a piece on the families of men who haven't come home from the war, or have disappeared."

"Willy hasn't disappeared. He just ain't come home yet."

"So you know he's alive?" asked Upham. "That's good news! I'm very happy for you, Mrs. Beech."

Her gaze dropped to her work-worn hands, one laid over the other on the table. "Never had no doubts about Wilson bein' alive. Question is, when's he comin' home?"

"He hasn't yet?"

She shook her head.

"Do you expect him to?"

She glanced around shyly. "I don't think he can. Or 'least he thinks he can't."

"Why do you say that?"

"I got fed up with no news from him—sends money but not a word! So I gone to Richmond to check with the army."

"And?"

"There's no record of Willy bein' killed. But I found out somethin' else."

"And that is what?"

"Clerk showed me his name in the book of the 62nd Virginia Infantry. Willy was in Company C, out of Front Royal. Somebody had writ 'deserted' next to it."

"Could he have been taken prisoner?"

"They wasn't fightin' when he left."

"Well, he could have been stunned in battle and just walked away, or gotten lost. All this happens to soldiers, Mrs. Beech. He might not have deserted."

"Clerk said he lit out on March 21st."

*Over a month before Booth was tracked to Garrett's barn.*

"They shoot deserters, don't they?"

Upham saw that she was wringing her hands. *She still cherishes the cad.*

"The war's over, Mrs. Beech. The Confederate army—indeed the Confederacy itself—is no more. So who is there with any authority to punish him?"

"That's what I been axing myself."

"You wrote in your letter that you heard from him."

She opened a blue ceramic box on the table, removed an envelope and handed it to him. "This come eleven days ago."

The envelope was postmarked *Ft. Benton, Montana Territory.*

"Look inside."

Upham held up a one hundred dollar bill.

"Just like the last time," she said. "Out of the blue. I figure he's 'fraid to come home and 'fraid even to write a proper letter, so he sends me money. He's now sent more'n we ever had at one time ever." She was quiet for a moment.

Upham was at a loss for what to say. "That's very thoughtful of him, I'd say."

"We have a boy to raise. We have a field to plant. And he made a promise."

"To do what?"

"What the preacher swore him to do—to cherish and protect me, 'til death do us part." Once again her gaze dropped to the table and she fell silent.

Upham studied the penmanship on the envelope. "Is this his handwriting?"

She shook her head. "Willy don't know how to write very good. Someone had to have writ it for him."

"Do you have the other envelope?"

"Dog et it. Thank the Lord I took the money out a'fore."

Upham could see that her name and address had been written by an educated hand, like the envelope he'd delivered previously. It looked to him to be the same handwriting, its flourishes suggesting—*Booth.* He made a mental note to track down an example of the actor's handwriting.

"So where do you think your husband might be?"

"Where it says there—in Montana Territory. Always was talkin' 'bout goin' out there, ever since cousin Wilma sent him that rock I showed you." She nodded toward the gold-laced quartz sitting on the mantelpiece. "Just like that, he got the gold fever, always talking about Bannack, how you dig up gold, how you tell if'n it's real—all the things we'd have when he struck it rich. He got drunk on those dreams without drinkin'."

"The cousin—her name, again?"

"Wilma Harrison."

"This postmark's from Ft. Benton, not Bannack."

"You take the boat there first, then a stage many miles away to Bannack. He told me that a score if he told me once."

"Mrs. Beech, believing your husband might be a fugitive, why then did you write to me about him?"

She looked off for a moment, then turned back to him. "I been married—legal—eight years come August." Her voice had grown angrier and her fists were clenched. "Those years ain't been easy, Mr. Upham, to put it mild. Willy has a wanderin' eye, a weakness for liquor, and a heavy hand. A lazy but hard man. In spite of that, I have kept my promises as a wife. So I think I got a right to half of whatever he's come into out there. If he can part with three hundred dollars this easy, think how much more he must have. He's struck it rich, all right."

Upham had to sigh. He had attributed her pensive manner solely to the loneliness of a neglected loving spouse.

"And why did you think I could help you, madam?"

"First time you come here, all dressed up so fine, like now, I figured you for a lawyer—somebody who could help me get what's comin' to me."

"I might indeed be able to help. As for what may be rightfully yours, however, I can't say. I know nothing about such things."

"It's not for me, you understand. It's for our boy. I want you to believe that."

"All right. I will."

"A widow I was when Mr. Beech come a'courtin'. I brung this 120 acres to the weddin'. And every dollar we made off'n it, Willy found a way to spend it. That man owes me and the boy, Mr. Upham."

195

"I see."

"Promise me you're not from the government or the police."

"Mrs. Beech, I assure you I am neither, but I do have connections that might be of use to you." He took a small leather case from a vest pocket, opened it, and presented her with his calling card.

"I would be much obliged if you'd let me know promptly when you hear again from your husband. If you're to have an equitable share of his fortune, such as it may be, you need to track him down. I might be of assistance in that regard."

She nodded, examining his expensively engraved card, turning it over in her fingers. "Pretty." She put it in the ceramic box with her money.

Upham stood to leave. "Was Mr. Beech political?"

She shook her head.

"Well, he enlisted as a Confederate soldier, did he not?" he said.

"We needed the money. Lost a harvest to blight. Every man around here enlisted."

"Did he ever talk about Lincoln in what might be considered hostile or vengeful language—say, wishing he were dead, or something like that? It's not necessarily a crime."

She gave a dry laugh. "You don't know Willy. He don't think nothin' 'bout that sort of thing. Only thing he hated was the army—and gettin' up early."

Upham put on his bowler and shook her hand, startled by its bony thinness. It felt like his dying mother's hand. He wondered what life had in store for this poor woman and her boy.

"Mrs. Beech, I wish you nothing but well."


While waiting at the Alexandria station's platform for the night train to New York, Upham pondered the timeline he had drawn across two spread pages of his notebook, tracing Booth's flight from Washington to Garrett's barn. To it he had added Beech's March 21st disappearance from his encampment. He could now presume that Booth knew Beech—either as a fellow conspirator or by a chance meeting during his twelve-day flight. Perhaps Beech had been mortally wounded and, knowing he was dying, asked Booth to deliver his money to his widow. And now he jotted further notes:

*Was Beech murdered by Booth and Herold, and his leg broken, so Booth's pursuers would find his body in the barn and take it for Booth's?*

*Was the money sent to Charlotte Beech to buy her silence? But she has not been silent. Perhaps the $300 was sent to salve Booth's conscience?*

*Is it folly to suppose that Lincoln's assassin might have a conscience?*

# CHAPTER TWENTY FIVE

Langford Upham shivered as he trudged through the January snow that had blanketed Manhattan over the weekend. He had just spent three hours in the public library, boning up on Western American geography. He had located Ft. Benton on a map and consulted train schedules to St. Louis. With disappointment he'd learned that Montana Territory was inaccessible by Missouri riverboat until April or May—at least four months away.

Crossing Broadway, he stepped into a grand portal. Carved in stone above the entrance was the proclamation:

## THE WORLD COVERS THE GLOBE

The minute hand of the big clock in the vast echoing lobby lurched to the top of the hour and struck twice: two o'clock. Still not entirely trusting Mr. Otis's new elevators, operated ingeniously by steam, he climbed the stairs to the third floor, quickly passing the entrance to his father's imposing suite of offices. The title *Langford Upham, Sr., Publisher* was painted large on the frosted glass of his tall door. Senior U would certainly disapprove of the latest chapter in Junior's quixotic crusade. However, always keen on publicity, the mogul might yet be cajoled into backing it.

In the newspaper's main editorial room, he found the editor, Chadwick Tompkins, at his paper-strewn desk, issuing orders to reporters amid the usual afternoon chaos.

"Lang! You're actually gracing the premises? Say, do you sleep in that derby? No, of course not. You have a dozen or two, right?"

Upham always suspected that Tompkins was consciously straining to be seen as the archetypal Managing Editor—a green eye shade pulled low, garters on his inky sleeves, a cigar jutting from his mouth, and a fathomless disdain for anything unconnected with journalism.

"Chad, I've got a splendid idea for a series."

"Really?" The editor looked skeptically over his glasses at him. "Not more Lincoln stuff?"

"No 'Lincoln stuff', as you call it."

"Readers are sick of the Lincoln stuff."

"I'll wager our readers have never heard of Bannack or Virginia City or Butte."

"I've heard of Butte, but not Bannack. Bannack sounds Canadian, and who the hell cares about Canada?"

"They're all towns out in the Montana Territory. How about Last Chance Gulch?"

Tompkins removed his cigar. "Last Chance Gulch? Sounds like something in a dime novel. We are not publishing dime novels, Junior. What's your point?"

"Last Chance Gulch is a hot gold strike in Montana Territory. A small city, Helena, has formed around it. You're going to be hearing plenty about Helena, Bannack, and a dozen other places. The world's rushing out there, just as they did to San Francisco in '49. It's the new Eldorado."

"So why do we need a series? The Erie Canal is a big deal, and closer to home."

"*The World* can't just be about New York. Everyone dreams of being rich, Chad. And getting rich quick—that's the new religion. Our readers want to know if it's easy to pick up gold, to amass a fortune with a pick and shovel. Could they do it? Sluice for gold, shake up nuggets with a pan—dig a proper mine shaft? What's life like out there in the barbaric West? Gamblers! Gun-fighters! Indians!"

"The dregs of society, Junior."

"A bold civilization determined to rise under the lofty peaks of the Rockies!"

Tompkins had leaned back in his chair, his arms crossed skeptically. But Upham was warming to his pitch. "Stampeding buffalo! Tribes on the warpath! Five million dollars in gold dust a year taken out of Helena alone by amateurs! Lynchings, armies of beautiful loose women for the asking, instant millionaires gambling away their fortunes at a poker table!"

Tompkins gave a mirthless laugh and held up his hands. "Enough, enough! Save it for your readers. What does Senior think?"

"I haven't told him. Matter of fact, Chad, I'd appreciate it if you didn't either. Just give me the assignment."

A frown creased Tompkin's face. "How much is this going to cost us? It's a couple thousand miles out there by riverboat, isn't it?"

"About four hundred dollars. Maybe five hundred. It's at least three months of traveling there and back."

Tompkins' lips pursed in a silent whistle.

"But think," said Upham. "You'll get a long-running popular series that no one else will have. We'll tell our readers the true story—direct from the Great Wild West!"

"Excuse me, sir," said a copy boy as he handed Tompkins the proof sheet of an editorial.

"Hang on, Junior," said Tompkins, pulling out a pencil.

Upham looked out the window at the skyline of Manhattan, catching a glimpse of the Hudson River. Tompkins read the copy in a muted, high-speed monotone. "Okay! Print it." The copy boy hurried away.

"What about it?" said Upham.

Tompkins looked at Upham blankly. "What?"

"The Great Wild West series."

"Want to get yourself scalped, do you? Now that'd be a good story." Tompkins burst out laughing and stood up. He held out his hand to Upham.

"Go do it," he said. "Better be great pieces, though, or I'll be out there digging for gold myself, because I won't have a job here anymore."

"They will be good," Upham smiled. "And you won't have to leave your desk."

"All right. I'm goldstruck. When do you go?"

"Not for a couple of months. The boats can't get up there until late spring. April or May."

"Great. Until then, I want you to cover the Tammany Hall scandals. Same as usual. But seek out a higher quality of crookedness. And there's this crazy poet Walt Whitman who's blowing the pants off the critics. Perhaps that's not the right phrase. But his books are selling out. And there's this young painter named Winslow Homer. . . ."

"Okay, I'll cover them all— as long as you get me out West."

"Good luck, kid. But do your homework before you go on holiday."

As Langford Upham left Chad Tomkins' office, he strode through the newsroom, passing men busy working on international news, obituaries, advice to the lovelorn, and accounts of rigged horse races and prize fights, and darted past his father's office.

He was heading up Broadway, negotiating the crowded sidewalk, when he heard a desperate voice calling his name. He turned and saw the Irish copy boy running after him.

"Mr. Upham," panted the youth, "yer fether wints to see ya immediately, sir!"

So much for Tompkins' vow of secrecy. Upham followed the clerk back into the building and up to his father's aerie. When he walked in, Senior swiveled in his chair, flashing what a stranger might take for a smile: a perpetual widening of the mouth, like a shark squinting into the sun. But it had nothing to do with the man's humor, mood, or disposition.

"Well, my boy."

"Yes, father."

The publisher wore pince-nez glasses on a blue ribbon. He doffed them theatrically and stared at his son as though he were a physician inspecting an unpleasant organism under a microscope.

"Too busy even to say hello to your aging patriarch?"

Looking at his father's handsome, sun-tanned face and abundant white hair, he thought it was indeed a visage suited to a senator.

Framing this living portrait of achievement and power was the office itself, luxuriously appointed by Upham's young stepmother, dear Blanche, who wished everything to be *just so*. Rare English hunting prints decorated the walls. Over the fireplace hung an ornately engraved shotgun and, above it, a print of an American Eagle by John James Audubon.

"I would have stopped by, Father," said Upham, sitting down, "but our visits always seem to end in a quarrel, and I wasn't up to that today."

"Come now, Lang," said the older man. "Didn't I send you a note on your interview with Davey Herold? And your description of the hanging? That was damn good reporting, lad!"

"You gave me hell for using the words 'purported' and 'alleged' in connection with Booth's death."

"Well, of course! His death is a fact! And in this business, facts are called facts."

"Father, Booth was not killed in Garrett's barn."

The publisher's eyes became slits. He slammed a palm down on the vast plain of his gleaming oak desk. "Nonsense! Boston Corbett put the sorry dog out of his misery."

"Father, Boston Corbett is an insane religious fanatic. I can't put this charming tidbit in the newspaper, of course, but I've found out that seven years ago Corbett castrated himself after an encounter with a prostitute."

"Good heavens. Is that true?"

"Unfortunately, sir, it is a *fact*, as you say, confirmed by a police report. Corbett told the doctor that God ordered him to make himself a capon. The man is a moonbeam from a major lunacy."

Senior appeared to shudder. "His *pecker*? Off?"

"Just the testicles. With a pair of scissors."

"My god! Corbett? The same Corbett?"

"The same peculiar man who will collect some of the reward money and is already staging lectures, proclaiming himself Booth's killer— Lincoln's avenger—'the swift sword of justice.'"

"Lafayette Baker swears it was Booth that Corbett killed. His cousin Luther saw it happen."

"Father, Baker was under orders from Edwin Stanton to produce a body fast, to placate President Johnson, and quiet the public's anger. Baker saw a promotion, a means to collect some reward money, and he got it."

"Mind whom you speak of, son."

"I do, sir. But people are also saying that the Secretary of War wanted a body—any body—in Booth's grave."

"Why would he want that?"

"Some people in Washington believe he is the black hand behind the conspiracy."

"Poppycock!" The elder man jerked back in his chair. "Ed Stanton is a fine man!"

"People on the inside tell me that eighteen pages of Booth's diary—a diary I saw intact that night at the Garrett farm—are missing. Stanton has those pages."

"Poppycock!"

"Father. These are not rumors. These are facts—not connected yet in a logical way, I will grant you. But they are *facts*. I am not trying to stir up controversy."

"But you *are* stirring it up!"

"Another thing, Father. One of the doctors who examined Booth's body on the *Montauk*, Dr. John Frederick May, had operated on Booth two years before to remove a tumor. He said the body looked 'much altered' from when he first met Booth, and that the body was 'much older and in appearance much more freckled than he was.' Booth was famous for his clear white skin! An Adonis! The surgeons who examined the body on the *Montauk* permitted a photographer to take a portrait of the corpse. Witnesses confirmed this to me. The man, Alexander Gardner, had his camera shoved up close to the body's head. But all the plates he exposed were confiscated and taken to the War Department. I'm told Stanton wanted proof the body was Booth's."

"Well then, he got it!"

"He got the plates, but no one's seen the images from them."

"I know Ed Stanton to be a man of integrity."

"I don't disagree. But look how quickly they got the body out of the way."

"Then may I ask who is in Booth's grave, down there in Washington?"

"A poor devil named Wilson Beech, a Confederate deserter. I've been in contact with his widow."

"And she says he's the man in Booth's grave?"

"She doesn't know he's dead."

"But *you* do?" The older man cupped his ear.

Upham could feel his anger rising. "Yes, father, I do."

The publisher gave a cold laugh. "Lang, you are truly a piece of work, you really are. Don't you know that the President of the United States has personally told me that Booth is dead?"

"Father, don't you realize the President of the United States is a drunken jackass from Tennessee?"

The publisher stood. "You will *not* slander my old and loyal friend. How dare you, boy!"

Upham sighed and shrugged. "I'll leave now, sir." He got up and went to the door.

"Not so fast, young man," his father commanded. "What is this new goose chase Chad told me about, this sudden lust of yours for the Golden West?"

"I feel it could be a fine series and sell a lot of papers."

"I'm sure it could be. But I worry about your asthma, and, frankly, the adventure strikes me as rather too rough for your—sophisticated tastes."

The tone of sarcasm in his father's voice stung him deeply.

"I'm going to the Montana Territory."

"I grant you permission, and I will pay for it. But, Langford, if you even once mention Booth and your cockeyed theories, the articles will not run in my newspaper. I will hold Tompkins responsible. Write one word, and both he and you are out of a job."

It alarmed Upham to hear his father struggle to control the tremor in his voice.

"Well then, father, perhaps *The Boston Globe* will be interested in what I believe could be the biggest story of the decade."

"Poppycock!" said the publisher. It struck Upham as an unmanly expression, unflattering to his elder. Why did he use that word?

"Father, did you know that your favorite word comes from Middle Dutch—*kacken*—which in turn derives from the Latin word *cacare*, meaning, essentially, shit?"

"By God, young man, you personify arrogance! You shout nonsense like that ridiculous cockatoo of yours, fancying you know everything, when in fact you know next to nothing!"

"Poppycock, father!" said Upham quietly. "Once more, unto the breach."

While pulling the office door shut, Upham had a brief glimpse of his red-faced father slapping the arms of his leather chair.

# CHAPTER TWENTY SIX

Booth and Fern spent an outwardly brutal winter in their cabin. In November the snow came thick and hard and rarely let up until February. Great drifts once prevented them from driving into town for a full week. Booth, however, thrived on the isolation, drawing and painting constantly, to the point where he had to use the pages of an old newspaper as a sketch pad, the words only partially obliterated by the water-colored images of bison and badger. After shooting a skinny deer that happened to wander by, he and Fern butchered it, and hung it in the shed. Venison kidneys and the liver were unexpected delicacies.

Several times Booth used snow-shoes to trek into town to sketch Fort Benton's characters. Yet most of his drawings were now of animals particular to the region, large and small. Years before in New York he'd seen an exhibition of John James Audubon's works. Though impressed with his paintings of birds, what stayed with Booth and influenced him now were the lesser-known animal studies, the quadrupeds. A local trapper had supplied him with pelts so he could observe the fur and claws first hand, but it was better to watch them alive. Even in winter Booth would wander out on the plains at first light to make sketches of the creatures, before the more nocturnal among them vanished for the day. In the afternoon and in firelit evening sessions he would render them in detail. On one of his outings he'd shot a heavy-footed lynx, with some regret, but praised its beauty and honored its soul with three sketches painted over the pages of a newspaper. Finally, with a cardboard purchased from I.G. Baker, he'd painted a personal masterpiece of the cat, its eyes large and yellow, as it held a rabbit under its paw.

I.G. Baker had been able to secure top-grade pigments from St. Louis along with good watercolor paper. Booth found it exciting to transfer his sketches into finished color compositions. He felt blessed by the unknown skills the projects brought forth from him. And Fern had been part of it.

In March the Chinook winds blew strong and warm across the prairie, melting the snow, and the land emerged as brown and shaggy as an old bison robe. By April green grass had fought its way through the brown crust. In May came wildflowers and birdsong. The Missouri River ran high, fast, and brown, and the first steamboat of the year, the *Chippewa*, hove into sight, loaded with freight and miners.

Booth celebrated the good weather by heading out onto the prairie with his sketchpad as often as he could. These forays to the faraway hills had become a cherished routine. He never knew what he might stumble upon.

One day, several hours ride from the cabin, he spotted a bear asleep on a rock ledge near a stream. It was not a grizzly, with that tell-tale hump on its back, but a common black bear. Still, it would more than do as a subject. He quietly tethered his horse to a stump. With his pad under his arm he stole slowly toward the slumbering creature, sliding down the embankment on the opposite bank of the stream. He found a low flat boulder to sit on and began to sketch. From time to time the near-sighted animal would raise its head, its small round ears turning, sniff the air, then doze off.

What a superb creation the animal was with its shiny ebony hide, its great claws and its huge head. In twenty minutes he completed a full-length sketch surrounded by copious color notes and a suggestion of background.

Suddenly the bear jerked up its head, wide awake. It growled, leapt off the ledge and lumbered into the foliage.

Booth turned. On the rise directly behind him were four half-naked horsemen staring down at him. Blackfeet. They wore bows slung on their backs and carried lances. One sported a headdress and a breastplate made of polished bones. All wore war paint.

They trotted to within a few feet of Booth. There was no possibility of escape—the Blackfeet were between him and his tethered horse. Their faces were almost expressionless, their eyes dark, glistening. Booth thought quite calmly: I am going to die out here today.

"Mah to toh pa," said the Indian in the headdress, raising his left hand. His tone was commanding, stern.

Instinctively, Booth mimicked the sounds perfectly, thinking it was a greeting. "Mah to toh pa."

All four of the horsemen laughed at this. Maybe it was a threat? Maybe it meant I will now kill you. Maybe it was the man's name. Booth pointed at himself.

"John," he said. "John." He slapped his hips to show he was carrying no pistol. "Friend!"

"John Friend," said the Blackfoot. Then he pointed to his chest. "Tall Elk."

He had a magnificent face. On either side of the scimitar-like nose glared eyes black as flint, as if they were chips taken from his spear point. Long braids hung from under a cap made of a wolf's face. Two black-haired scalps hung from his shield. Booth had never seen anything so weirdly wonderful.

"Tall Elk," said Booth. Smile, he told himself, stay calm.

Tall Elk raised his lance, then reached down, and jabbed the point at the sketch book. He motioned for Booth to bring it to him. Booth approached Tall Elk and gingerly handed the pad up to him. The warrior leafed through the book, talking to his companions animatedly and showing them the depicted animals. When he came to the sketch of a dead buffalo bull Booth had done on the steamboat, he held it up to Booth.

"Iliniiwa. Good medicine," he said. He pointed at himself and then at the drawing. "John Friend give Tall Elk."

"Of course." Booth nodded, and the Indian tore the picture out of the pad. He handed it to one of the braves. Then he cut one of the scalps off his shield and held it out as a gift.

"This good medicine for you, John Friend," said Tall Elk. "Belong Crow man." He handed the relic to Booth. "Great warrior. Horse not fast."

This sent the Blackfeet into paroxysms of laughter. Booth smiled with them; it seemed he might not die today after all. A wild thought came to him: if only they knew he'd killed the biggest Chief of all. Would they

209

not think him a mighty warrior and honor him?

"Thank you," he said and tucked the ghastly scalp in his belt. Now Tall Elk was looking at a portrait sketch of Fern in the drawing pad.

He looked at Booth, then pointed at the sketch. "Good." he said. "You do face Tall Elk same."

"Yes."

"Next day, I come to you, John Friend." He moved his hand in an arc, mimicking the passage of the sun.

"Tomorrow?"

"Yes. Here."

"Not here," said Booth. "At my house." He took back the pad and drew a little map showing the cabin in relationship to Fort Benton and pointed with his hand. He tore out the page and handed it to Tall Elk.

The Indian grunted something and wheeled his horse. The others followed with a clatter of hooves. In a moment they were up the ravine and out of sight behind a grove of cottonwood trees.

Booth found himself taking deep breaths and laughing with relief as he went to his horse and leaned his forehead against its neck. He looked down at the scalp tied to his belt. His drawings—at first figuratively and, now, in fact—had perhaps saved his life.

On the ride back to the cabin he thought of how he would pose the warrior, what colors he would use to capture that luminescent bronze skin. He would do the portrait, then make a copy for himself, perhaps several more for I.G. Baker. But the original would be large, it could be a masterpiece. If Tall Elk brought his friends tomorrow, maybe he'd sketch them also. Baker would surely buy these pictures. Especially now that the boats were running for the summer.

Arriving at the cabin he saw a buggy in front of it. He recognized the vehicle as Tobias Ledyard's. As he was dismounting, Emma Ledyard and her stout little husband stepped out of the cabin with Fern following.

"Here he is now, Mr. Ledyard," Fern said. "You must ask him yourself." Her smile at Booth was radiant.

Booth greeted the visiting couple as he tied up the horse. "Ask what, may I inquire?"

"Well, Marlowe," Tobias Ledyard said genially. "We're planning the annual July Fourth pageant. Just a month from now. A splendid affair that I seem to be chairman of this year. The money raised will build a little school. Not a shabby room, but a real school. My wife and I have a special interest in it since Tommy now attends this noble concentration of great minds." He turned to Fern. "Under the admirable aegis of Miss Fern. Forgive me—*Mrs.* Marlowe!"

"How is Tommy?" Booth asked.

"He misses his art lessons," said Mrs. Ledyard. "You must come into town more often, Mr. Marlowe."

"Ah, yes, of course," said Booth. "Or send him out here to us! A child would brighten up our hermetic life."

"You've been a great addition to our town and made Fern so happy."

"You are too kind, Mrs. Ledyard."

"Anyway, Marlowe," Ledyard went on, "this pageant will feature songs and skits and monologues. All to the glory of our historical United States. Many heroic parts need actors. And little men need heroic parts. I myself will play Benjamin Franklin. For obvious reasons, I'm afraid." He patted his bald head and ample stomach self-deprecatingly. "Mrs. Ledyard will be the effervescent Dolly Madison, both great beauties."

"Perfect," said Booth gallantly.

"Emma tells me she heard you recite poetry mighty well on the boat coming up here."

"We were rather starved for entertainment aboard the *Yellowstone*, otherwise I wouldn't have presumed."

"We would be much obliged if you and Fern were to play the important parts of Martha and George Washington."

So that was it! Booth held up his hands in protest. "Sir, I could never do that."

"But why?"

"I have always been filled with dread of appearing in front of people. When I was your son's age, speaking before the class was a nightmare." *That's the truth, actually.*

"Nonsense, Marlowe! We're talking about nothing more than standing up in a fake rowboat, wearing a wig, and saying a couple of lines about crossing the Delaware. No wooden teeth necessary—just look presidential. Nothing to it, though you might want to shave that beard."

Ledyard helped Emma step up into the box of the carriage. "It's not for a few weeks yet, so Miss Fern, you talk him into it."

Fern looked amused with the prospect. "I'll do my best. Thank you for visiting."

"Our pleasure," said Ledyard, slapping the reins down on the horse and turning the buggy around.

As Booth and Fern went inside the cabin, she took his arm and said, "The Father of Our Country."

"I don't want to make a fool of myself on a stage."

"Oh, please," Fern said. "It'll be good fun—and it's for a good cause, you know. Help the local schoolmarm."

He put his hand to the beard that now ran full under his jaws. "I would have to part with this."

"It is a small sacrifice for our only house of learning."

"It's my civic duty, then."

"Indeed it is, Marlowe."

He wondered how identifiable he might yet be. Before a crowd, the odds of discovery increased. He'd put on some weight, but his face appeared to him unchanged. Without a moustache, however, and topped by a Washingtonian wig of white hair, he doubted anyone would look twice at him, except perhaps to laugh. If so, just as well.

Booth took Fern's hands and kissed her. "We are going to have guests tomorrow, very interesting Sunday guests."

"Really? Who?"

"I will tell you all about it when I get back from town."

He seldom went to town these days. It was not so much the fear of being recognized—to the world, Booth was dead—as it was enjoying the freedom of anonymity. Fort Benton, despite his friendly acquaintances there, was still a very rough place, where strangers came and went, some benign, others sparking apprehension and gunfights.

Booth needed a large cardboard for the painting he planned of Tall Elk. He passed the *Yellowstone*, newly arrived at the dock and unloading passengers. As he guided his horse along the riverfront to I.G. Baker's store, it seemed to him much longer than a year since he had arrived on that same paddle-wheeler.

Inside the store he was selecting a cardboard from a rack when Isaac Baker spotted him and came over.

"Marlowe, my friend—such a hermit! Where are the new paintings? Customers are arriving. And all the gold bugs who have wintered at Bannack will be passing through on their way to St. Louis. Bring them in. T'is the season!"

Booth shook his hand. "I'll have glorious surprises for you soon, I promise."

"Is it true you're to be Washington in the pageant?" said Baker. "They've got me playing Jefferson. I can't act worth beans."

"Neither can I," said Booth. "I fear what little respect I might have in this town may vanish the moment I pretend to be Washington."

Baker chuckled, slapped him on the back, and strolled away.

Booth was walking back to the hitching post with the board under his arm when his sense of security evaporated altogether. He pulled his hat down and ducked into a doorway, breathing hard.

Could it be? It *was*.

The small man crossed the street in front of him, no more than a hundred feet away. His bowler hat, fashionable suit and tie, and small suitcase left no doubt as to his identity.

How in God's name had that bastard Upham tracked him to Fort Benton? Surely it couldn't be coincidence—the West was too big. No, the man had guessed. He knew everything. God Almighty. It had all been too good to last.

Hugging the storefronts, Booth followed Upham as the reporter made his way up the street. Where was he going? To Fern's cabin? Did he know that much?

Now Upham stopped in front of The Star. He took his watch out of his vest and appeared to check the time. Then he went into the saloon. Booth sidled up to the swinging doors and cautiously peered inside.

Upham stood at the bar, his suitcase on the floor beside him. Luke drew a beer and placed it on the counter. Booth saw Upham take something from his coat pocket, a piece of paper. Then earless but sharp-eyed Luke was studying it—a photograph, Booth realized. The bartender shook his head and handed it back to Upham, who slipped it back into a coat pocket. He drained his glass in one long pull, slapped a coin onto the bar, and picked up his suitcase.

Booth quickly went around the corner and hid in a doorway. Upham walked hesitantly away from The Star, then stopped, turning in a slow circle. It was as if the reporter had a sixth sense. Booth did not move. Upham stared at the Missouri river for a few seconds, then walked to Huntley's stage depot. Booth followed at a distance.

Seven men and two women stood in front of the small cabin as their luggage was loaded and lashed on top of the four-horse stagecoach. Upham handed over his carpet bag and stepped up into the coach.

Booth waited for five more minutes until the driver cracked the whip. The four big horses lunged forward, and the rattling stage headed toward the south end of town. He watched until it had disappeared from sight.

Booth was trembling. When he had caught his breath, he went to the depot cabin and found the dispatcher, a lean, tobacco-chewing man in red suspenders.

"Mind telling me where that stage was headed?"

"Scheduled for the fine and civilized metropolis of Bannack," the man said laconically. "Unless the Blackfeet get 'em first!"

# CHAPTER TWENTY SEVEN

There was no way out. Booth returned to the cabin after watching Langford Upham board the stagecoach to Bannack. He would have to confess to Fern that he was a murderer. It would be a relief to get at least that off his conscience. But no details, certainly not Ford's Theater, not *The Event.* No—not to Fern who held Lincoln in such high regard, who idolized the man. She would never understand that what he had done was no different than killing an enemy soldier in battle.

He would tell her of having seen the reporter, his pursuer, but he would only identify Upham as a witness, someone capable of alerting the community and the world that he was a fugitive criminal. They would discuss fleeing Fort Benton to start a new life far away. Perhaps in Canada. Yes, Canada, a vast country where no one could find them, not even Upham. The border was just two days ride north. It would be easy to disappear. But suppose she chose not to leave her comfortable life and beloved teaching to go on the run with a fugitive? He would have to slink away in the night. But that was unthinkable.

Things changed when he actually started to tell her. She looked so beautiful and vulnerable as she led him through the kitchen to the cabin's main room.

"Dear," he began, "dear Fern." He took her hand hesitantly as they sat on the deerskin-covered bench. "I must tell you something. Something very important."

"Yes, Marlowe?"

She was so gentle.

"Dearest—" The words would not come.

"You know you can tell me anything."

He took a deep breath. *Better not.* In his mind he saw the face of that little ferret, Upham. Sometime soon the reporter would be back in Benton to track him down.

"I have killed," he said. "I've killed another human being."

There—it was out.

But she didn't seem shocked. Not at all. "It was the war," she said. "The terrible war."

He didn't know how far to go.

"It was—yes— an aspect of the war," he said. "But beyond it. I wasn't innocent. And he wasn't innocent. He had harmed others."

"I understand," she said. "I also am a murderer."

"You?" he exclaimed.

"A failed one, but no less of one. I certainly tried my best to kill someone, and that is the same thing."

"Whom?"

"I told you my stepfather did worse to me than this," she said, pointing to her face. "It happened the last time my mother had to leave our house overnight." She spoke calmly, but her fingernails dug into the palm of his hand. "She went to tend my grandmother. As soon as she was gone, that bastard came into my bedroom, naked, again. But this time I had hidden the poker from the fireplace and when he came toward the bed I rose up and I hit him. Hit him down there. Then smack across the head as hard as I could. Then down there again." She was whispering now. "And I hit him and hit him and jabbed him in his fat stomach and chest until he was covered with blood and I fled that house. He didn't die, but I wanted him to. Oh God, I wanted him to die with all my heart." She leaned back. "So you see, I also am a murderer."

Booth held her tightly in his arms. "My poor Fern," he murmured. Then he said, "My crime was worse, far worse. I killed an unarmed— soldier. Actually, a high officer. A general. I shot him in the neck. I murdered him."

She put a finger to his lips.

"Shhh—dear Marlowe. That was wartime. That belongs to the past. I have my cruel past and you have yours. We have left that behind, in the East. We must think only of the future. Our future, and someone else's."

"Who would that be?"

She looked up at him with shining eyes. "Guess what, Mr. Marlowe? I am going to have your baby."

He didn't quite understand. "Well, that would be quite an idea," he said. "Wouldn't it?"

"It's already begun. I'm three months along."

He was stunned. She was serious. He felt as if he were falling into a pit.

"You're happy? I can feel it! You're trembling!"

"Yes, I am very happy."

He loved children, but now? A child would vastly complicate his life—their life together. His mind was spinning. Her pregnancy might slow their escape to Canada. *Damn Upham to Hell.*

Then the spinning stopped, and the despair lifted. It was as if the sun had broken through the clouds after one of those quick Montana thundershowers. And he suddenly knew that he loved this woman. He would never leave her. The mother of his child should never know whom he had murdered.

In the months since *The Event*, he himself had come to regret what he had done, for as bitter a thing as it was to concede, he knew he had accomplished nothing good by it. If only he had asked for a personal audience with Lincoln at the White House during the War. Perhaps he could have softened Lincoln's inflexible opposition to the Secession. *Perhaps Lincoln would have softened my fervor as well.* He stroked Fern's hair as she lay against his chest, squeezing his hand. *I do not deserve such love. I must make myself worthy of it, somehow.*

Booth sat at the kitchen table, thinking, as Fern prepared supper. Humming softly, every few minutes she would turn to look at him and smile—like a girl in love for the first time, he thought.

Perhaps if Upham found no trace of J. W. Booth in Bannack he would give up the chase. No. Not after coming this far. But perhaps he was here for an altogether different reason. Booth knew that was wishful thinking, too.

"John—are you listening? What shall we name the child?"

He was at a loss. "Let me think for a moment."

"If it's a girl," she said, "I would like to suggest Lillian, after my mother."

"And if it's a boy?"

"Of course, after you. John Richard Marlowe, Jr."

Should he not insist on their leaving Benton? But how could he? This was her life, a fine, worthy, purposeful life she'd made for herself, in a land of extraordinary beauty.

*It is just a question of time before Upham shows up. He's a yappy terrier, but with the tenacity of a bulldog.*

"Did you hear me? Named after you!"

"A boy should have his own name." The old man and his poor brother Junius.

"All right," she said. "Would you consider John Abraham Marlowe?"

He almost laughed. Then he nodded numbly. "Whatever you wish, dear."

*Are the gods doing this to mock me, or torment me—or both?*

He told her about encountering Tall Elk, and his arrangement for the Blackfeet to come here to pose.

"You mean tomorrow—here? An Indian in this house? Blackfeet?"

"Yes."

She frowned. "Oh John. Blackfeet are not to be trusted. The post Indians that hang around the fort are drunkards and thieves."

"These are not post Indians. They are glorious! You'll see," he said. "It will be perfectly all right. I have made friends with Tall Elk, such as two alien creatures may be friends. I would not dare to risk any harm to you." He decided then not to show her the scalp Tall Elk had given him.

They went to bed, turned out the lantern and, under the warm buffalo robe, made gentle love. Afterwards he kissed her still-flat stomach. She squeezed his hand and murmured sleepily, "John Abraham Marlowe."

"Lillian Fern Marlowe," he replied sternly.

As Fern slept, her breath warm against his shoulder, he prayed silently to a God he had never been able to fully accept: *I have sinned, but I ask that You not visit Thy wrath upon this good woman and our child.*

Tall Elk and two of his braves rode up to the cabin early the next morning. Silent in their arrival, they were suddenly just there at the gate.

"Good morning, Tall Elk."

"Good morning, John Friend."

The Blackfeet followed Booth into the cabin. Fern masked her terror by pretending to putter about unconcernedly as the warriors wandered wordlessly, running their brown fingers over objects that intrigued them, sharing quiet amusement over some, puzzlement over others.

"They are most courteous, aren't they," said Booth, squeezing her arm. "A savage gentility."

She looked at him in wide-eyed wonderment. "This is indeed a weekend of surprises," she observed softly.

Tall Elk was pleased to sit in a chair on the porch for his portrait. He sat motionless for forty-five minutes, as though made of granite. Booth completed one profile sketch quickly, then offered him coffee. He drew another, head-on, for himself.

The pose was heroic, the colors vibrant. Tall Elk's burnt sienna skin with bluish highlights contrasted with the yellow beads on the band of the headdress, the ivory eagle feathers standing out starkly against a greenish sky. Booth knew it owed much to Catlin but he was nonetheless pleased with the result. He would add more details later. He handed the first sketch to his subject. The Indian's stern expression barely changed, but he was clearly pleased. He held it close to his face and then at arm's length. He showed the picture to his two braves who studied the image and nodded solemnly.

Fern could not take her eyes off the Blackfeet. As they prepared to remount their horses, Tall Elk turned with an abrupt movement, and Fern jumped back in alarm. For the first time, he smiled. In his hand was a large knife with an elk antler handle in a beaded sheaf. He flipped the weapon around and held out the bone handle to Booth, who took it, and dipped his head in thanks.

"You come my tepees, John Friend," said Tall Elk, pointing toward the hills.

"I will come soon, Tall Elk," said Booth. "Thank you." He put a hand over his heart, hoping that might be a gesture transcending language. Tall Elk nodded and did the same. Then as if it were a novelty trick, the Blackfoot held out his hand.

Booth shook it heartily, and Tall Elk smiled.

He was thrilled to be invited to sketch an Indian village. It also occurred to him that it might afford an escape route if Upham got too close.

The Blackfeet leapt onto their ponies' backs and rode off without a backward glance.

"They seem to have absolutely no artifice," said Booth.

"You've made a formidable friend," said Fern as they watched the horsemen disappear around a bend above the river. "I have never actually spoken to an Indian before. Perhaps I've been wrong about them."

"We are often wrong about people," said Booth. "Especially ourselves."

## CHAPTER TWENTY EIGHT

As he bounced along in the stagecoach to Bannack, Upham conceded that his father was right in one respect: he wasn't cut out for the rough life of the Territory of Montana. The three days since walking down the gangway of the *Yellowstone* had been the most uncomfortable of his life. Now he was jammed in a lurching box with eight other people, six of whom had apparently not bathed since sprouting their first whiskers. Loud and hearty miners, they never stopped talking about gold they had found or were going to find or should have found. Their crude jokes involving mules, darkies, Indian whores, and latrines appalled him.

His other two traveling companions were a Methodist lay preacher and his prim wife who were returning to their home in Bannack. They rarely spoke to each other or anyone else, and blankly stared at the passing scenery. Made peevish by the jostling, dusty journey, Upham furtively studied the grimly pious couple with an unkind eye. With her red bonnet and long pointed nose, he thought, she looked like a woodpecker about to drill a pine. The Reverend's two prominent front teeth gave him the aspect of a beaver ready to attack an aspen.

The stage lurched, bounced, and shuddered so often he could rarely pencil observations into his notebook. The ordeal finally sapped him of any goal except to survive it. If one desired mountains, he mused, there were a plethora. If one sought mental stimulus this was the Sahara without oases. He was bored by the flora, the fauna, and the scenery, whose names lacked the heritage and sophistication of Eastern landmarks. They careened past Little Prickly Pear River, Niggerhead Mountain, Bloody Dick Peak, Rattlesnake Creek and Dead Indian Hill. During rest stops he dutifully scribbled notes for future articles.

The road was terrible from start to finish—a flash flood at a creek ford had waylaid them for seven hours—and the relentless rocking of the coach kept him on the edge of nausea. The food offered in the roadhouses at which they stopped was inedible. After three days, in late afternoon, Bannack hove blessedly into the distance.

In a rare burst of garrulity, the minister volunteered that, since the discovery of gold at Grasshopper Creek three years ago, Bannack had grown to a population of "about 2,000 souls."

Upham nodded politely, thinking, Hades or Limbo?

"Grasshopper Creek is a tributary of the Beaverhead River," added the preacher.

"Ah!" said Upham, "ah-hah!" He nodded as if this were a revelation that made sense of many of life's mysteries. When one miner broke wind loudly, all three howled with laughter. The preacher and his wife declined to react.

"It was originally named Willard's Creek by Lewis and Clark," continued the preacher, determined to uphold civility. "Way back when."

"Fascinating," said Upham. "Fascinating. Who was Willard?"

"Don't know," said the preacher.

All he could see on the outskirts of town were rows of tents. "As a resident here, Reverend, have you ever come across a woman named Wilma Harrison?"

The clergyman's beaver teeth jutted down over his lower lip as he pondered the question. Upham noticed his quick glance at his wife.

"We know Wilma," he said. "And we know Robert Harrison."

"Wilma," said Upham, "is the cousin of an army comrade of mine."

"They live in The Castle," volunteered the man's birdlike wife.

"The Castle?"

"Up on the hill," she said. "Biggest house in town. You can't help but see it."

The stagecoach passed the last row of tents and rounded a low hill where a row of freshly painted wooden tombstones marked what looked like a group burial. Nearby was a gallows, blessedly not bearing fruit.

"That's Boot Hill," said the preacher. "They buried the Plummer gang two years ago. And there's the gallows."

"Plummer?"

"Henry Plummer was our sheriff. Came out from Virginia City in

222

California. A gentleman, it seemed. Until he started robbing people in his spare time, when they went out of town. Gold brings sin if one's not careful. Thank God for Wilbur Sanders and the other God-fearing men who stood up to this menace and hanged him."

The stage delivered them onto the main street of Bannack. This was the territorial capital of Montana Territory. It was like Fort Benton but without the river. It was a bigger town, with several thousand miners. A series of saloons stood shoulder to shoulder with painted storefronts: Bakery, Assayer, General Store, Carpenter, Undertaker. The muddy street—why did every town out here have a stinking muddy street? Mud made up of equal parts of bovine, equine, and human urine mixed with earth. Bannack teemed with shouting bearded men, some laden with gold-washing pans hanging off their backs, and always a pick and shovel in hand or strapped to their packs. There was a throng of mud-flecked horsemen, clanking wagons, braying mules, snarling dogs, cackling chickens, and the occasional garbage-eating pig. It was all chaos and muck. The romantic Wild West of cowboys and Indians that Upham had read of was not apparent in this bustling outpost, founded and built overnight by wild-eyed greed.

The stagecoach pulled up in front of the two-story Goodrich Hotel. Upham was first out of the coach, landing on legs so stiff that as he hobbled up the steps and into the white clapboard hotel a prospector took his measure, spat tobacco juice, and observed to his partner, "There's a little cripple."

After registering and washing up, Upham ventured down the muddy street to the Skinner saloon and ordered a beer. The barber in the corner was singing a low ditty to his customer.

The bartender asked, "Is you paying in dust, coin, or paper?"

"Er, coin."

"That's best."

When the mustachioed barman slid the foaming glass in front of him, Upham held up the photograph of Booth.

"Any chance you've seen my friend hereabouts?"

The barman shook his head. "Bears the look of the actor fella—John Wilkes Booth, don't he?"

"Many people have said that to him," said Upham.

"Bad luck. Could get hisself shot hereabouts. Or honored. Lots of Rebs out here. I ain't one, in case you're asking."

"Is that so? But imagine the face without the moustache," Upham prompted. "Maybe lighter hair, or with a beard?"

"Lots of beards out here," said the man. "Haven't seen him. Sorry."

The bartender moved up the counter to take another order. Upham pocketed the photograph, picked up his glass, and stood by a window, watching the street traffic. *Who are these people?*


The large wooden house stood atop a barren hill directly behind the hotel. Surrounded by humble clapboard houses, log cabins, and tents—tents everywhere—the stolid two-story edifice proudly boasted gingerbread trim. It should have been in Providence, Rhode Island or Litchfield, Connecticut for God's sake. Not surrounded by tents and mud.

Upham trudged up the hill, quickly out of breath, and knocked on the ornate but somewhat crudely carved front door. He waited for about half a minute before it opened part way. A woman peered out at him. She was far taller than Upham, at least six feet tall. He blinked up at her.

"What do you want?"

"Mrs. Harrison?"

"What do you want?" she said suspiciously.

"I'm Langford Upham, a friend of your cousin Wilson Beech. I've come a long way."

She exhibited no trace of welcome. She had short sandy hair, a square mannish face, and wore a gaudy red and black dress. She looked more suited to a flannel shirt and dungarees, with a mule out back. This was no Mrs. Van Rennselaer or Livingston.

"We were in the army together," Upham said finally. "Charlotte sent me."

"Money? Is that what you want?"

"I'm a newspaperman," said Upham, handing her his calling card.

"You want money, don't you," she said. It was a statement, not a question. Only then did she glance at his card.

"I assure you I do not. I am employed by a New York City newspaper owned by my father, and I am here on assignment. May I have just a few minutes of your time?"

"Everyone wants something from us," she said. "No one has asked for time before. It's always money."

"I regret to hear that. I'm sure it's vexing. But I'm here only to inquire after my good friend Wilson."

The woman hesitated. Then she opened the door, motioning Upham inside. The large foyer and the parlor beyond were unlike the woman, excessively feminine and filled with *objets d'art* which looked to the reporter as expensive as they were tasteless.

"You have a lovely house, Mrs. Harrison. Very well-appointed."

"So what about Willy?"

"So many nice things. Such a nice house. You must be proud of it. I sense hard work."

She shrugged. "Robert and I were lucky. We got to Grasshopper Creek early, found The Golden Girl lode quick, and kept our mouths shut. This was our genius. No one, I mean no one, knew. We staked all the claims around the lode. I give us credit for that. The rest was luck. But that's life, isn't it?"

"How true."

She indicated a chair for Upham. She sat on the red silk divan opposite him and lit a cheroot. "So what about Willy?"

"Mrs. Harrison," he asked, in a tone as light as he could muster, "have you seen him lately?"

"Why in hell would I see Willy?"

"Well, he always said that, after the war, he'd come out here to Bannack and try his luck. It was nearly a catechism for him. He nearly chanted about the gold floating around the place. Manna from heaven, etcetera."

"Well," said Wilma with a dry laugh. "He better hurry. Gold's dryin' up fast everywhere. The Golden Girl's played out. Nearly finished. We sold half to an English fella at the peak. Old gal stumbled after that. But she did well by us in her day. Willy'd be better off in Helena or Butte. There's silver now. And copper's coming in with a big tune. But there's nothing like gold, is there, Mr. Upham?"

"Yes, madam," said Upham. "You haven't seen him, then?"

"Who?"

"Wilson Beech."

"The last time I seen Willy, he and Charlotte were living down there on that miserable farm in Virginia. That must have been at least six years ago, before he signed up."

"You mean joined the Confederate Army?"

She laughed bitterly. "He flipped a coin to decide whether he'd join the North or the South. Nothing ever seems to work out for Willy."

Upham took out the photograph of Booth and showed it to her. "May I ask you if you've ever seen this man?"

The woman squinted as she looked at the image. "Never seen him, no. But he looks like that actor who shot—"

Upham heard a ghostly moan from the hallway.

"Wilma?" A feeble voice cried from behind a half-open door. "Who's there?"

The door swung open to reveal a skeletal barefoot man wearing just a stained nightshirt. He shuffled on bird-like legs. Upham recoiled at his bluish-white pallor. Unsteady, the man clutched the doorjamb with a bony hand.

"Just a friend of Willy's," she said tenderly. "Here on business. Go back to bed, dear. I'll bring you some soup in a few minutes."

"Hello," said the man in a hoarse whisper.

"Hello, sir," said Upham. "Please excuse my intrusion."

Robert Harrison's eyes were sunk so deep in their hollows that Upham could see only the highlights reflecting from them. His blue lips moved soundlessly. Then a few seconds later, he said, "Put a little brandy in it, Wilma. Not much, just a little."

"I will, dear."

He gave Wilma a little wave, then turned slowly and shuffled back into the bedroom, leaving the door ajar.

"There's all kinds of luck, isn't there, Mr. Upham," said Wilma, her manner much softened. "God says, 'take what you want, but pay for it.' All that gold Bobby and I found, nuggets and shovel-loads and a wheelbarrowful in a week! But it can't cure cancer. It's in his stomach. All through his stomach. You have to wonder why."

Upham shook his head. "I'm truly sorry, madam."

Tears welled in her eyes. Upham reproached himself for his earlier assessment of her. He thanked her for her hospitality and left.

Discouraged, he trudged back down the hill to the hotel and reserved a seat on the morning stagecoach back to Fort Benton. He did not bother to canvass the noisy bars that stretched to the end of town. Why bother strangers with the photograph of Booth? He knew his was a lost cause if Wilma Harrison and the bartender hadn't seen him.

Back in his upstairs room at the Goodrich, he quickly wrote a two-page description of his impression of "the new Eldorado," the town of Bannack, including a "buzzard's eye view of a superb example of the nouveau riche, the Robert Harrisons." He felt a pang of guilt depicting them as parvenus, but he faced the requirement to justify an expensive wild goose—or prairie chicken—chase, as they'd no doubt call it back at *The World*. Another episode in "Junior's Follies." Besides, by the time it would be published, Robert Harrison would be dead, and the odds that a copy of *The World* would ever find its way to Bannack were slim.

He described their house as "inappropriately elegant in this Godforsaken land as a Christmas tree decorated in the Gobi desert by a demented Midas, including several *gen-yu-wyne* Tiffany lamps all the way from New York. If you don't believe it, why, just look at the price tag still affixed."

It would be the first in the series of articles he had promised Tompkins. He was not particularly proud of the mocking tone, but his mood was foul. He handed it to the hotel desk clerk with instructions to send it immediately.

"Sorry, sir. There ain't no telegraph service in this part of the Territory."

Upham lowered his head to the counter and groaned. That possibility had not occurred to him. His dispatch would be put in a postal pouch and carried by stage to Fort Benton, thence taken by steamer downriver to Omaha, where the Pacific Telegraph Company would wire it to Tompkins. "Omaha's only about eleven days from Fort Benton, sir," the clerk said proudly.

This part of the world is twenty years behind the rest of America, Upham thought. He strode miserably from the lobby into the hotel bar and, for the first time in years, got thoroughly drunk. *This is an ignoble trade I pursue.* He laid the photograph of Booth down in front of him on the polished wood of the counter. Somewhere behind him piano keys tinkled in a macabre manner.

"There's some connection," he murmured to himself. "There's got to be a connection."

"Sure there is," said the young but gray-faced bartender, who proceeded to match him drink for drink.

"I mean, it's all connected," said Upham, slapping the bar with the earnest desire of the inebriated to convince. "Beech—Booth—Bannack, all connected! All B's! Cosmic . . . cosmically . . . connected."

"'Course they are," said the bartender.

"Damn right," said Upham.

"Bet your life."

"But how?"

"Got me, pardner."

"Got me too."

"Have another shot?"

"Is that some sort of trick question?"

It was past midnight when Upham wobbled up to his room, almost reached the bed, but fell to the floor and passed out.

His hangover was such that he could not face the prospect of a stomach-churning stagecoach ride back to Fort Benton until three days later.


Back finally in Benton, he wrote his articles in the comfort of his tiny room at the freshly built Overland Hotel—luxurious compared to Bannack. He took long walks down by the Missouri and up to the bluffs. He used interviews and his imagination to fill in for what he lacked in personal experience of the Wild West. So he stayed on in Fort Benton, penning his articles and putting them in the pouch for Omaha. Two more weeks passed. He kept a calendar on his wall to track the progress of his dispatches down the river. Once he knew that six had likely been wired to Tompkins, his sense of isolation began to lift. One afternoon, as he deposited an envelope holding a pair of articles at the steamboat office, the clerk noted his name.

"Langford Upham? Telegram for you, just arrived. Brought upriver from Omaha."

He took the envelope from the agent's hand apprehensively.

*Lang—400 dollars quite a sum for 12 pages. Your father disappointed. Need more unusual people, why there, expectations, costumes, color. Details! More Indians, mountain men, enterprises. No comedy. Where Eldorado? Remember what we need from afar. Cheers. Tompkins.*

His temper simmering, Upham had a glass of beer at The Star, re-reading Tompkins' wire, then throwing it down again. He had sent them a profile of The Star's earless bartender Luke; another on the peculiar English spoken by the Blackfeet braves who came to town to trade; and one humorous piece on the exotic pleasures of Wild West stagecoach travel. He had also revisited the Plummer gang's rapine exploits in Bannack. There was an especially good one on the perils of piloting a riverboat on a shallow river where buffalo created traffic jams—he had interviewed the captain of the *Lady Parkinson*. And a tongue-in-cheek discussion on how to avoid getting shot while making a living as a one-legged, half-scalped saloon gambler with shaky hands who went by the name of "Lucky Pete." *Wasn't that color enough?*

He left the saloon and wandered idly along the waterfront. A sharp hoot echoed from the whistle of a packet boat about to depart. *I will be damned glad to leave with your sister ship, my dear.*

Seeking inspiration or color—*something*—he ambled along the waterfront's mercantile row. *Not exactly Fifth Avenue.* As he passed the I.G. Baker general store, he noticed some paintings and colored sketches in the window. Most were of animals, but there were also studies of Indian braves, surprisingly well done. A portrait of a fierce warrior in a feathered headdress caught his eye. *Almost as good as Catlin. Almost.*

He was still admiring it when I.G. Baker stepped outside.

"I see you have good taste, sir," said the merchant, introducing himself as the proprietor and welcoming him to Fort Benton with a warm handshake.

"Who made these, Mr. Baker?"

"Fellow named Marlowe, artiste extraordinaire. Brilliant young man. I can let you have that one of the chief for only forty dollars. It's his masterpiece. A Blackfeet warrior called Tall Elk. Wonderful color, no?"

"Forty?" Upham exclaimed.

"An investment, sir. We'll be hearing from this artist, I'm certain of that."

In a boom-town in the middle of nowhere, mused Upham, everything was expensive. The shovels for sale behind the paintings were offered at twenty dollars—triple their usual price back East.

"Does he live around here?"

"Yes, a fine addition to the community. As you can see for yourself, we're fast becoming an outpost of culture as well as a hub of commerce. The future of the Territory is bright indeed, sir."

*Boosters*, thought Upham. *Carnival barkers all.* "Where is this artist?"

"Lives out of town. Bit of a loner. Friendly enough, though, when you get to know him."

Upham pondered the drawings. *The newspaper wants visuals? I'll give them visuals.* He would buy several and send them East, as illustrations for his pieces, and charge it to the paper.

"I'm a reporter for *The New York World*, Mr. Baker. Here to chronicle the Wild West, as it were."

"You don't say! Well, sir—if I may say so—we have here in Fort Benton a wealth of local color certain to be of *special* interest to your many readers. We are not without refinement. And perhaps not as wild as we were just a year ago."

"I might do a piece on this fellow. He's good."

"I sell his pictures faster than he paints 'em."

"His name again?"

"John Richard Marlowe."

"An illustrious theatrical name."

"That so?" said Baker. "Well, I hope he has talent in that direction as well—he's to play the part of George Washington in our Independence Day pageant. Now there's another story for you."

Sudden as a lightning bolt, Upham felt the pieces falling into place. Could it be? He recalled his meeting with Edwin Booth—*Johnny had a talent for drawing.* Upham felt his heart accelerating.

"When did this Marlowe arrive?"

"Well, let's see. Bought this buffalo picture—a year ago. August? Thereabouts. Now you must attend the July Fourth Pageant, Mr. Upham. Many of our leading citizens are taking part. I'll introduce you around, and I fully expect, as an artiste yourself, you'll find it inspirational."

"Mr. Baker, by any chance do you sell firearms?"

"I carry the very finest. What's your pleasure?"

"What should I have, you know, for protection at close quarters?"

"A good revolver, for starters. Essential. A rifle too, if you plan to venture far. Despite the sophistications here in town, this remains a wild region. Brigands. Indians galore. Not that long ago, this was a very dangerous place," said Baker. "See that tree?" He pointed to a tall cottonwood up the street. "Seventeen men have been hanged from it. Murderers, rustlers, highwaymen, common thieves, despoilers of women. Last year there were only four, and so far this year only one. Fort Benton is getting to be as safe as any place you can name."

"That's a testament to progress."

"The criminal element knows it has no place here," said Baker. "For the most part. Here in town, you needn't carry a piece. Except when there's trouble. Then you'll bless that iron."

"Mr. Baker," said Upham. "May I please see one of your revolvers?"

# CHAPTER TWENTY NINE

In the afternoon, Booth and Fern hitched the small wagon to Sagebrush and drove into Fort Benton for a rehearsal of the July Fourth pageant. They walked hand in hand past the makeshift church, past the big cottonwood "hanging tree," and entered an empty warehouse behind the I.G. Baker store.

The space had been swept clean, and its rafters echoed with the chatter of women sewing costumes. Partially costumed men and women rehearsed their lines on the hastily-constructed raised stage. The piano player from The Star, the coal-black man with the mischievous face of a born entertainer, played the tinny upright in accompaniment to a coloratura singing "Come Where My Love Lies Bleeding." Somewhere a banjo player was tuning up and a violin sang out "Jeannie With the Light Brown Hair."

*What happens if I come face to face with Upham, and he reveals me? I cannot let him wreck this happiness I've found. Fern's happiness. I might have to kill him.*

Emma Ledyard was there, her face powdered, her hair hidden under a white Dolly Madison wig, standing on a box while her maid stooped beside her, lowering the hem of her elaborate dress. Tommy Ledyard, dressed as a drummer boy, waved enthusiastically to his two teachers.

Tobias Ledyard, dressed as Ben Franklin, spotted Booth and Fern from across the hall and bustled up to them.

"Ah, here are the Washingtons!" he said cheerily. "Your costumes aren't quite ready. But, General, your Delaware-crossing boat is."

He led them over to where a carpenter was nailing the last board to the frame of a one-sided longboat on wheels. A young woman was painting scalloped waves on a long board that would be placed alongside it, to be rocked and pulled back and forth by stage hands tugging ropes in the wings.

"Now, next Wednesday, the big night, all you have to do is stand in the boat with the oarsmen and soldiers and look determined and presidential as the National Anthem is played, and you're wheeled across the stage."

Fern looked at Tobias Ledyard. "You mean he won't be saying anything?"

"He told me he didn't like to speak."

"But you're so good at it, John!"

"A wife's blind pride," said Booth.

"But it's true," she insisted.

"Well," said Ledyard, "why not say something like 'Onward men, across the Delaware!'"

"I could probably manage that," said Booth. "But no more."

At that moment he saw a tall man in a black suit, a stovepipe hat, and false chin whiskers walk out on the stage. Although the man had a round face and a bulbous nose, there was no doubt who he was supposed to be. Booth looked away.

Clearing his throat the man began to recite in an unpleasant nasal twang. "F-four score and t-ten years ago."

A fat woman behind him, holding a script, hissed, "Seven!"

"S-seven years ago," he intoned, "our fathers brought f-forth on this c-continent . . ." And on he stumbled, mangling the Gettysburg Address.

Booth closed his eyes and took a deep breath, as he had often done to suppress the effects of stage fright. It was the stutter that rattled him; in the dark stage behind his closed eyes appeared Davey Herold, struggling to speak, then dangling from a rope. *I shall always be haunted. It is the penance. May God spare me. For Fern's sake. And for the baby's.*

Fern leaned close to Tobias Ledyard's ear. "Is this the best Lincoln our town has to offer?"

Tobias looked pained. "I'm afraid so. That's Dudley Gunn. He begged to play the part. Well, his wife insisted, and he had the right costume."

"The undertaker?"

"As noble and necessary a profession as any other," said Booth. He had a terrible notion of what Fern was thinking.

"With all respect to Mr. Gunn," she whispered, "his performance is an insult to Lincoln's memory. It is comic."

"Perhaps I could rehearse him," Booth said, grasping for a way to deflect her.

"You could do it so much better yourself," she replied.

"Not a bad idea," said Tobias.

Booth held his hand up in protest. "No—no. I'm honored enough to play Washington. And Mr. Gunn's feelings would be greatly hurt."

Fern smiled at him, shook her head, and rolled her eyes as Tobias took her arm.

"Marlowe, or should I say General Washington! I'll take Mrs. Washington here over to the other First Ladies and rehearse her briefly. Terribly simple, my dear, never fear." Prancing in a courtly fashion, the round little man escorted her across the room.

Waiting for Fern's rehearsal to conclude, Booth tried not to listen to the words of Lincoln's battlefield address, as Gunn struggled to commit them to memory. Claiming to need some air, he stepped outside and watched the late afternoon sun play on the river.

When Fern was finished, she came looking for him. He took her firmly by the elbow and, smiling and nodding graciously to the townsfolk, urged her toward their buggy.

Crossing the street they saw Moody Suggs confront Isaac Baker dressed as Thomas Jefferson.

Swaying drunkenly, a near-empty whiskey bottle in his hand, Suggs had the merchant's lapel firmly in his grip and was rudely shaking him. "Who's the sorry son of a bitch playing Lincoln in there?"

"We're just rehearsing a play, Moody. Now let go of me!"

"I will not let—nobody! Gah-damn Lincoln!" The bottle slipped from his fingers and fell to the street.

"Calm down, Moody," said Baker, pulling his coat from the drunkard's paw. "It's just play-acting, for God's sake!"

Suggs stepped back, stumbled, and looked around as if he were lost. He flung an arm sideways, then turned and reeled away in a stupor.

Booth steered Fern away from this bathetic scene. "Suggs is hopeless. Let's go."

From his vantage point in a dark narrow alley, Upham watched his quarry walk arm-in-arm with a woman dressed as Martha Washington. He saw them cross to the opposite side of the street to avoid a drunken altercation between the storekeeper Baker and a rowdy hothead with a Southern accent.

*Got you now, Booth. I wasn't imagining it.* He wished his father could be here to witness his moment of triumph.

From the shadows Upham watched Baker, still in the street, tucking in the shirtfront the drunken lout had yanked from his waistband. The merchant stepped up to a storefront and stood before his reflection in a window, positioning his tricorne hat and adjusting the scarf around his neck. As he resumed his walk toward the hall, Upham stepped out of the shadows and hurried to overtake him.

"Mr. Baker!"

Baker turned. "Ah, the intrepid newspaperman."

"An interesting outfit you're wearing tonight, sir."

"We're rehearsing the pageant. Finding things to write about in our little town?"

"Oh quite, quite," said Upham. "Mr. Baker, that gentleman who just passed—the one with the lady—was that the artist you told me of?"

"Exactly, that was Marlowe. You must write about him."

Upham had seen him for but a few seconds. He looked profoundly different from the man who had claimed to be Beech, the one he had seen leaving Lee's house over a year ago. That man had been blond and clean-shaven. This one calling himself Marlowe was dark-haired with a fringe of beard around his jaw. He appeared older, his face gaunt, the dark eyes deep-set and brooding. *But the less he looks like the so-called Beech, the more he looks like Booth.*

"He reminded me of someone I knew," said Upham.

"Soon he'll remind all of us," said Baker. "He plays President Washington in our upcoming pageant. He's ever so clever."

"Ah, frontier theater," said Upham. "Now there's an article."

"Why don't you come on inside with me, Mr. Upshur—"

"Upham."

"Mr. Upham, of course! Tobias Ledyard is our director. He's looking for someone to play John Adams."

"The whole pantheon, eh?"

"By any chance would you care to join our little troupe for Wednesday's performance?" said Ledyard.

"I might," said Upham, absently looking down the street where Booth had just walked. "I just might, sir, though I must tell you that my histrionic talents are limited."

"Nonsense, sir. You will have an uplifting, patriotic experience, I promise you. The experience of your life!"

# CHAPTER THIRTY

The next morning, Booth slid his sketch pad and pencils into the leather bags behind the saddle, preparing to ride out to Tall Elk's village. Fern watched him with a peculiar foreboding.

"Be careful, Marlowe," she said as Booth put his foot in the stirrup and swung up onto Sagebrush. "Take the rifle."

"They won't hurt me."

"They are not really our friends. You don't know them. Take the rifle."

"I trust Tall Elk, he knows that," said Booth. "A rifle would tell him differently."

"Indians are Indians," she said. "I have seen what they can do."

"I'll be all right."

"I am barely a bride, Marlowe. Don't make me a widow. Think of your child."

"I think of little else," Booth said. "Except the child's beautiful mother."

He leaned down from the horse and kissed her. Then he cantered off. She stood on the porch and watched him get smaller and smaller, then disappear into the cottonwoods.

Fern spent the morning cultivating her little garden behind the cabin. Summer had come to the prairie, bringing long hot days. She took pride in the lettuce, beets, and carrots that stuck their heads out of the black earth.

Putting away her trowel, she washed her hands by the well, then went inside to work on her Martha Washington costume. Adding a white lace collar to a simple black gown gave it the look of a century-old dress. As she sewed, she thought of Marlowe, the strange, wonderful unknown quantity that had come into her life and changed it so profoundly.

Long before he confessed to her, she'd sensed he was running away from something or someone. Lately it seemed to have been pressing down on him again, but this weekend his mood was lighter. She didn't want to know what black demon might lurk in his past. She had taken him as he was, a kind, sensitive—and perhaps damaged—person; she knew he would be a good father to their child and a loyal husband.

She stood at a window to watch a pair of crows fighting noisily over a small fish one had brought up from the river. The birds cawed raucously at each other and flapped their wings over the silvery carcass. *So wary of everything and yet so full of bravado.* What actors, she mused.

She was finishing the costume when she heard a soft but insistent knock on the door. Obliquely, through the window, she saw a stranger. She flipped a scarf over her head and knotted it under her chin. She lifted the rifle from its pegs, cocked the hammer, and held it in one hand, out of sight behind the door, while she lifted the latch.

Opening the door, she found a small man in a black derby and a well-tailored city suit framed against the wide river and massive bluffs. He looked comically out of place.

"Yes?" she said.

The man gave a bow and flashed what he fancied to be an ingratiating smile.

"Miss, I am a reporter from *The New York World*. My name is Langford Upham."

She disliked him immediately, though she couldn't have given a reason.

"I am interested in talking to Mr. Marlowe. Does he in fact live here?"

She nodded.

"May I ask your name, Miss?" he said.

"I am Mrs. Marlowe," she said for the first time in her life. It felt good and strengthening to say it.

Upham's eyes widened in surprise. "You are Marlowe's *wife*?"

"Yes."

"Madam, may I ask how long you have been married?"

"May I ask you, sir, why that should matter to anyone?"

240

Upham was at a loss for an answer.

"What do you want of my husband?"

"I admire his work," he said.

"Good," she said. "If you wish to purchase some of it, see Isaac Baker in town."

"What I want is to talk to the artist—Mr. Marlowe."

Fern felt certain that this man boded ill.

"Why do you wish to speak with him? He only does his trade through Mr. Baker's store. They have an arrangement."

"I find it interesting to encounter such talent out here in the wild. I'm in the Territory to write a series of articles for my paper—sketches of frontier life, that sort of thing. I thought it would make an interesting article."

Fern didn't respond.

"It might also enhance his reputation in fine art circles back East," urged Upham.

"I don't know that he wants his reputation 'enhanced', as you put it. He prefers to be left alone to paint and draw. We both prefer that."

"And where is he now, may I ask?"

"Painting and drawing. On the prairie."

He peered beyond her into the cabin.

"What a charming little home you have," he said. "Might I have a look around? For the article, you know."

Without waiting for an answer he stepped inside. She felt a panic at not having kept him out, and leveled the rifle at his chest. Upham froze.

"Ma'am, I mean no harm at all."

*Good God! She knows and is going to kill me.*

"I did not invite you in, sir."

"I—I thought you did."

"You weren't listening. People get shot out here for not listening."

"Very sorry. I misunderstood."

Fern studied him. His frightened eyes kept dropping to the muzzle of her rifle. *A cocksure city boy far from his element. We must all seem like peasants to him.*

Upham's throat was dry, and he backed up a step. He had a sickening image of his limp body sliding into a grave as she and Booth stood over it with shovels.

"Mrs. Marlowe, I assure you I meant no harm." He indicated her costume and wig on the kitchen table. "We're fellow actors, you know."

"I don't know."

"Yes! Mr. Ledyard has pressed me into the ranks, to play John Adams. In the pageant tomorrow. I understand your husband is to play General Washington. I wondered, since General Lee was a cousin of his wife, Martha Custis, if there was some connection? Perhaps he is an admirer of Lee?"

Something about Upham did not feel right, and it drained Fern of any impulse toward civility. When she did not respond, he made a show of eagerly surveying the sketches and unfinished paintings displayed around the room. She kept the rifle leveled.

"A beauty, that one of the bear. Sleeping bruin. Delightful!" His voice was tremulous with fear. "Ah yes, a lovely sky there!" he said in a frantic chirp. "And that charming eagle with his scornful beak."

Fern was surprised by the strength of her resolve. *I have so much to protect now.*

"I have work to do, sir."

"Yes, of course, but getting back to the pageant, they say Mr. Marlowe is quite good as Washington, quite the thespian. Is that so?"

"I don't know why they'd say that," said Fern. "They haven't seen him perform it. The part has practically no words."

"Mrs. Ledyard insists that he recites poetry beautifully."

"How would she know?"

"From their days shipboard. Six weeks."

Fern stared at him.

*What cold gray eyes she has. Merciless. God help me.*

"Did you hear me when I said I have work to do, Mr. Upham?"

It took Upham a moment to comprehend that she was not going to shoot him. Immediately the terrier in him returned. *She's frightened of me!* "Will Mr. Marlowe be along anytime soon?"

"By sundown, I suppose."

At that moment Booth appeared in the doorway, his sketchbook under one arm, his saddlebags over the other. "You suppose wrong, my dear," he said, glancing at Upham and just as quickly ignoring him. "I'm back early."

He strode into the cabin, brushing by the reporter, to lay his sketchbook and equipment down. He gently put his arm around Fern's shoulder. "Hunting up dinner, darling?" he asked lightly, nodding toward the rifle.

Puzzled by his insouciance, which she knew was false, she gave him a searching look. "As you see, we have a visitor."

"Upham," said the newsman, holding out his hand. "Langford Upham. I've come to see you."

"And so here you are," said Booth, neither warmly nor coldly, ignoring Upham's extended hand. "What can I do for you, sir?"

"I admire your work," said Upham. "I would like to write about you for *The New York World*."

"Why would you want to do that? I am not the New York sort."

"It would be interesting to our readers. A fine artist in the Wild West."

"An earnest amateur would be closer to the truth, and an article would not be of interest to your readers. Nor to me."

Booth took off his hat and hung it on a peg, turning his back on Upham. His casual disregard of the stranger's presence alarmed Fern; she still sensed the man was dangerous.

Booth poured himself a glass of water from the clay jug in the kitchen and returned to the front room where Fern and Upham stood facing each other in awkward silence. She was still holding the rifle but had lowered the muzzle to the floor.

"Fern, you should have seen that village! Teepees—wonderfully decorated teepees. Squaws and children going about their daily life, such as few people have seen them. Braves racing their ponies. Artisans making headdresses and bone ornaments and weapons and chipping flint arrowheads. Teepees painted with a panorama of their gypsy existence following the buffalo. Dogs that are half-wolf. A tame eagle. It was astounding. A caravansary of life on the plains."

Fern nodded, trying to share his enthusiasm, but Upham's presence in her home was oppressive and disturbing. *Doesn't Marlowe feel it, too?* She sensed something going on between them and was utterly bewildered.

Ignoring Upham completely now, Booth opened his sketchbook on the table in front of her and flipped through his quick studies and impressions. "I have weeks of wonderful material here," he exulted. "Tall Elk said I can come back any time I wish. You, too! Think of that. And Fern, you were wrong about him. We really can trust him. He offered to let me stay for a week."

"I gather you intend to stay here in Fort Benton for a while, Mr. Marlowe," interjected Upham.

Booth looked up at him as if surprised to find the man still in his house.

"Forever, actually."

There was another brittle silence as Booth turned the pages. Neither he nor Fern were really looking at them now.

"Well, I should be going," said Upham.

But he did not go. Instead he walked up close to Booth, too close for civility, and studied his face. Booth thought of his Bowie knife, tucked under their mattress. *How easy it would be to end this forever.*

"Mr. Marlowe, have we not met before?"

Booth met his gaze unblinkingly. "I have never met you, Mr. Upham."

"Could we not have met in Richmond?" Upham said.

"We could surely have met in Richmond," said Booth, "had I ever been in Richmond."

"You did not—fairly recently—go to a saloon there called The Black Rooster?"

"I do not drink, sir. And I have never been to Richmond."

"You did not have an interview with Robert E. Lee in Richmond last April?"

"As a Virginian, I would consider it a rare honor to have met General Lee, but as I told you, and you seem to have trouble remembering, I have never been in Richmond."

"You have a fine voice," said Upham, unfazed. "Mellifluous, I'd call it. Even trained. Have you never been on the stage, sir?"

Booth registered a thin smile. "Not even on the stage to Bannack."

"So I have not seen you in a theater?"

"I abhor the theater."

"You have never been an actor?"

"I am an artist," said Booth, "who prefers to be as far away from his audience and his critics as possible."

Upham glanced down at Booth's left hand. "You have a scar on your left hand."

"I injured myself rather foolishly picking up a hot shovel on the steamboat. I worked my way up river, you see. Shoveling coal in the boiler."

"That must have been painful."

"For a short time, but inconsequential," said Booth. "And now, Mr. Upham, at the risk of appearing rude, I must get to work. I need to make notes on my sketches while my memory is fresh. I must sing—on paper—for my supper."

Upham moved to the door. "Perhaps we can talk more at the pageant tomorrow."

"Perhaps." Booth held the door open. "Good day, sir."

As Upham stepped from the cabin Booth saw Tobias Ledyard drive up fast in his buggy, alone, at the reins of his matched bays. His usually jovial face was somber.

"A crisis, Marlowe, a crisis!" Ledyard blurted, as he struggled down from the buggy. Spotting Upham, he said "Ah, there's John Adams himself. Well, *mes enfants*, the town has had a bit of a disaster."

"Not another fire!" Fern gasped.

"No, no, it's Dudley Gunn," said Ledyard. "He's succumbed to a panic of stage fright. Bolted! Hiding someplace."

"Oh my," said Fern, relieved. "No Lincoln." She was smiling.

"I thought he volunteered," said Booth.

"He did, but you heard the poor fellow's feeble attempt at rehearsal. Overmatched," said Ledyard. "I feel bad for him."

"So what on earth are we going to do?" asked Fern, looking at Booth.

"He left us his costume, the stovepipe hat, and this book of Lincoln's speeches," said Toby, retrieving it from his buggy.

"So who can take his place?" asked Fern.

"I will volunteer my services," said Upham, his eyes never leaving Booth's face.

"You don't quite look the part, sir," said Ledyard bluntly. "You are

245

one foot too short. No offense intended. It has to be Marlowe here."

"No!" Booth said. The notion was horrifying. "No."

"Yes!" said Fern clapping with joy. "Yes, oh, yes!"

"You'd make a fine Lincoln!" said Ledyard. "You even have a beard rather like his. Some make-up will age you."

"I am already playing Washington," said Booth.

"Washington's almost a silent part, and Sheriff Johnson is more than willing to take it over. Marlowe, the Lincoln scene is the most important one! It cannot be made ridiculous, with all respect to our fine undertaker. It must be dignified. I believe you possess that quality."

Fern turned to Booth. "For the school, dear." she urged. "Please—for the children."

"No."

"Please, Marlowe."

"I am not worthy," he said, barely audibly.

"Nonsense," said Ledyard.

A sweat broke on Booth's forehead. He didn't dare glance at Upham. Making a scene over this would only stoke the little ferret's suspicions. He saw the disappointment in his wife's beautiful gray eyes. He never failed to react to them.

"All right," he said finally. "I would be honored to play him. But don't expect a miracle."

Fern squeezed his arm. "Thank you, Marlowe."

"Bravo!" exclaimed Ledyard.

Booth saw that Upham was studying him intently, the hint of a smirk on that callow face that said: *This is too ridiculous.*

*Quick,* thought Booth. "Please understand my reluctance—all of you," he said, mostly for Upham's ears. "I believe it the height of presumption to assume the persona of someone so... so consequential to our Nation, even in celebration. Our late... murdered ... martyr must not be trivialized, least of all when so many of our countrymen remain in mourning."

If Upham was convinced of Booth's sincerity, nothing in his face indicated it.

"Good man!" said Ledyard, handing him the book of Lincoln's speeches. "The Gettysburg Address is marked with a ribbon, and I have the costume and hat in the buggy."

He turned to Upham. "Come along, John Adams. Tie your horse to my rig, and I'll rehearse you on the way back to town."

Upham looked disconcerted by the prospect of leaving his quarry but obediently tied his rented mare to the back of the carriage and climbed into the box. Tobias took off his straw hat and put it behind him. He reached under his seat and retrieved a cloth bag from which to Fern's delight he pulled his Franklin-esque tricorne and donned it.

"Once a year I am allowed to pretend I'm a great man. Indulge me."

Booth and Fern stepped back as Tobias lifted the reins. Upham noticed that each had an arm around the other. *Either she has no idea, or a murderer has found his murderess.*

"I'll be here at five sharp to pick you up," Tobias said, turning the buggy around. "After the pageant there'll be a fine outdoor beef roast in the Fort Benton yard, courtesy of my good Emma Ledyard and all the other ladies."

"We'll be there," said Fern.

"You are the fairest of all, Mrs. Washington," said Tobias, lifting his three-cornered hat and bowing. "And good afternoon, Mr. Lincoln."

Booth managed a wan smile and waved them off. But his other hand was clenched in a trembling fist. Watching Upham climb into the buggy, he had seen the little man's coattails rise to reveal the handle of a revolver.

# CHAPTER THIRTY ONE

Early the next morning was Wednesday, July Fourth, and Booth picked up the book of Lincoln's speeches as reluctantly as if it were a poisonous mushroom.

He sat out on their little porch and watched Fern ride off to church. She had urged him to come with her for this special mid-week service but he demurred. Though baptized an Episcopalian, he had found formal religion difficult. He had once attended Mass with Mrs. Surratt, who had been a devout Catholic. He did not feel right stepping into a church these days. And out here on the prairie it seemed disconnected from the natural world that had renewed him. In any case, he had Lincoln's speech to memorize and had no desire to risk another meeting with Langford Upham.

The un-Christian idea of killing the reporter drifted in and out of his mind. With Davey Herold dead, no one save Dickie Garrett knew for sure that he was alive. And who would believe that an eleven-year-old boy had spoken with the assassin after the tobacco barn was torched? Official Washington wanted Booth to stay dead and buried.

In all of America, why did only this odd fellow Upham believe in a living John Wilkes Booth? What drove him to question the official story? The trail must be swept clean forever.

Booth had sworn he would never kill again, but that vow had grown from emotional weariness and the horror of killing Wilson Beech in a moment of desperation. He was more threatened by what harm might come to Fern, than to himself. And to their baby. *You set the stakes, Upham. This is not a game from which the loser walks away.*

As he sat on the porch and opened the book of Lincoln's speeches, he felt a gentle puff of summer air. Near the banks of the Missouri the cottonwoods were bright green, and the river's surface was suddenly corrugated by a gusting wind blowing downriver. Storm clouds were gathering, great purple-black clouds unlike any he had ever seen back East, accompanied by distant rumbling thunder. Such weather thrilled him, made him feel as if he lived in a world still ruled by great mysteries.

He leafed through the book of Lincoln's speeches, looking for the Gettysburg Address. The speech had been delivered almost three years before, to consecrate the thousands who fell on that Pennsylvania killing field. Booth had had friends who died there fighting for General Lee. How very bizarre, he marveled again, this macabre turn of events—forced to resurrect the man he had murdered! It was a ghastly joke beyond the imagination.

Into these dark thoughts scampered a chipmunk, running along the porch rail to where Booth sat. The little animal, a regular visitor over the last week, was completely unafraid of him, almost a pet. He was looking for a handout of pine nuts. Booth coaxed it to his hand, pleased to postpone his theatrical task. He studied the tiny creature, noting the perfect symmetry of the black and white stripes along its tan back. It was like a toy from the Divine.

Despite his disdain for those who gushed over God's hand in Nature, Booth's sudden immersion in the Western country had got him wondering—rationally, he would insist—if there wasn't, perhaps, a Master Architect, even a Supreme Artist, who had created the myriad denizens and landscapes of this blessed part of America. Who designed that beautiful pattern of color on this little rodent? *If I knew only that, I would know the secret of all Life itself.* Instead, he thought, he was happily destined, as an artist, to make pale copies of a beauty beyond description. Even a very great artist was merely an apprentice to the genius of, well, whoever designed this beautiful little chipmunk.

He gently waved the animal away. He couldn't stall any longer. He found Tobias's ribbon in the book and opened it to The Gettysburg Address.

Its brevity surprised him. Less than a dozen sentences. He read aloud, as was his practice when learning lines. Certainly the language was *adequate*—not the Immortal Bard, of course—but *sturdy*. Actually, quite good to read aloud. But was it original? After all, hadn't Daniel Webster, decades before Lincoln, spoken of "a government made for and made by and answerable to the people?" Not so new an idea really, but.... He read it again. The rhythm and force of the short sentences, followed by a long one, impressed him. It was nearly the stuff of poetry. Lincoln possessed a frightening facility with words, able to mesmerize a whole nation, draping political enslavements with high-minded language. Still, Booth had to concede, it was pretty compelling stuff.

Breathing hard, he read it a third time. Always a quick study, he nearly had it committed to memory. He turned the book over, resting it on his thigh, and began reciting, projecting his voice as though on a stage. Another rumble of far-off thunder made him laugh, as if the gods were reminding him who commands the stage here.

"The proposition that all men are created equal. Now we are engaged in a great civil war, testing whether that nation or any nation—"

He hesitated. "Or any—nation—"

He started to pick up the book to see the next words when a voice prompted from behind the cabin:

"—So conceived and so dedicated can long endure."

Booth jumped up from his chair as Langford Upham stepped around the corner of the cabin, applauding.

"Very nice," said the reporter pleasantly. "Very nice, Mr. Booth!"

"What are you doing here?" Booth looked at him coldly. "Why do you call me that name?"

"The game is up, Mr. Booth. I have heard that voice of yours on the stage. Many times. One doesn't forget it."

"My name is Marlowe," said Booth. "John Richard Marlowe, and I ask—I order you to get off this land."

"You see, Mr. Booth, I used to follow your appearances. I was a fan! Fancy that! A great fan!"

"My name is Marlowe."

"Ah, yes, *Marlowe!* Well-chosen. Always thought, unlike some critics, that your potential was far greater than your father or your brothers. You had that blazing passion in your breast. They merely had the technique—in my humble opinion."

"I do not sense a humble bone in you, Mr. Upham."

"Nor yours, sir. How I enjoyed your Othello to your brother's Iago that night—in *Richmond.* Thank you, Mr. Booth."

"My name, sir, is and always has been Marlowe."

"Are you willing to go to New York with me and tell your brothers and your mother that your name is Marlowe?"

"I am not willing to go to New York or anywhere with you," Booth said. "I do not have a brother. Nor a mother. I have a pregnant wife. And if you do not leave immediately, I shall be forced to throw you off this property."

Upham stared at Booth, a smile on his face. "I have no intention of leaving without you. You don't realize, sir, you have become an historical figure. And of a type we shall never see again. Caesar, Brutus, *et al*. It is too rich! And you don't remember that we crossed paths earlier this year, at Ford's Theater. I was in the very front row when you made your leap. '*Sic semper tyrannis!*' Very dramatic."

Booth stared back at him, unblinking. "I do not speak foreign languages."

"You'll be interested to know," said Upham, "that your brother Edwin told me—"

"—I have no brother, Mr. Upham."

"Your brother Edwin told me that you have a considerable scar on your right shoulder. It was a sword slash administered by your brother—on the stage. If you are not Booth, you'll bare your shoulder now. I challenge you. Show me. If there is no scar I shall leave and never bother you again. I give you my word."

Booth glared at him.

"Show me your shoulder, Booth."

"I will show you a boot—a boot to your backside if you are not gone from this place instantly."

The rifle was inside the cabin, only ten feet away, behind the door. *Kill him! Kill this spawn of Satan. Bury him in the garden, and no one would ever know, not even Fern.*

"Your shoulder, Mr. Booth."

"I want no trouble, Upham. You must not be here when my wife returns. She is with child, and nothing must upset her."

Upham made no move to go, and now his smile was gone. "Tell me, Booth, what did it feel like when you fired the shot into the head of our president?"

"Sir, I am not that man," said Booth steadily.

"You were," said Upham. "You may not be now, but you were that man then, that night."

"You've had your ... fun, Mr. Upham." said Booth calmly. Now, leave."

"One thing I would really like to know—the world would like to know—was Secretary Stanton a part of the conspiracy? For some reason he removed eighteen pages from your diary."

"I shall count to three," said Booth. "And then you will be gone, or I shall be forced to get my rifle. One ... two...."

The little man suddenly had a revolver in his hand. An Army Colt .44. "You will get no rifle," he said between clenched teeth. "You will come with me to town, to Sheriff Johnson's jail. The jig is up, Mr. Booth."

Booth looked at him in wonder, shaking his head. "You are out of your mind," he said.

"It is you who has taken leave of sanity," said Upham. The revolver was shaking in his hand. "Sane people do not kill presidents!"

"Of course, Upham. And all those other war dead—six hundred thousand poor wretches, Upham—were they killed by insane men as well? The insane killing the insane, is that what you're saying?"

"Shut up!" barked Upham, struggling to hold the heavy Colt steady. He placed his other hand under its long barrel to ease the strain on his arm, but the muzzle of the revolver danced.

Booth stepped off the porch. He walked slowly toward Upham, his hand extended.

"Give me the iron."

Upham backed up, cocking the revolver.

"Don't come any closer!" said Upham. "I'm going to shoot."

"Think how ridiculous you will be when my body is identified as John Richard Marlowe. You will not only be a laughingstock, but face the gallows for murder. There's your news heading: 'Deluded Vigilante Scribe Hanged in Frontier Village.'"

"Halt, or I'll fire!" Sweat was streaming down Upham's face like tears.

"No," said Booth quietly. "You will not."

Standing directly in front of Upham he reached out slowly and took hold of the barrel of the gun. He turned it to the side, shook it once, then again. Upham's fingers loosened, and Booth gently pulled the weapon from his hand.

Upham froze as Booth turned the pistol around and pointed it at the reporter's chest. *So this is how it ends for me.*

Booth broke open the pistol and extracted the cartridges. "You see, my friend," he said, offering the weapon, handle first, back to Upham, "it is not easy to kill a man. I am gladly giving you back your life."

Upham, his face glistening, grabbed the empty revolver and shoved it under his belt buckle. Breathing hard, he backed up, pointing a trembling finger. "You are John Wilkes Booth!" he said. "I know it, and you know it."

"Sir, you're free to say what you will about me, true or not," said Booth. "But consider one fact. I could have killed you just now. Easily. And buried you in the back yard. No witnesses but the crows. John Wilkes Booth would have killed you. What would you be to a man like Booth? But I did not kill you. I am not that man. However, and hear me now: if you ever menace me or my wife again, in any way, near or far, I *will* track you down and kill you."

Booth watched as Upham clumsily mounted his horse and galloped away toward town. *For once*, he thought, *I should have killed a fellow human being.*

# CHAPTER THIRTY TWO

Riding back to Fort Benton, Upham spotted Fern on horseback, trotting through the sagebrush above the Missouri. He slowed and collected himself as she approached him on the road.

"Good day, Mrs. Marlowe," he said, tipping his hat to her. "Looks like rain, doesn't it?"

She stopped her horse and fixed him with a cold look. "I hope you haven't been out pestering my husband again."

"Not at all."

"He's preparing for his part in the pageant."

"A great admirer of our late president, is he not?"

Fern didn't answer. She resented the way Upham asked questions. They seemed less questions than traps.

"Isn't it ironic, Madam, for a Southerner like your husband to want to play Lincoln?"

"Southerners are not simple-minded, sir," she said. "They are perfectly capable of appreciating a great man's qualities without embracing his politics. And my husband is in no way a political man." She spurred her horse forward, cantering toward the cabin.

*If only you knew, madam, what you owe me. I spared your husband's life.* Then Upham felt the empty pistol in his belt, and his face began to burn, for he knew he had done nothing of the kind. He had proved himself a coward. Booth had spared *his* life.

*It is not easy to kill a man.*

Upham had never killed anything, not even a duck or grouse. Firearms unnerved him, their recoil a jarring reminder of the impact on the receiving end. And for all the torments of his asthma, of attacks that made him feel as if he were drowning, the affliction had saved him from the folly of war.

Letting his horse walk to Fort Benton at its own pace, he felt as though the revelation at Booth's cabin had rendered him a different man. After a year of nursing a deadly contempt for the assassin, he had suddenly found himself holding this man's life in his hands—and been unable to pull the trigger. Yet when the tables were reversed, when Booth could have killed him, he had not begged for mercy. Quite the contrary.

Only two men stood at the bar when Upham entered The Star. The bartender was reading a month-old newspaper from Omaha.

"Where's everybody, Luke?"

"Gettin' ready for the pageant," he said, drawing a glass of beer and placing it in front of the reporter. "Bad for business." He went back to his newspaper.

At the heart of Upham's turmoil were Marlowe's words: *John Wilkes Booth would have killed you*. It had the weight of common sense. Upham could not conceive of the man who shot Lincoln in cold blood hesitating to kill a mere reporter who threatened to expose him.

Yet Marlowe had not pulled the trigger.

But, damn it all, Marlowe *was* Booth. That unmistakable voice. A reformed and transformed man had faced him, released him from death. A good husband, perhaps, and an artist of some skill—but this was still the murderer of an American Titan, and the callous exploiter of the luckless Wilson Beech.

Did it matter that Booth tried to salve his conscience by sending money to Beech's widow?

Tankards of beer fueled Upham's inner dialogue. Why persecute this man? He was an artist of exceptional talent—a man whom, once upon a time, you wished to emulate in style. Would killing Booth be an act of justice? Or am I, like Booth, driven by dark vanity to bring down a famous figure?

Upham studied his reflection in the mirror behind the bar. What he saw was a diminutive reporter wearing a dusty bowler. *I am just that. A reporter. Neither a moralist nor a philosopher—nor the final judge and hangman of a misguided soul.*

The thought of physically confronting Booth again filled him with dread. Somehow the man calling himself Marlowe would have to be presented—alive—to Booth's family for identification. He could well imagine Edwin Booth slamming the door on him. Did a witness still live, somewhere? He would never find that person now.

His choices narrowed to one: He would defy his father's warning and write the story with all its facts and conjecture, send it off to *The World*, and weather the storm.

As he counted out change to pay for the beer, he become aware of the foul odor of sweat and tobacco in a concentrated form just off his left shoulder.

"Have a drink with me, pardner."

It was the loathsome Moody Suggs, gazing at him unsteadily with those angry, self-pitying bloodshot eyes.

"I have to go, Mr. Suggs," said Upham.

"How come you ain't in the pageant—like a good Yankee?" rasped Moody, dropping his hand over Upham's arm. Upham recoiled from the man's fetid breath.

"I'm playing the part of John Adams," replied Upham, yanking his arm free. He pulled his watch from his vest. "And I must get dressed."

"I hear tell some son of a bitch-dog is gonna stan' up an' talk' like Lincoln!"

Upham slid off his stool, leaving Suggs growling at his own reflection in the bar's mirror.


Back in his room, Upham went to the table where a stack of blank Pacific Telegraph Company message forms lay. He took off his jacket, hung it on the back of the chair, and sat down wearily. He pulled his revolver from his belt, looked at the empty chambers, and put it back in his jacket. He'd buy more cartridges tomorrow.

He picked up the pencil and took a deep breath. This would be the most difficult and momentous article he would ever write. It might rend his relationship with his father, for better or worse. To say nothing of the lives of "Mr. and Mrs. Marlowe."

*Even readers of Edgar Allan Poe will have trouble believing the story this reporter must recount. If I were to tell you that John Wilkes Booth is very much alive and living in a small town in Montana Territory, would your credulity be strained? I expect so. But wait—there is more. Much more. Suppose I told you that the thespian-assassin is, as I write, taking time out from his new career as a painter of Blackfeet warriors and buffalo stampedes to play the leading role in a frontier pageant of history and patriotism? Suppose I told you—hang on to your stovepipe hats and the better angels of your natures—that the character he is playing is the late Abraham Lincoln?*

Upham envisioned Chad Tompkins' incredulous face when he received this wire, imagined the editor's groan, and his father's apoplectic rant. "More cockeyed theories! And now Booth dressed up as Lincoln? Poppycock! It's an abomination! Poppycock!"

Upham unfolded his pocket-knife, sharpened a pencil, then abruptly laid it aside. Suddenly oppressed by a colossal fatigue, he pushed back his chair and rolled onto his bed, gazing up at the mottled ceiling.

Suppose Marlowe was who he said he was. Would it not be inexcusable to destroy his life by accusing him of being an assassin? Upham imagined a lynch mob forming. But if Marlowe was indeed Booth, for the rest of his life and times, Upham would be the most famous reporter on the continent and command princely sums from the greatest newspapers in the land.

Booth, Beech, and Marlowe were one and the same. That was as certain as the dark-eyed, mustachioed phantom, now standing at the foot of his bed, laughing as he aimed the muzzle of a derringer at him.

Then he was asleep, dreaming of a darkened stage.

# CHAPTER THIRTY THREE

"I can't do it," said Booth. "I swear I can't do it!"

Fern saw him pacing the cabin. Marlowe had been restless all day, exhibiting symptoms she took for stage fright.

"Dear Marlowe, of course you can—and you'll do it well."

Booth had spent the morning immersed in the book of Lincoln's speeches. He had committed the Gettysburg Address to memory. It was what he discovered on other pages of the book that fascinated and troubled him.

"These are—quite fine," he conceded in response to Fern's observation that he seemed taken with the president's oratory. That was the most he could manage. "Quite good, indeed." He had never been so conflicted.

"Listen to this, Fern," and he read her a passage from Lincoln's first inaugural address.

"I like the less important things that he said," she replied. "You know, when he said 'The happiest people are those who think the most interesting thoughts.' Things like that."

Booth nodded distractedly. Fern watched him recede into his reverie again. She saw that his eyes glistened. *Tears.*

She knew so little about her husband's origins and background, or the dark matters he had spoken of. She sensed that those buried secrets were what drove him to work so determinedly at his art.

Whatever hardship or brutality he had suffered, Marlowe was resourceful and kind; she knew he would be a good and loving father to their child. He had already fashioned a cradle, with great care, using nothing but a few tree limbs and the knife Tall Elk had given him, notching and grooving the pieces of wood so they fit together without screws.

"Were you a carpenter in your other life?" she'd ventured once, breaking their rule of not asking about what he called "other times." He'd laughed and said, "Among other pursuits." He remembered the many stage sets he'd helped build as a teenage apprentice for his acting troupe.

On this Wednesday, he seemed more withdrawn and introspective than usual. For the first time since they had known each other, he did not sketch or paint. He sat with the book on his lap, rarely speaking. Occasionally he would read a passage out loud.

"Listen to this, Fern. 'When again touched, as surely they will be, by the better angels of our natures. ...' What a lovely phrase that is! 'The better angels of our natures.' It's poetry, musical."

And later: "How did this man write such words?" He shook his head with an expression of pained discovery. "'With malice toward none; with charity for all; with firmness in the right, as God gives us to see the right.'"

Fern watched him in fascination. He shook his head again, as if chagrined. Then he stood up, abruptly, went into the bedroom and shut the door. Fern remained sitting, perplexed. He had never closed a door between them. Then she thought she heard a soft moan, a muffled sob. *Dearest Marlowe. How he must have suffered in the war, in his life.* She wanted to go to him. But she did not. She knew enough to leave him with his darkness for now.

Booth put a handkerchief to his eyes. He looked again at the gravure of Lincoln in the book. Then he went to the mirror. Using his straight razor, he shaved away some of his hair to give himself a higher forehead. Taking a pair of burned sticks from the fireplace, he daubed dark circles of soot under his eyes and rubbed them in with a finger. He used the charcoal to thicken his eyebrows, to deepen the lines around his mouth, and to accentuate his cheekbones.

With deft, experienced fingers, he used flour to add streaks of gray to his hair and the beard around his chin. He mixed flour with water, and from his paint box took yellow ochre, burnt sienna, and raw umber, working the ingredients into a putty-like compound roughly matching the color of his skin. With repeated glances at the images of Lincoln, he used it to slightly build up the bridge of his nose, to wrinkle his brow. Then he was done.

He dressed in the ruffled shirt and knotted the black velvet bow tie. He donned the suit with the long coat and draped the shawl around his shoulders. Standing in front of the small bedroom mirror he slowly, carefully, placed the tall satin stovepipe hat on his head. He studied his mirrored image. *Good God. It is almost too good.*


When he stepped from the bedroom Fern gasped at the transformation. It was more than physical, for he seemed to have grown taller and taken on the presidential demeanor of Lincoln. She looked at him, open-mouthed with amazement. "I'm not sure whether I should genuflect, or curtsy!"

"I'd most gratefully accept a drink of water, Mrs. Marlowe," he chuckled, and then she saw again the man she loved. Yet he was Lincoln. Even his voice had changed—a higher register, but solemn and commanding.

She pressed her hands to her face, astonished. "Oh my, Marlowe. Oh my!"


Fern donned her costume quickly. She was reluctant to put herself on display, but at least Martha Washington's large white-powered wig and linen bonnet would mask her disfigurement. When Booth saw her dressed in the lacy gown, he spun his finger in the air, her cue to turn a circle.

"Lucky old George Washington," he said, admiring her figure as she obliged him with a shy turn-around.

They sat on the porch, holding hands silently, he in her old rocker, she on a little chair she had borrowed from the Ledyards. The vista before them was magnificent, the sun making the fluttering leaves of the cottonwoods sparkle green and white.

She felt the peculiar tension in him still. She let him sit in his thoughtful silence until they heard Tobias Ledyard's carriage coming up the road, precisely on time. "A penny saved is a penny earned," called out the little round man. "Early to bed, early to rise...."

Ledyard was now a credible recreation of Ben Franklin. The half-bald wig and wire eye-glass frames recalled the inventor-printer-statesman quite accurately. The jabot of lace at his throat and brown tailcoat evoked the century past.

Booth stood, put on his high hat, and offered his arm to Fern. They walked arm-in-arm out to the road, where Ledyard waited, his eyes widening.

"Amazing!" said Ledyard. "Absolutely amazing! You see, Marlowe? I was right! You *are* Lincoln!" He looked at Booth in wonder. "Aren't you proud of him, Mrs. Washington?"

"Yes," she said. "I married the wrong president!"


As they drove into town Tobias Ledyard bubbled over with excitement about the costumes and sets and the singing he'd heard in rehearsals. Along Fort Benton's main street it seemed all were gravitating toward the "auditorium," a former warehouse. Booth surveyed the tableau, an audience such as he had never had—miners, cowboys, trappers, the town's few respectable ladies, and a frilly retinue of "soiled doves" seated at the back near a few of the tamer post Indians.

As the buggy passed, one man shouted "Hooray for Abe!" The mother of one of Fern's students waved at them. "Good evening, Mrs. Washington!" Fern waved to her friends. His thoughts churning, Booth sat stiffly, his eyes unseeing. *My friend, if indeed you are my friend, this may very well be the queerest thing you have ever got yourself into.*

As they pulled up to the warehouse, a woman standing outside the door hurried over.

"Dudley Gunn's wife," said Ledyard, as he reined up his team. "Good God," he sighed. "What now?" He tipped his hat to the lady as she charged up to him.

"Dudley's changed his mind, Tobias! He's ready to play Lincoln."

Ledyard dropped his head in exasperation, then shot her a look. "My dear Mrs. Gunn, it's too late to—"

"He's learned the words perfect! I'm sure he can do it just fine this time."

Booth looked away, embarrassed by the poor woman's humiliation. Ledyard turned to him. "What say, Marlowe?"

Booth shook his head. "No."

Mrs. Gunn's voice took on a ragged tone of hysteria. "He's got it down pat! He doesn't stammer when he says it now! Says he's ready to—"

"No!" said Booth with such firmness that she fell silent. "When he bolted, Mrs. Gunn, I was pressed into service to replace him, much against my wishes. But I, too, am ready now. Next year and for all the years to come, your husband may have the role with my blessing, but today it is mine."

Pressing her handkerchief to her mouth, Mrs. Gunn turned and rushed away.

Fern squeezed Booth's arm. "Well done, Marlowe."

They stepped down from the buggy and went into the hall.


The pageant was ten minutes late in starting. In the crowded space behind the stage, Booth stood stoically in a corner next to Fern, while others in the cast paced and rehearsed their lines or chatted in nervous whispers.

Finally the pianist from The Star, accompanied by a lady violinist, began to play "Hail, Columbia," alerting the audience to take their seats.

When the anthem ended, Tobias Ledyard stepped out on stage and greeted the crowd. "Fellow Bentonians!" he announced, "This patriotic show is staged for the benefit of our worthy school program," and the hall filled with applause.

Backstage, standing beside her distracted husband, Fern heard the applause. She looked up at Booth, who seemed in a world of his own. Noticing her gaze, he leaned close to her and said, "I'm sorry, but I need a few moments alone."

She moved away, taking up a position behind a curtain where she could watch the action on stage without being seen by the audience. There was another round of clapping as Tobias hurried into the wings.

The first number featured Phineas Canby, the town's elderly physician, who clawed his way through the rude canvas curtains and appeared as top-hatted Uncle Sam.

"Yay for Doc!" someone called out as the medic expertly juggled three balls, then four potatoes. That done, he bowed to cheers, whistles, and foot-stomping.

Next the medic juggled three cigar boxes and an apple, ending his performance by setting his Stars-and-Stripes top hat spinning on a cane, and then balancing the stick on his forehead, bringing down the house. A miner, overcome with enthusiasm and more than drunk, took out a revolver, pointed it at the ceiling and fired it. Four men sitting nearby overpowered and discreetly disarmed him as the sheriff, Meriwether Johnson, dressed as George Washington, directed them to the jail at the rear of the building.

The next act was a cowboy who first twirled two ropes at a time, then jumped in and out of a great vertical loop spinning beside him. He ended his act by snagging Tobias Ledyard around the neck and pulling him to center stage, as the master of ceremonies pretended to choke.

The audience howled. Fern glanced again at her husband, who stood as if entranced, eyes closed—Lincoln in meditation, she thought.

Musical acts followed. Despite her diligent rehearsals, the coloratura who sang "Come Where My Love Lies Bleeding" forgot the lyrics, but improvised valiantly.

Then Fern herded her students' little group onto the boards and directed them as they sang a medley of Stephen Foster songs, starting with "Old Black Joe." In the audience, the black pianist from The Star caught the eye of his very white, red-haired and freckled violinist, who blushed at his all-too-familiar smile. The children sang earnestly if off-key, and garnered enthusiastic applause.

After the incident with the trigger-happy miner, Meriwether Johnson took up a position in the lobby, watching the audience from behind, his sheriff's star pinned on the lapel of his Colonial era waistcoat. He was not pleased when Moody Suggs ambled up the steps to the front door. The lawman planted his considerable bulk in the drunkard's path. "That's far enough, Moody. I can't let you in."

"Wanna see the show."

Suggs tried to push past him, but Johnson pushed him back outside. "Not when you're drunk as a skunk. Out—go!"

Suggs stumbled down the steps of the building. Johnson watched him walk splay-legged into the darkness. Tomorrow he would put Moody Suggs behind bars for a month, to forcibly sober him up.

A trio playing a violin, a banjo, and a whiny saw wrapped up the musical portion of the program with a spirited rendition of "Turkey in the Straw," rousing the audience to tap their feet and clap along. As they were cheered off the stage, Tobias Ledyard ducked through the curtain, as much frontier Falstaff as Franklin.

"Glad you folks appreciate the amazing talents we have right here in Fort Benton," he said. Another burst of applause. "And now for the historic portion of our pageant, beginning in modern times and working back through some previous great presidents to the beginning of our glorious country."

Booth had finished his preparation and joined Fern in the wings. He no longer appeared nervous. He seemed detached, almost ethereal, his faint smile and thoughtful gaze at the audience suggesting to her a wry and tolerant acceptance of all mankind.

As the lights dimmed, the piano began very softly to play *The Battle Hymn of the Republic*. Out of the corner of her eye Fern saw Upham, dressed in his John Adams costume, standing alone backstage.

The stirring music swelled. Tobias Ledyard, across stage, assured that all was ready, nodded his head at Booth.

There was an audible gasp as Booth appeared on the stage. He walked tentatively, holding himself like a strong but weary fifty-six-year-old president, and slouched to the lectern. Ignoring the audience, he turned up the flame on a large oil lamp. His face was now uplit, while a great top-hatted shadow projected onto the curtain behind him. Fern scanned the faces of the audience. They were rapt, so astonished by the living apparition before them that none thought to clap.

Slowly Booth removed his hat and put it on the lectern. He adjusted the shawl around his shoulders. "Gettysburg," he said, contemplatively, as though to himself. "Getty's Burg. Getty's town."

He shook his head. Then he picked up a pencil and a piece of stationery from the lectern, and walked away from it slowly, scratching his beard as if deep in thought. He turned his back on the audience and heaved a deep sigh. A great sorrowful sigh.

He turned around, not gazing directly at the audience, but through them. He was not only the war-exhausted president, he was a man with an immediate and important literary problem to solve. Then his eyes shifted downward, and he began to slowly write on the card in his hand. As he wrote he murmured, loudly and clearly enough for the crowd, who were leaning forward in their seats to eavesdrop on this historic moment.

"Eighty-seven years ago ... our forefathers ... brought forth upon our continent ...."

He stopped, held the card next to the glowing lantern as if to read what he had written. Frowning, he crossed out lines and began again, walking away from the lectern. He stopped and struck a thoughtful stance.

"Four score and seven years ago . . ." He paused and kneaded his forehead with his fingers. "Four score and seven years ago, our fathers brought forth upon this continent a nation."

He stopped and made a quick note. "A *new* nation, conceived in liberty and . . . dedicated to—what?" Then, firmly and with conviction, "Dedicated to the proposition ... the proposition that all men are created equal."

He nodded in satisfaction, then began walking slowly around the stage, jotting down the words, speaking quietly but with his authoritative voice projecting, carrying easily to everyone in the hushed room, even the crowded back rows. Fern marveled at their faces. *They are in thrall.*

"Now we are engaged in a great civil war," Booth intoned, "testing whether that nation, or any nation, so conceived and so dedicated, can long endure. We are met on a great battlefield of that war."

No one stirred as he went on, his voice rising and falling, pausing, sometimes almost whispering, as though still in the process of composing, blacksmithing the great address on an anvil of sacrifice and hope.

Fern saw that many people in the audience now had tears in their eyes, including the ebony-cheeked piano player from The Star, who sat quietly at the piano. Handkerchiefs appeared, and men blinked determinedly. Bursting with pride, she held a fist to her mouth to contain the emotions welling up.

Standing in the wings next to Ledyard, Upham felt his emotion rising as well. He knew the Gettysburg Address by heart, but never had he heard such a rendition of it. Here was proof. Only a trained actor, a master thespian with the rarest of gifts, could marshal these words in such a manner.

Now Booth's voice changed. It shifted subtly from a conversational, reflective tone to a strong and forceful urging. He no longer pretended to be writing. Instead he looked straight at the audience, as though seeing them for the first time. They straightened up in their chairs as the actor made the electrical connections for which he was famous. Holding his lapel with his left hand, he swept his right hand over the crowd.

"It is for us the living, rather, to be dedicated here to the unfinished work remaining before us ... that from these honored dead we take increased devotion—"

The audience, even the children in it, sat frozen as if transfixed by a shaman. Sheriff Johnson had left his place at the door to check on his prisoner. No one noticed as Moody Suggs slipped into the back of the auditorium.

"—to that cause for which they gave the last full measure of devotion—"

Suggs started down the aisle toward the stage.

"—that we here highly resolve that these dead shall not have died in vain—that this nation, under God—"

Booth's eyes locked on the man advancing toward him, but kept speaking.

"—shall have a new birth of freedom—"

From the wings Fern saw Moody Suggs striding fast toward the stage, muttering oaths as he came.

Booth's voice boomed from the lectern.

"—and that government of the people, by the people, for the people—"

Upham saw Suggs reach for his revolver.

"—shall not perish from the earth."

"Stop him!" shouted Upham, hurling himself from the stage.

Too late. The revolver belched flame. Upham's falling body slammed the gunman to the floor. Other men swarmed over the bellowing assailant, pummeling him with their fists.

Men were now standing on benches, some holding revolvers, as a few women wailed or shrieked in horror. Most of the audience sat in mute shock. Then came the rumble of feet as a rush for the doors began.

For a moment after the shot, Booth stood, one hand gripping the lectern, the other rising to his forehead. As Fern rushed to catch him, his knees buckled. He sank to the floor, pulling Fern with him.

"Marlowe, oh Marlowe," she moaned. "No! No!" She held his bleeding head in her hand. "My God, what has he done to you?"

Upham fought his way back through the throng surrounding the lectern. He found old Dr. Canby crouching over the actor, pressing a blood-soaked handkerchief to the side of Booth's head.

Booth's eyes were closed, but his lips were moving as if he were speaking. "What's he saying?" whispered Tobias Ledyard.

"I don't know," said the doctor.

Upham knew—he saw the whispered words form on Booth's lips: "*Sic semper tyrannis.*"

Fern was kissing Booth's face, desperately stroking his hair. "Don't die, Marlowe. Please, darling—*please*. You have to stay with me!"

"It's grave, but I don't believe he'll die," said the doctor. "Quick, Tobias, go out to my buggy and get my medical bag!"

"Yes, doctor," said Ledyard.

Booth opened his eyes and, searching, saw Fern.

"Won't die," he muttered to her. "Won't die. Not now."

"You'll be fine, son," said the doctor, his thumb pressed on the bullet hole. He spoke to Booth as he might have consoled a child. "Just fine."

"Stay with me, darling," said Fern, her voice breaking. "You've got to!"

Booth's eyes met Upham's. His mouth opened with a gasp. "Don't let them hurt Moody. Have mercy upon him."

Upham was stunned by Booth's words. But no one else seemed to pay attention.

Fern was kissing his face again. "I'm right here. You'll be all right. I'm going to take you home."

Upham looked down on the wounded actor with wonder and even anguish. *Who is this man?* It was no longer enough to say he was Booth.

The answer was vastly larger.

Ledyard was down among the benches, urging stragglers out of the hall, apologizing, calming them, assuring them that Marlowe would survive. Darkness was falling. As he herded the last man out the doorway and scanned the street for the doctor's buggy, he saw that it was filling with men, many of them holding torches. Nearby stood Sheriff Johnson, still dressed as George Washington, but with a gun belt buckled over his waistcoat.

A lynch mob was forming down by the river. At least a hundred men were gathered around the big cottonwood, shouting and brandishing revolvers, rifles, and clubs.

"Good Lord." Pulling off his wig, the sheriff went down the steps and strode toward the hanging tree.

At the roots of the cottonwood knelt Moody Suggs, his face bleeding, bruised, and swollen, his arms tied behind him at the elbows. A rope noose dangled above him. His eyes were wild with terror. The sheriff walked slowly through the quieting mob and stood before the cringing man.

"Damnation, Moody. Look what you've done."

"Help me, Sheriff. Oh, Jesus, you got to help me!"

Johnson said nothing.

"I jus' meant to scare him! I never shot nobody ever, I swear to God on that, sheriff!"

Johnson surveyed the hard faces staring at him in the torchlight. He saw what they wanted. He looked back to Suggs's body, convulsing with sobs.

"I'm sorry I did that," said Suggs.

"He's only talking to save his neck," said a man in the crowd. "Jus' let us be done with it, Sheriff."

Johnson stepped back. "Don't do this, boys."

Two men looped the noose around the prisoner's neck and pulled in the slack. Moody threw himself sideways onto the ground, howling in stark terror, his churning legs turning him around in a circle. The men grabbed him under the arms and pulled him upright. One spat in Moody's face.

"Hoist 'im high!" shouted someone from the back of the crowd. A hundred voices roared agreement as the rope around Moody's neck snapped taut. A dark stain was advancing down the inside of his pant legs.

"Gentlemen!" came a command. "In the name of God release that man!"

It was Upham's voice, so authoritative that the men holding the rope eased up and turned their heads. Upham was pointing his pistol at them. "You will stop now!"

He strode into the crowd, turning for no one, bumping a few aside. He walked straight to Moody, who was back on his knees, quivering. Upham loosened the noose and pulled it up over the man's head.

A voice shouted. "He killed Marlowe!"

"He's a murderer!"

Upham looked over the crowd with a fierce gaze. "Marlowe is still alive! And he asks you to have mercy."

A murmur of surprise rippled through the throng.

"Remember Lincoln's words toward the Confederacy, men. 'With malice toward none, with charity for all.' Even this sorry excuse for a human. Don't worry—justice will be done. Won't it, Sheriff?"

"Damn right," said Johnson, lifting Moody Suggs to his feet. "By the law."

The mob hushed. Upham could hear impassioned discussions all around him, arguments over Suggs's fate, and his own.

"Go home, fellows," Johnson said in a booming voice. "I'm taking Suggs to jail. We'll let the circuit judge decide when and where we get to hang him—but accordin' to the law. Now let's all go home, or go have a drink. But no more of this!"

There were mutterings and profanities, but the crowd dispersed. Johnson jerked Suggs around. "One goddamn word, Moody, and I'll throw you back to 'em. Hear me?"

Tobias Ledyard arrived, breathless. "You did a brave thing, sir," he said to Upham. "And with just a pistol."

"I did it without thinking," he said. "The pistol isn't even loaded."

"We're trying our best to make Fort Benton a civilized place, fit for women and children." Ledyard looked around at the town, where torches were receding in every direction. "One day this will be Benton

City. Perhaps the capital of a state. I hope your newspaper won't give readers the impression that shootings and lynchings happen here every day. That would be untrue."

"You have my word on that, sir," said Upham.

On the lamplit stage in the old warehouse, Fern cradled Booth's head in her lap, rocking back and forth in her anguish. The bleeding would not stop. The old doctor sat in a chair beside them, helpless, defeated.

"How is he?"

At the sound of Upham's voice, Booth's eyes fluttered open and fixed on the reporter, who knelt beside him. Tobias Ledyard did the same, putting a hand on Booth's shoulder. Booth's gaze at Upham was fierce.

"The truth is," said Booth, his voice a whisper now. "The truth ... is ... I'm not...." He gasped deeply, blinking several times. Then he looked up at Fern, trying to speak to her. "Home," he whispered. "Take ... me ... home."

"Yes, soon, darling."

Then the lids on his dark eyes closed halfway, and he was still.

Fern bent over him, pressing her tear-stained face to his bloody cheek. "Marlowe, oh, Marlowe!"

For a long time no one spoke. Tobias Ledyard sighed and squeezed Fern's quivering shoulder.

"He's gone," he said. "Gone home."

# CHAPTER THIRTY FOUR

Upham's voyage back down the Missouri to St. Louis took only twenty-nine days. Clear skies allowed a luminous moon to shine on the most dangerous stretches of the river, and the *Chippewa* made record time.

From there to New York, Upham spent three tedious days in rail transit, mostly reclining in his berth on a sleeper car, reading, and only occasionally looking out at the sliding green landscapes framed by the windows.

Stepping off the railroad ferry onto Manhattan Island in mid-August, his spirits soared. It was a hot, sticky day but he was thrilled to be back in the big city. He savored the hustle and bustle of hansom cabs, oysters being hawked by street vendors, and all the fine shops displaying the latest fashions. Then into his apartment—a welcoming screech from Calpurnia, the glint of his antiques and the rich oily scent of leather-bound titles lining his bookshelves. The fine texture and tailoring of the clothes in his closet nearly reduced him to tears. At last, civilization.

The following day he treated himself and a group of friends to an evening of theater, then a late supper of champagne, oysters, and beefsteak at the Brevoort Hotel. At some point he raised his cognac in a toast: "To hell with Horace Greeley's travel suggestions! Stay East, young men, stay East!" Upham swore he would never venture west of the Hudson again.

The next day, he went straight to the Broadway offices of *The World*. He had not sent the newspaper the final story he'd written in Fort Benton, the wild tale revealing the escape and transformation of the actor-assassin named Booth into the artist, husband, and martyr known as Marlowe. For reasons not yet clear to him, he had folded the longer story up and sealed it in an envelope that he hid inside the lining of his valise.

During the night of the tragic pageant, Marlowe's body had been given to Dudley Gunn, the undertaker. Fern returned to the Ledyards house. Two days later Upham was due to leave on the *Chippewa*, bound for St. Louis. With just an hour to go, he had hurried to the log cabin that served as the morgue and knocked on the door.

Dudley Gunn appeared in the doorway, wiping his hands on his apron. "Ah, Mr. Upham," said the undertaker, "come to pay your respects?"

Over Gunn's shoulder Upham saw a sheet-covered form lying on a table. There was a freshly milled coffin on the dirt floor.

"I was just getting ready to close Mr. Marlowe up. Funeral's at noon. Want to come in?"

How easy it would be to prove once and for all who this Marlowe was, or who he had been. He either had a scar on his right shoulder, or he didn't. The positive proof of his yearlong quest for truth lay just ten feet away under a rough sheet of cloth.

But suddenly a voice was speaking. "No, thank you, Mr. Gunn," said Upham. "I merely came by to say I can't attend the burial. I must head downriver in an hour. Would you please give my condolences to Mrs. Marlowe?"

"I will, sir. That good woman is suffering the loss of a fine man, to be sure," said Gunn.

"A real shame," said Upham.

"Just to think," said the mortician quietly, "if I'd g-gotten the part of Lincoln, it would have been me that was s-shot."

"There are many kinds of luck, Mr. Gunn," said Upham. "And now I must head to the steamboat. Goodbye."

"A safe voyage to you, sir."


Several times on his long journey back to New York, Upham regretted not examining Marlowe's body. But what point would it serve? They would still bury Marlowe out on the great prairie above the bluffs of the river. Why interfere with a widow's grief? Nothing would bring back Lincoln. And Booth was dead—once, if not twice.

To fulfill his reporter's duty he'd written a colorful description of a modest homespun pageant in a wild and woolly frontier town. During the boat's brief stopover in Omaha, he had wired it to New York. The piece ended with a heartfelt account of the shooting of a promising young artist named John Richard Marlowe at the hands of a drunken unreconstructed Southerner. He did not mention his own actions in preventing the lynching of Suggs. Nor did he mention that, in an effort to support the widowed Fern, he had purchased several of Marlowe's watercolors from I.G. Baker. His favorite was a lovely sketch of a chipmunk gnawing a pine nut.

Upham bypassed his father's office, walking directly into the newspaper's main room. When Chad Tompkins saw him, he sprang up from his desk and greeted him with unaccustomed warmth.

"By God, it's himself returned safe and sound from the Great Wild— and with scalp intact! Sit down, heroic fellow, sit down! Let me take your coat."

Upham sat and accepted the fine fifteen-cent cigar the editor offered him.

"Well, Lang, you really did it. That piece on the murder of the artist fellow created quite a stir, quite a stir. Even your father liked it."

Upham was surprised to discover that he preferred the less friendly Tompkins, the prickly, distant, skeptical managing editor to this ingratiating version gushing with bonhomie. Managing editors weren't supposed to be nice.

"That's good news," said Upham, guardedly. He was unused to praise in this great noisy room and was conscious of the sly glances from staffers pretending not to notice the return of "Junior U." Something funny was going on.

"The color was great, so were the characters. Wonderful descriptions. But what really impressed us was your sense of drama, the way you built up to that shooting, your classical allusions and comparisons—ever the Yale man, eh? *Lux et dramatis?*"

"*Veritas*," Upham corrected.

"Good theatrical presentation. Splendid stuff, really."

Tompkins struck a match and leaned across his desk to light Upham's cigar. The reporter watched his editor closely. *Something's up.*

"Lang, we feel you're being wasted as a reporter."

"I see."

"I assume you haven't heard that Morely Haight died while you were away."

"Sorry to hear that. He was very good."

"The best. My point is, we think you'd do the newspaper proud as the new drama critic."

Upham sat back in his chair. Drama critic of *The New York World*!

"Chad, I am overwhelmed," he said. *Six months ago I would have been overwhelmed. And grateful. And eager.*

"Your new office is right down the hall. Haight's stuff has been moved out, and the floor waxed."

Upham looked down the corridor. His name had already been painted on its frosted glass pane.

"I trust you'll find it comfortable. Your first assignment should be right up your alley. Lincoln and all."

"Yes?" said Upham.

"They say Edwin Booth has decided to return to acting. Go interview him and find out the truth about it."

He remembered Marlowe's dying words, *The truth is . . .* What truth was Marlowe — Booth — about to reveal?

"A great way to jump into the job, Lang."

"Ah, the truth, Chad," said Upham. "Always the truth. But—"

The editor interrupted him. "One more thing, Lang." Chad lowered his voice, his hand to one side of his mouth. "Just between us," he said conspiratorially, "that business about Booth being still alive—you know. I almost kind of believed it. Your father thought it was all fabrication, not a grain of truth in it."

"I recall."

"But this came in a few days ago." He handed Upham a letter. "From that farmer in Virginia, Garrett, remember?"

"Yes." Upham felt his heart picking up speed, the old feeling.

"Garrett says that right after they burned the barn, his young son Dickie saw Booth escape, met up with Booth and even gave him half a roast chicken. He swears it was another man the soldiers killed and that Booth got away. What do you think? Worth following up, talking to the boy?"

Upham pushed back his chair and stood up. "Just between us, Chad," he said, "in the words of my esteemed father—poppycock!"

He turned and started in the direction of the stairs. Tompkins rose and followed him.

"Aren't you going to inspect your office?"

Upham kept walking.

"You're going the wrong way, Lang."

"No, I'm going the right way. I'm going to Boston."

The editor looked at him in puzzlement. "Boston? You mean, for a story?"

He shook his head. "For a job."

"But, you have a job, old man," said Tompkins. "I would say the most coveted job in the shop!"

"Chad, my friend—and you have been a good friend—you can take that job and—" Upham gave him a smile—"give it to someone else."

"No! No! I understand. You've been out West. You need time to settle back in here. Take your time. Take a holiday."

"I'm going to work for *The Globe*."

"*The Globe*! Good lord! Why?"

"To become, I hope, a first-class reporter."

"But you are one!"

"No I'm not. Not yet. Meantime, tell Senior to read the out-of-town press, if you would. Goodbye, Chad."

Tompkins' hand was limp with shock as Upham shook it firmly, then turned away.

Upham descended to the lobby and walked out of the building, his hands trembling, but his stride confident and strong. He knew a truth that no one else in the world knew, something no one else needed to know.

And, God willing, they never would.

This is to testify that Sinclair Lewis and
Barnaby Conrad have agreed that all profits(including
book, serial, dramatic, motion picture, and radio rights)
from a story, whose plot, devised by the former is to be
written by the latter, shall be divided 30% for Mr. Lewis,
70% for Mr. Conrad. The story, tentatively entitled "Thus
Ever to Tyrants," deals with the supposition that J.W.
Booth was not killed shortly after assassinating Lincoln,
but instead escaped, migrated west, and died from a crank's
bullet while impersonating Lincoln in a small town pageant.

It is agreed that the story is not to be offered
for sale unless Mr. Conrad devotes at least three months
preparatory study to the work and unless it be a story of
at least 40,000 words.

*Sinclair Lewis*
SINCLAIR LEWIS

*Barnaby Conrad*
BARNABY CONRAD

AUGUST 9, 1947

*Williamstown, mass*

# AFTERWORD

This book might be called a posthumous Sinclair Lewis novel, though he neither wrote nor read a line of it.

It all began in 1947 when I met Lewis, America's first Nobel Prize winner in literature, in Santa Barbara, California. The author of such classics as *Main Street, Arrowsmith, Babbitt,* and *Elmer Gantry* was sixty-two and in the twilight of his career, but he was still producing novels. He hired me, then a twenty-five-year-old fledgling writer, to serve as his personal secretary, chess opponent and protégé at his great estate in Williamstown, Massachusetts.

I asked Mr. Lewis what my duties would be and he replied, "To get up at 5:30 every morning, have coffee with me, and then work on that damned novel of yours. In the afternoon you'll answer all my correspondence and then play two games of chess with me."

It was an extraordinary offer for a young would-be writer. I learned to respond to Mr. Lewis's fan mail in his voice and even to forge his signature for autograph seekers. Lewis was mercurial and irascible, but he was never dull. He would make up little stories almost every day, mostly for his own amusement or mine. As a young man he'd sold twenty-seven plots to Jack London for $137.50, which the author of *The Call of the Wild* fashioned into four published stories.

One morning, over our 5:30 thermos of coffee, Mr. Lewis mused, "Y'know, he really didn't die in that barn in Virginia at all."

"Who?" I asked, blinking. It was awfully early.

"Booth," he replied, his piercing blue eyes fixed on some distant spot over my shoulder, as if he were viewing his own private motion picture.

Then he began to ramble: "Boston Corbett claimed he shot him after they set fire to the barn. But that isn't what happened. Oh no, not at all! When Booth first took refuge in the barn he found a soldier sleeping there. Booth killed him with the man's own pistol, fearing that the soldier would turn him in for the reward for Lincoln's assassin. Then he switched clothes with him, and fled. Then where did he go? Where would you go if you were Booth?"

I found myself caught up in his enthusiasm and said, "Not North, certainly."

"Exactly! They'd lynch him in the North. So he heads South, right straight for the one man he counts on to treat him as a great hero, to give him the rewards he had risked his life for. He slips out of the barn before Boston Corbett and the soldiers even get there and limps off directly to see Robert E. Lee. 'I've come, my General!' Booth exults to Lee. 'I've come to help you rally the armies—the war's not over yet!' Lee stares at him. 'Who are you, my poor friend? The war is virtually over and we have lost.' Booth shouts, 'I am the man who killed Lincoln! Make me a general and together we can still defeat the North!'"

Mr. Lewis was now so wound up that he was imitating the flowery Southern accent of the actor. And then he'd switch expertly to the weary tones of the defeated general: "'You—you did that?' Lee is horrified. 'You infamous madman, you've killed the best friend the South could have at this tragic time. Get out of my sight before I shoot you myself!' So in a state of disillusionment and shock, Booth reels from Lee's headquarters and starts his lonely hegira west. He comes across the funeral train slowly carrying Lincoln's body to Illinois. He sees the thousands upon thousands of people weeping as they watch, and the enormity of his crime begins to become clear to him. He somehow makes it to the Midwest and settles in a little town. He lives a recluse's life on a little farm with a girl he has taken on as a wife.

"He becomes stranger and stranger, brooding, gaunt, and he grows a Lincoln-esque beard. One day the town council comes to him and asks him to play in their annual Fourth of July pageant. They have heard his wife boast of her husband's beautiful recitation of poems and because of his beard and gauntness they want him to play the lead part—that of Abraham Lincoln. At first he demurs, saying he is not fit to play the great man, but finally he agrees. An unreconstructed Southerner, the town drunk, threatens to kill anyone who plays the part of the President, but Booth goes into the makeshift theater anyway. He is on the stage reciting 'Four score and seven years ago,' when a shot rings out. Booth topples from the stage and dies, murmuring '*Sic Semper Tyrannis.*'"

It was impressive. In about ten minutes he'd told the story almost as though he were reading it in finished form. He would make up almost as good a story as that at least once a day.

"Mr. Lewis," I said, "you should write that."

"I've got a better idea," he said. "You write it! You're almost through with your Spain novel, right? So we'll write this one together."

I'd spent three years in Spain in the consular service and had transformed my experiences into a short novel which Lewis had been helping me with.

At lunch he produced a contract that he'd typed up; we would write *Thus Ever to Tyrants* together. He would get thirty percent of any profit, I would get seventy. We signed in high spirits; both of us bursting with gimmicks and touches to improve the story.

"We'll tell Bennett Cerf about it," Mr. Lewis said. "My publisher—he's coming up this weekend. And we'll also show him your Spain book."

I started to work on *Thus Ever to Tyrants* that afternoon. But after the first flush of enthusiasm had worn off, it was heavy going. For one thing it wasn't my story, I didn't really feel it. Another thing was that I didn't know enough about Booth and that period of the Civil War to write about it convincingly. Then too, Mr. Lewis was adamant that the plot be expanded into a novel. I felt that its anecdotal quality meant it was better suited to be a short story for the *Saturday Evening Post*. The next day, after writing a few pages, I decided I'd better study at least the last volume of Carl Sandburg's *Abraham Lincoln*; and I put the manuscript aside with relief.

Mr. Lewis asked me every day how much I'd worked on "our novel" and was irritated by my total lack of progress. But I still had to polish my own novel for Bennett Cerf, who had agreed to publish it under the title *The Innocent Villa*.

Though always hard to please, Lewis now began to find more and more fault with me. He was compulsively fastidious and I was compulsively sloppy. If I left the lid up on the piano after playing it, he would berate me—often in front of guests—growing empurpled as he ranted. Like a cranky schoolmaster, he gave me "room orders" for an unmade bed or leaving tennis clothes on the floor. He was furious that I had not progressed more on *Thus Ever to Tyrants*, even though I was reading about the period and also making the many extensive changes that Bennett Cerf and his editors suggested for my own novel.

"You'll never make a writer," he bellowed once. "If you don't write that Booth story you'll never make a writer!"

After three months Lewis left for Europe, and I was out of a job. I eventually published *The Innocent Villa*, for which Lewis congratulated me in a letter, but he still brooded about the Booth novel. I saw him a final time while in Paris on my honeymoon in 1949. He had begun to drink heavily, and his alcoholic decline shocked and saddened me. At the end of our evening in a Left Bank café he slurred, "Finish that damned Booth novel!" and collapsed into a taxi. He died of a stroke in Rome two years later.

I went on to write over thirty books, a number of them bestsellers, but it took me over sixty years to get around to the Booth story. So here, Mr. Lewis, is your—*our*—story at last. I offer it with admiration, gratitude, and affection.

BARNABY CONRAD, JR.
Carpinteria, California
*May 16, 2010*

## ACKNOWLEDGEMENTS

I gratefully acknowledge the encouragement and enormous creative input from my son, B.C.III, who is also my editor and best friend. Without him there'd be no book. I also wish to thank a fellow writer and friend, Mark Hugh Miller, for his historical insights and fine editing. And finally, I thank Maurice Kanbar for his belief in this project.

There are many fine books on the Lincoln Assassination but three masterful histories were essential to this project: Michael W. Kauffman's *American Brutus: John Wilkes Booth and the Lincoln Conspiracies* (2004); James L. Swanson's *Manhunt: The 12-Day Chase for Lincoln's Killer* (2003); and Edward Steers, Jr.'s *Blood on The Moon: The Assassination of Abraham Lincoln* (2001).